DANIEL LINGFIELD WAS CAGED IN A LION'S DEN OF QUESTIONS

Had he sent the beautiful girl he loved to her death at the hands of the Nazis after betraying her with another woman?

Had his ravishing twin sister broken the most sacred laws of God and man to gain control of a vast family fortune and the enormous power that went with it?

Was his father a weakling coward or a martyred hero—and was the gigantic business empire that he was heir to founded on a devil's bargain with Hitler himself?

The key to the perverse puzzle lay in a single word. A word buried in Daniel's lost memory. A word that could mean death, or even worse, to decipher.

Janus.

THE HOUSE OF JANUS

THE HOUSE OF JANUS

A NOVEL BY

Donald James

A SIGNET BOOK

SIGNET
Published by the Penguin Group
Penguin Books USA Inc., 375 Hudson Street,
New York, New York 10014, U.S.A.
Penguin Books Ltd, 27 Wrights Lane,
London W8 5TZ, England
Penguin Books Australia Ltd, Ringwood,
Victoria, Australia
Penguin Books Canada Ltd, 10 Alcorn Avenue,
Toronto, Ontario, Canada M4V 3B2
Penguin Books (N.Z.) Ltd, 182–190 Wairau Road,
Auckland 10, New Zealand

Penguin Books Ltd, Registered Offices:
Harmondsworth, Middlesex, England

Published by Signet, an imprint of New American Library,
a division of Penguin Books USA Inc. This is an authorized reprint of a
hardcover edition published by Donald I. Fine, Inc.

First Signet Printing, April, 1992
10 9 8 7 6 5 4 3 2 1

PUBLISHER'S NOTE
This novel is a work of fiction. Names, characters, places and incidents are
either the product of the author's imagination or are used fictitiously. Any
resemblance to actual events, locales, organizations or persons, living or
dead, is entirely coincidental and beyond the intent of either the author or
publisher.

To the World's End,
Chelsea

PROLOGUE

~ ~ ~

He could see light. A rectangle of soft opaque light before his eyes and shadowy figures moving above him. A woman's voice, American, one of the moving shadows, said: "We'll finish this one and break for coffee, okay?"

A warm, rounded shape leaned over him. For a moment he felt scented breath on his chin and neck. A covering was drawn back from his body. He could feel cool drafts of air set up by the woman's arms and legs moving around him.

"He's been dreaming again," one of the nurses said. "Betty Grable by the size of it."

Warm water sponged his chest; someone took his erect penis, holding it aside as the sponge flicked between his thighs.

One of the women laughed. "Carrie told me," she said, "that Henderson comes in here to practice on him when she's on night duty."

"Poor darling." Soft lips touched his forehead. "He deserves better than that."

For days or hours or minutes he watched the sunlight pass across the gauze that covered his eyes. He was content not to try to move. Sleep came in deep drifts from which he awoke to savor the proximity of the women who attended him. He smelt their freshly soaped skins and imagined crisp white uniforms as they leaned across him. He listened to their talk as they worked around him. He was a blind voyeur, an uncomprehending eavesdropper.

When the doctor came, the women's banter stopped. Temperatures were discussed; the regularity of breathing reported on. One nurse claimed that he had been weighed yesterday. How could that have been? He knew nothing of that. Was there a part of his life hidden from him? The doctor's voice announced the start of one course of drugs or the termination of another. The nurses called him "Colonel."

Drifting on the wings of sleep, he once heard footsteps, the many steps of many feet clattering towards him on a tiled floor. He listened acutely. The high heels of women mixed with the measured heel-rap of men. He distinguished three, four, five different persons.

"So this man could well be the last American casualty of the war," a deep voice said through the tumbling mists of sleep.

"Could well be, General," the colonel-doctor answered.

"Is he going to make it? I mean will he pull through?"

In the bed the soldier waited, indifferent through the long pause.

"He's come through surgery," the colonel-doctor said. "In that sense there's no reason he couldn't stand up and walk out of here."

"I mean will he come out of the coma?" the general said testily.

There were many people round the bed. Pipesmoke and perfumes mingled nauseously.

"I can't say, General," the colonel-doctor said. "This is beyond our precise medical knowledge. He was torn to pieces by an explosion. We gave him all the necessary surgery. Now his body and his mind, working together, or maybe fighting it out, for all I know, will either bring him out of the coma. Or not. Sorry, General, I can't say more than that."

Suddenly time had passed on; there was the yellow

haze of night lights through his window of gauze, and nurses whispering by his bedside.

"The general today was trying to get Colonel Buck to say he definitely wouldn't wake from the coma. That's what the general wanted. He wanted him to die."

"So the old bastard could get him for his monument to the last GI casualty of World War Two."

"There must be plenty of other candidates."

"The general thinks this one's perfect. If he dies without speaking he'll not only be the last GI casualty of the war. He'll be the unknown soldier thrown in. That's why the general wants this one."

"Screw the general," the third girl's voice said softly. "We're not going to let this baby die."

When was it now? The next day—the next week? The excitement was terrific. Three or four nurses and the colonel-doctor were there. Curtains ran on rings along a bed-bar as others joined them. "He moved twice," a young voice said breathlessly. "I noted it all down, sir. Two distinct movements."

"Describe them please, Nurse," Colonel Buck said.

"First"—the pages of a notebook fluttered—"the very slow turning of his palm down onto the blanket. At 0734 hours."

"That was the first movement?"

"Yes sir." There was eager triumph in the girl's voice. "After that I sat by the bed watching. Thirty-five minutes later he drew his leg up, normal speed, didn't jerk it up, just brought it up like he was getting more comfortable. And his mouth moved at the same time. Not really a word. A sort of croak."

He could sense the girls all clustered round. "Does that mean he's going to make it, sir? Does that mean he's going to be all right, Colonel?" He knew from their voices how much they wanted to put one over on that sonofabitch general.

There was no escape now. The light gauze was re-

moved from his eyes and he stared up at Colonel Buck
to find he was narrow-shouldered in his white coat
with blond receding hair and pale eyes. He leaned
forward. "Do you hear me? Do you hear me, soldier?"

The man in the bed stared up at the colonel, trans-
fixed. His mouth moved.

"Moisten his lips, Nurse," the colonel said, his voice
now edged with excitement.

The colonel bobbed aside from his vision and it was
filled with a small, neatly featured nurse, a white cap
balanced on her dark slightly frizzy hair. Her large
soft breasts labeled in olive green, Nurse C. O'Dwyer
pressed down on his upper arm as she held a china
beaker, dipped her hand into the water and gently
drew her wet fingertips across his lips.

"Get inside his mouth," Buck's voice urged from
the sidelines.

The girl's fingers worked themselves gently past his
lips and between his teeth. Within the secrecy of his
mouth he moved his tongue against her fingertips and
she smiled down at him.

After this Colonel Buck came back every two or
three hours, taking his shoulders and looking pale-
eyed down at him. "Do you hear me, soldier? Who
are you? What's your name?"

Each time he stared up at him in terror. He could
hear his own breath sloughing back and forth past his
lips.

"Can you hear me, soldier? Your name. Just tell
me your name."

But how could he tell him his name? How could he
tell him when he didn't know himself?

His temperature rose and fell erratically. He sweated
drops of fear whenever a doctor or physiotherapist
came near him. Only Nurse O'Dwyer gave him comfort as she sat beside him asking no questions. Only

with Nurse O'Dwyer did he communicate—secretly tonguing her fingertips as she moistened his mouth.

There were no deep drifts of sleep to conceal his hunted self now. All day he lay there listening for the approach of footsteps. When they next came it was a tall figure in a strange uniform, a man who stared at him, thin-lipped, while Colonel Buck's voice behind him said. "This is Captain Oliver Sutchley, from the British Army in Austria. They have several liaison officers with Patton's Army who still are missing. He's been asked to check our wounded."

Sutchley looked at the man in the bed and consulted the photographs on his billboard. "Not one of ours." Suddenly he smiled, big white teeth below a trim moustache. "Take my advice, old chap," he said. "The war's over. Go away and forget it. Somewhere with sun, wine, women, a peacetime atmosphere. Lisbon's the place. Know it?"

Buck was tugging at Sutchley's sleeve. "Leave it, Captain. We'll decide on treatment."

Between visits the days were sweet. The soldier listened to the warm bustle of nurses around him, the clatter of metal instruments in bowls, the soft squeak of a trolley as it was pushed past the open doorway of his room. It was summer and the air was warm. Outside in the gardens GI's talked of home and of the war that had lost them arms or legs. Places and names were mentioned that he knew—the battle for Nuremberg and Pilsen, George C. Patton's Third Army. But none of the things related to him directly. Between him and events that he could describe to himself in quite reasonable detail lay a veil, a thin wall of mist. In no incident of his memory did he himself play any part whatsoever!

Sweetest of all was the morning Nurse O'Dwyer came in smiling and bidding him good morning as she always did, as if he were responding.

"It's a beautiful morning, Daniel," she said. She

had christened him Daniel for reasons known only to
herself. "Now let's get you all freshened up."

She drew back the covering and turned away to
busy herself with a sponge and bowl of warm water.
"Now if we knew when it was your birthday, Daniel,
all the girls would want to send you a card," she said
inconsequentially.

She turned back towards him, her small hands bubbled with soapy water. "My! Betty Grable again, is
it?" she said as she reached down and smoothed her
palm under his testicles. "I think, Daniel," she said,
"you must have very naughty dreams." Her left hand
masturbated him with smooth regular strokes. "Don't
pretend, Daniel. Don't pretend you don't like it."

It was irresistible. His back arched and lifted from
the mattress, his fingers twisted the sheets. As the
sensation flooded him, he jackknifed his legs, groan-
ing with pleasure but also with the knowledge that she
had betrayed him.

Because Colonel Buck stood smiling in the doorway. "Thank you, Nurse," he said. "Excellent. Well
done!"

He was in hell. It was as if one half of his mind saw
him lying in a hospital bed in South Germany while
another darker element took part in a Dantean scene
from the other side of midnight. In his vision yellow
fumes rose from everything, from the ground, from
the dead trees, from the three long columns of people,
men, women and children, their heads lowered, their
feet dragging, as they marched through this sulfurous
landscape.

Perhaps he was part of these dread columns or perhaps he stood outside them watching, he was not sure.
But he was searching the faces with an intensity of
yearning that he could feel even now, fully awake. He
was searching for a face which seemed to settle on
one pair of shoulders after another, ever moving away

from him until it was lost among the columns of the damned.

There were better times, times spent talking to the nurses or with Colonel Buck. Exhausted after his first unaided walk, he watched as Buck crossed the timber planking of the veranda and threw himself into the easy chair beside him. A man small in stature, the colonel liked to behave like a big man. Looking across at the gleaming snowcap of the Unterberg, he drew a deep breath of the mountain air. "Any complaints, Daniel?" he asked.

"It's as good a name as any," the soldier said.

Buck grunted, took out a pack of Chesterfields and offered one. The other man took it automatically, accepted a light from the colonel's Zippo and inhaled smoke.

Buck was watching him, the blue flame of the Zippo wavering around the wick. "It's hard not to play detective," he said.

"Listen Colonel," the soldier said as he eased his chair around. "I'm holding back nothing. But you know things about me, like where I was picked up, and I can't think for the life of me why you won't tell me."

Buck had capped the Zippo. Uncapping it again he spun the wheel and lit his cigarette. "You were picked up in the middle of a minefield," he said. "The field had been set around a big house, a mansion they say, between here and the Austrian border."

"Were there army units in the area?"

He shook his head. "None really. No U.S. Army units within twenty miles. No, looks as if you went there alone."

"I walked?"

"No. You went by jeep."

"The jeep must have had unit markings."

"The jeep was blown from under you, exploding one mine after another as it landed." He paused. "I guess it was like a firecracker." He nodded, pleased with the image he had evoked. "It was disposed of after they'd taken you away to the field burial station."

"Burial station?" the soldier said.

"When they picked you up the Medics thought you were dead."

"What about my tags?"

"They followed procedure. They cut your ID tags and threw the body on the blood wagon."

"My body?"

"The one you're sitting in. The ID tags went into the bin with a few hundred others. In those last days Third Army lost three hundred men."

"Are you telling me you have *nothing* to go on?"

"Not a lot yet," he conceded. "But when we get full lists of men supposedly killed in action on that last day I'll get you to check out the names. Maybe one of them will mean something."

"Did I say anything under anesthesia?"

"Nothing comprehensible. Nothing in English that is. You've got a pretty solid linguistic background. You speak good French and even better German. Try it out." He nodded towards an old man in a faded peaked Wehrmacht cap tending the flower bed beneath the veranda.

The soldier tried a few sentences, passing the time of day. He understood the old man as he might a film in which the characters were supposedly speaking in German but were in fact Hollywood actors. It meant he was fluent in German. As the old man touched the long peak of his cap and returned to his flower bed the soldier saw that Buck was smiling at him. "You got more secrets like that tucked up your sleeve, Colonel?"

"The psychiatrists advise we let the rope out slowly."

"Tell the psychiatrists I want Nurse O'Dwyer back on my section."

"I could maybe arrange it if you really tried hard to remember your name."

The soldier turned his face away. He could not tell the colonel that he was not, as they all imagined, consumed with curiosity, desperate to know who he was.

Later that week he stood in front of a mirror, the first one he had been allowed to approach. Colonel Buck stood to one side as the soldier examined himself in the reflection. That he was tall and underweight was no surprise. What he was not prepared for was his face. By now clean shaven, it was long with deep set eyes heavily eyebrowed. A neat but not too sharp nose led down to a good wide mouth. He bared his lips. The teeth looked good.

"Don't get carried away Valentino," the colonel said. "We gave you four bottom crowns and a bridge San Francisco wouldn't be ashamed of."

"How about the nose?"

"I modeled that on my own."

The soldier looked and grinned. The smile faded as his attention was caught by his hair. He took a few strands and rolled them between fingers and thumb, observing that they were strong, wiry stuff. "It's not a wig?" he said suspiciously.

"All your own," Buck assured him.

"But for Chrissake, Colonel, it's *white*."

"Sort of blonde," Buck said.

The soldier scowled, found he was really taken by the effect, and scowled again. "Apart from the white thatch," he said, "I'm not a bad looking guy."

"Captain Daniel Lingfield," Buck said.

"Lingfield? Where did you get that name?"

"You were picked up in the grounds of a mansion called Haus Lingfeld just north of Munich. Foundlings get named after the place they were found."

"Daniel Lingfield . . ." The soldier rolled the name

slowly off his tongue. "Daniel Lingfield . . . Okay
Colonel, I'll go with that."

On his first night away from the hospital Daniel took
a jeep from the motor park and drove slowly through
the ruined streets of Munich.

There were people on the sidewalks, mostly old
women pushing small wooden carts or carriages piled
high with household goods, a few young palefaced
hookers. He drove on down Leopoldstrasse and turned
into the Marienplatz. A post in the center of the
square had nailed to it over twenty black-and-white
painted signboards. The one that caught his eye was
Special Services HQ, Lingfeld.

Should he continue down the Lingfeld road? Should
he continue past the looming signpost that would have
directed him back to the hospital? Or should he face
his fears and drive on down this narrow road where
the trees almost joined above his head and where the
long whipping radio aerial of the jeep sliced off apples
that danced and rolled on the moonlit road behind
him.

He was afraid. A different sort of fear. Afraid not
of the future but of the past.

Why had he been in the grounds of Haus Lingfeld
on May 8, 1945? In the vast sweep of a world at war,
when inconceivable crimes were committed by simple,
ordinary men, what had he been running from?

He stopped the jeep at the entrance to the drive
beside a gatehouse of perhaps four small rooms and
a gabled roof, the tiles of which had been torn and
scattered by mortar fire. A green painted door
slumped inwards on a single remaining hinge. Every
pane in every window was broken. Before him the
drive curved away in parallel lines of linden trees. The
gravel surface was pitted with shallow holes. A crudely
painted notice said in English and German: "The
drive to the house has been cleared of obstacles. You

are warned that the woods on either side still contain mines."

He moved the jeep down the broken drive at five miles an hour. Just past the first gently curving bend the moonlight caught the full length statue of a figure in Roman breastplate chipped where the name might have been. But the date was able to be read clearly in the incised stone: 1694.

Gravel crunched under the jeep tires. The moonlight brightened as the linden trees seemed spaced wider apart. A screech owl burst into lights from the jeep and rose, banking menacingly above his head. In the distance dogs barked and were silent.

A sense of private menace hung over the place. As the wheels of the jeep rolled slowly forward the hair on the back of his neck stiffened and rose. He reached over and hauled his pistol belt from the back seat and one-handedly clipped it around his waist.

The drive now opened steeply before him into a cobbled forecourt, enclosed on the three sides by a stone balustrade topped at intervals by weathered stone urns. As the jeep rolled forward the roof of a large house became visible.

Haus Lingfeld was a stone mansion, large but not enormous. Part of the roof had collapsed and window frames hung outwards, shattered by the force of some explosion within. Along the lower floor the stone was chipped where the facade had been raked by heavy machine-gun bullets.

The house was deserted. No lights shone from even those few windows that were intact. He stopped the jeep and got out. The steps before him were of worn stone and the wide terrace in front of the house was flagged and balustraded. He climbed the steps and stood on the terrace. Away to the east high hills rolled towards the mountains. On the west side of the house a huge ornamental lake gleamed in the moonlight. In

the middle a wrecked German army truck stood, the
water level above its wheels.

The crunch of gravel somewhere around the side of
the house focused his attention. He strained his eyes
into the deep shadow beside the house. He could see
a shape there, unmoving. Then the crunch of gravel
as the figure came forward. In the shaft of moonlight
the shape seemed to be without a face!

He knew he was looking deep into his own fear. He
called out. The figure came forward. Two paces and
stopped.

In the moonlight he could now see it was a woman.
Tall, seven or eight years older than himself, her hair
drawn back from a hard but beautiful face. She stood,
one hand resting on the rusticated stonework of the
corner of the house.

"What do you want here?" she said.

She had spoken in English. Turning towards her,
looking past her to see that she was alone, he said:
"On the last day of the war, I was blown up by a
mine in the grounds of this house."

She barely moved, but with one almost impercepti-
ble lift of the shoulders she indicated her indifference.

"I want to come in," he said. "I want to go into
the house."

"Why?"

"I'm an American officer," he said. "I don't have
to explain why."

Again she shrugged, this time more obviously. Then
she turned and led the way around the side of the
house. "We live in the kitchens," she said. "Or what's
left of them. The house was hit by shellfire. As you
have probably seen, most of the roof has collapsed.
The upper floors are uninhabitable."

She turned through a porched doorway and led the
way along a passage. The kitchen at the end of the
corridor was a huge room, the ceiling height lost in
diminishing candlelight. Dark recesses suggested great

oak cupboards or other doors that led into the interior
of the house. A fire was burning in a tiled stove and
woodsmoke drifted into the candlelight and was lost
in the darkness above his head. As he watched the
shadowed outline of her body before him he was
seized by curious, unmeasurable feelings. Distaste?
Yes. Familiarity? Certainly.

She turned, the line of her cheekbones caught in
the candlelight. She was in her mid-thirties, dressed
in a skirt and flowered blouse of some quality beneath
a rough plain farmworker's apron. Her eyes, wary,
intensely proud, caught his.

Then some surge passed through his body or brain,
far more than familiarity. Instead, an overwhelming
sense that he had once slept with this woman.

"Is this your house, or are you a squatter here?"
He felt no friendliness towards this woman. That first
single shrug of the shoulders had told him all he
wanted to know about her attitude to Americans.

She hesitated a long time before answering the
question. "It's my house," she said at length.

"What's your name?"

"Frau Elisabeth Oster." She pronounced it with deliberate emphasis on each syllable.

"You live here alone?"

"No. My husband lives here with me. Tonight he is
in Munich preparing for the Victualienmarkt tomorrow. The home farm produces a little extra food. Not
much."

"Were you here in the last days of the war?"

"Yes."

"Do you know me?"

"No."

"Are you sure, Frau Oster?"

"Why should I know you?"

She was trembling faintly, which somehow increased
this strange intimacy he felt towards her. He had no
doubt that he disliked her, but for men at least some

feelings are more potent than dislike. Again he felt that surge of warmth, that near certainty that he had slept with her, like meeting a woman the morning after an erotic dream in which she had unwittingly played a part.

"The explosion of a Teller mine in the driveway of this house," he said carefully, "left me temporarily incapable of remembering what I was doing here." He paused, then added as a shot in the dark. "I think you know."

She was now shaking violently.

He leaned forward until his face was only a foot or two from hers. "Do you know me, Frau Oster. Have you ever met me?"

She shook her head.

"Why had I left my unit? Why was I making my way towards this house?"

But she was recovering, fast. "I can't help you, Captain," she said. "I do not know you. We have never met." Again she pronounced the words with that same deliberate pacing she had used when she had first given her name. "We have never met."

Without saying goodbye the soldier turned and walked back to the jeep. As he drove down the driveway his headlights picked out patches of broken branches and shattered upturned roots.

P A R T I

MARTIN

CHAPTER 1

When Martin Coburg was a young boy he believed all young boys lived as he did. He believed first of all that all young boys lived with their grandfather, although he wasn't absolutely sure he thought that all grandfathers were tall, suntanned white-haired men who insisted that their grandchildren call them Pierre.

Martin knew many things for certain. He knew that Kansas City was the whole world, which could be seen between the two rivers from the very top room of their house on Quality Hill. He knew that fathers and mothers were not half as important as grandfathers named Pierre and he knew that a twin sister was a great burden for a young boy to bear.

When he was five the family moved to New York and that confused him a great deal about the size of the world. He knew he was five and his twin sister was five, which led him to believe that all children were five. But he also knew, because he had asked him, that Pierre was forty-five. This led him to believe that all adults were forty-five. When he told his mother at a grown-up party that she must be forty-five because she looked it, Pierre and the others burst out laughing but his mother slapped his face.

His mother often slapped Martin. She didn't slap his twin sister Celine, however naughty she was. His dad didn't slap anybody but that's because his mother said his father was as weak as water.

Martin's mother was named Rose. Everybody, especially the servants, were always saying that his mother was very beautiful. Certainly she was always buying new clothes but it didn't really matter how much they cost because the family business was printing bank-notes. In his secret box under his bed Martin had saved up several dollar bills that had been made especially for him in the family's Kansas City printing plant.

The truth was that he kept the dollar bills in his secret box because he was planning to run away. He had four dollars and two French francs with holes in the middle and he was only waiting for the weather to get warmer before he ran away.

The problem was not so much that he was unhappy at home. It's true he didn't love his mother as much as he should and his father was as weak as water, which left only Pierre whom he loved and who was big and suntanned and forty-five. The problem was the German Coburgs who were coming to stay for the summer and Martin couldn't stand the thought of that.

The German Coburgs spoke German. Emil was the head of the German Coburgs. He was Pierre's twin brother and was tall and suntanned, and like all other grownups, forty-five. His wife was a big fat lady in a red shiny dress who was always hugging Martin and trying to put his eye out with the sharp things she wore around her neck. Those things were like stones but were more sparkly and shiny. Dorotta, as he was instructed to call her, in the family tradition of using first names, was a very nice lady who didn't like his mother slapping him. Once she had spoken to Emil about it and Emil had gotten very angry with his mother. This only led to more slaps when Martin was in her presence.

No, the problem with the German Coburgs was not Dorotta's stones or the fact they spoke in German. It was the two girls—Alexina, who, being a child, was also five, and Elisabeth, Dorotta's younger sister, mysteriously suspended between child and adult.

The problem was that he and Celine and Alexina and Elisabeth were to go away on a special children's cruise for the whole summer and sail up to Canada and look at things and sail back. Him and three girls!

He had asked Pierre if something could be done. It was after lunch and Emil and Pierre were sitting at the table telling stories about when they were five-year-old children in some place they were born called the Waldviertel where everybody spoke German. Pierre had told him to have a word with his mother about the summer trip when she got back from New York City.

Pierre and Emil really did look alike. They had the same sort of loud voices and told jokes that everybody laughed at. Since the German Coburgs' visit, Martin had been busily revising his view of the world. It seemed clear enough now that it was divided into two parts. One was called Europe and the other was called America. Emil, he was now certain, owned Europe and Pierre owned America.

This was a very comfortable cosmography for Martin until the table talk began to turn to places named China or Russia or England.

That afternoon he waited until his mother had returned to the house; then he ran upstairs, into her bedroom and out onto the balcony where he liked to press himself among the ivy and look out over the gardens where the gardeners worked all day with their sleeves rolled up and their caps pushed back on their heads.

Below him he could see his mother walking arm in arm with his father and a friend of theirs named Jack. They came along the rose alley, which his mother loved because her name was Rose, and Martin tried to wave to them, but they turned onto the broad west lawn where his dad and Jack left his mother's side and started some horseplay, rolling about on the lawn in their city clothes. His mother soon got annoyed. He noticed her mood even from where he was watching.

For quite a while longer he stayed where he was, until the two men stopped fooling around, brushed themselves off and came towards the house. As they disappeared into the main hall under the balcony he was standing on, he tried to wave to them again but he wasn't quite tall enough to make himself seen over the stone balustrade.

If he asked his mother and she said he didn't have to go on the ship to Canada he would try to love her more. He sat down and thought about it. If he made her a real promise perhaps she would say the girls could go alone.

There was movement on the driveway below him. He stood up again and strained to see over the top of the balcony. Martin's father was at the wheel of his sportscar. "Be back in an hour," he said as he waved to his friend Jack. The white car screeched away and Jack walked back into the house.

Only a few minutes later he heard voices behind him in the bedroom. He tried to remember the promise he was going to make. His mother's French door onto the balcony was open slightly and he could hear her voice.

Martin frowned. His mother was putting on the silly, baby voice she sometimes used with Celine. "You lamb," she said, "just come here and let me kiss it and make it better." He heard a man's voice say something and he edged forward to look through the crack in the door. His mother was certainly making it better. Red-faced, she was kneeling in front of Pierre, not only kissing, but gobbling away like a turkey!

Along the drive he could hear the German girls coming back from their horseback riding. Sometimes they took Celine with them but today they were alone. What was the promise? He couldn't go into the bedroom without having his promise ready. To love her more. Prepared, he stepped forward and flung open the French door. Pierre and his mother were under the silk cover having a wrestling match. All the grown-ups were having wrestling matches today! Then his mother started screaming at him, calling him nasty names and yelling at him to get out. After that he never dared to ask her if he could stay at home when the girls went sailing to Canada.

When Martin Coburg was fourteen Pierre decreed that his grandson should accompany him to Kansas City. It was the spring of 1935 and Martin was the heir to Coburg Banknote. Nobody bothered to ask why John Coburg, Martin's father, was not in the line of succession. John simply was not interested. He painted, he played cello, he wrote poetry. These activities excluded him from succession. Celine was excluded too, because she was a girl. It had never been put into words but Pierre had made it clear: his grandson was his heir.

Martin Coburg stood in total awe of his huge, domineering grandfather, in awe of him when they visited the governor of Missouri, in awe when he starved his striking workers into submission at the Coburg Banknote plant on the Kaw River, in awe when he drank whiskey and hammered the table with Tom Prendergast, the acknowledged boss of Kansas City. Pierre Coburg might live in New York, but he was still a rich and powerful figure in Kansas City and he had no plans to let anyone forget it.

It had not always been so. Pierre Coburg was twenty years old when he had left his homeland, an area in the middle of the old Austrian Empire, to seek his fortune in America. His only real regret was that he could not persuade his twin brother Emil to come with him. The two boys were tall, powerfully built young men with big faces and thick blonde hair. They spoke the languages of central Europe, German, Hungarian, Czech, and although their parents had been peasants, they themselves had been apprenticed to a master printer in Budapest. The company's speciality had been in the printing of bonds and banknotes. A Russian fifty-rouble note with the Tsar's head in the right hand corner excited their craftsman's pride.

But one day Pierre sneaked a look at the company's accounts and discovered how much the Tsar was paying for his fifty-rouble notes, and how much the Serbian Central Bank paid for its annual order of one million five-dinar notes. Thereafter it had been the brothers' ambition to own the foremost specialized printing business in the world. Their views were split on how to do this. Pierre favored taking their talents to America; Emil was convinced that Vienna could prove the foundation for their fortune.

In the autumn of 1900 they had traveled together down to the Imperial port of Trieste. On the dockside the freighter *Udine*, bound for New York, was already crowded with emigrants pressing against the rails, waving goodbye to relatives below.

The two brothers strolled along the wharf reiterating promises, underlining details of the plans they had been making over the last few months.

"I'll miss you, Pierre," Emil said.

"I'll write."

"By the time we meet again you'll be an American."

"So?"

Two girls, baskets of apples in their arms, eyed the twin brothers as they passed.

"Just don't forget where you come from, Pierre. Don't forget the hills of the Waldviertel, don't forget the land we grew up in, the old ways, the old customs."

Pierre looked past the bustle of the port to the hills rising above the city. "Count on me," he said, "I won't forget."

They turned and began walking back toward the *Udine*. Men were taking down the gangplank flag. The last passengers were boarding.

"You worry too much, Emil, you know that," Pierre said. "I'm not going to let America change me. We come from the heart of Europe. I'll never forget it. My sons won't. My grandsons won't."

"America may be the land of dreams," Emil said, "but I've heard that New York is the city of lost illusions."

Pierre put his arm round his brother's shoulder. "Are you afraid I won't fight?"

"No, you bullock," Emil said. "I'm not afraid of that. But I don't want you to lose hope, forget what we've talked about all these months."

"Together, but apart," Pierre said, "we will build the greatest printworks business in the world."

Their plans were set. Each brother was to work to establish a Coburg banknote printing company. The two companies were to be independent yet linked in their division of orders received. There was to be no poaching; there was to be annual open examinations of the books; technical advances were to be shared equally. Both companies, although carrying different names, Imprimerie Coburg in Europe and Coburg Banknote Corporation in America, were to share as their company symbol the head of Janus, the Roman god with two faces, separate yet linked, looking, the boys told each other, two ways, a vigilant guardian of both Coburg enterprises.

It was a dream. A dream of two boys who were barely more than peasants. But it was a dream backed by the Coburg will to succeed.

Pierre arrived in New York City at the beginning of the bleak winter of 1900. Even though he first lived in tenements on the few dollars he had, he bubbled with ideas for becoming rich. When he talked of printing banknotes, fellow immigrants sat back and laughed. The

big German had a sense of humor. But Pierre was not
interested in schemes to roast chestnuts or sell worn
boots. He was looking for bigger money. One day an
old drunk came to the tenement and rambled on half
the night about life in the heart of America, about the
prizefighting and gambling and spending money. For
four hours Pierre listened in the communal kitchen
until long after the fire had burnt out. By dawn he
had decided that the free and easy life of frontier
America was where he could make his first fortune.

Chance and odd jobs as a conductor and pullman
porter took him to Kansas City.

In 1900, Kansas City was a strapping young town,
barely fifty years old. Its character reflected the Indian
tribe for which it was named. The Kansas or Kaw
Indians were known for their roistering, feasting,
dancing, speechmaking, gambling and drinking. By
1900, Union Avenue greeted visitors with skills whose
task it was to separate the newcomer from his money
in the shortest time possible. Prostitutes swung their
hips as they roamed the streets. Cattlemen in high
boots and gamblers in high hats joined the riffraff.
Music, gambling, women and drinking were Union
Avenue's specialities.

Calls for a cleanup of Union Avenue and the whole
of the West Bottoms district of Kansas City were frequent, but little was done. However, another Kansas
City was already in existence. Up on Quality Hill,
Colonel Kersey Coates had established an area featur-
ing the Coates House Hotel with its copper-roofed
towers and a white-marbled swimming pool, the large
and ornate Grand Opera House, and exclusive
residences.

It was on Union Avenue that Pierre Coburg began
his career, but it was always to Quality Hill that he
aspired.

Just down from the old Union Depot, was Doyle's
whorehouse, which needed a shill and a bouncer,

someone who was big and fearless. "You bring 'em in," Mrs. Doyle said, "you make 'em pay, and you carry them out." When she saw Pierre Coburg she decided he was the man for the job.

She decided within a short time after he was hired that there were other jobs he could do, also. Pierre showed himself to be a competent bookkeeper and part-time runner. He was a natural politician and was befriended by Boss Jim Prendergast. And he kept his hands off the girls, at least as far as Mrs. Doyle could see.

She married him in 1901 and died in childbirth at the age of forty-two just nine months later. Pierre Coburg sold the whorehouse he had inherited and moved with his baby son and a nurse to some rooms above a small new printing plant in the West Bottoms. The American branch of the House of Janus was born.

To celebrate attaining American citizenship in 1908, Pierre held an enormous party in the banquet room above Jim Prendergast's Main Street Saloon. Every member of Prendergast's Democratic Club was there. The entree was wild boar and the wine was the best imported vintages. The women, Pierre claimed, had been brought in from New York.

That party took Pierre to the edge of bankruptcy, but in the following years it never ceased to pay dividends. The Prendergasts liked a man who made clear which side of the fence he was on. Printing work came Pierre's way from his political connections. In 1910, Coburg Banknote printed its first currency bill, a Haitian ten-franc note. The business resulted from an introduction by a former U.S. senator for Missouri.

Pierre Coburg by then looked the part of a banknote printer. A tall, well-dressed, distinguished looking young man with prematurely gray hair, he inspired confidence in his discretion and the utter reliability and quality of Coburg banknotes. At the same time he was a ruthless fighter for foreign currency contracts, prepared to lie, bribe or cheat to get them.

By 1917, the House of Janus in both Europe and America had grown so that it was uniquely positioned to seize the opportunities presented by the war and the even greater opportunities brought by the peace. The Treaty of Versailles had created some ten new countries in central and southern Europe and almost every state needed new currency. The contracts were there for the taking. While Emil gained contracts for the new Czechoslovakian crown and the marks of the Kaiserless new Germany, Pierre specialized in the profitable China trade. Here the grand names of European and American currency printing, De la Rue of London, Banque de France, American Banknote, all engaged in a vicious cutthroat scramble under a veneer of dignity and discretion for the more obvious contracts. Often, Pierre came away with the order for the more obscure Macao dollars or Shanghai bank bonds.

But not all elements of their boyhood dreams were realized by Pierre and Emil. They remained as close as ever, the greatest of friends, but also the greatest of rivals. Within ten years of the end of the Great War, Emil had infiltrated the immensely profitable China trade; Pierre was dabbling in the Balkan lands of southeastern Europe. Sometimes, rarely, they cooperated as when they snatched twenty percent of the huge secret Soviet Union rouble contract from under the noses of American Banknote and De la Rue. But cooperation was not the name of the Coburg game. The twin brothers brought vastly different qualities to the House of Janus. Pierre was a master salesman; Emil, a brilliant administrator and printing technician. They should have combined.

Instead, they chose to compete.

For Coburg Banknote and Pierre the years on either side of the Great Crash were spectacularly successful.

His personal life was a series of affairs with some of the greatest beauties of the day. He seduced the Duchess of Manneringham on a *Queen Mary* voyage from London to New York. On the same voyage he seduced the brilliant new Swedish film star Karen Targa. He was completely ruthless in taking to bed the wives of his subordinates or the stenographers in the New York home office. He still had a slight accent, but to women there was something rich and raffish about it. He was a world-traveled captain of commerce, a man of steadily increasing wealth.

Yet Pierre Coburg still retained much of his central European peasant upbringing. He was careful to disguise the fact, but he was highly superstitious. He furtively crossed himself whenever a German sheperd crossed his path. That particular breed reminded him of the werewolf myths of the old Waldviertel hills. Full moons affected him, too, not inducing madness, but making him uncomfortable, extra watchful in family and business matters. A Sunday falling on the seventh of the month was especially dangerous.

His son, John Doyle Coburg, was in every way overshadowed by the father. At the age of eighteen John had been sent to Oxford and had there met and impregnated a young American girl from a good but only modestly wealthy family. From the day John brought Rose back to meet his father, their marriage, if it ever had a chance, was doomed.

CHAPTER 2

For Rose Coburg life in Kansas City was as close to perfect as she could imagine. She had grown up in Boston, the third daughter of a former Beacon Hill family that had long ago fallen on hard times. They were not really poor. Her father was an effete and unsuccessful lawyer who fortunately received an annual sum from a family trust that enabled him to maintain a gentleman's lifestyle. He drank vintage port, hunted, and traveled once a year with his wife to London to stay with a cousin in Wimbledon. Each of the three daughters was given one chance in life to establish themselves. At age eighteen, they were sent to London to find a titled husband. The first daughter had sadly miscalculated and become engaged to a tailor on Wimbledon Hill. The second daughter had been unsuccessful in her quest and had received no offers at all. Rose, a striking rather than beautiful girl, had met John Doyle Coburg at a Commem Ball in Oxford. Seducing him was not easy, but marrying him in his college chapel a week after the "discovery" of her pregnancy had been as easy as pie.

He was, she decided, almost certainly more comfortable in the company of men than he was with women. And that suited her plans. But, most importantly, his family was extremely rich. It's true that she had little more than his word to go on, but he offered the information so casually that she was convinced he was telling the truth.

She believed that her return to America as a pregnant bride and her forthcoming meeting with her new husband's father would be a massive ordeal. But from the day she met Pierre Coburg, she began to formulate her plans.

She intended to seduce him. But, when the time was ripe, he beat her to the punch. Perhaps, she thought, they seduced each other, if that were possible.

When she first arrived in the big house on Quality Hill, Pierre was cold to her, making no attempt to disguise his disapproval at the haste in which the marriage had taken place. A few days later, two men arrived at the house wearing collars too tight for their bulky frames, brown tweed suits and brown derbys. They looked like cheap detectives or, at best, Pinkerton men. Pierre was closeted with them for an hour. When they had gone he took Rose's arm and told her he wanted to walk in the garden. "I hope," he said, "your father can be persuaded to come out to Kansas City for a visit. I'm planning a belated wedding breakfast for you at the Coates Hotel. Everybody in Kansas City will be there."

Rose was not fooled. "What did your two detectives have to report?" she said, looking up at him. "That we were a respectable but not very wealthy Boston family, I trust."

He smiled. "That's about what they reported."

"Just as I said."

He squeezed her arm. "Just as you said honey."

That first wedding breakfast had also been the scene of the first real confrontation between Pierre and his daughter-in-law. At the age of forty, the slender but powerfully built Pierre was still a young man, although streaks of gray could be seen in his hair. He was accustomed to absolute obedience from his son and from his employees. His servants trembled before him, and he treated them with a rough kindness. Few had ever been dismissed from the Coburg household, but few had ever chosen to leave. Women who had become old women in his service were kept on. The large stable block contained small apartments for Coburg pensioners.

The young woman who now entered this household was to be completely unprotected by her husband. From the first she knew that she could fight Pierre or join him. She was realistic enough to understand that she could not fight him.

Her assets were her youth and good looks. Her problem was the pregnancy. By her own calculation, she had less than a month to get Pierre into bed before the swelling distorted her shape too much to make her desirable.

She knew enough about the world to realize that this man who considered no opinion but his own would nevertheless be titillated by a display of spirit. At the wedding breakfast her husband John made a six-line speech of hesitant thanks to his father. It was not the family custom for the bride to speak, so when she rose, a wave of whispering rolled through the banquet hall.

"Kansas City, as we all know," she began with an air of shyness, "is named from the Kaw or Kansas Indian tribe that hunted the Blue Hills and fished in the old Blue Muddy when time began. These Kaw Indians, it seems, were renowned for their festivals of speechmaking and, I believe, several less mentionable enjoyments."

The men at the wedding breakfast let out a loud cheer. Pierre's set face softened.

"As a newly married Kansas squaw," Rose said, "I know enough to know I can't duck my speechmaking obligations."

Pierre smiled in response to the mutters of encouragement all around him.

"This is the Heartland of America," she said firmly. "The East can talk about its big cities, its big schools.

Texas can talk about its size and the West Coast can talk about its opportunities that are always, *always* around the corner. But here in Kansas City the opportunities are here today. And I'm telling you I may have been born in the East. I may have even been to Europe. But my place is right here in the Heartland of America." She paused for effect. "Beside my husband."

Then she slowly transferred her glance to Pierre. From that moment, some sort of pact began to form between her and Pierre. Friendship had nothing to do with it. How far their alliance would take them neither knew exactly. But both knew that their agreement had to be sealed.

Of the two, Rose, already more than three months pregnant, had the greater sense of urgency. When her husband John went to New York for a week, Pierre was mostly busy away from the house. She did not want to be too open about her intentions, but she made efforts to send all those messages that she knew she had to send. When they were alone, she would carefully arrange and then rearrange her slim legs for his pleasure. Leaving the pool, she would let her robe slip negligently from her shoulders. He acknowledged all this with a hard, wry smile. More than two weeks after the wedding breakfast she was still far from sure that she could have him.

Then one afternoon John left to visit a friend who had just bought a farm down the Raytown Road. The friend, Jack Aston, was a wealthy young man who had yet to do a day's work in his life. But the early death of both parents had enabled Jack to draw up plans to demolish the family farm and erect a house with formal English gardens.

Rose declined her husband's offer to take her for a drive. "My dear John," she said in that haughty tone she had adopted to distance herself from him, "don't you know what this heat does to a girl from the East?"

"I'm sorry, Rose," John said hurriedly. "Of course you must rest. I'll explain to Jack."

He set off in his Lagonda, happy to get away for a few hours from the pressures his wife was able to exert.

John Doyle Coburg was one of those men who had absorbed a sense of personal failure from his father's success. At school he had done modestly well and studied archeology at Harvard, after Pierre made a large contribution to the institution's general fund. But in the rough and tumble world of Kansas City politics and business he was completely lost. People like the redneck Prendergasts who ruled Kansas City shook his hand and turned away. Nevertheless, this tall slender young man, shy at parties and particularly with women, had one ambition, to please his father. To this end he had dabbled in the business but he had been shocked on his first selling trip to Peking to see how bribes were distributed and reluctant officials beaten. He would never, he knew, make a banknote salesman. And after his first month in the central printing plant in Kansas City he also knew that he would never be able to control the tough Irish overseers that security banknote printing demanded in the wild post-war days.

He was twenty when he arrived at Oxford, cloaked in his sense of failure. Then he had met Rose, beautiful, American and from Boston. After the ball, they had taken a boat ride on the river. It was a warm June night an hour or so before dawn and they had allowed the flat bottomed punt to drift and nestle among the reeds on the bank. Boats full of other revelers moved past them, as Rose undid the buttons on his fly. He was deeply shocked but he lay back, helpless on the broad corduroy cushions. It seemed to him that she was possessed as she knelt above him, pulling off her English knickers. When she straddled him the folds of her ball gown obscured his vision. He struggled to pull it from his face and when he was once again looking straight up at the checkerwork of black leaves against the lightening sky, he was aware that his penis felt enjoyably warm. She had enclosed him for fully two minutes before he realized that for the first time in his life he was experiencing sexual intercourse. His spasm coincided with the realization. Rose rolled off him and lay beside him on the corduroy cushions. As a pink dawn rose behind Magdalen Tower, she snuggled closer to him. "Wasn't that just wonderful, darling?" she said as she urged him awake. "When we're married," she said happily, "we'll be able to do it whenever we like."

Back in Kansas City his father's anger had at first been terrible. He had raged up and down the room like a bull, swiping at ornaments and kicking at oriental carpets. But he was faced with a fait accompli and he knew it. Whether he would accept it depended on what the Pinkerton men reported and what the brazen offer of alliance contained in Rose's wedding breakfast speech had in it for him.

On the afternoon that John Coburn left to look at the plans for the conversion of Jack Aston's farm property, Rose took the gravel path that would bring her past the open garden doors of the room where she knew Pierre was working. Before she rounded the corner of the house she stopped in the shadow of a great wisteria and arranged her broad-brimmed sun hat and smoothed her hands down over the faint swelling in her belly. Then she walked slowly on.

She knew he was there in the deep shadow of the room. Her heels crunched on the gravel. She stopped and picked at an imaginary snag in her stocking, but still he didn't call.

Continuing as slowly as she dared, she passed the garden room and reached the main entrance to the house. Still he didn't call.

She felt furious. Humiliated. She had offered herself

to an old man and he had *refused*. She stood indecisively before the vast front door, then let herself in.

Pierre was standing in the doorway of his work room, cigar in hand. He smiled at her and she swallowed hard and smiled back.

"I think I drank a little too much wine at luncheon," she said. "I feel quite light-headed."

He drew on his cigar without speaking. His eyes roved over her body and she became infuriated. She was on the very edge of turning, flouncing out, when, with his free hand, he reached for a servant's bell and pushed it.

She heard the ringing in the rear of the house. Then again and again as he pushed on the button.

They heard hurried steps on the servants' stairs and Jacob, one of the younger footmen, raced into the hall and stopped.

Pierre turned towards him. "Ask Henry, for me," he said, "to take a bottle of champagne up to Mrs. Coburg's bedroom."

Jacob half-bowed and turned quickly away.

"Come in," Pierre said.

She walked ahead of him into the room. "And just why," she said as he closed the door after him, "have you had champagne sent up to my room?

"If you feel a little light-headed, Rose," he said nonchalantly, "an hour's sleep in a cool room and a glass of good champagne upon waking, will do wonders for you. I'm sure your dear mother would agree."

He had dropped into one of the armchairs.

"You've assumed of course, that I don't enjoy this state of lightheadedness. On the contrary I find it refreshing, liberating even." She sat on the arm of his chair. It was a perfectly open invitation. Again he did nothing and again her anger began to rise. Then he placed one enormous hand on her thigh and began to caress upwards. She shifted her legs a fraction, opening them. His hand moved down the inside of her thigh and she felt his thumb between her legs.

"I think perhaps we should go and drink that champagne together," she said.

He smiled. "What a pleasurable daughter-in-law my son has presented me with," he said, rising to his feet and offering his hand.

For a long time afterwards she wondered about his use of the word pleasurable. Was he aware that the word was used not to describe a person, but rather an event, an occurrence, even a *thing?*

CHAPTER 3

The family that Pierre Coburg moved to Long Island in 1926 consisted of himself, his son John Doyle Coburg, his daughter-in-law Rose and his grandchildren, the twins Martin and Celine.

It was a privileged existence. Through the 1930s Martin grew up unaware of the grimness of the depression years. An athletic boy, comfortable in his body, he was devoted to tennis, swimming and especially boxing. By the time he reached his teens, his looks and his easy manner ensured a ready acceptance at the family's Long Island country club.

But there was a darker side. Surrounded by friends of his own age, he could avoid the problems of his home, the problems of family love and affection and the sources of authority. If he hated anybody it was his mother. If he admired anybody it was his grandfather. If he loved anybody it was his sad, nervous father.

Yet he and his father had little or nothing in common. John Coburg played the cello to performance standards, but he played for himself, alone in his rooms. As Martin got older he came to realize that music and whiskey were his father's main supports in life. Music and whiskey and Jack Aston.

Martin had, over the years, tried to become close to his father. At dinner each evening he would pretend not to hear the jeering note Pierre's voice naturally adopted when he spoke to his son John. As Martin grew older, each evening became an excruciat-

ing exercise in speaking politely to his father without
offending his mother or his grandfather. Celine, of
course, sided openly with her mother. Pierre's business friends or Rose's Boston relatives who visited
always gravitated towards the strong. Evening after
evening Martin would watch in misery as his father
sat at the table, totally ignored by all the adults.

It was music that opened up a tenuous line of com-
munication between them. On his phonograph Martin
often played the newly available records of the jazz
bands of Chicago and St. Louis. He had none of his
father's formal knowledge of music, but something in
him responded to this Negro music with its humorous,
liberating rhythms.

One day, passing each other on the wide staircase
of the house, they both stopped and realized that they
could not really pass each other without speaking.

"I heard your phonograph all morning," John said.

"Sorry, Dad."

"No, no that's not what I meant, son. I like the
music. At least I find it more interesting than I at first
thought it was."

"You like jazz music?" Martin had looked at him
in surprise.

"I think I might grow to like it," his father said
cautiously. "I might just grow to like it quite a lot,"
he added, desperate not to break the slender thread
between them.

There was a long pause. "Bix Beiderbecke is playing in New York," Martin said. One hand was rubbing
up and down the bannister rail. He was ready for
rejection.

"In New York, you say?"

"At the Honey Club. I couldn't get in by myself."

John Coburg felt a throb of excitement. "Would
you like me to take you?"

"Would you?"

"Why . . . sure I would. The Honey Club, you say."

Two days later they had sat at a table not twenty
feet from Bix Beiderbecke himself. Martin was transported. His father, who had begun the evening with
a skeptical demeanor, ended it with foot-tapping enthusiasm. "I think I am beginning to see," he said in
the back of the limousine on the way home, "what a
young fellow like you sees in this music. I think this is
something we ought to explore a little more together."

Martin felt a warm glow of gratitude, a sense that
he had been able to give something to his father.
"Next week at the Honey Club," he said, "Armstrong's playing with Ella Fitzgerald."

"Then we must go hear them," his father said gaily.
"Let's see, Tuesday before Christmas, marvelous.
We'll have dinner at the Harvard Club and go to hear
ourselves some jazz."

The feeling for his father generated by their visit to
the Honey Club remained throughout the preparations
for Christmas. There was between them, for the first
time, a certain complicit warmth.

Shortly after Pierre had moved his family to Long
Island, Jack Aston, Martin's father's friend, had
turned up there with beachfront property near Montauk Point.

He now came to the house quite often and Martin
began to get to know him for the first time. A slender
man of medium height with light brown hair that fell
across his forehead, Aston wore quite different clothes
from Pierre or most of the men Martin knew. He
never wore heavy dark suits. In summer he wore
cream linen with large red or deep green handker-
chiefs that cascaded from his top pocket.

Martin had grown up with the sense that there was
something undesirable about Jack Aston. His mother
and Pierre were always scathing about him. At times,
having drunk a little too much Armagnac after dinner,
Pierre would begin a strange prancing imitation of
Jack Aston, which was not like him at all but which

made Martin's mother shriek with laughter, and sometimes made his father rush from the room.

When Martin was younger, Jack Aston had offered to tutor him in Latin. But Pierre, Martin knew, had forbidden it and instead hired some seedy English clergyman who arrived twice a week to torture him with the dreadful complexities of Bradley's Arnold.

Only at prep school in Westchester had Martin begun to understand, however vaguely, the attacks on Jack Aston and his father. They were pansies, one of the older boys said. And he began to prance around much as Pierre did when he was imitating Jack.

At that moment Martin was still ignorant of what his father was being accused of. The bigger boy, Barrington, had nudged others in the group gathered around Martin. "Well, Coburg," he said, "what do you say about that?"

"My dad isn't a pansy," Martin had said, defending himself desperately from the pushing group of boys. "He ran the hundred yard dash for Oxford."

"He's a pansy," Barrington said menacingly. "What's he do, Knight?"

Eric Knight sucked in his lips. "He goes kiss, kiss with other men."

"He doesn't. He is not a pansy," Martin had shouted in Knight's face. But Barrington had seized him from behind and with Knight's help had twisted Martin's arm until he screamed with pain.

"And what does your dad do, Coburg?" The boys twisted Martin's arm. "Kiss, kiss with other men. Kiss, kiss with Jack? What does he do?"

Martin clenched his teeth, throwing his head back from side to side.

"What does he do?" Barrington leaned harder on his arm.

Intense loyalty to his father rose like a spurt of anger. Struggling violently, Martin kicked backwards, his heel rising between Barrington's legs. As the boy

screamed the armlock broke. The games master, at-
tracted by the shouts, came into the locker room.
"Stop that horseplay," he said. "I want you all outside, changed, in two minutes."

A few days after their visit to the Honey Club to
listen to Louis Armstrong, John Coburg had come up
to his son's room. Outside, it was snowing heavily and
Martin was sitting in the window seat, reading.

"Martin, I've got a great idea. Jack Aston says that
Fats Waller's playing at the Courtesy Club right until
Christmas. You like to go?"

Martin put down the book. "Fats Waller? Sure I'd
like to go."

"These tickets are like gold dust," John Coburg
said. "But I have influence in high places."

"I'd really like to go, Dad."

John Coburg was delighted by his son's rare display
of enthusiasm. "Okay. Dinner jacket. We eat at the
Harvard Club and go on to catch the midnight show
at the Courtesy. How does that sound to you?"

"Really great."

Martin's father smiled as he moved back towards
the door. "Just one thing, Martin. Perhaps there's no
need to mention to your mother or Pierre that Jack's
coming with us. Jack's not their favorite person."

On the night they were to go to see Fats Waller,
Martin dressed in his first dinner jacket. Pierre had
insisted that, now that he was fifteen, he should be
properly dressed for the huge Christmas Eve dinner
Pierre always gave. A dinner jacket for the young
Coburg boy was now essential.

Standing in front of the mirror in his bedroom, Martin looked himself over with pleasure. Thrusting one
hand deep into his trouser pocket, he left his room on
the second landing and came slowly down the staircase
into the hall. The butler was helping his father on with
his blue overcoat. John Coburg looked up and smiled
approval at his son. "Looks good, doesn't he, Frank?"

The butler, an ally of Martin's mother, looked at Martin without a word. "Impeccable, sir," he said after a perfectly-timed moment of insolence.

From the drawing room came the sound of voices as the door opened. Pierre, Rose and her sister Bette, came out into the hall.

Rose stopped, staring angrily at Martin. "That dinner jacket is for Christmas Eve," she snapped. "Who gave you permission to wear it tonight?"

Martin looked towards his father whose lips were pressed tight together, unable to speak.

"Dad said you have to wear dinner jackets at the Courtesy Club."

"We're going to listen to some jazz music," John Coburg blurted.

"I'm not having the boy wear that dinner jacket before Christmas Eve," Rose said coldly.

Pierre stood with Bette a few steps behind Rose. He was smoking a cigar, content to let Rose exert her authority.

"Rose,"—John Coburg's voice took on a note of pleading—"I can't take him without the right clothes. You know the Courtesy Club."

"Get out of that dinner jacket," Rose said quickly.

Martin hesitated as his father struggled to protest. "Listen, Rose," her husband said. "Just this once."

She turned away.

"Okay Dad," Martin said. "You two go on alone."

Rose swung round. "You two? Who else was going? You, Martin and who else?"

The butler smiled down at the black-and-white tiled floor. Pierre waved his cigar under his nose and inhaled the smoke. Bette's eyebrows lifted inquiringly.

"Jack Aston," John Coburg said, "Jack was coming with us."

Rose took a step towards him. "You were allowing my son to go with *Jack Aston?* A fifteen-year-old boy going with that pederast? Are you out of your mind?"

She threw down the drink she was carrying and the glass shattered on the tiles.

"Are you insane? My good God," she exploded, "it's bad enough having a nancy boy for a husband. Do I *have* to put up with him taking my son to socialize with his nancy friend?"

Martin turned and blundered wildly up the stairs.

Barely checked, a violence roamed Rose Coburg's spirit. It was not directly sexual. She did not demand her lovers should be abased. Certainly, Pierre with his huge masculinity left her no choice. But she enjoyed suffering, she enjoyed the helplessness of the sufferer, she enjoyed most of all her part in inflicting suffering.

It was, of course, not that clear-cut even to Rose herself. She was fully aware of the extent of her harbored resentments against others. She was equally aware of that strange, exhilarating tingle of satisfaction she received when she reduced a maid to tears.

Most of her anger was directed towards her husband. The high points of her satisfaction were gained from inflicting pain on him.

Yet he rarely left himself vulnerable. He had learned, over several years, how to protect himself. He never took part in family discussions; he accepted Rose's decisions without comment. But his relationship with Jack Aston was, everybody in the family knew, his Achilles' heel.

The Christmas of 1936 was, as usual, to be spent at Island House. Apart from the immediate family, Rose had invited her unmarried sister Bette (who arrived in mid-November for the celebrations) and her married sister Zoe and her husband, a Boston lawyer named George Ackroyd. They brought with them three colorless teenage girls whose presence embarrassed, bored and irritated Martin in turns.

Pierre's guests were all men of political or business importance and their wives and children. There was a

British ambassador and his wife, two governors of the Federal Reserve Bank, half a dozen politicians from Kansas City, a senator from New York State, and as a special sign of Pierre's favor, Merril Soames, the young up-and-coming vice-president from Coburg Banknote.

Notably absent from Rose's guest list was Jack Aston. Martin had been reading in the corner of the library, trying to escape the attention of the Ackroyd girls, when his parents walked in. They were so rarely together that Martin looked up in surprise.

John Coburg stopped somewhere near the middle of the room, ill at ease as he always was if a confrontation loomed.

Martin looked from his mother to his father. "If you have things to talk about," he said as he rose from his chair, putting aside the book.

"If you don't mind old chap," his father smiled an apology.

"Stay where you are, Martin," Rose snapped. "We're talking about the guest list, for God's sake. So what is it John, what's troubling you?"

She had swung around to face him.

"I talked to Jack today," he said.

"Yes?"

"He told me he hadn't received an invitation yet."

Rose reached over slowly to take a cigarette from a silver box. "That doesn't altogether surprise me," she said.

John Coburg lit her cigarette. "I don't understand, Rose. Why hasn't he got his invitation?"

"Because he wasn't sent one."

Martin lifted his eyes quickly. His father's face was crumpled with distress.

"Jack is my best friend," John Coburg said. "I insist he be sent an invitation to this house for Christmas."

"You can insist all you like. He won't get one. Would you like me to tell you why?"

"For God's sake, Rose," John flushed in rare anger. "I will not have you repeating gossip and rumor that you pick up at cocktail parties."

"The picking up was done entirely by your friend Aston, as I understood the story," Rose said cooly. "Two Yale freshmen. Very fresh, I was told."

"Listen to me, Rose. Swill all that malicious gossip from your mouth. If Jack is not invited here for Christmas, I won't be here either."

He looked down at his son. "I'm sorry, Martin. I'm sorry for your sake."

"Just one thing," Rose said as he turned for the door. "Obviously you're going to tell Pierre . . ."

John Coburg paused.

"Obviously you're going to tell Pierre you can't bear to spend Christmas Day away from Jack . . ."

Defeat showed in his stance.

"Shall I get Mabel to wake Pierre from his nap?"

John Coburg lifted his eyes once more to his wife's face and shook his head slowly. "Forget it," he said and turned and walked from the room.

"There," Rose threw her cigarette into the fire, then turned to her son. "Don't let that upset you, Martin. Some men like the rules laid out to them. Some men are as weak as water."

The Coburg Christmas traditions dated back to Kansas City days. Christmas Eve was the high point of the holiday when the family and guests would gather in the long library at about five o'clock. Drinks and canapes were served. Martin in his new dinner jacket and Celine in a superb dress from Contrain-Laffont were for the first time invited to join the adult guests. The children were, meanwhile, entertained at a lavish party in the kitchen.

The scene was etched with acid in Martin's memory. Rose, his mother, floated from one group of guests to another, talking of business, politics or clothes as seemed appropriate. Young Merril Soames flirted cautiously with her, one eye on the Coburg Banknote president. Pierre and Celine stood before the great fireplace where huge logs of silver birch burned with bright blue-and-white flames. Champagne and martinis were offered from silver trays by waiters in white gloves. Christmas music played on a new phonograph gadget that Pierre had acquired during the summer.

Waves of talk and laughter swelled through the room as the drinks began to have their effect. At seven o'clock, as tradition dictated, Pierre would call for silence, would bow his head and briefly ask for the Lord's blessing on their Christmas. He would then offer Rose his arm, the double doors would open and Pierre would lead his family and guests across the great hall with the lighted Christmas tree and into the dining room. On the table would be a centerpiece of an enormous three-foot-long stuffed carp.

Martin was fretting. His girl cousins fluttered around him, all slightly older than he was, all anxious to please. Barrington, the boy from his Westchester prep school, was there with his parents. Now a young man with dark smoothed hair, the boy cultivated a disdainful manner. "You ever run into Eric Knight these days?" Barrington asked. "Remember him?"

"Oh, I remember him," Martin said. "Is it true he couldn't get accepted to law school again?"

"He was never much of a brain," Barrington conceded.

"He was never much of anything," Martin said, looking over Barrington's head from the extra three inches he had over the older boy.

His mother touched his arm, indicating he should come closer. "Where in God's name is your father?" she hissed.

"I haven't seen him," Martin said.

"For God's sake drop your lifetime habit of telling lies. You saw him after lunch."

"I meant I hadn't seen him since. I'm sorry, I don't know," he muttered, "I don't know where he is."

Her head came up, nostrils flaring.

"I want the truth," she said. "Or you go down now in your smart new dinner jacket and you eat Christmas jello and ice cream with the kiddies in the kitchen."

Pierre came sauntering over to her side. He stood opposite Martin, not more than an inch or two taller now. "What's the trouble?" he said in a low voice.

"Martin refuses to tell me where his father is."

Pierre's deep blue eyes narrowed. "You want to celebrate Christmas with a whipping, boy?" His voice was loud now. In his anger he didn't care who heard.

"It's the truth, Pierre," Martin said desperately, "I don't know where Dad is."

"Is he in his room?" Pierre asked Rose.

She shook her head. "I just sent someone up to look."

"He won't be far away," Pierre said. "I told Dawson to lock his car in the garage." He smiled grimly. "And to make sure he didn't get the keys to any of the others. In this weather he's not going to walk to Aston's place."

Rose frowned. She turned to her son, reluctant to believe he knew nothing about his father's where-abouts. "And he said nothing to you? Nothing about what he was going to do this afternoon?"

Martin shook his head.

She stared at him in frustrated anger. "I just know you're lying." Then a thought struck her. "Your mo-torbike," she said.

Martin paled.

"That's it, of course," she hissed triumphantly. "You gave him the keys to your motorbike."

The children's excited screams were deafening. Jello and lemonade mixed with cake crumbs. Paper hats wagged on once well-brushed heads. Balloons rose and were popped by jabbing forks.

"Sit down," Rose ordered, pushing two children aside to open a place on the bench. "Sit down there. If you're not to be trusted to behave like an adult, you get treated as a child. Understand?"

For a moment he contemplated rebellion. For just one moment. Then he put one leg over the bench and slid down between the two little girls.

When his mother left, he sat red-faced with pointless fury. If only he'd said no. Just no.

"Anything I can get you, Mr. Martin," one of the maids said. The concern on her face was almost too much for him.

"No," he said. "No, for Christ's sake."

From the direction of the open staircase he heard laughter.

Harry Barrington and one of the Ackroyd cousins were leaning on the bannister. Barrington raised his champagne glass to Martin. "Sorry we're not staying, old fellow," he said laughing, "but I think we're just about to go in to dine."

Martin pulled himself from the bench. "If my mother wants to know where I am," he said to the maid, "I'm in my room."

The girl nodded expressionlessly.

He walked slowly to the bottom of the stairs. His head lurched with the humiliation of being made to sit with the children while his stomach churned with guilt at having given his motorbike keys to his father. He stood at the bottom of the stairs. Pierre was right. He knew where his father was going and he knew it meant he would not be back that night, or, if he did return, he would be drunk.

Martin started up the stairs to the main hall. He could hear sounds up there, strange scuffling sounds. He took two more steps up. His father and Jack Aston were embracing in the middle of the hall, their mouths locked together.

At that moment the double doors opened from the long library. Pierre stood there with Rose on his arm. Celine screamed, guests surged forward and Martin stared with horror at his father's white face.

CHAPTER 4

The news that arrived by cable from Shanghai was a shattering blow. The Coburg Banknote agent there had changed sides, been bought by another company just as he was negotiating what would have been a highly profitable contract for Pierre.

In the head office in New York confusion reigned for several hours. Desperate telephone calls were placed to everyone who knew anything in the world banknote community. Westfall of De la Rue in London denied his company would ever descend to such an ungentlemanly level. Pierre snorted and put in a call to American Banknote. Again, a similar response. Contacts in Mexico were cabled but claimed to know nothing. The French payee of Coburg Banknote inside Imprimerie d'Orient knew nothing. For ten minutes Pierre raged at him while the members of the board of directors of Coburg Banknote sat watching.

"We pay you a fat bribe to know," Pierre shouted down the transatlantic telephone line. "So goddam find out."

Merril Soames, Pierre's vice-president responsible for contracts, suggested they fly to China immediately. He knew the key man in the deal, Pan Ku-Yan, well. The great problem of dealing with him was that he was endlessly shifty and totally on the make. It would need a watertight deal and Pierre must be prepared to go high.

Pierre calmed slightly, as he was inclined to do when money was mentioned. "I'll stake a million to win eight," he said. "You leave for China right away, Merril. I'll join you as soon as I can discover who the hell bought our man."

The call came late that afternoon. "To the victor, the spoils," a familiar voice said in German.

Pierre flushed with anger. "Emil, you bastard. It was you? You'd undercut your own brother?"

"Why not?" Emil said easily. "You've done the same enough times to me. Or worse."

"I have eight million dollars riding on this deal," Pierre's voice rose in fury.

"Had," Emil corrected him. "Now I have."

"What the hell are you doing, Emil?"

"I'm trying to bring you to your senses."

"You want me to throw money away on your new machine."

"You've got more capital than I have. Spend some of it, for God's sake."

"Waste it on you tinkering with new machines? Listen, the presses we use have not changed in fifty years and they'll go on for another fifty."

"You're a pig-headed fool," Emil yelled down the transatlantic line. "Do you know what the fattest contract in the whole of Europe will be next year? Spain."

"Perhaps."

"If Franco wins," Emil said, "he has promised the contract for a complete new Spanish currency to the Italians. A contract worth millions of dollars to a small printing house in Milan. And why? Because they have a young engineer improving on the old Serge Beaune machines. This young man is the future, you dolt. He's the future unless we put money into development."

"I'm not changing my mind," Pierre growled, "and I'm reminding you that you're breaking our solemn agreement on China."

"You're breaking an equally solemn agreement on technical cooperation. So as far as I'm concerned that leaves China up for grabs. Unless you change your mind. How are Martin and Celine?" He changed the subject abruptly, provocatively, as if now turning to more important matters.

"They're not so bad," Pierre said sulkily. "Martin's turning into a business-like young fellow. Bit on the serious side sometimes. Needs a woman I expect. Celine follows the family tradition. Or *part* of it," he said, heavily. "She'd double-cross her own grandmother if she had one. How're the girls?"

"Elisabeth's entering the marriage stakes. She's set her sights on a young man named Rolf Oster. Fairly bright, but a bit too Englishified, you know."

"I know," Pierre grunted, thinking of the types from De la Rue. "And Alex?"

"She's become quite a serious young lady, too. Politics has got its hand in her knickers."

Pierre grunted. He would leave for Shanghai now. It was going to be tough going. Perhaps he should take young Martin to show him something of the unpleasant end of the business.

"No hard feelings," Emil was saying.

"You treacherous sonofabitch," Pierre said.

"See you in Vienna this summer?"

"Doubt it. Try to make Long Island in the fall. Give my love to Dorotta."

"*Auf Wiedersehen* Pierre."

"*Auf Wiedersehen* you cheating bastard."

Hung with candle lanterns, the two painted barges were poled across the glistening darkness of the Imperial City's Lake Pei Hai. In the leading boat His Excellency the British Ambassador sat with Sir Neville Hatton, the British Naval Attaché, and an American who was later to become famous as "Vinegar Joe," Colonel Joseph Stilwell, the United States Military Attaché and his wife.

In the prow of the second boat, lagging thirty yards behind, Martin sat next to Joe Stilwell's daughter

Nance. He was in a state of acute embarrassment. His embarrassment was not occasioned by Nance, a friendly, easy going American girl. It was because of the necessity he felt to block the view that the group of adults in the lead boat had of the stern of his boat. There, in the stern, he could see his grandfather Pierre and Sir Neville Hatton's wife. Pierre's hand was clearly visible against the dark material of Lady Hatton's dress, undoing buttons until it slipped out of sight under the ruched material of the bodice of the evening gown. He could even hear Mollie Hatton gasping encouragement.

From across the lake came the sound of a guitar and the faint yellowness of a string of lanterns announcing another barge. The attention of the group in the lead boat was diverted. They called in English to the other barge and American voices answered.

"You can't leave yet," Lady Hatton whispered urgently in Pierre's ear.

Martin turned, tried not to hear anything but the greetings exchanged across the water and the inexpert twanging of the guitar.

"I have to go, Mollie," Pierre said in what seemed to Martin like a recklessly booming voice. "Unless the British government is prepared to sell me those rust-buckets in Shanghai, I've no excuse to remain in China."

"I'll do something," she said firmly. "I promise you I'll talk to Neville. They're not his boats. Why should he care who buys them?"

China in 1937 was the land of opportunity for the tens of thousands of foreigners who fought, lied and bribed their way to concessions, franchises and rights to fulfill almost any function in the Chinese economy.

The country was disintegrating. The Japanese had invaded Manchuria. The principal port of Shanghai was a British concession with its own army and police force, currency and laws. Bandit warlords controlled large tracts of land, recruiting peasants into their private armies. An American regiment was permanently stationed in the Imperial capital of Peking. British gunships sailed Chinese rivers. Japanese planes shot down commercial airliners and confiscated Chinese merchant shipping.

Almost without exception, banknote printing contracts were bought; that is to say, Chinese officials were bribed. But this was not by any means a simple, crude process. Only those salesmen who could tread the delicate path between offending and satisfying Chinese pride would succeed. There were recognized experts like the Bulgarian Avramov of De la Rue and there were plainly gifted salesmen like Pierre Coburg of New York. Sometimes they divided the spoils, sometimes they double-crossed each other, sometimes, they conceded defeat, but not often because the stakes were too high.

To Martin the trip to China was the strangest experience of his life. A dozen things disturbed him. Most of all the Chinese girls strutting the Bund in their tight black skirts and flowery blouses, emitting their strange and frightening shrieks of laughter when they saw a potential customer like himself. But even these girls who made his penis harden as he sat at a sidewalk cafe and drank a *citron presse,* even these girls were made more strange and alien by the smells of shredded duck, the shouts of merchants, the shuffling of old ladies, the screams of the rickshaw boys, the constant tinkling of bells and the blaring horns of ancient delivery trucks and shiny western limousines.

Sitting in one of the big window alcoves of the Hotel Woodrow Wilson that looked down on the endless stream of vegetable sellers, old mandarins, rickshaws, and bakery boys, Merril Soames watched with amusement as Martin picked out the street girls' slow, sure swinging strut from among the mercantile hustle on the Bund.

"Pretty, some of them," he nodded towards two girls passing.

"I guess so," Martin said.

Soames drank his *café au lait*. "But if you start getting hot about them you ought to know the score."

"The score? You mean how much they charge?" Martin said tentatively.

Soames brushed the question aside. "That's not the score. A dollar will take you where you want. I mean risks."

"Risks?"

Soames nodded. "Less than half of them are girls." He smiled as he saw the flush rise on Martin's cheeks. "So unless you like the idea of finding yourself in bed with another boy, feel first."

Martin's eyes opened. "First?"

"Before you buy."

It was at that moment that Martin knew that his sex life would not begin in Shanghai.

Behind the facade of street energy the hotels and private houses of the rich were sunk in an oppressively dignified silence. To Martin it seemed a metaphor for the banknote printing business itself. Out on the street where the contracts were won and lost, it was the most persistent, the most cunning, the fastest tongue that triumphed. Once gained, the contract was carried on a silver plate back to the banknote printing houses of America and Europe where men in wing collars genteelly toasted their success.

Martin and Pierre had arrived in Shanghai in the early summer of 1937.

They had rented a house on the Avenue Pétain in the French concession. Within a week Merril Soames had arranged a meeting with Pan Ku-Yan, a senior official of the Bank of China, the man targeted by both Coburg brothers.

"Now I'm going to show you, Martin, what doing

business is about in China today," Pierre had said minutes before the door opened to show Pan Ku-Yan into the salon.

Martin sat as far from the center of the room as he could while first Pierre and then Soames greeted the tall round-faced Chinese in the long embroidered robe. It seemed to Martin that the smiles, the many small jokes, the inquiries after the health of families was all, on both sides, utterly insincere.

When tea had been served the smiles faded as Pierre began talking. "We in New York have taken great interest in your rise to deserved prominence in the banking world of China," Pierre began. "We have looked with pleasure as you were appointed first to the office of the Minister of Finance, Mr. H. H. Kung, and then to the post of representative of the Central Bank here in Shanghai."

"Only time itself can limit the possibilities for Pan Ku-Yan," Soames said politely.

The Chinese gravely inclined his head in agreement.

"From Washington I am able, personally, to bring the congratulations of the U.S. Secretary of the Treasury."

Again Pan Ku-Yan inclined his head. Martin, watching from the far end of the salon, wondered if the Chinese actually believed Pierre or perhaps decided it didn't matter because this gross flattery was all part of the game.

"Secretary Morgenthau offers his best wishes on the marriage of your daughter Ping."

Did the Chinese stiffen slightly? Martin watched his eyes rest on Pierre over the raised teacup.

"The Secretary has consulted me on the subject of a suitable gift to your daughter and her new husband."

Silence.

"Mr. Merril Soames informed me of the interest of your son-in-law's family in merchant shipping."

"His family is prominent in this area," Pan conceded.

"Let us all hope," Pierre said piously, "that the new Tokyo demands will not result in the transfer of all China's commercial shipping to the Japanese merchant fleet."

Pan's eyes fluttered.

"My advice to Secretary Morgenthau," Pierre said carefully, "was that in normal circumstances an appropriate gift to the young couple might be an addition, or perhaps two, to the shipping interests of the Li family."

Again the hooded eyes fluttered.

"But Secretary Morgenthau considered this might not be wise."

"Ah . . ."

"His question was how to ensure that the ship or ships might remain in the possession of your daughter's new husband now that Japan and China are at war."

"Ah . . ."

"I therefore offered to have the tonnage registered in my name, thus giving the protection of U.S. ownership to the ship or ships. In practice, of course, the gift is a gift like any other. Your son-in-law will be free to use the tonnage as he wishes."

The Chinese breathed in deeply to indicate a change of subject. "I understand there was an attractive bid from your sister company, Imprimerie Coburg."

Merril Soames was watching Pan closely. Pierre's face was set, waiting. Was the gift of two merchant ships a higher bribe than Emil's?

"At a time when China's fortunes seem cast on a turbulent sea," Pan said, "it is good to have trustworthy friends."

"We can count on the Central Bank's endorsement, then," Merril Soames said.

"I am sure so." Pan rose to go. "Allow me to convey to Secretary Morgenthau my daughter's gratitude for a handsome gift."

The men shook hands. Pan bowed briefly to them all and Soames opened the door.

"I will arrange for a signed copy of the provisional endorsement to be delivered this very afternoon, Mr. Coburg."

The door closed behind him. For a moment Pierre stood, smiling to himself. Then he took a cigar from a box and offered one to Soames as he re-entered. "So we made it, Merril."

"It's only provisional," Soames said.

"A perfectly balanced deal," Pierre smiled. "The ships are his, but in my name. The contracts are mine, but only as long as *his* name remains on the endorsement. This way neither of us can doublecross the other."

"And the ships that we're presenting to Pan Ku-Yan? Where do we get them from?"

Pierre grinned. "That might be the most difficult part of the deal."

Martin Coburg spent his seventeenth birthday with a notebook on Shanghai's waterfront. He had never seen such a confusion of ships—Chinese red-sailed junks unloading into sampans, old tubs from the last century that listed and belched black smoke. Between anchored cargo ships registered in Liverpool and San Diego and Hamburg the slow sea sucked and fell, heavy as the oil that glistened on it.

He had talked to grizzled skippers in bars, to the sad patient rickshaw boys, to sampan loaders and to street girls. "We need two old coasters," Pierre had said. "Three or four thousand tons each. Go out and find 'em, Martin. But don't go to any shipping office, or regular official. You just find them and let me know where they are. We've hooked this fish and we've got to keep it on the line. Emil is here with a bunch of German salesmen. I don't want anybody to know you're sniffing around the old freighters in the port."

On the second day he got lucky. A sampan boy had told him that two rusting freighters, one with its smokestack collapsed, the other with part of its bridge eaten away, had been moored there since the end of the Great War. Careful inquiries had revealed they belonged to the British Admiralty. Martin sat on a stone wall amid the frantic bustle of the Chinese port flowing past him and began to sketch the two ships.

Surrounded by the screech of laughter from the shop women, the clank of anchor lines, the shouts of Europeans and the rattle of provision carts, Martin was unaware that someone was standing over him until a girl's voice said, in English, "I didn't know you were an artist."

He looked up in surprise to see a very tall, slightly angular European girl of about sixteen, her face shaded by a wide-brimmed sunhat. She wore a pale yellow silk dress belted with a white sash to show a figure poised on the edge of adulthood. In the way she stood, looking down at him, he could feel an adolescent uncertainty in her.

"You remember me," she said. "I'm Alexina, your cousin."

He snapped shut the notebook and stood up. He wasn't thinking how pretty she was, although she certainly was that. He was wondering just how much of his sketch Emil's daughter had seen.

Alexina turned to a young Chinese behind her. "You can go now, Lee," she said, giving him a coin from her purse. "Mr. Coburg will escort me back to the hotel."

"What are you doing in Shanghai?" he asked as they walked along the waterfront.

She laughed, taking off her straw hat and letting tawny blonde hair billow in the offshore breeze. "You know perfectly well what we're doing in Shanghai. And I for one think it's utterly ridiculous."

"Ridiculous?" he echoed carefully.

"Two brothers with the whole world to divide up between them and they can't agree which market belongs to whom." She had lost any uncertainty she might have had. She was telling him now, firmly, her forehead lined in concentration, her eyebrows pressed down over her dark blue eyes. Physically, he thought he could see a resemblance to Celine, although his sister's mouth was different, usually set in a thinner, more self-absorbed line. If one thing was totally absent in the face of Alex and dominant in Celine's it was calculation.

They turned into the Imperial Boulevard and Martin asked her if she wanted to stop at a tea house. She nodded briskly. "But don't *you* think it's stupid, this rivalry?"

He found his deep sense of loyalty to Pierre touched at a sensitive point. "Emil started it," he said. "China has always been recognized as Coburg Banknote territory."

They sat down and ordered tea from the wraith-like girl who appeared from behind a screen of tinkling bamboo.

"You believe it was Emil who first stepped out of line? What about Pierre's bid for the Luxemburg contract. And the Kroner contract from Norway?"

"They were nothing contracts, a few thousand dollars profit in each," Martin said. "You know why Pierre bid for Luxemburg and Norway?"

"Because they couldn't agree about a joint research budget."

Martin nodded. "Pierre believes printing presses have remained basically the same for a hundred years and will do so for another hundred. So, who wants new ones?"

Her young face tightened in concentration. "I think

my father's right," she said. "We can't afford to be left behind. De la Rue in England, the Italians, the Dutch, they're all working on new machines."

Martin shifted uncomfortably. The truth was he had never agreed with Pierre's refusal to create a Coburg research fund. And when Pierre had lunged into Emil's territory and snipped off two small contracts he had thought it childish.

"But don't you see the way it's going?" she said earnestly. "Whoever's right about developing new machines, the important thing is that sooner or later Emil and Pierre will fall out. Seriously. And that's the end of the House of Janus."

Martin looked at her uneasily. This was territory that Pierre would not appreciate him getting into. "I can't see Emil and Pierre ever seriously falling out," he said. "They're brothers. Twins."

"You'll never fall out with Celine? Is that what you're saying?"

He looked at Alexina in surprise. For a sixteen-year-old she knew how to hit below the belt.

The tea arrived and the ceremony of pouring saved him from having to give an answer.

"You know that one day," Alexina said, sipping the hot tea, looking at Martin over the edge of her cup, "you and I will own the House of Janus. Me, because I'm the only child. You, because you're the male heir."

Neither of them mentioned Martin's father.

"Perhaps we'll hate each other," he said grinning.

Her face was totally composed, totally regular in that slightly rounded bloom of extreme youth. Her tongue searched her top lip. "Perhaps we won't," she said.

Leaving the tea house they walked back to her hotel.

He felt her eyes boring through the covers of the

notebook, exposing the sketches of the two British freighters.

She smiled. "When Pan Ku-Yan finished his meeting with Pierre," she said, "he came straight to Emil."

"Jesus! So Emil's upped the offer?"

"Not yet."

"Is he looking for ships?"

"Desperately."

"Has he found any?"

"Not yet."

Martin gripped the notebook. "There aren't that many around," he said.

"There are the two you were sketching," she said.

She stood silent, looking down at the notebook. "Those are your two ships," she said. "You saw them first."

He stared at her unbelievingly. "You mean you're not going to mention the ships to your father?"

"I'm not even going to mention that we met. Between the two sides of the House of Janus there must be no competition. If Pierre and Emil are too stupid to see that, it's up to us. Do you agree?"

"I guess so," he said.

She gave him her hand. "And don't do anything silly like getting engaged to some American girl before you next come to Germany, will you?"

"No," he said as she turned briskly away. "No," he said to the retreating back of her pale yellow dress.

CHAPTER 5

~ ~ ~

Celine Coburg was always going to grow up beautiful. Her mother told her so, the servants told her so, but most of all her grandfather Pierre told her so. "When you're a full-grown woman," he had said, "you'll drive men wild."

At the age of twelve she had desperately wanted to know when that would be. Her mother had not helped much with talk of tufts of hair between her legs and under her arms. She already knew about monthly periods; it was, however, beyond anything, breasts she was interested in.

And then, it seemed almost suddenly, one day they had arrived. No longer just a faint plumpness on either side of her breastbone, but now something definite, shaped almost rounded.

The phonograph was playing a new piece by the Harry James Band. A new singer named Frank Sinatra was crooning "Once upon a Time." Even on the balcony of her bedroom looking out over Montauk Point Celine Coburg had felt the summer of 1934 was proving horribly hot and humid. She had danced about in her shift, her new breasts jumping against the light material of her nightdress.

She could see, almost on the shoreline, that the pickup truck used by Culver, the sour-faced head gardener, had turned and was making its way up to the house.

God it was hot! She lifted her nightgown up above her knees and kicked out her legs like a showgirl. At twelve years of age she was already tall, with Coburg features and tawny blonde hair.

Culver, she noticed, had stopped the pickup in the main garden aisle and had gotten out. No more than fifty yards separated them, and he looked up at her with his usual sour-faced disapproving expression. Then he smiled. She stopped dancing.

"Good morning, Miss," Culver said, still staring unblinkingly up at her. His hand was rubbing slowly at his groin.

This she could not understand. Culver never called her Miss unless Pierre or her mother were present. She came to the balcony rail, leaned on it, and looked down at him. "Good morning, Culver," she said in the most haughty accent she could remember from the movies.

She expected him to get back in the pickup, or tie his shoe, or roll himself a cigarette, but he did nothing. Just stood there. And still rubbed slowly at his groin. She began to feel uncomfortable. "Why are you looking at me like that, Culver?" she said sharply.

"I was just thinking, Miss," he said slowly, "that you look mighty pretty, dancing away like that." Again he smiled.

In her room, behind her, the phonograph clicked off. She stood up, stretched her arms above her head, and pretended to yawn. She knew that was the best way of showing off her breasts, because she'd stood in front of her mirror a thousand times trying to assure herself they were not shrinking back into her chest.

There were voices somewhere along the front of the house. Culver turned abruptly back to the door of the pickup. "If there's anything you want, Miss" he was looking up at her again.—"Anything you want me to do for you, you just come down to my cottage and tell me. Okay?"

She turned back into her room but she could feel the flush of excitement in her cheeks. Culver was over

twenty. Maybe even *thirty*. And he liked her. Suddenly
he liked her.

After that she did it to amuse herself. She would
stand at the top of the garden steps when Culver was
working below. She knew that with the sun behind
her he could see the shape of her body through the
muslin dress.

Or in Shoreline Wood she would stop before him
when he was pruning and command him haughtily to
help her onto a tree trunk. To give her a better view
over the ocean, she said. But she would turn her back
to the sea, and to him, and enjoy the awareness of
him standing there, behind her, sweating.

By the end of the summer Rose Coburg had begun
to organize a few parties of selected friends of Celine's. The boys would arrive in ties and white trousers
and would stand one hand in their pockets trying to
imitate their fathers. The girls would gather at a separate end of the garden and giggle together while Culver prepared the grill for the hamburgers and one of
the maids served fresh lemonade into which the boys
poured moonshine they bought in Montauk.

The parties usually ended in disaster, with fourteen-
year-old boys reeling sickly around the garden and the
girls shrieking in alarm or an imitation of alarm.

On one evening when it seemed to her that not one
of the boys was sober and the girls were all exceptionally stupid, Celine watched Culver clean up the barbe-
cue, then stand wiping his hands on a rag.

He said nothing. But there was a very faint smile
on his face, contempt perhaps for the behavior of the
rich kids reeling and vomiting around him.

She watched him turn away and walk slowly toward
the garden aisle where he had left his truck.

It was not yet dark, though the shrubbery was a
thick mass of shadow as she followed Culver along the
twisting path. He walked fifty, sixty yards before he
stopped and turned toward her. "You ain't enjoying

your party, Miss?" he said. She saw he was rolling a cigarette.

"The boys are drunk and the girls are too young."

He nodded, tongued the paper and stuck the cigarette into his mouth. With a brass petrol lighter he lit the wisps of tobacco hanging from the paper and inhaled.

"Don't you think they're all appalling?" she pressed him.

"Not for me to say, Miss. Anyways, they're your guests. Not mine."

"Do you like my dress?" she said suddenly, swirling around until it lifted above her knees.

"Sure," he said. She saw that he was again rubbing slowly at his groin.

"Why do you do that?" she pointed.

"Because it makes me feel good, Miss."

She nodded. "Would it make you feel better if I did it?"

He threw the cigarette away. "It might at that," he said.

She returned to what remained of the party in a state of turmoil. She had never as much as petted with a boy before and now she had done things with a grown man. She had reached out to rub his groin and been surprised at the hardness pressing against his blue jeans.

His hands, the fingers wide, had engulfed her breasts. She recoiled, slapping his hands away. "You take your hands off my dress," she said. "Stand there against the tree."

She had watched the anger in his face. He hesitated, half turning.

"If you go now, Culver," she said in her movie voice, "don't ever come back for more."

He swung back towards her, then leaned against the tree. Very calmly, though her heart was beating wildly, she unbuttoned his fly. Slipping her hand inside she began to caress the heat and hardness, her eyes on his face as he threw back his head and gulped great mouthfuls of air. Then she smiled, withdrew her hand and turned away. Before he was fully aware of what was happening, she was several yards down the path.

He came blundering after her. "For Christ's sake," he said, grabbing her arm. "You're not going to leave me like that."

"I'm not?" She peeled his fingers from her arm and walked back down the darkened path to where the girls were dancing to the phonograph while the boys looked on, their ties askew, their eyes barely focusing.

For a few moments Celine stood hugging herself, encompassed in an utter feeling of triumph. Only when the high tide of her feeling began to recede did she leave the party in the garden and walk rapidly back to the house.

In the days that followed Culver pursued her with an expression of yearning. The cool superiority of just a few weeks before had gone. If she played tennis he contrived a gardening job near the courts. If she went riding he tried to follow her in the pickup. Within a month first the maids and then Rose herself noticed it. "That man Culver," she said to Celine, "has got to go."

"Go?" Celine said innocently. "go where?"

"He's got to go," Rose snapped. "Leave. I'll tell Pierre to fire him tomorrow."

"What's Culver done?" Celine asked smiling. "I thought you always said he was the best gardener we had."

Rose put her arm around her daughter's shoulder. "What a little bitch you are," she said affectionately. "What a little bitch!"

Ambition seemed to Celine as if it had been with her all her life. As she entered her sixteenth year she would have been hard put to describe it in specific, comprehensive terms, but she knew beyond doubt that it was part of her as she recognized it was part of her mother.

She was not afraid of Pierre. Why exactly she did not know. Her grandfather was capable of towering rages, of striking servants or even once attacking her father last Christmas when they had all walked into the hall to find her dad kissing Jack Aston under the mistletoe.

She wasn't sure how shocked she'd been herself. She had pretended to cry and her mother had started to scream or something and Pierre had barged his huge shoulders between the two men, striking his son to the ground.

Weak as water her mother always said about her father. Weak as water she said about Martin too. Celine wasn't by any means so sure.

Inadvertently, it was Martin who had introduced Celine to Harlem. Long Island Mission was a clapboard building off Lexington Avenue founded in 1930 by a group of Long Island businessmen (among them Pierre Coburg) as a sports club and boxing hall for the children of Harlem. As the grandson of one of the founders and himself developing into a competent amateur boxer, Martin spent an evening or two a month at the Mission, teaching some of the younger boys, sparring with those his own age.

His coach most nights there was Joe Williams, a young Negro not more than two or three years older than Martin himself; a strongly built boy whose ambition, stated candidly and without boastfulness, was to become cruiserweight champion of the world. He had already performed brilliantly in last year's Golden Gloves and his first professional fight had already been arranged for him at the old Masonic Hall in Queens. He was a quiet, self-contained youngster who knew that boxing was one of the few and quickest

ways out of Harlem, even if you were only moderately
successful.

They became friends, awkwardly given the differences in their background. Some nights Joe would
take Martin down to Henry O's where they heard
some of the best musicians in New York.

To Celine her brother's forays into Harlem were
intriguing and spiced with danger. Her friends at
school, Suzie van Meegren in particular, claimed Ne-
groes were naturally more virile than white men and
that every girl should try one at least once.

Celine's dreams were stimulated further by the photographs of black boxers Martin kept in his room. Joe
Louis was appealing, but too dome-headed; he had
nothing of the svelte blackness of a middleweight
named Steve "Bomber" Hartley, who posed with a
great swelling in his boxer shorts and an expression
that was somehow both haughty and humble. Sometimes she would remove the picture and take it to her
room.

During the spring in which she was to turn seven-
teen, Celine had begun to go into New York to visit
her friend Suzie. She would be driven into Manhattan
by the chauffeur, Oates, and dropped on Madison Avenue at what he was told was the van Meegren's apartment block. At around nine o'clock Oates would
return, collect Celine and drive her back.

All Suzie's mother knew, since her family spent the
summers out of New York City, was that *their* chauffeur deposited his charge at a Manhattan apartment
building. She thought the address was that of the Coburgs' town house. It required no more than an occa-
sional ten dollars to the hall porter for the whole thing
to operate like clockwork.

Free now for the afternoon and early evening, the
two girls would head for Harlem.

Henry O's was called a lunch club. Occupying the
whole of a faded but elegant building on Lenox Ave-

nue, the lunch club welcomed guests, or at least some guests, from about midday until the early hours of the morning. In the rear rooms you could relax with a drink on large comfortable sofas and back horses running anywhere from New York to Florida.

It was Suzie van Meegren who had found the name of the club after overhearing Martin talking about it at a cocktail party. Since then, having used Martin's name while he was away on a junior club tennis tour, the two free-spending girls were welcomed guests. Henry O, a big light-skinned Negro, even kept a mostly benevolent eye on them.

Joe Williams was a Saturday waiter at the club. After the first two visits to Henry O's, Celine, in her best movie voice, insisted she would be served by no one other than Joe.

By mid-afternoon Henry had called Joe into the kitchen. There were only the Chinese cook and a couple of women washing dishes at the sink there. "You know what she's doing, don't you, Joe?" Joe shrugged uncertainly.

"She's prick-teasing a colored boy. It's one of the least edifyin' sights I know."

Joe didn't answer.

"Stick to your boxing, son, you're a good fighter. If you're going to get your head scrambled, get it scrambled by a left hook, not by some white girl." He flicked Joe lightly under the nose. "And for this advice *I'm* paying *you* sixty-five cents an hour!"

The week after Henry O had delivered his advice, Suzie and Celine arrived for lunch to find their table waited on by an apologetic regular waiter. "Joe don't come in till afternoon now, Miss," he said in answer to Celine's questions. "Henry O's moved him into the gaming room."

At six o'clock Celine watched Joe come out of Henry O's and look hurriedly both ways down the street. She pressed herself back into the shadows and watched as, after a few moments, he began to walk north on Lenox Avenue towards 134th Street. When he had almost reached the corner she ran quickly across the road, calling to him.

He turned quickly, stopped and moved his shoulders inside his jacket like a boxer loosening up. She stopped in front of him. "Are you going to show me where you live, Joe?" she said.

The boy shook his head. "I can't do that."

"Why not, Joe?"

"You know why not, Miss."

"Call me Celine," she said. "So why not, Joe? You live with your family?"

"No."

"What do you have, an apartment? Or a room?"

"It's a room," he said. "Just a small room. The house isn't that clean."

"This way is it, Joe?" She started down 134th Street. "I don't think I've ever been in just a room before."

He had stopped before a closed bakery with wooden shutters. Through an open doorway beside the shop Celine could see a tobacco-brown plaster wall with a haphazard pattern of deep scratches. There seemed to be no front door.

"Please," he said desperately, "you can't go up there."

"This is it, is it?" She looked past his shoulder. She felt totally confident, unworried by the stares of passersby as she stood with Joe outside the bakery.

"Listen," the boy said, "if a cop comes along now, I could be in trouble."

"Nonsense," she said.

"Believe me, it's not nonsense."

"If a cop comes along now, Joe, I'll tell him to mind his own business." She walked past him and entered the hallway. The sweet smell of poverty floated around her. It was the first time she had smelt it.

He had run after her.

"Which floor?" Celine said, plunging up the oil-cloth covered stairs. He caught her at the first landing, angry now. "Look, I don't have to show you where I live," he said. "In the restaurant it's bring me this, bring me that and I have to do it. But this is where I live. This is different."

"Why is it different, Joe?"

A door opened before he could answer and a thin black woman in a flowered apron stopped in astonishment, then stepped back, slamming the door.

"I'm not here to be laughed at," Joe said. "I'm a poor man, but I'm a fighter and a good one. When I get me my own apartment in Jersey somewhere, then you can come. If you want to, that is."

Ducking quickly under his arm, she was in the room before he could react.

"You'll have to be faster than that at the Masonic Hall, Joe."

He followed her through the door. "You certainly know how to get what you want," he said grudgingly.

She stood in the middle of the room. It was small, with one long well-shaped window looking down into the bakery yard. The ceiling was high and the walls were plain green, newly painted.

"I did it when I took the room," Joe said. "I said to myself, does this place need a paint job! And I did it right off."

She nodded, letting her eyes wander over the single bed with a fresh clean pillow in evidence, the two straight-backed chairs, the old brown painted chest of drawers and the dark green oil-cloth covered floor.

"It's a nice place, Joe," she said at length. "You got one of those rubber things here?" she said.

"What rubber things?" he stared at her.

"Rubber things you put on you?"

"Oh . . ." he said.

"Yes or no? You know what I mean."

"Yes," he said. "Yes."

She began taking her clothes off. "I've chosen you, boy," she said with deliberate offense, "to be the first one."

CHAPTER 6

~ ~ ~

When Martin returned from the tennis tour, he rang the Mission to speak to Joe Williams.

"Joe's not here," the gym manager said.

"When can I reach him there?"

"You can't, Mr. Coburg. Joe wouldn't want that."

"I don't get it," Martin said. "Why shouldn't Joe want to speak to me?"

"You mean after what's happened, Mr. Coburg?"

"Call me Martin, for Christ's sake," Martin said. "You never called me Mr. Coburg before."

"We learn fast, Mr. Coburg," the manager's voice was loaded with irony.

"Listen," Martin said carefully, "I gather something's happened. What?"

"I don't know what, Mr. Coburg. I only know that you can't reach Joe Williams here."

That same evening Martin took his father's car and drove into Harlem. At Henry O's his reception was brief, and not welcoming.

"Henry," Martin said as he ordered a Scotch and water at the bar, "where's Joe?"

"He doesn't work here any more."

"What?"

"I dismissed him, okay with you Mr. Coburg?"

"You dismissed him," Martin echoed.

"On account he couldn't do his job, I let him go." He pushed Martin's money across the counter. "No cause for you to be coming round any more. Okay with you, Mr. Coburg?"

"Where is Joe?" Martin asked desperately.

"I think he's taken off for Chicago. Okay with you, Mr. Coburg?"

Martin got off the bar stool and walked towards the door, baffled by Henry O's hostility.

"You like Joe, right?" Henry O called across the room.

Martin turned at the door. "You know I do. He's a friend."

"If you're a friend don't go looking for him at his rooming house. Joe's got the message."

Martin shook his head. "Message, what message?"

"The message was loud and clear: you stay away from the white folk," Henry big-mouthed the words, parodying his own accent.

"Who sent the message?"

"I don't know and Joe don't care. Goodbye, Mr. Coburg."

The day Martin returned from his tennis tour Joe Williams had been found badly beaten up in the hallway next to the bakery on 134th Street. It had happened, an unnamed witness reported, at about ten o'clock in the evening as Joe was getting back from the training run he put in every night. A car full of white men had pulled up outside the bakery. The witness wasn't sure, but she thought there may have been another car behind the first. Four men had got out as Joe came running towards them. The first had hit him with something without speaking. The others had baseball bats and they hit him too. Joe had managed to get into the doorway before he went down and stayed down. The doctor called by Henry O reported that Joe's right arm was broken in four places between the elbow and the wrist. Most serious was the broken elbow. There was no chance he'd fight in the Masonic Hall or any other place after this.

The morning after Joe Williams was beaten in Harlem, Pierre Coburg called Celine to the library. She took her time after her maid told her, dressing in a leisurely way, rubbing rouge into her cheeks and reddening her lips. When she was ready she went down to the library.

Pierre was sitting behind his desk. When he looked up she felt a spasm of alarm. She should have got down here more quickly. His face was dark and rigid with anger. "If that girl can't deliver a message from me more quickly than that, I'm going to have to fire her," he said.

It seemed best to say nothing.

He got up and began to prowl the length of the library. She stood watching the broad shoulders as he moved away from her, and then the mass of gray white hair turned and his face had a ferocity she could not remember seeing before. "Why in the name of God?" he said, stopping five yards from her.

"Why?"

"Why in the name of God do you choose a colored man for your paramour?"

Her principle was to admit nothing until it was proved against her. "What colored man," she said. "What paramour?"

He took two enormous strides and hit her.

She fell backwards against a table and down painfully across a pair of library steps. Her face was stinging, her head thumping with pain and anger.

"You're seventeen-years-old," Pierre roared, "and you don't have the common sense to realize that a Coburg girl *cannot* be seen screwing a colored man. Don't you understand that? Don't you see you can bribe, steal, even arrange murder, but you cannot be known to be screwing a colored man in Harlem. Oh, my good God," he shouted. "Thank the Lord you were seen by someone close to me. Thank the Lord you weren't seen by anyone else. Don't you know that if the muckrakers had got onto what you were doing

half our business connections would have faded away
before our eyes."

The pain was changing now, deepening. She had
half risen onto one knee, still afraid that he would
strike her again. A silence fell in the long room. He
reached out a hand and pulled her to her feet.

They stood close together, he with his arms around
her. "I've dealt with the situation," he said. "There'll
be no blackmail. You just keep away from Harlem
from now on," he said as he slid his hand down across
the curve of her hip, "or I'll have your beautiful ass."

"What happened to Joe?" she said, although she
thought she could guess.

"Taken care of," he said, "by a few friends of
friends from the Kansas City days. Remember, you
talk to no one. Not to your mother. Not to Martin.
No one."

She felt his arm tighten round her. "A girl like
you," he said slowly, "can have just about any man
she wants." His hand came up and brushed her breast.
Deliberately, she relaxed into it. "As long as it's not
a colored man," he added, his lips pursed
disapprovingly.

"If it was anyone in my family, I swear I'll call the
cops," Martin said.

Joe Williams lay propped up in the hospital bed.
"It could have been anybody," he said flatly.

"If it was anything to do with us . . ."

Joe nodded, heavy-lidded. "Listen," he said. "I'm
pretty tired now. D'you mind?"

Martin stood up. "I've taken care of the hospital
bill."

"Did you speak to the doctor?"

"He said you'll be fine. He said you'll be able to
shovel coal in no time."

Joe looked at him. "I'm not aiming to shovel coal,"

he said. "Did the doctor say I could deliver a right hook?"

Martin hesitated. "He said you'd be fine, Joe."

"As long as I didn't want to fight again."

Martin's eyes moved across the dingy gray-painted walls and back to the scratched iron bedstead.

"Now why don't you just leave me be?" Joe said.

Martin left the hospital ward with anger boiling inside him. Running along the tattered corridors, he burst through the swinging doors out into the afternoon sunlight.

There was too much for him to absorb. Celine and her friend at Henry O's. Celine chatting up Joe. The appalling sight of Joe in splints and bandages.

And most of all the recurring thought that it was all connected. That Pierre had paid for Joe Williams to be given brutal warning.

He got into his car and drove back to Long Island. Afterwards, he could remember nothing but the whining of the car engine and the screech of tires and the wind plucking at his face. But, somehow, passing along the familiar coast road, seeing the house up in the distance, his earlier certainty that Pierre was involved began to decrease. He thought of his grandfather at the center of jostling friendly crowds, joking at dinner tables, drunk and mellow after a big family evening, and he could not believe he had stooped to ordering a vicious beating for a young boy in Harlem.

And then he thought of China and the double-dealing he had seen, had even been part of, and he had to recognize that for Pierre none of the normal limits seemed to apply. He was larger than life.

Martin turned into the driveway, and pulled up outside the house. Through the corner of his eye he saw his father gardening among the rose bushes. Briefly, it crossed his mind to ask his help. But he quickly dismissed the thought.

On this he would have to face Pierre alone.

As he crossed the hall, his anger rose. Usually he knocked before entering Pierre's domain, but this time he twisted the handle and walked straight in.

Pierre, standing alone next to his desk, looked up, irritated.

His face lightened when he saw Martin. "Come in, boy," he said. "You haven't really told me how the tour went. You did pretty well I hear."

Martin walked slowly down the length of the library. Why hadn't Pierre been angry that he hadn't knocked?

"What is it, Martin?" Pierre asked. "Face as black as thunder." His hand rested on the servants' bell. "Want something to drink?"

Martin shook his head. "A friend of mine from the Mission, a boxer named Joe Williams . . ."

"You talked about him," Pierre said, nodding. "Very promising fighter."

"Not any longer."

"No? Why so?"

"He was beaten up outside his apartment last night. Beaten with baseball bats."

"Sorry to hear that, Martin. It's a hard neighborhood. Arrange with my secretary to send him something. Whatever you think's right in the circumstances."

"That depends on what are the circumstances."

Pierre sat on the edge of his desk looking at the young man in front of him. "What's on your mind?" he said. "Something about your tone I don't like much."

"Did you know that Celine was seeing Joe Williams?"

"What does that mean?"

"I'm not here to tell tales, or even home truths about Celine. I'm just asking if you knew she had been seeing Joe Williams."

"The little bitch," Pierre said tonelessly. "I'll have a word with her. That's what was bothering you."

"I'm still looking for an answer to my question, Pierre." Martin stood in front of his grandfather, his fists clenched in an effort of self-control.

Pierre came off the edge of the desk. "What are you asking me?" he said, an edge of menace in his voice.

It would have been easy to capitulate. Very easy. Instead, he took a deep breath. He knew he could not live with himself if he didn't speak up.

"I'm asking you flatly if you paid someone to have Joe beaten," he said.

They stood in total silence.

"And if I did?"

Martin hesitated. "If you did," he said slowly, "then I'm going to call the cops."

"I didn't." There was no attempt to persuade him. Pierre's face was flushed with anger.

"How can I be sure?"

"You know it boy, because your grandfather tells you. Understand?"

Martin shook his head. "I'm sorry Pierre," he said. "Not good enough."

"I did *not* arrange for your boxer friend to be beaten up. Is *that* good enough?"

There was a taste of ashes in Martin's mouth. He knew he would never be certain, and because of that would never again be certain about his grandfather.

"A professional boxer getting a street beating is common enough stuff when so much money rides on even small fights. You got the picture, Martin?"

Martin nodded stonily. "Okay . . ."

Pierre broke into a broad smile. "Okay. Now you come in here handing out accusations again," he said jovially, "I'll have to give you a whipping."

Martin shook his head. "Either way, I think you know, the time for that has passed."

CHAPTER 7

Until he met Jack Aston, John Doyle Coburg's life had been devastatingly unfulfilled. He did not love his wife; he feared his father; he could not talk to his children; he hated being a member of the powerful Coburg family.

He had not worked in the family business in years and had no expectations of a major inheritance from his father. For tax reasons, Pierre had transferred a hundred thousand dollars to him at the age of twenty-one and John knew that that was a sufficient bulwark against the poverty people spoke of after the Great Crash of a few years back.

He had thought many times of leaving his father's house. It was not the long-running affair with Rose that troubled him. He knew of his father's greedy sexuality and it did not concern him even when it was directed towards Rose.

But he also knew that Pierre's existence as an American business tycoon was only skin deep. He felt his father to be still a man of the woods and hills of the Waldviertel. He had never forgotten a story Emil had once told him of a farmer from a small Waldviertel hamlet whose wife had died leaving him with a daughter in her early teens. Within a year or two, Emil claimed, the village generally acknowledged that the farmer and his daughter were sharing the same bed. Within two years the girl was pregnant. Within days of the birth the girl was addressed as Frau rather than Fräulein and as other children were produced the original relationships dropped to the back of the folk memory. The girl became, to all intents and purposes, the farmer's wife.

John Doyle Coburg was afraid for Celine.

He was ashamed of himself for not having the courage years ago to intervene when Pierre had whipped John's son Martin with the leather cords. He was ashamed of many things. But he was afraid for Celine.

For many years, the most stable element in his life had been his relationship with Jack Aston. The relationship had undergone and survived strains, it is true. When Rose's sister, Bette, had come to live at the Coburg house on Long Island she had set her cap at Jack . . . And Jack had for a month seriously considered marriage. On Jack Aston the pressure from his family bore heavily. Elder sisters and childless uncles urged him to ensure the continuance of the line.

He was not repelled by women and had from time to time conducted one or two affairs. His choice had tended to alight on strong-minded girls who had soon required that Jack's friendship with John Coburg be ended. For a week or two Jack would try to avoid his friend. But it was not a life he could contemplate.

These crises passed. John Coburg and Jack resumed their relationship, which was only occasionally physical and was mostly a calm, companionate friendship. Whiskey heightened their feeling for each other and sobriety keyed it down to what they both regarded as a respectable level.

There had been only one public error, that Christmas Eve when they had seized each other like teenagers, kissing under the mistletoe at the very moment Pierre had been leading the family out of the dining room.

It was an incident he had since paid deeply for in sneers and contemptuous glances. It had made it impossible for him to play any real role in his children's upbringing. The mere presence of Jack Aston in his life had debarred him in the eyes of Rose and Pierre and the children themselves.

Even so he had refused to end his friendship with Jack. Apart from anything else, Jack Aston was the only one he could talk to about what was becoming an obsession with him.

When he had first told Jack, they had been walking along the shore, shoes tied by laces round their necks, bare feet splashing through the shallows.

"I'd believe a lot of things about your father, Johnny," Jack Aston said. "But not that he was having some sort of sex with his own granddaughter."

"I'm not saying that yet," John Coburg said in an agitated voice. "I've no evidence, Jack. But the way he looks at her, the way he touches her is bad. And she responds. The girl responds, Jack. For all I know she could be leading *him.*"

They splashed on for a few moments in silence.

"You think I'm making too much of it," John said. "Is that right?"

"Too much or too little," Jack Aston said. "If he were . . . no," he shook his head. "I can't believe it, John."

"Even after Rose?"

"Rose was an adult young woman. She wasn't related to him."

"Jack, you see Pierre as he wants you to see him. I still remember him before he made his fortune. Then he'd stand up and fight bare-chested with any union man in the plant who refused his orders."

"Okay, he clawed his way up."

"It's more than that, Jack. He doesn't just come from another continent. He comes from another century."

"Suppose you're right. Suppose even it looks as though you might be right. What are you going to do, John?"

"I suppose I gave up my right to protest," John

Coburg said bitterly, "when I acquiesced in his affair with Rose. He got away with that. People knew, business people, politicians that came here, they all knew he was sleeping with Rose. Just nobody ever mentioned it. To his face."

"Celine would be different," Jack said. "With Rose it wasn't incest."

"He believes he makes his own rules, Jack. You know him. He's devious and clever behind the exuberant appearance. He won't flaunt it. The way he'll behave in public anybody could put him down as a doting grandfather. Nothing more."

"And are you sure there's something more?"

"I don't know," John Coburg said in anguish. "I just don't know."

When, later, he was trudging up alone in the woods towards the house, John Coburg's sense of self-esteem, never high, had reached the lowest point he could remember. He knew what he should do. But he wasn't sure, absolutely sure, that anything was really happening. And within the family he was isolated.

There was Rose, of course. But she would respond with utter contempt. A prurient old fool, she had called him after that incident at Christmas.

If he had one glimmer of hope it was with Martin. Especially now, since Martin was so obviously the Coburg heir. It had happened slowly over the last year or two. Gradually he had seen that Pierre was changing his views of Martin, confiding in him if not actually consulting him about the business.

And Martin, as curious and complex a person as he was, could respond to Pierre, at least with some of his concentration and commitment. They could talk of contracts and delivery dates over drinks in the garden. One day a week Martin would travel to New York City and attend board and sales meetings at the Madison Avenue offices. Yet he seemed to maintain a central position in the family. Most important, Martin had never, like Celine, shut himself out of daily discourse with his father.

John Coburg was infinitely grateful for this, touched, because he didn't understand how his son seemed able to maintain a core of independence among people like Pierre and Rose and Celine.

If Celine was completely unapproachable, if he had forfeited all right to take part in her life, he still saw the possibility of talking to Martin.

After a rare game of tennis with his son, they sat one day in the arbor next to the tennis court overlooking the ocean.

"Rose tells me that Pierre is sending you to Europe this summer," John said hesitantly.

"I'm representing the family at Aunt Elisabeth's wedding."

"Of course," John said. "Europe's a strange place right at this moment for a young man like you, Martin."

Martin waited. He had an awful feeling that his father was about to try to give him some advice about life. Or women. He knew he would never give him advice about Pierre.

"You know there could be war this year."

Martin shrugged, relieved.

"I just don't want you getting tied up in Europe, son," John said heavily. "The place is a mess. Everywhere. England as much as France or Germany or Italy. You're an American boy."

What *was* his father talking about?

"I just as soon you didn't go," John Coburg blurted out, then toweled his face furiously.

"Pierre says I'm to go," Martin said with the brutal finality of youth.

"And that clinches the matter?"

Martin got up. "Can you manage another set?"

John Coburg stood, dropping his towel on the bench. "I guess so," he said, and followed his son back onto the court having said not a word about Celine. He was, he acknowledged, as Rose always said, *as weak as water*. Was Martin? Would Martin be able to stand up to Pierre? Ever?

Martin placed his feet carefully just outside the baseline, bounced the ball once or twice, then came up with a smooth movement as he tossed the ball high above his head. At the right moment the racket struck the ball with an explosive *pock*. The ball cleared the net with an inch to spare and struck deep and perfectly placed way outside his father's reach. But his father had in any case turned away, his arms hugging his ribs, his racket on the court at his feet.

Martin walked to the net. The ball had not hit him. "What is it, Dad?" he called. "You okay?"

His father walked to a shaded corner of the tennis court and Martin rounded the net and came quickly across to where his father was standing, arms still hugging his ribs, his back towards Martin.

A yard or two away Martin stopped. He could see from the heaving shoulders that his father was weeping.

"Dad," he said tentatively. "You okay? You want me to go?"

His father turned and used the back of his hand to wipe tears from his eyes. "No, don't go Martin," he said. "I can't imagine I'll lose anything in your estimation by a few tears."

"What is it, Dad?" Martin asked, desperately hoping at the same time that his father would not say.

What he did say baffled Martin completely: "I'm sending Celine away to college," he said. "There's nothing else to do. You're going to Harvard this year, Celine can go to Sarah Lawrence."

"Celine doesn't want to go to Sarah Lawrence, Dad. She's studying accounting and working in the business. That's what she wants."

"I insist she goes to college this year, Martin."

They stood facing each other, locked in a tension Martin could not understand.

"I want your support, Martin."

"My support?"

"Your grandfather is not a good influence on Celine."

Martin looked at his father in astonishment. Nobody in the Coburg household had ever said anything like that before.

"I don't know why you say that, Dad," Martin said carefully.

Did he know? Was his father referring to the way Pierre touched Celine these days. He would reach for her, she would laugh and duck away from him. Rose ignored it. Did it mean anything?

Martin's stomach lurched. "I tell you, Dad," he said, "I don't know what you're talking about. If you think Celine ought to go to college, why don't you take it up with Pierre yourself?"

The boy picked up a ball and bounced it. "You want to play, Dad? Or do you want to call it a day?"

John Coburg looked at his son for a few moments. He was trying to decide whether he was strong or weak. It had become an obsession trying to understand the terms. He knew they were easily confused. Weak people sometimes seemed to behave like the strong. But that was just in panic or perhaps an outburst of viciousness. Why don't you take it up with Pierre, yourself, Martin had said. Was that strength or weakness? The strength to reject his father's pathetic appeal for an ally. Or the weakness which paralyzed so many men faced by Pierre Coburg.

"What's it to be, Dad? Do we play or not?"

His father shook his head. "I guess not," he said. "It's late."

CHAPTER 8

In the spring of 1939 Martin Coburg was pleased to be going to Germany. He was happy to be getting away from his mother who now bored rather than frightened him. He was pleased to be getting away from his sister Celine who was rapidly becoming as assertive as his mother was. He was pleased too, to be getting away from the Long Island gossip about Jack Aston and his father. But most of all he was excited about his trip to Germany because Alexina would be there.

The accepted family reason for Martin's visit was that he was going to Germany to represent Pierre at the marriage of Emil's young sister-in-law, Elisabeth.

But the visit to Germany had a deeper significance. It was the journey that would affirm Martin, as the heir apparent in the Coburg Banknote Corporation.

From the time Martin and Celine were fourteen, Pierre had made it clear to both of them that Martin alone would inherit Coburg Banknote. Celine had screamed in a tantrum of envy and injustice. She had done what she had never done since. She had begged and sobbed and fallen to her knees, pleading to be allowed a real position in the Coburg family business.

But the ancestral lines of Pierre Coburg were stronger than his granddaughter's grief. If there was a son, or a grandson, he must inherit. It had been that way with the sparse farmland of the Waldviertel; the tradition was deep in Pierre's blood.

Pierre talked openly about such things. The problem, Pierre said, as they sat in his study the week before his grandson was due to leave for Germany, was that Martin was still unproven.

"You're a good young fellow," Pierre had said. "You're loyal, discreet, hardworking and intelligent. Now, if I wrote that recommendation for one of my employees, most employers would think it was all there. But it isn't. It never is. The question is, Martin, one of *will*. You understand me?"

"I think so."

He hammered his fist on the table. "Your father," he said, "was once a good young fellow too. But now he's as weak as water. Are you?

"No sir."

"Celine isn't."

"I know that."

"Your mother isn't."

"I know that too, Pierre."

"But are you?"

"I'm sure I'm not."

Pierre had sat back watching the boy. "You remember our troubles in China with Emil. Poaching our Shanghai contract?"

Martin stayed silent.

"Things aren't the way they were with Emil. You remember his idea of a Coburg research fund? I didn't go along with the idea."

"I remember."

Martin nodded.

For a moment Pierre remained silent, watching Martin across the library table. "I was wrong. Emil is developing a printing press," he said suddenly. "A press that could print the rest of us out of business."

"Emil wouldn't do that," Martin said. "He wouldn't put *us* out of business."

Pierre looked at his grandson, irritated that he had been taken so literally. "I'll never give him the chance," Pierre grunted. "In any case, the full development of Emil's press could be years away."

"Did he tell you about it himself?"

"Yes. Mockingly. He told me last month that in two years he will have a press that other companies will have to adopt. Or fade away."

"You think it's true?"

Pierre nodded. "Several people have been working on a fast multicolor press of this type. The original work was done by a French engineer named Serge Beaune. His patents have now lapsed, but he showed the road ahead. He showed people like Emil what is possible."

Pierre got up and walked the length of the room. To Martin he seemed more agitated than he had ever seen him. More agitated even than when he had ordered the pickets at the Kansas City plant to be beaten up at the gates.

"Germany's growing fast," Pierre said. "Not just adding territories like Austria and the Sudetenland, but growing fast in influence. Influence on markets like Bulgaria, Romania, Hungary, Spain. Influence on countries much further afield. Like Argentina, Ecuador, Peru. Germany's influence is spreading right into our backyard, Martin. And in our business that mostly means Emil's influence. Especially if he *has* developed an improvement on the old Serge Beaune press."

Suddenly Martin knew the real reason why he was going to Germany. He was going as a spy. He was to report back on the new presses. He was to report back on Emil's position as a leading banknote printer in the newly powerful Reich.

"Listen, Martin," Pierre leaned across his desk. "Isolation might be the best war policy for America. But it is definitely not the best commercial policy for the Coburg Banknote Corporation. Our markets are mostly overseas. And they are threatened by the political punch Germany can deliver. If Hitler ever invades

France and England we could be done for. Get over to Europe and find out all you can. You've got to grow up quickly, boy. Or your sister takes the prizes." It was the first time he had put the threat into words.

The Martin Coburg who left for Europe in the spring of 1939 was a tall, well-formed young man just eighteen. Fair-haired and good-looking in a long-headed Germanic way, he had eyes of a strong blue color and a smile that, though infrequent, was disarming.

He was unaware that his manner might have been described as charming. He would have disliked the word to be applied to him, because it evoked his father and all the softness that Pierre despised.

He had never slept with a woman, although he was wracked by periodic lusts. On this trip to Europe he had promised himself the experience he lacked. But he lacked knowledge, too, mostly because his father was in no position to give him advice and his mother had no inclination. Pierre, in a straighforward peasant way, assumed that the barrier had been long surmounted.

But Europe beckoned. As full of hope to Martin Coburg as America had been to his grandfather.

Oliver Sutchley, the Coburg representative in London, came aboard the *Queen Mary* when the liner docked at Southampton. Martin found himself greeted by a tall, slender man of about thirty, with thin dark hair in a widow's peak, and a Ronald Coleman moustache. Within minutes, Martin found himself disliking the man.

"Drive you to London," he said in his clipped speech. "Set you up in the Dorchester and tonight take you out on the town."

They had driven at high speed in an open roadster up through the county of Hampshire and into London. For the most part the wind made conversation impossible. Martin settled back to look at the countryside and the market towns en route, each with a smattering of Tudor pubs and shops among the modern styles of the chain stores on the high streets. But mostly, as he told Sutchley when they were established in the bar of the new white-stone-faced Dorchester Hotel, his impression had been of a quiet prosperity and propriety.

"Quiet and complacent, Martin," Oliver Sutchley had said. "These people don't know the world's moving on its axis. The British middle classes have got to be shaken out of their apathy. And we're the ones to do it."

"We?"

"The upper classes. We'll do it in an alliance with the lower orders if we have to. But it's the only way to save our bacon."

Martin looked at him. "You won't mind me saying, Sutchley," he said, "but I haven't understood a thing of all that you're saying."

"You must know that Europe is on the move."

"Who's saving whose bacon? Let's start there."

"Adolf Hitler, old boy, that's who's going to save our bacon."

"How is Adolf Hitler going to save Britain's bacon?"

"Through his ideas. People who can see further than the hand in front of their face belong to the British Union of Fascists. All this anti-Hitler stuff is cutting our own throats."

"Your Winston Churchill doesn't think so."

"A windbag," Sutchley said.

"He's got a lot of friends in Washington."

"Mark my words," Sutchley said. "Within a year or two there's going to be a new Europe. And I want to see us in the forefront of the movement. Now drink up. Pierre asked me to show you a bit of night life before you catch the boat train tomorrow morning."

CHAPTER 9

As the train steamed into the Vienna Hochbahnhof, Martin shook hands formally with his fellow passengers, took his single suitcase and swung himself down onto the platform.

The noise struck him first, the hissing of the locomotive, the shouts of porters and railroadmen, the clash of cymbals from the brass band on a podium in a crowded concourse.

He was almost at the ticket counter when he heard his name shouted. He had played with the hope that Alexina would be there to meet him—or at least that she would be with her father. Turning, he saw Emil pushing his way through the crowd towards him. But it was a different Emil.

Instead of one of his usual English tweed suits, Martin saw to his surprise that his grandfather's twin brother was wearing what at first looked like the outfit of a stormtrooper. Under an open brown leather overcoat he wore high-laced boots, corduroy breeches and a short brown jacket. In his hand he carried what appeared to be a flying helmet of soft brown leather.

"Martin, my boy," Emil shouted in German. "You've grown so big, so handsome."

A waiting porter took Martin's bag as Emil embraced him. "I've given instructions for your steamer trunk to be sent on to us," he said. "Martin, it's good of you to come all this way."

"I have been looking forward to it," Martin said.

"But a family wedding. What young man of your

age wants to attend a wedding. Unless he could find his own bride there."

They were following the porter past a line of automobiles. Martin was looking for something open-topped. A Mercedes, supercharged, like the car Adolf Hitler rode in on newsreels. But instead the porter reached the end of the line of cars and stopped.

He was standing beside a BMW motorcycle with a large bullet shaped sidecar.

"Your grandfather Pierre insisted," Emil said mysteriously. "There's a leather coat in there. Put it on and we'll go for a drive."

The drive took them out of Vienna to the west towards that unknown region of Austria between the Danube and the old Bohemian border. Head down against the wind, knitted scarf flying, Emil Coburg drove at seventy miles per hour, taking bends at a speed that made the sidecar rise in the air to descend with a thump and screech of tires as the road straightened.

To Martin, crouched in the sidecar wearing goggles but no helmet, his grandfather's brother was driving like someone possessed, laughing, shouting into the wind, accelerating past farm carts and ancient, listing trucks loaded with hay.

They met the Danube at Melk before lunch and stopped for beer and sausage at a simple Gasthaus on the Danube at Pochlarn. It was the first time Martin had had an opportunity to speak. Or at least to be heard. Stretching his cramped legs and pulling off his goggles, he followed Emil toward the half-timbered Gasthaus. It was still a fine morning although dark clouds piled up above the hills to the north.

Emil was in good spirits. "A sausage," he said, "some black bread and a stein of beer, that's the standard fare of this part of the world. Nothing French, nothing fancy here. Good?"

Without waiting for an answer, he ducked under the low doorway and entered the Gasthaus.

Martin could sense in Emil something not quite secretive but not yet revealed. When the plates of steaming sausage and sauerkraut were put before them, Emil plunged into questions about the family in New York. He had not seen Pierre since they had met almost a year ago at a banknote conference in Mexico City. There, he said, the Coburgs had seen off the competition, the American Banknote Company, Givierke & Devrient and the British from De La Rue in London. He plied Martin with questions about Pierre, his health, how hard he worked.

"Martin, I don't mind telling you that sometimes my brother worries me."

"Don't worry, he keeps fit," Martin said. "He plays tennis, swims. Last winter he was checked over by Doctor Cunningham and given a clean bill of health."

"I'm not really thinking about his health." Emil stared down into his beer. "We Coburgs are oxen, all of us. Hard work never harmed us."

"What is it that's worrying you, if not his health?"

"It's his well-being, Martin. And that depends on the success of Coburg Banknote."

"So what's the problem?"

"The problem is, Martin, that in a world I don't welcome, but I see just around the corner nevertheless, Coburg Banknote could be squeezed out."

"You're talking about technical advances."

"I'm talking about technical changes and political changes. The most potent, exciting or damaging conditions for a business to face."

Before Martin could ask more Emil drew in a big breath. "Even the air up here smells better," he said.

It was a clear message to change the subject.

Martin looked out across the river to the country beyond. "I was surprised to see that you're still a motorcycle buff, Emil." He addressed his grandfather's brother respectfully despite using his first name.

"Anything technical my boy. Motorcycles, cars, but most of all printing presses. They have a beauty, you know, beyond many paintings. Some of them approach a work of art." He stopped, a forkful of sauerkraut in midair. "But you're asking me, of course, why I didn't collect you by car. Why this mad drive along the Danube with a geriatric road hog."

"I wondered about the car," Martin said carefully. "How far are we from Lingfeld."

"It's fifty kilometers or so to the border." He stopped. "Ah, a common error." He lifted the fork, this time carrying a fat slice of sausage. "Until last year you understand, there was a border between Austria and Germany. Now, since the Anschluss, since Herr Hitler brought the two countries together, there is none."

"You don't approve of the Anschluss?"

Emil leaned forward and tapped Martin's nose with the end of his now empty fork. "You were asking me how far it was to Lingfeld?"

"Yes." Martin took the rebuke without clearly understanding the reason for it. If his uncle didn't approve of the joining of Austria and Germany, why not say so.

"If we were going direct to Lingfeld, which is just this side of Munich, it would take an hour or two more."

"We're not going direct?"

Emil shook his head. "First there is somewhere you must see."

They left the Gasthaus and drove north across the Danube toward the old Bohemian border.

They now entered an area of wild and desolate country where peaks rose toward low clouds from a high plateau of rock. Great slopes of pine forest led the eye up to tiny isolated villages or to even smaller farmhouses, the grim enclosed stone bastions of the area.

After half an hour or so it had begun to rain, cold, slanting and wind-driven. In the sidecar, the chill air swirling round his shoulders, the rain flattening his hair, Martin could see that Emil was indifferent to the cold. He drove the motorcycle like a young man, swooping down roads that were now no longer paved, hurling gravel from under the wheels as he took a bend. On the top of a hill he brought the machine to a skidding halt. Climbing off the saddle, he motioned to Martin to get out of the sidecar.

"Here Martin," he said when they stood together, "is where you hail from."

He swept a huge hand outwards encompassing the thick wooded hillsides, the narrow ribbon of road and the stone villages under a brooding sky.

"This is the Waldviertel," Emil said. "The people here believe it's closer to the Mist-Life than anywhere in the world."

Rain slashed their faces. Martin only wanted to get back into the minimal cover of the sidecar, but he felt he ought to ask. "The Mist Life," he said, "what's that?"

"It's the land of evil," Emil said. "It's a land of perpetual rain and mist, deep, impenetrable forests and unfished streams. It's the land of the dead, the domain of the goddess Hel. Its entrance is guarded by the monstrous wolf-dog, Garm."

Emil walked back to the motorcycle. "You will see," he said, "that even now, every crossroad is provided with a wolf spear. Of course now it's just a staff of ashwood tied across a tree. Nowadays they call it a cross."

Martin climbed back into the sidecar. Emil stood for a moment, one gloved hand on the handlebar. "Living so close to the Mists, the people of these parts *know* evil. Their Christianity is mixed with pagan tales. When we were boys, Pierre and myself, our great-grandfather was the storyteller of our village. He was born in 1775, Martin. More than a decade before the French Revolution. A year, even, before America began to struggle for its freedom."

Emil climbed onto the saddle. "The people of these villages have an enormous potential for good, Martin. The stories tell us so. But they also have a great potential for evil." He looked down at Martin, his face hard. "You laugh at me, Martin. You laugh at Pierre and myself as old men unable to throw off the shadows of the past."

"Of course not," Martin said hurriedly.

"That village below us," he pointed to a miserable straggle of stone houses, "Strones, it's called. From October to May it lies deep in the mists and mountain fogs. A man was born there in the last century, at house 13, the father of Adolf Hitler."

For the first time, Martin felt a chill, unconnected with the blasts of rain, pass down his back. Good or evil? It wasn't difficult to see where Emil stood.

They stayed that night in a farmhouse outside the village of Weitra. It was a farm occupied by Coburgs still, the males, huge hulking men, the women big, broadfaced and dour. Generations of inbreeding had given them all a familiarity of feature. Martin saw, uncomfortably, how much he resembled the males of the family, how much his sister Celine shared the dark blue eyes, the broad shoulders and narrow waists of the Coburg women.

There were six members of the family at the farmhouse, and other Coburgs came in to see Emil and Martin during the evening. When they sat down at the planked table for dinner they were fourteen or fifteen, all Coburgs and those married to Coburgs.

The evening passed, with much drinking and a harsh sort of jollity rather than gaiety. Emil and Pierre were held in almost god-like reverence, and the women,

Martin noticed, lowered their eyes respectfully when they passed even him.

The farmhouse itself was astonishingly primitive. In the one large, flagged room a log fire roared. Blackened cooking pots swung over it. Beyond the rough-hewn panelled walls, cattle and horses shifted and stamped in the barn. In a stone chamber off the main room was an enormous brass bed. It was the only bed he saw for the six members of the family.

After the soup and sauerkraut were consumed, the family sat around the fire talking of the late snow this spring, the loss of lambs to a pack of wolves that had crossed from the Bohemian Hills, the death of this or that member of the commune. But, as the schnapps was passed around and one by one the older women slipped away, the men began to recount stories of the past. Of apparitions seen at crossroads, of a company of dwarfs seen feasting in a ruined castle hall, of the disappearance of a young girl, selected by the demon-goddess, Hel, for her pleasure.

Bemused by the fumes of the schnapps, Martin found it impossible to guess whether or not they believed these tales. Certainly they believed accounts of betrayal and treachery in families or villages and certainly they believed in retribution.

By midnight the talk grew bawdy. Martin's neighbor on one side was a big Coburg girl with a flat ugly face. She nudged him. "I wouldn't mind," she said to the room at large, "if this one was my wedding guest, my first invited."

The assembly around the fire roared with laughter.

Martin frowned. "I didn't know you were getting married," he said, politely. This time the assembled Coburgs could hardly contain themselves, slapping their great knees and shaking with laughter. "Tell him, Traudi, *show* him!"

Taking pity on him, Emil came over to where Martin sat.

"What's going on?" Martin said. "I'm lost."

Pouring them both another glass of schnapps, Emil said, in English, "In Waldviertel the custom is for the first invited to arrive early."

"Before the wedding?"

"Sometimes even the night before."

"And?"

"He will always be a member of the family. It is his responsibility to take the bride's virginity."

"You're not serious."

"You've heard of the old *droit de seigneur*, when the local lord or sometimes priest assumed the pleasant duty of deflowering the brides?"

Martin nodded, dry-mouthed from the bite of the raw schnapps.

"Then this is simply the *droit de famille*. Until recently it was practiced by every peasant family in the Waldviertel." He smiled. "For all I know it still is."

The talk around the fire swept on. Out of it Martin saw arising the shape of a strange semi-pagan world. They told stories of the end of the earth when the Valkyries, young women in silver armor, rode their steeds across the sky to take part in the last great battle, the *Götterdammerung*, the twilight of the gods.

How much of this they believed Martin did not know. Most certainly they believed in wood spirits and the ability of those spirits to create natural disasters.

"Up on the Waltersberg," a young man, Martin's neighbor, said, "the earth was split open, throwing hot rocks up to the sky."

One of the girls pulled a face. "Burning rocks," she said dubiously.

The young Coburg farmer bridled. "Haven't they sent the soldiers up there to warn off farmers and passersby?"

The girl shrugged. "Perhaps," she said.

Emil leaned across to where Martin was sitting. "You don't have to believe all the Coburgs say," he said in English. "It's a camp the government is building up there. One of the new prison camps."

Emil and Martin slept in the hayloft above the barn. In another section of the loft, as Martin drifted into sleep, he heard women's voices, and the deeper voices of men demanding, and scuffling and laughter and long grunts of pleasure.

It was almost mid-morning the next day when he and Emil arrived, crumpled, unshaven, smelling of hay and woodsmoke, at the newly acquired family house at Lingfeld just inside the old German-Austrian border. The contrast with the stone farmhouses of the Waldviertel could hardly have been greater. As the motorcycle swept up the driveway and past the house, Martin saw gardeners straighten and touch their hats, maids at the long curtained windows peer out at the newcomer's arrival and Emil's wife, Dorotta, in a peach-colored dress, come out on the terrace to wave a welcome.

With Dorotta greetings were always effusive. As Martin came forward she ran down the terrace steps, threw her arms around his neck and placed two or three loud kisses on each cheek.

"What a man he's become," Dorotta burbled to Emil as she held Martin at arm's length.

"In Waldviertel," Emil said proudly, "he couldn't walk down a village street without being recognized as a Coburg."

"That wicked man my husband took you off to Waldviertel when you should have been here in comfort after your long journey." She punched ineffectually at Emil's huge chest. "But he insisted, you know. 'A Coburg,' he said, 'should see Coburg country first'. He loves all those great shambling peasant oafs."

Martin laughed. It was some years since he had seen Dorotta, but he always felt the same ease in her ebullient presence.

"And how are you, Dorotta?" Martin said. "Winning the battle against the pastries and the chocolates, I see."

"The boy is a born flatterer." She laughed, smoothing her muslin dress over the amplitude of her hips.

A movement above them behind the windows of the long terrace room caught Martin's eye. He turned as Alexina came out on the terrace, shielding her eyes against the sunlight.

"Alexina," Emil boomed, "come out and say hello to Martin."

She stood for a moment, then dropped her hand from her eyes. She was no longer the slightly angular adolescent he had met in Shanghai. She moved forward with a sensuality that was not quite conscious. Her dramatic tawny gold hair framed a face dominated by cobalt-blue eyes and a wide, almost Slavic mouth.

Her impact upon him was immediate and engulfing. He was suddenly aware of a level of perception he had never experienced before: the movement of the folds of her blue dress, the flare of the skirt as she came down the steps, the fernfoils of golden hair on the brown arms as she stretched out a hand to him.

Martin Coburg had read that some girls possessed an improbable beauty, but he had never before felt himself in its presence.

CHAPTER 10

~ ~ ~

Alexina Coburg was an adopted child. Like the Coburgs of Weitra, she had origins in the desolate forests
of the Waldviertel. Her mother Hanna was a Coburg
from Strones who had traveled to Vienna to take a
domestic post. In Vienna there was a perpetual short-
age of what were described as reliable servants, and
country girls were favored as being more readily
teachable. To the master or son of the house this
might often have been translated as bedable. But
Hanna was not bedable. In her first week at the magnificent merchant town house in Vienna, she had refused the eldest son's advances. She had even stayed
awake until she knew he was safe in bed two floors
below. Then, in her second week as a parlor-maid,
the son of the house had left for a week hunting wild
boar in Czechoslovakia and Hanna Coburg had finished her duties and retired to her room exhausted
but relieved.

The turning of the door knob ten minutes later had,
at first, terrified her. Then when she saw the master
of the house standing in the doorway, a lighted candle
in one hand, his nightshirt at the front draped over
his erection, she had burst into nervous laughter.

She was not afraid of men—no girl from the Waldviertel was—but she liked to choose her own man. At
first, she begged the master to return downstairs but
he refused. He was still not an old man and he possessed that steely determination that made him a successful merchant. She succumbed twice, succeeded in

blackmailing from him a respectable reference, and left to take another post in Vienna. But she was already pregnant.

Her daughter, Alexina, was born in 1921. For the first three years of her life, she lived with her grandmother in Weitra. When the old lady died, Hanna Coburg was desperate. She could not support the child herself, her work as a domestic in Vienna made it out of the question for Alexina to come to live with her. Hanna took her problem to an old lady they called Grandmother Coburg. Within a week the little girl had been adopted. Within a year her mother had died in a second childbirth.

Many times in the years following, Emil asked himself why he had agreed to the adoption. His own war service had resulted in a flying piece of shrapnel severing a vital duct and achieving its own crude form of vasectomy. Thus, a son was out of the question. If he wanted an heir he might have adopted his wife's young sister Elisabeth, still a child when he and Dorotta were married. Perhaps he might have adopted a boy. But he didn't. In the end he accepted what was in fact the truth of the matter, that he had adopted Alexina because she was a child of the Waldviertel in need.

She had grown up in many ways as much of a Coburg as Emil himself. She was tall and well-shaped as she came into adolescence. Her eyes were of that same dark blue shared by so many people of Waldviertel, and her hair was a dark tawny blonde, again a common enough color in Upper Austria but rarer further northwest where Emil Coburg and his family had now settled.

She no longer remembered her mother, though both Emil and Dorotta were careful at first to try to keep the memory alive. But by the time Alexina began to emerge from childhood both Coburgs had given up the uneven struggle and come to regard her as a daughter of their own.

Alexina had first visited the United States when she was five-years-old and again every three or four years in her childhood and early adolescence. Though easy and outgoing in her manner, she was a young woman capable of making her own judgments on the circumstances she found herself in. She liked but was wary of Pierre. She felt with that subcutaneous instinct of women that there was something beyond friendliness in his touch. She felt uncomfortable at his arm draped around her shoulder, the huge hand covering, but not touching, her breast. She did not like Rose, Martin's mother. And she reacted in adolescent shock to the discovery that Pierre and Rose, from time to time, slept together. She did not like Celine. Though girls of the same age, similarly formed, sharing the interests of their age group, they did not get on well. Alexina usually felt this was mostly her fault. Celine had made the advances, the offers of friendship, several times, but Alexina had politely rejected them. The reason probably was because she felt that to side with Celine was to take sides against Martin and his father.

It was a standing joke among the Coburg adults that at the age of five Alexina had decided to marry Martin. It was not a joke either of them found easy to endure in their early adolescence. To Martin it created an acute sense of discomfort when the idea was bandied around the dinner table. Alexina dealt with it more firmly, telling Pierre and Emil that she was capable of making up her own mind.

Was Martin? She had never been able to talk to him. At fifteen she felt things stir in her when she saw the tall young man loping across the tennis court to drive the ball down the line. Even she recognized that at fifteen he was a little overgrown, too tall, a little gangly perhaps, but she knew he interested her.

The difficulty was that he was a boy of few words, someone difficult to get close to, someone impossible to talk to about Emil or Dorotta, or Pierre or his father, about the things, in short, that concerned her most in life, that is being a Coburg, coming from the Waldviertel forests with all their history and myth.

On her last visit, in the spring of 1936, she had been fifteen. Like Elisabeth, now twenty-five, her interests lay in the romance and hope and ambition for a better future that the Nazi Party inspired in the young. She knew Emil and Dorotta did not share these hopes or ideals and she found that difficult to accept in those she so much trusted. But she was much more baffled by the fact that Martin appeared to have no views of the future *whatsoever*. He was neither for nor against Adolf Hitler. He seemed to understand nothing of the desperate plight of Germany from which Hitler was raising the nation. He seemed to know nothing of the depravity of the Zionists and their secret plans, contained in the *Protocols of the Elders of Zion,* to dominate and plunder the Aryan race. She found her feelings about him veered erratically. Sometimes she saw herself marrying him in the Munich Frauenkirche. Sometimes she sadly concluded that he was just a big, beautiful and completely empty-headed American boy.

They had had one conversation that pleased her. They were sitting on the great trunk of a fallen elm drinking the cook's own lemonade. They had just completed a set of tennis in which he had beaten her by a humiliatingly vast margin. "You should become a tennis player," she said, mostly to cover her own loss. "You know, travel around the world. Go to Paris, Wimbledon, that sort of thing."

"I'm not good enough, I know that. Pierre says I'm a long way from that standard."

"What does Pierre know about it?" she had asked casually.

"I guess he knows about sports."

"You think Pierre knows everything. He doesn't."

"What do you mean?"

"He doesn't know for example," she said with icy

fifteen-year-old female deliberateness, "how to keep
his hands to himself."

During the following year Alexina was called for her
League of German Girls training. She had worked on
a farm and met other girls from the poorer districts
of Hamburg and Berlin, as well as the young women
from the Junker class of the eastern Prussian Marches.

With eight hours work a day in the fields, she had
grown trimmer and fitter. The sun had made her body
browner and turned her hair a deep tawny gold. But
most important to her were the evenings when everybody gathered in a meeting hut and sang songs and
talked about Germany and its future and Hitler's gift
of pride to the German people.

On these occasions the group would be mixed. Boys
from the Hitler Youth camp in the mountains would
come down to attend the talks and lectures. There was
strict supervision, but some fraternization was allowed
under the eye of the Party supervisor.

Hans Emden was from the north, from Bremen. He
was medium-sized, dark-eyed boy who failed in every
way to live up to the physical standards of a Nordic
master race. But he had a fast, irreverent wit. He sang
different words to party songs. He told scurrilous
jokes about party officials. And he was of a tempera-
ment to help anybody out at any time.

Some of the young people were wary of him, but
Alexina took to him instinctively. She liked to listen
to his stories of life in the industrial suburb of Bremen
and the grinding poverty of life there even now. To a
girl brought up in the luxury of the Coburg household,
the stories of Han's mother dividing the bread every
day among the four children was infinitely moving. It
was a window on life that neither home, nor school,
nor tutors had given her.

Sometimes he went further. He would take a lecture
or a piece of party literature they were learning and

invert its meaning, make fun of it or simply deny that it was true. One day they left a lecture together and he walked with Alexina to the corner of the club-house. The subject of the lecture had been those same *Protocols of the Elders of Zion* that she had talked to Martin about in America last year.

"What do you think?" he said, inexpertly lighting his pipe.

"About what?" She was swinging her satchel of lecture notebooks, looking up towards the great peaks of the distant Swiss mountains. She felt she had not a worry in the world.

"About the lecture," he said deliberately.

"Excellent."

"Just that, excellent?"

She turned to him, surprised. She was wearing her brown uniform jacket, white shirt and tie, and her tawny hair was restrained by the regulation two pig-tails. She looked infinitely innocent to him. "What would you say the lecture was about, Alex?"

"You know what it was about, the *Protocols,* the document that proves conclusively that the Jews . . . oh, you were there, why do you ask?"

"If I told you it was about a cheap forgery," he said quietly. "What then?"

"How can it be? It's in the Führer's book, *Mein Kampf.*"

"We are to believe that these documents were recently discovered and prove that the Jews were determined to destroy the Nordic race?"

"Why not?"

"To begin with," he said casually, "they're pretty old documents, even if you believe they're genuine."

"Of course they're genuine," she snorted.

"They were first known of over seventy years ago. In France. That's where the forgery originated," he said. "A false document written by anti-Semites. The Tsar's secret police found this trash useful to stir up further anti-Jewish feeling. The Gestapo finds the so-called *Protocols* equally useful."

"You don't believe all this, Hans."

"I believe it. The London *Times* believes it and most eminent historians in the world believe that your precious *Protocols* are what I said they are. A cheap and vicious forgery."

Alexina heard her supervisor's voice calling through a mist of tears and panic. How could Hans say such things? She turned back to where her supervisor stood, tapping her foot, at the entrance of the clubhouse.

"Alexina," Frau Busch said severely. "I want you to stay away from that young man."

"Stay away from Hans?"

"Yes. What was he talking to you about so earnestly just then?"

"He was discussing the lecture, Frau Busch," she said, dry-lipped. "He was saying that he thought it was . . . excellent. Excellent in every way."

The supervisor frowned. "Stay with your own group," she said. "There's something I don't like about that young man, Emden. Something unclean about his thoughts, I suspect."

One late summer morning as her period of service was coming to an end, Alexina was sent by an organizer to gather kindling in the woods by the stream. The main group of girls had gone for an all-day hike and her own supervisor had gone with them. She knew she had all morning if she wanted to wander by the stream or sit and read in the clubhouse.

She had chosen to collect her kindling first and was making her way down the steep path, the mountains rising distantly from a pale blue haze of heat, when she thought she heard something in the thicker part of the woods ahead. She knew that some caution was necessary. Wild boar were common enough in these woods and if a sow was leading her young down to

drink in the stream it was dangerous to get in their
way. She stopped and listened again. Without doubt
there was something moving there. She could hear the
shuffle of leaves and the crackle of twigs. She called
out in order to warn the boar of her presence, if indeed it was a wild boar. "Hey! Hey! Hola!" she
shouted, using the calls she had heard on her visits
with Emil to the Waldviertel.

She moved forward cautiously. She was about to
call out again when she heard a voice whispering her
name and Hans Emden stepped onto the path in front
of her. For a moment she looked at him in alarm. She
could see an ugly tension in his face, his mouth set,
the brow furrowed.

"Hans," she said. "What is it, Hans?"

He seemed to relax a little at the sound of her voice.
He stepped forward, no taller than she was, his hands
coming out to rest on her shoulders. "I shouldn't do
this to you," he said. "I know that. But I've no one
else to come to. I'm on the run."

"On the run?" she said. "Who from?"

He shrugged. "Supervisors, police, local Gestapo."

"Police, Gestapo. What have you done, for God's
sake?"

He smiled. "You still think it's necessary to *do*
something to be on the run in the new Germany?"

"You're splitting hairs, Hans," she said curtly. "All
right, what *haven't* you done?"

He glanced up the path to where the outline of the
girls' clubhouse was visible through the trees.

"They're on an all-day hike," Alexina said. "Nobody can see you from here."

"All the same, let's go down to the stream. It's safer
there."

They walked quickly down the path to the stream,
he slightly ahead of her, making it impossible for her
to press her questions. At the water's edge he stopped,
turned towards her and opened his arms wide as if

exposing his chest. "Last night they found out," he
said. "They found out I'm a Jew."

Alexina stood in front of him in shock. He smiled
his crooked smile and reaching forward with one index
finger, pushed up the jaw of her gaping mouth.

"Oh Hans," she said. "I'm so sorry."

He burst out laughing. "You're so sorry I'm a Jew,
uh?"

The laughter cleared her head. "You know what I
mean," she said. "You know what I mean."

He sat down on the grass by the bank of the stream
and looked up at her. She was wearing a white blouse,
a dirndl skirt and sandals. He thought, irrelevantly,
that she was the most beautiful girl he had ever seen
in his life.

"There's no one else I can ask," Hans said. "I need
a little money and a little food. There's no one else."

She crouched down beside him. "What you told me,
Hans. About the *Protocols of the Elders of Zion* being
a forgery. That was true, was it? You didn't tell me
that just because you're . . ."

"A Jew myself? No." He looked into her extraordinary eyes, so dark a blue that he could see his own
reflection there. "No, I swear it."

She nodded. "Your sisters," she said. "Your mother.
Can't they help?"

He laughed. "Oh my lovely Alexina," he said. "My
parents were put in a camp somewhere early this year.
A work camp. My mother bought the papers of a dead
boy my age. It's good business now in Germany to
have a dead son. I became Hans Emden. Until last
night, when a new Hitler Youth section arrived from
Bremen. As luck would have it, one of the boys had
been to school with the real Hans Emden. He was
even present at the canal bridge when Hans was
drowned."

For Alexina what she would do was never in question. Hans Emden, *this* Hans Emden, was a friend.

She was too young for an ideological division to have any influence on her. And she brushed aside the danger to herself. "I'll get you money and food, Hans," she said. "Of course I will."

"You know it's dangerous," he said. "You know *how* dangerous. German you may be, Nordic you may be, but there are hundreds of thousands of honest Germans, Nordics like you, already in concentration camps."

"Is this true, Hans?"

"This and much more is true," he said bitterly. "Much, much more."

She looked at him with a mounting sense of dread. "But surely," she said urgently, "Germany has a *right* to be free."

"Germans have a right to be free," he said. "If Germans are free, then Germany is free."

The simple statement was a revelation to her. The stream trickled on through the woods. She thought of what he had said. Even then she knew it would be a burden to her. But it was a burden she would willingly bear.

"Where will you go?" she asked him.

"I'll head for Switzerland."

She was on the edge of tears. "But Switzerland is turning back Jews."

He was standing, looking down at her. "We'll see," he said simply. "There's nowhere else to go."

She gave him a sapphire ring, a necklace with three large diamonds, one hundred marks, and cheese and bread from the club foodstore. Then she walked with him through the woods. She reached out and held his hand. "It's not far," she said, "to the border."

He stopped. "You must go back now."

She nodded. Tears were running down her cheeks. "When you get to Switzerland go to Imprimerie Coburg in Zurich. As soon as I get back home, I'll make sure they know who you are."

"I'd like to kiss you," he said.

She nodded. "Kiss me." She held her lips out to him. He kissed her puckered lips. "So that's it," he said. He smiled a smile close to tears and turned, climbing quickly through the forest towards Switzerland.

For Alexina it was an instant conversion.

CHAPTER 11

~ ~ ~

She had watched from the terrace of the drawing room as the motorcycle had drawn up and Wilhelm, the head mechanic, had come forward to take it around to the garages. Emil was looking up at the terrace where Dorotta waved. The American boy had clambered out of the sidecar and was peeling the goggles from his eyes.

She had somehow not expected to find him greatly changed since she had last seen him, in China. He was, if anything, taller, but he was also much more obviously a Coburg. In the line of his jaw and in the high cheekbones he closely resembled Pierre. Except for a certain refining of the features, he seemed to have absorbed very little from his mother, Rose.

Alexina came forward onto the terrace and watched Dorotta embrace Martin. She rested one hand on the balustrade and came slowly down the terrace steps. She could see his eyes were upon her, as she had intended. She had carefully chosen her frock for the occasion. In English did one say frock, or dress?

"Go and give Alexina a big kiss hello," Emil said as he pushed Martin forward. Martin regained his balance just as Alexina reached the bottom step.

She held out her hand to him. "Hello, Martin."

They shook hands formally. "You've changed," he said.

"I should hope so."

"Now," Dorotta said, coming to Martin's rescue.

"Now we shall send for Rolf and Elisabeth, the young lovers we call them, and have some tea served. No," she corrected herself looking at Martin's crumpled clothes. "First Alexina will show you your room. Your things are already here. You can bathe, change, then join us for tea in the terrace room. So much to show you, so much to talk about," she said, raising her hands in the air in excitement.

Alexina showed him to the magnificent guest room overlooking a long slope of woodland and the mountains beyond. She stood in the middle of the room for a moment watching him. He moved easily for someone so big. Easily and confidently. Then, as she often did, she thought of Hans Emden last year struggling through the mountains alone. In his pocket he had the ring and necklace she had given him and the two fifty-mark notes. She knew she did not love Hans, or even have any trace of that sort of feeling towards him, but he remained strongly in her consciousness as someone she respected, a yardstick against which to measure other boys.

For Martin Coburg that first tea taken with the family was one of the most uncomfortable experiences in his life. It had began well enough with Dorotta plying him with questions and Alexina offering cakes and comments on his account of his trip via London to Vienna.

"I've never been to London," she said. "What sort of city is it, magnificent like Vienna or the pictures I've seen of Paris? Or fog-bound and grimy?"

Martin felt like the world traveler. "No," he said judiciously, "not like Paris."

Alexina waited.

He cast around for any sort of phrase to fill the gap. "More homely," he said. "Not as many public buildings in evidence." He was enjoying this now. "Of course you see a great deal of private affluence in Britain. But unemployment is high."

"Here in Germany," Dorotta said, "the Führer has abolished that. And crime of course. We no longer have crime."

Martin looked towards Alexina. He knew her enthusiastic opinion about the new Germany from their last encounter on Long Island. But this time she said nothing.

The door opened and Elisabeth entered with her fiancé. She was much as Martin had remembered her, much older than himself, quite attractive rather than flamboyant. Her husband-to-be wore a well-cut uniform with black collar tags. "May I present my fiancé," Elisabeth said as Martin rose from his chair. "SS Standartenführer Doctor Rolf Oster."

They shook hands. Oster was a tall, distinguished-looking officer with the faintest line of a scar at an angle across his cheekbone. Older than Elisabeth, perhaps in his mid-thirties, he conducted himself in a totally relaxed manner, pouring tea for her and himself, praising the cakes set out on the silver tray. "So Martin, if I may call you that, have you had an opportunity yet to form an opinion of our new nation?"

"Not yet," Martin said. It was not the last time he was to see that politics was the principal subject of conversation in Germany. "I hope to while I'm here."

"If there's anything I can help you with, any books I can lend you, don't hesitate to ask me. The SS library in Munich is particularly fine. It's said to contain the most comprehensive collection of the literature of racial matters in the world."

"Thank you very much, Doctor."

"You must call me Rolf," he said amiably. "We're about to become related after all. In any case," he said, fixing Martin with a smile, "it is generally ac-

cepted that SS Standartenführer is a title that takes
precedence over doctor."

"Will you live in this part of the country when
you're married?" Martin asked Elisabeth.

"So much depends on Rolf's military posting," she
said. "But, in any case, if there's war I am registered
as a member of the Foreign Ministry. I should expect
to be posted to a legation or embassy somewhere
abroad."

"War," Martin said. "You expect a war?"

"We do."

"We don't," Emil interjected flatly. "That's to say
we don't *want* a war, Martin. That's the message to
take back to the United States."

"The message to take back, if you don't mind me
saying so, Emil," Elisabeth said, "is that we hope we
shall not be *forced* into war."

"But that if we are . . ." Oster left the sentence
hanging menacingly.

"I'm quite sure," Dorotta said soothingly, "there
will be no war. I saw enough of the last one to last
me a lifetime."

Martin looked across at Alexina. She sat with her
face composed, looking directly at him as if waiting
for him to speak, to reveal himself.

"In America public opinion is divided," Martin
said. "A lot of people see Adolf Hitler as a man of
his word. Others just don't trust what he seems to
want for Germany."

"And what do you think he wants for Germany?"
Alexina asked.

Martin saw Elisabeth shoot an angry glance at her,
but the meaning of the look eluded him.

"I'm not ashamed to say I haven't made up my
mind yet. I've just arrived. I don't feel qualified to
come down on one side or the other."

"There's no time for dithering," Oster said with a
broad unfriendly smile.

"I'm not dithering," Martin said calmly. "I'm making up my mind. Not surprisingly, on as big a question as this one it's going to take some time."

"Adolf Hitler is looking for justice for Germany," Oster said with finality. "For Germany and all Germans."

"Including German Jews?" Alexina stared coldly at Oster. Emil stood up. "Enough of all this political talk," he said. "Come with me, Martin, I want to show you Lingfeld. Like all self-made men," he said, "I'm inordinately proud of my property. It's different with an old family like the Osters, they've never known what it's like to be without a great mansion somewhere." He clapped Rolf Oster on the shoulder as he passed him on the way to the door. "Come along Martin, let's leave Rolf and the ladies to get this wedding organized."

That evening after dinner Martin found himself alone with Alexina for the first time. He was helping her water plants in the conservatory, which ran along one side of the house. Now in the light filtered through the leaves of plants he watched her moving along a row of cuttings giving each a cupful or two of water. She knew he was watching her.

She looked up at him. Light danced across her hair as she moved.

"I didn't get engaged to an American girl when I got back from China," he said.

"No . . ." She smiled enigmatically and poured water on the cuttings.

"You asked me not to."

"A silly joke," she said, moving behind a tall fern plant.

He waited until she reached the end of the line of cuttings. "Pierre told me that Emil is working on a new machine, a new printing press."

"Is Pierre afraid?"

"I think maybe he's concerned."

She nodded, put the watering can on a shelf and brushed drops of water from her hands. "I can see why he's worried," she said. "So much has changed since we were in Shanghai. Germany has become so powerful."

He frowned, not sure what that had to do with Pierre and Emil and the Janus printing press.

"If Germany is powerful, German industry is powerful," she said. "You know that of the two parts of the House of Janus, the American company, Pierre's company, has always been stronger, more successful."

"I guess so. I guess there aren't so many opportunities in Europe."

"With new machines and Germany's new position in the world there will be more opportunities in Europe than anywhere."

"You think they could become out-and-out rivals?" Martin said uneasily. "I can't see that myself."

She began filling the watering can at the tap. "You know what those Waldviertel peasant feuds can be like?"

"Emil and Pierre are not exactly peasants."

"Sometimes I think they are at heart," she said, watching the level of water in the can and turning off the tap. "All my life I've heard stories of feuds over tiny strips of land. Fighting. Burying brothers or uncles at night."

He stared at her, baffled. "Something I have to get right," he said. "You've no love for what we come from."

"I hate it," she said passionately.

"When you were in America it's all you wanted to talk about, blood and soil and that stuff."

"It's evil," she said stubbornly. "It's what Hitler rants about all the time."

"But it's the family's origins," he said. "Whether we like it or not."

"We have a choice. A choice about whether or not we succumb to medieval ideas no civilized modern person would do anything but laugh at." She hurled the half empty watering can into a corner and, before Martin could stop her, ran past him into the house.

CHAPTER 12

~ ~ ~

It was idyllic August weather. Throughout the month the sun shone, drawing out Alpine flowers and grasses over the high hills behind Lingfeld.

During the first weeks after his arrival, Martin spent a lot of time with Alex. They rode, swam, played tennis together. And throughout that time, Alex struggled not to speak of what preoccupied her, of what, as the days passed, soon began to terrify her.

She found it difficult to keep her eyes off him. She prayed that it wasn't obvious to everyone else. Most of all, she prayed it wasn't obvious to him. If he were calming a horse in the stables, she watched him; while he swam or talked to Emil her eyes never left him. Once, as they played tennis, she had let the ball pass, unaware of it, mesmerized by the way he moved across the court.

That day he had noticed.

He walked slowly towards the net, towards her. "I don't think that you're the best tennis player in the world," he said. "But you could easily be the best-looking one. That was a pretty wild shot of mine. I wasn't concentrating."

She wanted to reach out across the net and touch his hand for saying that.

Behind his head the hills rose to mountain height. For a moment she thought: He is going to kiss me. He has only to bend his head forward to kiss me.

But the sound of laughter and Elisabeth's voice calling caused him to step back.

Alex watched Rolf Oster and her aunt come down the stone steps to the level of the sunken court. Dressed in a pale blue top and a brief tennis skirt, Elisabeth waved her racket towards Martin. "Will you give me a game?" she said. "Rolf's decided his wife-to-be is too good for him." Elisabeth patted her fiancé on the backside of his tennis shorts with her racket. "Why don't you challenge Alex?"

"Alex?" Oster lifted his eyebrows to her.

"Love to." Alex turned abruptly and walked towards the second court.

"You weren't playing a set?" Elisabeth's voice was husky with concern.

"No, I guess we'd abandoned it," Martin said.

"I wouldn't want to upset Alex."

"Let's play," Martin said, uneasy at Elisabeth's tone.

"She's young of course, and very headstrong. And she has this embarrassing crush on you. But you know that already, I'm sure."

She looked up at him, smiling.

The smile died slowly. "You're a very beautiful young man, Martin," she said. "I'm sure you're already turning the heads of all the young women of Long Island."

"Hey, Elisabeth," he said, jumping the net. "Do you want to play tennis?"

"I want to play tennis," she said, the smile again touching her lips.

It was a good game. She played fast and strongly enough to make him work at it. Losing the set six-four was no humiliation for her. She came over and shook his hand across the net. "Excellent," she said. "Excellent game. Only your service is too strong for me."

They walked towards the wooden hut at the far end of the court. Taking deck chairs out onto the stone

terrace in front of the hut, they watched Alex and
Rolf finish their game.

When the last ball crossed the net Alex thanked
Oster briefly, waved towards Martin and Elisabeth
outside the hut and walked quickly off the court.

As she disappeared along the wooded path that led
to the house, Elisabeth leaned towards Martin's chair,
a hand on his arm. "My adoptive niece does not like
to lose," she said.

In her room Alexina struggled with the feeling of
gnawing emptiness in her stomach. She paced back
and forth between the door and the window. She
hurled herself on her bed. She rolled into a sitting
position and jumped to her feet taking deep breaths
until she was dizzy.

But still the dull gnawing inside her would not go
away.

She knew it was jealousy. She knew that one look
passing between Martin and Elisabeth could cause her
hands to start shaking.

She was not sure when she had fallen in love. Perhaps when she and Martin were still children; perhaps
in those few hours in Shanghai the year before last;
perhaps she had simply fallen in love with the photographs Pierre sent regularly of the American Coburgs;
or perhaps it was that moment when he first arrived
at Lingfeld. She had come out onto the terrace expecting to see him, yet never expecting to be dazzled
by the way he looked up at her.

But no singer, no poet, had adequately described
this feeling. No one had ever told her that it was a
feeling that could take a balanced, confident,
eighteen-year-old girl and tear at her like some clawed
animal. Make her lie awake wracked by fear of what
she was certain was about to happen. Wracked by
doubt about how Martin would react when the moment came. The moment she knew would come.

At times she herself had doubts. Doubts about her own fears. This was usually when they were riding or swimming together, with the sun shining over the mountainsides.

But at night it was different. Then she felt certain that she knew what was planned, that Martin was to sleep with Elisabeth before the wedding in accordance with the old Waldviertel tradition of the first invited and, she was certain that Elisabeth already knew. She had thought about going to Emil, telling him she knew what was going to happen. But her pride prevented her.

She could do nothing. She could do nothing but wait.

For the willfull destruction of all she had come to hope for.

During the week before the wedding, Martin and Alexina never came as close to each other as they had just before Elisabeth had arrived at the tennis court. The tone between them was not cool, not really distant, but Martin could see that Alexina was deliberately maintaining some barrier between them. Deliberately preventing things developing from that moment on the tennis court. In particular she refused to talk about the Waldviertel. Horseback riding through the woods on the estate, she blocked every attempt by Martin to find out what it was about the family's background in Upper Austria that upset her so much. "I told you what I think," she said finally. "I think these old cults and customs, these old feuds and peasant obligations should be left to rot in the past."

"Emil and Pierre don't believe that."

"Too bad," she said, kicking her horse into a canter. "Perhaps one day they'll learn. In the meantime what about you?"

Before he could answer she had turned the horse

into a narrow path and was galloping through the woods ahead of him.

It took nearly ten minutes of hard riding through narrow forest paths, under low hanging branches and across rock-strewn streams, before he drew level with her and grabbed her horse's bridle hard enough to bring the animal down to a walk.

They were both breathing hard.

"Let me go," she said fiercely.

"Not until you stop behaving like some ten-year-old kid. If you've got something to say, say it now."

She looked furiously away from him.

"What is it for God's sake?" he said. "What happens to you when you talk about the family?"

"I reject the idea that that world is where I come from." She said as she swung off her horse and began to walk it through the woods.

"Listen," he said as he swung down beside her. "You don't have to go along with it but it was their past, Pierre's and Emil's. You can't take it away from them."

"I'm not worried about them," she said. "I'm worried about you."

"Okay," he said. "I'll tell you. I'm an American, do you understand that?"

"Of course."

"I don't think you begin to. I think it's *you* that's stuck in fear of the old ways. See me for what I am. These things are interesting to me. Of course they are. But they're interesting at a distance. What's got into you? You think Emil's corrupting me? You think I'm going off to be a peasant farmer in Upper Austria?"

"Perhaps you're right," she said. "Perhaps I am just stuck in fear of the old ways. And I'm worried about you."

"You're crazy," he said angrily. "I'm an American from Long Island. Does that give you my answer?"

She smiled. "It's the answer I wanted. But it took a hell of a lot to provoke you into it."

"There's still something you haven't told me."

"True."

"When will you tell me?"

She looked down at the path. "When I'm no longer afraid," she said.

Martin took her hand. "You won't tell me more?"

She shook her head and he could see tears in her eyes.

"I also have a feeling this is some sort of test."

She shrugged, pulling her hand away.

"If it is," he said quietly. "If it's anything to do with the way I feel about you, I'm going to pass that test."

She reached up a hand and rubbed at her eyes. When she looked up at him she was smiling. "I feel better," she said, and putting a riding boot into her stirrup she swung up above him.

But, mostly, the days of brilliant August sunshine before the wedding passed in large family picnics by mountain lakes, drives through deep forests, a lot of laughter, champagne and good food.

The only real flaw in Martin's view was Gregor Stot, a young neighbor of the Coburgs, newly commissioned in the Luftwaffe and undergoing pilot training at Augsburg Airfield.

His interest in Alex was obvious. On a good day Martin could persuade himself she only responded as a friend. On a bad day it seemed she encouraged Stot outrageously. Worse was the fact that Martin himself found Gregor a friendly and likeable young man. Two nights before Elisabeth's wedding it came as a shock to Martin to discover Gregor was to take Alexina to a Luftwaffe dance in Munich.

He had come to collect her in his English sports car and stood in the drawing room at Lingfeld, far too good-looking for Martin's taste, in his pale blue Luftwaffe dress uniform. When Alexina came down the curving staircase in a low cut ballgown everybody in the room stopped talking.

"I have a lovely daughter," Emil said, advancing to the foot of the stairs to take her hand. "Look after her, Gregor. And not too late, uh?"

After a strained dinner with Emil and Dorotta, Rolf and Elisabeth, Martin went up to his room with a large whiskey. It was still only nine o'clock. He turned on the radio but it was mostly politics. Poland was mistreating some ethnic Germans in the Polish border areas. He changed stations. The Swedish singer Lale Anderson was singing a new German hit, "Lili Marlene."

For a few moments he walked about the room, sipping whiskey, thinking of Alex, puzzling over the way she behaved.

Sometimes she seemed interested. Sometimes she seemed to be thinking about something else altogether. She was worried about Pierre and her father falling out.

Well, so was he.

But most of all she was caught up in this Waldviertel thing.

Why?

Why not let Emil and Pierre sort out their own problems? They were brothers, twins even. Grown men. It couldn't get that serious.

He finished his whiskey. It was just after ten. What time did Luftwaffe balls end? Midnight? He went downstairs and refilled his glass. No ice, no water.

His watch showed two-thirty as Gregor's car drew up, and it was at least another half an hour before it rattled off down the drive.

Cool air streamed through the open window.

His hand reached for the lamp switch. He hesitated. He could hear Alex coming up the stairs. The familiar creaks of the old floorboards.

Then silence. And a gentle tapping. The handle turned and the door opened.

He sat up in bed, naked from the waist, and switched on the light.

Alexina took a step into the room and closed the door behind her.

He began to ask if she had had a good evening but broke off at the look in her eyes.

"What is it?" he said.

She leaned back against the door. "Gregor has asked me to become engaged to him," she said.

Martin's mouth went instantly dry. He forced words rasping across his tongue. "For Christ's sake, you didn't say yes?"

She half-turned and reached for the door handle. "I told him," she said, deliberately, "that I didn't know yet."

"You told him you weren't sure?"

"I told him I didn't know."

He grabbed his robe, got it round his shoulders and swung his legs out of bed. "And when will you know for God's sake?"

"He's invited to Elisabeth's wedding of course. The day after tomorrow."

"So what?"

"So by the day after tomorrow . . ." She left the rest of the answer hanging.

He stood up, wrapping the robe around him. "You'll have the answer. You'll have made up your mind?"

"I'll know by then." She seemed to be correcting him. His mind was fuzzy with sleep. Did that mean she had made up her mind already?

He stood in the middle of the room. "Listen," he said. "I'm just a straightforward American. I can't understand this double-talk."

"If you're just a straightforward American, why not just be straightforward?"

"Okay." He walked towards her and put his arms around her waist. "I love you, Alexina," he said. "I don't know when it happened. The first day I arrived here. Or maybe I always have."

She lifted her head as if to kiss him, then suddenly, broke away and reached for the door.

"Have I offended you, for God's sake?" he exploded.

He could see how close she was to saying something.

"Tell me that again when you've had time to think about it," she said finally. "After Elisabeth's wedding."

She opened the door. Before he could reach her she was out into the corridor. He pulled open the door. As a clock struck the quarter somewhere in the house he watched her reach her room and, with a final glance at him, open the door and disappear inside.

The next morning, with the wedding now only one day away, Emil invited Martin to go for a drive. "We're not wanted here," he said. "I've something I want to show you."

Emil took the wheel of the supercharged Mercedes and Martin sat next to him in the deep leather passenger seat.

"Let me tell you about making banknotes," Emil said. "Rag paper and Swiss inks we will put aside for the moment. When I talk about making a banknote I talk as a printer, I talk about *printing* banknotes. You know, Martin, a printing press that could print five colors with a hairline registration would sweep the competing banknote companies of the world into the sea."

Martin looked at him. He knew of course that Emil was talking about the press he was working on himself. "Has anybody developed such a machine?" he asked.

"For the most part the great banknote printing organizations of the world have not yet appreciated the possibilities of such a machine," Emil said. "Even giants like De La Rue in London have not yet appreciated the impact of this press. Should anyone ever succeed in building it . . ."

"Will they? Ever?" Martin said carefully.

Emil shrugged, clearly enjoying himself. "A French printer-inventor named Serge Beaune had made some steps in the right direction. But at the moment, Martin, the field is open."

The car swept through the wooded countryside. The signs read Augsburg.

"Are we going far?" Martin asked.

"A few miles. To Augsburg."

"You have a factory there?"

"Not really," Emil smiled enigmatically.

"Why are we going to Augsburg, Emil?" Martin asked at length.

"My old friend Willy Messerschmitt has a testing airfield there. This afternoon he's putting his new Me 109 through its paces. The sort of thing a young man likes to see, isn't it?"

To the young American the afternoon's low flying test program was riveting. Three of the new 109s made passes and rolls over the airfield, then climbed steeply into the sun, banked and power dived at what the commentator said was just over six hundred kilometers, four hundred mph. Emil and the American boy stood among a group of civilians to the left of the main party, which consisted of Goering and his wife, three Luftwaffe generals and one of the heroes of Martin's boyhood, Colonel Charles Lindbergh.

When the main party withdrew to the offices, which made up three sides of a square behind the forecourt in which they were standing, Emil took Martin's arm and led him to the car. "This is a time in German science and technology when enormous advances are being made. You saw the 109. Perhaps Britain's Spitfire and Hurricane are as good. Let us hope we never find out for sure. But the 109 is a fine piece of engineering." He gestured Martin into the car and himself climbed into the driver's seat. "I said I have something to show you. It is in its way as secret as the specifications of the 109 we have just seen." They drove across the airfield and pulled up in front of a small hangar. Leaving the car, they walked towards the small inset door.

"I've no doubt you have already guessed, Martin." Emil knocked and they were admitted. "My old friend Willy Messerschmitt has allowed me this hangar. It's guarded by Luftwaffe soldiers night and day."

Martin looked into the depths of the windowless aircraft hangar. A row of half a dozen large lights hung from the ridge of the metal roof. In the middle of the concrete floor was a brightly lit wire cage twenty feet by twenty feet. Inside it ten men were working on a long low machine shining with steel fittings.

Broad sheets of thick paper passed across slow moving rollers. Ascending from the depths of the machine the sheets emerged printed as small rectangles, banknote size.

Emil walked to the end and tore off a sheet. He folded it for Martin to see. The rectangles were dollar bills printed in an improbable pink.

"A test sheet," Emil said. "Forget the color."

For some moments they stood reverently outside the cage. "That press, Martin, will give the Coburgs the power to sweep aside every banknote printing company in the world. It is the most sophisticated printing press in existence. Tell Pierre that in honor of the symbol of our family house I have decided to call it *Janus*."

They took a different route back, a road that climbed up above the Augsberg autobahn and turned and twisted through the high summer woods. They drove for over an hour towards the Austrian border until darkness fell and even the Mercedes' powerful headlights showed Martin no more than the shape of the road ahead.

They had not seen a light or any real sign of habitation for over twenty minutes when Martin realized they must be driving through some private estate. "Where are we, Emil?" he asked, puzzled.

Emil laughed. "You know how much I love a little mystery, my boy. Don't press me with questions."

Martin sat back in his seat watching the tops of the trees fly by against the very faint light of the late summer twilight. He thought of Alexina and the way she had ignored him this morning. He could not believe that it was politics. She'd found in Gregor someone else she liked better. What other answer could there be. The politics was an excuse. Anger began to overtake jealousy. When, suddenly, the car stopped before a long low wooden building with a string of lights along its veranda, Martin realized he was unaware even that they had turned off the road.

"I'm lost, Martin," Emil said. "Go and ask at the house where we are while I turn the car around."

Martin got out and walked across the gravel towards the house. Behind him he heard Emil turning the car, the tires crunching over the gravel.

Martin mounted the roughboard wooden steps. Behind him the engine note changed. He looked, and saw the Mercedes moving swiftly away down the narrow track.

For a few moments he stood, dumbfounded. The taillights of the Mercedes twisted with the track—and disappeared.

He stood uncertainly. What was Emil doing? He looked out across the woods to where he could pick up the lights of the Mercedes again. The faint glow of light fled along a bank of trees and continued on until it dissolved into complete darkness.

He walked along the veranda and tried to look into the windows, but where there were lights the curtains were too thick to see anything inside. He walked back to the pine door. His footsteps on the veranda boards echoed loud on this silent summer evening.

Taking the brass lion-head knocker he hesitated a second, still baffled by the course of events, then let the lion head fall against the brass stud. The noise seemed to thunder along the veranda and out into the stands of fir trees. He waited.

After a few moments he knocked again and stood listening. Inside he could hear footsteps on bare boards approaching the door. There was a rattle of a bolt being withdrawn. The handle turned and the door was opened. Elisabeth Coburg stood in the doorway. "I thought it would be you," she said, "the first wedding guest. To tell you the truth I'd rather hoped so."

They sat in the main room of the chalet beside the log fire. "Of course you have the right to say no," Elisabeth said. "It's not a duty you know."

Martin looked at her without answering. He could feel himself already responding. Elisabeth was older than him but full-figured and long-legged. What she was offering made fumes like brandy rise to his head. He was still absurdly unable to speak.

"Nobody knows, of course, who the guest is. Or even if there's one. This is the way it's done in the villages of the Waldviertel. Rolf will never know. Only the head of the family, the one who makes the choice."

She got up and poured two large glasses of brandy. His eyes were on the shape of her body under the wine-colored woollen dress. She turned, saw him looking at her and smiled. "You'll be more relaxed in a moment," she said. She handed him the glass.

"But what about you?" He drank some brandy. "On the eve of your wedding . . ."

She acknowledged the thought crisply. "Some modern girls find it hard perhaps," she said. "But I've never heard for certain any woman from the five villages who has ever refused. They often claim afterwards that they ran away into the woods, but it's only for the benefit of their husbands." She stood sipping her brandy. "Yes," she said reflectively, "some modern girls find the custom distasteful." She paused. "I am not a very modern young woman. I'll not be running away into the woods."

"You really believe this custom is important?"

Her eyes narrowed. "All German customs are important," she said. "Even more so now when the Jew is trying to take them away from us."

"The Jews are trying to destroy the old customs?"

"Of course," Elisabeth said. "There is an attempt to de-Germanize us until it is impossible to tell the difference between a German and a Greek. Our old customs are our shield against this attempt to detribalize our race."

"Does Emil believe this?"

"He brought you here, didn't he?"

She was aware that she had destroyed the warmth between them. She took his glass and refilled it. "Don't you approve of our old customs, Martin?"

What in God's name was he doing here? Images of Alexina flashed across this mind. Alexina riding, Alexina standing in the ballgown in his bedroom. He let the brandy burn the roof of his mouth.

"Even in a practical sense it is often better that a woman is not introduced to physical relations by her husband," Elisabeth was saying.

He found her words deeply disturbing.

"I'm not a very experienced woman," she said.

He watched the movement of her body under the woollen dress.

"Of course," she said, "humiliating as it would be for me, you have every right to decline."

He stood up. One single step toward the door would have been enough.

"I think you have to understand that this is not an infidelity on my part. Or on yours," she added, watching him. "This is part of a ritual. Don't confuse the two."

One step toward the door.

She put a record on the phonograph, a slow Berlin nightclub piece. "I've seen you watching me, I think."

"Perhaps."

"Even Rolf noticed that."

"I'm sorry."

"You don't have to apologize. Drink your brandy and come and dance with me. Like this we shall relax a little together."

He was mad with lust as perhaps only a very young man can be. In bed he hurled himself at her, wrestling her down onto her back, forcing her legs apart with his knee. She laughed and sometimes squealed with pleasure as he plunged into her, hammering at her like a man-bullock.

Underneath him she rolled and swore and pulled his head down onto her breasts and bucked and shouted jeering obscenities until he drove deeper into her, sweat thrown from their bodies by the sheer vigor of their union.

Morning came to Martin as bright sunlight from the drawn curtains. Elisabeth stood beside the bed in a severe gray dress and heavy flat shoes. To Martin she looked so old.

She gave him a cup of coffee but she did not sit on the bed. "You'd better get up," she said in a completely neutral tone. "Emil will be here in a few moments. Neither of us will talk about this, ever."

He struggled onto one elbow, his head swinging slowly from the effects of too little sleep and too much brandy.

"As far as the rest of the family is concerned," she said, "you and Emil took the wrong road back. You were forced to spend the night in a hotel. Emil has already telephoned Dorotta of course."

Martin stretched out a hand to touch her thigh, but she backed away as his fingertips brushed the woollen dress.

"You do understand that from midday today I shall be a married woman."

He fell back onto the bed. "Of course."

"It is not the custom to make reference to last night ever again. Even if we are alone."

She walked across the room to the door. "Now please get dressed, Martin," she said in a hectoring tone. "Emil will be here any moment."

At that moment it hit him like a thunderclap.

Alexina knew. She had known from the beginning that he had been brought from America to be the first invited.

And now by his absence she knew that he had accepted.

CHAPTER 13

~ ~ ~

When Emil and Martin got back, Lingfeld had been transformed. Yellow-and-white striped awnings now shaded the long terrace. Lines of trestle tables with white cloths held silver dishes and nearly two hundred place settings. Maids and footmen hurried back and forth. Small crises developed: the smoked salmon flown by airmail from Scotland had barely arrived in time; an eddy of wind was plucking at the long red swastika flag on the east corner of the house; the SS general who was to marry the couple according to the rites of the SS Black Order had not yet arrived.

Alexina, running at full pelt across the front lawn with an instruction for some part of the massive operation, stopped when she saw Martin.

"Hi," he said. It was the first time he had talked to her since she had come into his bedroom.

They stood in the middle of the lawn, the activity of the house servants and caterers swirling around them. "Where did you get to last night?" she asked casually.

"Last night?" His stomach twisted.

She knew.

"Emil got lost," he said. "We had to find a hotel."

"I see." She didn't move, kept her dark blue-eyed stare upon him. "Waldviertel," she said. "It won in the end."

"I don't know what you mean."

He did. Clearly. He gasped as the meaning flooded him. She meant he had been suckered by the peasant fantasies—just like Emil and Pierre and even Elisabeth, too. It's what she had been telling him in the conservatory, in the forest, up in his bedroom. She *knew* why Pierre had sent him to Germany. To play the part. To be the first invited at Elisabeth's wedding. To reinforce for two old men the meaning of the House of Janus.

But it had lost him Alex.

"Alex," he said, his heart pumping, "I'm sorry. You understand what I mean?" he said desperately. "I hate myself for it. For what I've done to you."

She stood watching him, without speaking.

"Try to understand."

He thought her face had been turned to stone. "I understand," she said. "I'm sure you do, too. There's nothing to apologize for. You behaved as a young Coburg should."

She turned and hurried towards the house. There was nothing for Martin to do. He watched while the SS guard of honor rehearsed the arch of rifles the bridal couple would emerge to. They seemed to be so utterly perfect that by the third rehearsal Martin moved on. Old Wilhelm, the mechanic, had been watching too. "I wonder," he said. "I wonder how those parade dummies would have done in Flanders mud?"

Martin went up to his room, showered and sat naked on the edge of the bed smoking a cigarette. He could make no sense of the emotions that flowed over him, confused and contradictory. One idea kept returning: she had known all along that he was to be the first invited. She had used it to put him to the test.

And he had behaved as a jealous kid. *Weak as water.*

He got up from the bed and dressed in his formal clothes—tailcoat and striped trousers, dove gray vest and silk cravat. He looked in the mirror, thinking about how he would congratulate Rolf Oster after the wedding. Or what he would say to Elisabeth.

He was downstairs half an hour before time. The immense long windowed room, with its pale gray, swagged curtains was the ballroom of Haus Lingfeld. Stucco work graced the interior walls and four great chandeliers were suspended from the ornate ceiling. Guests swirled around, greeting each other; SS adjutants hurried back and forth, conspicuous in their formal black dress uniform. Looking around him, past the girls in their pale dresses and crimped blonde hair, Martin was surprised to see how many of the young men were in military uniforms.

Twenty minutes before the ceremony was due to begin the senior SS aide, an immensely tall young man named Gunsche, rapped his billboard for silence. "Ladies and gentlemen," he said, "may I ask you to take up your positions. Herr Coburg has an announcement to make."

The guests shuffled and bumped against each other to get to the position they had each been assigned, up on opposite sides of a long corridor between the door and a small table covered with a black and silver SS flag.

Martin was positioned quite close to the door. Gregor Stot, in Luftwaffe cadet officer's uniform, was beside him.

"Alexina tells me you've asked her to marry you," Martin said.

"I thought I'd get in before you did. Was I right?"

"She said yes?"

"Not yet," Gregor said. "She wanted to wait until after the wedding."

Martin stood there looking towards the exhalation of light around the long window in front of him. He was short of sleep and desperately in need of another glass of champagne. His thoughts drifted to last night. Perhaps he closed his eyes for a moment because he leaned against Gregor who pushed him upright. "Don't go to sleep on me yet," he said with his easy grin. Martin forced his eyes open.

"Ladies and gentlemen," Emil said, "dear friends and members of the family, I have an announcement to make to you. You will understand that for reasons of security, we were unable to tell you before." He paused. "The Führer has kindly consented to give Elisabeth away today."

A shiver ran through the guests and a flutter of low excited conversation. In their enthusiasm no one had noted the flatness of Emil's statement.

The guests now stood like soldiers, silent and upright. Anyone who dared to speak received harsh, penetrating looks. At five minutes to midday the great oak doors opened and Rolf Oster and his escort walked stiffly down between the guests, Oster's black uniform impeccable, his sword held tightly to his side. From somewhere among the guests near the table, the SS general stood with one outstretched hand lightly grasping the flag.

The minutes ticked past. Now no one spoke. Then a small organ, which had been positioned in the hall beyond the oak doors, began to play softly. It was a piece that Martin did not know, somber, heavy.

The doors opened to reveal Adolf Hitler, dressed in a simple brown jacket and black trousers with a silk stripe. On his arm, taller than he was, Elisabeth Coburg looked splendid in her ivory wedding dress. The music swelled. Adolf Hitler stepped forward with Elisabeth.

It was only then that Martin saw Alexina a few steps behind the bride.

Her face was composed, set even. It seemed to Martin that she looked like a Greek goddess with a rope of pearls banding her forehead and her long cream dress cut deep between her breasts. Carrying Elisabeth's train, she walked with long slow steps behind her aunt and the Führer of the Third Reich.

From his position near the door Martin was unable to see the progression of the SS wedding ceremony. Stretching his neck he was just able to see bread broken on the black flag and salt sprinkled on the hands of the bridal pair. The SS provided wedding rings and, as they were placed on the third finger of the left hand of the bride and groom, the presiding SS officer intoned an oath of mutual fidelity and respect.

Throughout the ceremony Adolf Hitler stood slightly to one side, staring fixedly at the proceedings. Next to him stood Alexina, and to Martin with the knowledge of last night now a source of overwhelming guilt, more classically beautiful than he had ever realized.

At the end of the ceremony Adolf Hitler shook hands with the bride and groom.

Then the room fell silent as the Führer took up a position at the far end of the room between the two lines of guests. For a moment it seemed possible that he would speak. Then, seemingly deciding against it, he began to pace slowly between the lines of guests towards the door at Martin's end of the room, his face grim, his hands clasped almost awkwardly in front of him. From time to time he stopped in front of one of the guests and shook hands. Then his somber expression would suddenly change so that, by contrast, the smile that illuminated his face seemed all the more friendly, more human. As he approached, stopping to nod gravely to one guest, courteously shaking hands with another, Martin felt some sense of the unpredictable nature of his personality. When the set look and the unseeing blue eyes were suddenly replaced by an almost playful smile, the whole room seemed to sigh with relief, to relax for a moment, before the Führer, turning abruptly, continued on towards the door, his thoughts seemingly far from Haus Lingfeld and the marriage ceremony that had just taken place.

At the door he stopped again and the smile and handshake for Oster and Elisabeth were brief and courteous. Then he was gone.

For a moment the whole room of some three hundred persons held their breath; then, as if with one exhalation of tension released, everybody began to talk at once.

Suddenly, Martin heard Alexina's voice. "What an odious little man," she said in a voice loud enough for three or four people around them to hear.

"For God's sake, Alex," Gregor hissed in her ear. "Are you mad?"

"I think we're all mad," Alexina said. "Have you heard the news?"

"No, what news?"

"One of the beast's aides whispered it to me as he passed. This morning the German army, *our* army, invaded Poland. You don't need to be a world statesman to know that this day is the beginning of another world war." Alexina's eyes flashed fury toward Martin, then she burst into tears and ran from the room.

Within an hour the chauffeur was loading Martin's cases into the car. Martin himself, pressed by Emil to hurry, had been able to say no more than a word or two of goodbye to Alexina and had had to do so when Dorotta was present.

When the chauffeur was ready, Emil took Martin into a small office off the salon. His agitation was evident as he poured himself and Martin a glass of whiskey. "I have instructed the chauffeur to drive straight to Switzerland," he said.

"Is that necessary, Emil? I could take a train from Munich."

"Listen to me, Martin," Emil said gently. "You're a young man, you're learning all the time, but you haven't learnt enough yet. Within hours, or days at the most, Germany will be at war with France and

England over the Polish issue. If President Roosevelt can bring in the United States, he will."

Martin stepped back in shock, as if he had been struck with a blow. In all this talk of war in the last weeks he had never imagined the United States having any part in it. It was a European affair, politics was a shady European business, it had nothing to do with America.

Emil was nodding slowly. "Yes," he said, "It may take your president months or even years, but he is determined to enter this war on the side of the democracies. He will not stand on the sidelines for one second longer than he has to."

"Do you know this, Emil? Do you know this is true?"

He nodded gravely. "I am far from alone in thinking so. Listen to me, Martin. Chance has insisted that you play a part in these events."

"Me? Play a part?"

"When I showed you the Janus press, you saw it printing banknotes, but you didn't see what kind it was printing."

"Pink dollars. A test run."

"No, the whole conveyor was covered."

Emil opened a drawer in his desk. "The Janus press has received its first order, Martin." He slid a green banknote across the desk.

It was a brand new U.S. twenty-dollar bill!

Martin stretched out a hand and touched it.

"Pick it up, Martin. You know banknotes. Feel it, smell it, run your thumbnail across it, look at it against the light."

Martin's mind reeled. "You've got an order to print U. S. twenty-dollar bills?"

Emil nodded grimly.

"But the American continent is agreed to be Pierre's area. In any case the Bureau of Engraving and Printing prints money for the U.S. government."

"The order for one million U.S. twenty-dollar bills did not come from the Federal Reserve Bank."

"Where did it come from?"

"It came," Emil said somberly, "from our own Reich government, in Berlin."

From the woods beside the drive, Alexina watched the car carrying Martin, sweep through the gates, hurling dust and gravel from its wheels. He had played the part Pierre and her father had assigned to him. He had proved himself, in all ways, a Coburg.

And, his duty done, he had been sent home.

She was no longer sure what she felt. Everything that she feared most had happened. She stood among the scents of summer in the depth of the narrow woods. She knew she was indulging her misery but there was nothing she could do to stop herself. At the core of her sadness was her knowledge that Martin Coburg was the man she still wanted, that there were still some strands of the Coburg inheritance in her, too.

She walked back to the house by the path through the woods. The noise of the guests on the terrace rose like the chatter of starlings.

She had told Martin that she understood. But that was bravado. She knew the truth was that she understood nothing. She was certain he loved her. So how could he have done what he did?

Her wide-brimmed straw hat in her hand, her head held higher than was natural to her, she emerged from the woods and followed the path around the lake towards the house.

She could see the guests now, packed, brightly colored on the long terrace. The women's dresses and the men's summer uniforms, sparkled in the sunlight.

She had not picked out Emil before she saw a figure in a cutaway coat coming down the stone steps towards the drive.

He had seen her and she stopped by the side of the lake as he waved solemnly and walked across the cropped grass towards her.

At first last night, when Emil had phoned to say he and Martin would not be back, she had been overwhelmed with fury, with a black sense of betrayal. She could not contain it. She had screamed at her mother and run through the house sobbing.

Maids who only knew her as warm and even-tempered recoiled as she ran past them. Only a few of the oldest servants, recruited in Waldviertel itself, guessed the significance of the master's telephone call that evening.

But now she felt numb.

She watched the huge figure, white-haired, broad-shouldered and now thick around the waist, cross the grass and stop in front of her. For a moment they stood like combatants in the ritual pause before the attack.

"I will never be able to tell you how sorry I am," Emil said slowly. "You might ask why I didn't realize what I was doing to the daughter I love, but I didn't. If I had told your mother in advance she would have known what my stupidity meant to you."

Alexina looked down at the toe of her cream silk shoe. "I know why you did it, Papa," she said, her lips barely moving. "But why did he?"

Emil shrugged heavily. "The instincts of men, especially young men, are not like those of women," he said. "There are sudden storms of lust and rapaciousness that obliterate everything else."

"Even love?"

"Even love," he said. "Men act with nobility, men are capable of self-sacrifice or altruism. But it is not in their *nature*. It has to be learned, my darling Alexina. In their nature lies their instinct—lustful, greedy, insolent of others' feelings. At this very moment, Martin is regreting last night more than anything he has ever done. But he'll learn, Alex. I promise you if you give him a chance, he'll learn."

"And you Papa, will *you* learn?"

He smiled. "You're too bold, my darling. It will lead you into trouble. Two or three people have already had a word with me concerning your comments about the Führer this afternoon."

"A lot of people feel as I do. In Munich, at the university, we already have an organization."

"Alex," he said, "go to America. Marry Martin."

She shook her head.

"Forgive him. He will not betray you again."

CHAPTER 14

~ ~ ~

By the time Martin arrived back in the United States, the first part of Emil's predictions had materialized. Germany was now at war with Britain and France. The beginnings of another world conflict were there for all to see.

Yet, on the surface, there were few signs of the impending catastrophe. Traveling from Switzerland to Paris, Martin saw French troops assembling at every station he passed, but the atmosphere was festive. Something approaching a holiday spirit prevailed. No one among the young conscripts marching up to the German border believed the war would last for more than three months. It was, in fact, all grimly reminiscent of August 1914.

From Paris, Martin took a train from the Gare d'Austerlitz south through Limoges and on to Bordeaux. From there a Norwegian freighter took him to Lisbon and from Lisbon he caught the Pan American flight to New York. The whole journey took less than four days.

It was after midnight when the limousine pulled to a halt outside Island House. On the bedroom floors the lights were out. Only in the library, where Pierre liked to sit over brandy and a cigar, did the lights still burn behind the heavy silk curtains.

Inside the library, Celine and Pierre heard the automobile pull up on the gravel forecourt. She was sitting, as she often did now, on the arm of his chair. She wore a robe and bell-bottomed satin pajamas of the latest fashion; one foot resting lightly on the seat of the chair so that her leg was lifted to about the height of Pierre's shoulder. Absent-mindedly, it seemed, his hand stroked the inside of her knee.

Both of them knew the movement to be far from absent-minded. It was, rather, part of a complex process, infinitely slow, that had been building up each time Rose stayed the night with friends in New York. He had never yet touched her bare flesh, but there were landmarks she remembered vividly. He had once stroked the inside of her thigh almost to the groin; once he had fondled her breast through no more than the satin pajama jacket. And once, while they talked of the New York stock exchange and banknote contracts and new technical developments, she had allowed her hand to fall and rest, very lightly, in his crotch.

"Do you want to see Martin before he goes to bed?" Celine asked Pierre as they listened to doors opening and closing and the muffled sound of voices in the hall.

"I'm enjoying just sitting here with a glass of brandy," Pierre said, smiling up at her. "Anyway, I guess Martin'll be tired after his long flight. I told Frank to say I'd see him in the morning."

Her hand was now around the back of his collar, a finger curling the hair on the nape of his neck. Not for the first time in her life, she was astonished by men. However banal or Hollywood the caress, they reacted immediately. "No," Pierre said firmly, "I don't think we need Martin barging in here tonight."

The knocking on the library door caused his expression to set with annoyance. He could hear Martin's voice calling.

"Shall I tell him?" Celine asked, half rising.

"You stay where you are," Pierre said. "Frank'll tell him."

The knocking continued. The brass handle turned. The locked door was rattled.

Pierre stood up furiously. "Goddam Martin," he was shouting long before he reached the door. "You heard what Frank said!"

Celine watched him with pleasure. She had been worried by this homecoming. Emil had cabled Pierre several times to say how well Martin was shaping up during the summer in Europe. She had watched Pierre nod his own confirmation to his twin brother's estimate and she did not like the implication for her own future. Because by now she had decided that there was a chance, however slender, that she would inherit Coburg Banknote when Pierre died. Or at least part of it.

The knocking ceased. Pierre unlocked the door and threw it open. "Did Frank tell you or not?" he demanded.

The butler was standing nervously behind Martin. "I gave Mister Martin your message, sir."

"Of course you did," Pierre snarled. "Goddam it, of course you did." He looked at Martin. "So why did you choose to come knocking down the door when I'm having a quiet little talk with your sister Celine?"

Martin looked past his grandfather down the length of the library to where Celine was standing in her robe and satin pajamas. She was lighting a cigarette, her eyes on him over the lighter's flame. For one second the memory of his father's concern crossed his mind, but he thrust it aside immediately.

"Well . . . ?" Pierre was demanding.

"I have a message from Emil."

"Can't it wait until the morning."

"Emil says it couldn't be more important. He asked me to deliver it to you the moment I got back to Long Island."

"Well, deliver it, then." Pierre still blocked his way into the library.

"I have to speak to you alone. I gave Emil my word."

With intense exasperation Pierre stepped back and gestured to Martin to enter. He turned and walked towards his chair. "Shut the door behind you," he growled over his shoulder.

Martin came into the room. "Hello, Celine," he nodded in her direction.

"Hi," she said casually. "How was Europe?"

"Europe was okay."

"And the lovely Alexina?"

"Knock it off," Pierre said crudely. "He's got a message for me. He insisted on bursting in here because he has a message for me."

"I heard," Celine said. "What's the message, Martin?"

"It's for Pierre. Alone."

She looked at her brother and drew sharply on her cigarette. Then she swung around towards Pierre. "Do I have to put up with that?" she asked icily. "Am I a member of this family? Or not?"

Pierre lifted a hand to placate her. He still hoped that once Martin's message was delivered he would be able to persuade her to resume her place on the arm of his chair. "I don't think it's very polite to your sister," he said, "to exclude her from a Coburg business matter. I take it that's what it is."

Martin reached inside his jacket and took out a billfold. Celine watched him remove a twenty-dollar bill and place it on the corner of the long library table.

Pierre looked down. As ever, he could not resist examining a newly printed banknote. This one was without even a single center fold.

Celine crossed the room to stand next to her grandfather. Below the peach shade of one of the library reading lamps she looked down at the Abraham Lincoln twenty-dollar bill and shrugged. It was a brand new bill. So what?

Pierre raised his head slowly. He was, Celine noticed, breathing heavily. "The serial number," he said.

Martin nodded. "Emil said you would see it, immediately."

"Go to your room, Celine," Pierre said as he dismissed her with a wave of his hand. He had not even looked at her.

She straightened, unable to understand. She made the error of an attempt to protest. "If it's Coburg business . . ."

"Go to bed, I said," Pierre roared at her.

She stepped back in alarm, then threw her cigarette into the fire and ran angrily from the room.

As the door slammed after her, Pierre's eyes rose from the banknote. "The serial number is the birthday of me and Emil, repeated three times. The Imprimerie Coburg in Germany printed this twenty-dollar bill? Is that the message?"

"Yes."

"But printed the bill on a new intaglio machine. Is that the message from my goddam brother."

"The engineers in Germany, mostly Emil himself, have developed a printing press. Emil is naming it *Janus* in honor of the Coburg symbol."

Pierre's expression suddenly lightened. "Will we in New York have full access to the machine?"

"Emil says those are matters for discussion between you and him."

Pierre's face flushed darkly again. "Discussion, is it? A *diktat* more like, with Emil calling all the shots."

"Pierre," Martin said, "I don't believe Emil intends to call all the shots."

His grandfather strode across the room and poured himself more brandy. As an afterthought he held up the decanter to Martin.

Martin shook his head. "I'll get some coffee," he said as he moved towards the bell beside the telephone.

"Forget the goddam coffee," Pierre said. "Either drink brandy or nothing."

"Nothing," Martin said. "I guess I'll have nothing."

"So Emil does not intend to call the shots you say? Yet how does he send me a message? He sends it on a twenty-dollar bill printed by his Janus, his new wonder machine. I get the message, you hear me? I get the message loud and clear."

Martin stood stock still. He had seen his grandfather in a rage before now but he had never seen him quite like this. He felt he wanted to do something, to help him over his anger so that he could deliver the rest of Emil's message. "Pierre," he said. "You haven't heard everything yet."

Pierre stopped his restless pacing. "There's something else?"

Strange emotions flooded through Martin. The eagerness in Pierre's voice made him feel a twinge of pity for his grandfather, for a man who had been so dominant a figure in his own life. Who still was. Yet the edge of pity was there for Martin to feel.

"What did Emil say to you? What else?" Pierre went to the fireplace and rang the bell. Lifting the ancient brass speaking tube he blew into it and held it to his ear. A girl's voice said: "Yes, Mr. Coburg."

"You got some coffee on down there?"

"Yes, Mr. Coburg."

"Bring a pot to the library for Mr. Martin."

He put down the speaking tube. Martin felt a curious sense of elation. As if he'd won some struggle. And yet at the same time he did not want this man to be defeated.

"Sit down, boy," Pierre said. "Let's hear from Emil in full."

Martin crossed the room and sat on the arm of one of the big library chairs. "Emil didn't just print one twenty-dollar bill to demonstrate the Janus."

"Go on."

"Emil didn't intend to give me the twenty-dollar bill. His plan was to show it to you himself. But the outbreak of war in Europe changed that. Emil believes it is essential that you take this bill to the president."

"To Roosevelt?"

"Yes."

"Why in God's name?" He stopped. "Because it's not the only one!"

Martin nodded. "There are one million others," he said.

"Jesus!" Pierre got up and went to the door in response to a hesitant knock. Opening the door he took the coffee tray and kicked closed the mahogany door. "Twenty-million dollars! What in God's name is happening to my brother?"

"The order for the counterfeits came from Berlin," Martin said as he watched Pierre pour coffee for him. Again that mix of elation and pity struck him as he reached forward and took the proferred cup.

"These false bills, where are they now?"

"On the high seas. Heading for the United States."

Martin leaned forward to give proper emphasis to the story, to savor the first moment in his life when he had Pierre's absolute and undivided attention. "Emil believes that Roosevelt will want to bring the United States into this war."

Pierre nodded. "He's left no one in doubt about what he thinks of Adolf Hitler. Sure, he'll want to bring in the United States. But first he has to win next year's election. The way I see it, Martin, this will be America's most important election ever. Politically, I've always been a Democrat. I just hope FDR knows what he's doing."

"Emil also believes that this is America's most important election. He says *who* wins will alter the history of the world. Berlin knows this. Berlin wants a president who will not take America into the war. Any other president but Roosevelt."

"And the twenty million dollars?"

"Are to defeat President Roosevelt in the 1940 election."

"How?"

"Nobody has ever spent that much money on a presidential election. That money can buy air time, newspaper coverage, rallies, meetings, even people. With twenty-million dollars the Reich believes it can tip the balance against Roosevelt, against the United States entering the war."

Pierre whistled through his teeth. "And Emil—what does he want?"

"He wants Roosevelt to win."

In the late evening of March 15, 1940 Pierre Coburg and his grandson, Martin, climbed into the back of a black limousine and were driven along the north shore of Long Island towards Queensboro Bridge. There was between them a shared sense of excitement, and for Martin an excitement that was that much sweeter since his mother and Celine had been excluded from all knowledge of what was happening.

Both had protested violently. Rose, by now a mature woman with heavy shoulders and a thickening waistline, had been shaking with rage. Celine, more diplomatic—craftier, Martin would have said—had adopted a hurt, silent manner, but neither woman had succeeded in swaying Pierre.

"I refuse to accept," Rose had said haughtily, "that my son should have secrets from me." She was angry, too, because she knew she was slipping back in the Coburg race for power. It was over a year since Pierre had shared her bed. She knew he had innumerable other women in New York City, but lately an intrusive, frightening suspicion had been forming in her mind when she watched her daughter and Pierre together.

But this night the opposition was clearly and simply her son Martin. Since his return from Germany she had seen him move into a different relationship with Pierre. Celine claimed it was because Emil's Janus machine was about to change the balance between the two Coburg companies and Martin formed some sort of bridge between them. Bridge or not, Rose could have screamed with fury when Pierre and Martin left for their unknown rendezvous.

She turned to her daughter. "Sit down, Celine," she said. "It's time we had a talk."

"What do you want to talk about?"

"Let's start with Martin," Rose said. "He's getting too uppity, too big for his boots."

"What do you expect me to do about that?"

"I expect *us* to do something about it. Not just you. Not just me."

Celine shrugged. "He's grown up at last, I guess. Don't they say boys grow up more slowly than girls."

"You know it's more than that."

Celine had seldom felt more in command of a situation when talking to her mother. She knew her mother wanted something. But as yet she still didn't know how far her mother was prepared to go. "Let's have a drink," she said to her mother.

Neither of them drank very much and Rose accepted the gesture as it was intended. "Yes," she said. "Why shouldn't we have a drink together."

Celine poured the drinks.

"You know," Rose said, "when I was a little girl, my mother's uncle died . . ."

"The one that owned the prosperous law firm that your mother *didn't* inherit?"

Rose's head came up. How much she disliked the sharpness under Celine's smile. "I guess I already told you about it."

"You did, Mother."

"Did I ever tell you why my mother didn't inherit?"
Celine turned away.

"Listen. She didn't inherit because she was a
woman. It all went to some distant cousin, a *male*.
You know what I'm talking about now?"

"You're talking about me and Martin."

"I'm talking about getting what's fairly yours. A
half share in Coburg Banknote. A half share *at least*.
I'm talking about your interest and mine."

Celine recognized the proposal of alliance to be as
far reaching as Rose intended. She was by no means
sure that an alliance was possible between them, but
she nodded and said: "Go on. I'm interested."

Rose stood in front of the mirror and looked at
herself. A woman still capable of attracting men. But
capable of attracting Pierre again? She doubted it. She
had always been a realist. Since long before the night
she had seduced John Coburg in a punt on some pid-
dling river in England, she had been a realist. That's
why she had got Pierre into bed and maneuvered her
husband onto the sidelines. But realism required that
she look at herself as harshly as she might a rival.
And she didn't like what she saw. Lines across the
forehead; pouches of skin, soft and rather charming
like a chipmunk's at the moment, but clearly poised
to droop and become jowly.

She was aware that her daughter was watching her
as she smoothed her hands over her widening hips.
Her daughter, whose hips were slender, whose legs
were slender, whose neck was slender. She flushed
with anger. If Pierre had died two years ago she,
Rose, would have inherited the company. She was
sure of that. Her husband was then and always would
be a despised fag, her son was then a weak and watery
figure easy to keep in a state of subjection, and her
daughter at that time was a flat-chested teenager desperate to seduce the gardener.

She swung away from the mirror. "You know what I'm talking about?" She stretched her hand for her glass.

"I'm not sure."

Her eyes glittered. "I'm talking about Pierre."

"Pierre?"

"Has he been playing around with you?"

"Mother!"

"He tries to touch you sometimes. I've seen it."

Celine sat down. "Do you realize what you're saying?" she said slowly.

"Of course I do. Don't get on your high horse with me. Pierre Coburg comes from a part of central Europe with different standards from ours."

"I come from Kansas City, Missouri, or that's what you've always told me."

"You're ambitious, Celine," she said, a note of desperation in her voice. "I don't mind admitting I am, too."

"Is that why you abandoned your husband and started sleeping with his father?"

"How dare you!"

"It's no secret."

Rose frowned a wry smile. "I suppose not."

"You didn't answer my question," Celine said. "Is that why you changed sides—*naked* ambition?" Her lips curled.

There was a long pause. "Yes," Rose said. "Yes."

Celine nodded her head slowly. She recognized the moment. The jugular had been exposed.

"There's no reason in the world why Martin should inherit Coburg Banknote alone," Rose said.

"It's the way Pierre wants it."

"Don't be so goddam demure. I know you want Coburg Banknote."

"And I know I'm not going to get it," Celine flared. "Because I'm a *woman*."

Rose stood stock-still, staring at her daughter. "You know what to do," she said.

Celine stiffened. "Do I understand what you're saying?"

"I think you do."

"You're suggesting I take over where you left off."

Again Rose paused. "Yes," she said finally. "I'm suggesting it."

"You dirty-minded bitch."

But Rose saw Celine was smiling. It was not the first time she had been called a bitch. Why should she care? "Well," she said. "Will you?"

Celine stood up, looking at her mother. Then she turned away. "I don't know. I might," she said. "If only to find out what the two of them are up to tonight."

The black limousine passed through the dock gates on the nod of the civilian standing next to the uniformed port authority cop. It swerved across the pavement and ran along the silent, lighted piers.

In the car, Martin turned to his grandfather. "Where are we," he said. "I'm lost."

"Hoboken, New Jersey," Pierre answered.

A figure in front of them flashed a dimmed light and Pierre rapped on the window for the driver to stop. Then, opening the rear door, he got out, waiting while Martin joined him. They stood on the eerie waterfront for a moment, two big men in dark overcoats, the shadows concealing Martin's youth.

They walked forward as figures came towards them. Pierre extended his hand. "Good evening, Inspector," he said. "Pierre Coburg of Coburg Banknote. This is my grandson, Martin Coburg. He's had a very great deal to do with us all being here tonight."

"It's a pleasure to meet you, sir," the FBI inspector said. Martin realized with a flush of pleasure that the inspector was talking to him.

They walked on, further along the waterfront, their footsteps echoing on concrete slabs that were cracked and puddled with dirty water. Mist caught the lights and swirled around it. It was not much past midnight. There seemed to Martin no sign of activity, no stevedores or longshoremen, no seamen on the high boat decks of the rusting freighters that lined the waterfront.

They had stopped now in shadow. The FBI man pointed at a small black freighter with a lighter color band painted along its middle and a squat red funnel illuminated by a single light bulb. Its port of origin read Lisbon, Portugal.

"Five minutes," the FBI man said looking at his watch.

The group of men stood in silence. By straining his eyes Martin could detect movement further down the dock. Mist rolled in from the black water beyond the freighter. Could he see the outline of a port patrol boat, lights out, riding the choppy surface of the water? Mist and excitement played havoc with the senses.

The FBI man said. "One minute."

Martin waited while the long seconds ticked past. But even beyond the excitement of the moment Martin felt something else. Emil had stressed that the Coburg name must be kept out of this. Pierre had announced their names. Only to the FBI certainly. But could it go further?

"Now," said the FBI man and simultaneously searchlights hit the freighter from the waterfront and from three patrol boats in the mist beyond.

At the same time a group of about twenty men detached itself from the shadows and headed for the freighter's gangway. From below Martin watched them reach deck level and fan out around the ship.

There were already shouts coming from the seamen, and deck lights began to flick on. Below, Pierre passed around cigars.

They stood there for almost an hour. There was much talk of loading levels and ships' manifests, but Martin paid little attention. He was waiting for his own private moment of triumph.

It happened when a line of men came along the deck, each carrying a wooden crate. Descending the steep gangplank with some difficulty, they piled the crates on the dock. The FBI inspector came forward with a crowbar, inserted it under the nailed-down top of the nearest crate and levered. The nails groaned, the wooden cover rose and in the beam of a flashlight Martin looked down on the neat packs of green twenty-dollar bills.

"Okay boys," the FBI inspector said. "Let's head for home."

CHAPTER 15

~ ~ ~

The events of the spring of 1940 hit Pierre Coburg like blows from a pickhandle across his back. On April 10, when the New York *Tribune* delivered the news that Germany had taken both Denmark and Norway, Pierre had laughed bitterly. "Another opportunity for Emil," he had said, looking up at Rose and Martin from his place at the end of the breakfast table.

"What's that, Pierre? What opportunity for Emil?" Celine had asked as she entered the breakfast room.

Pierre showed her the headline. "They'll need new currencies, ration books, identity cards. You don't imagine these orders will go to De la Rue in *England*, do you? They'll go to German companies. And with the Janus press the chances are that Emil will get a fat share of the pickings."

Celine spooned some scrambled eggs onto a plate and brought it to the table. She sat next to Pierre and reached out and touched his hand. "What's the latest news on Janus?" she asked gently. "When will Emil be sending you the specifications?"

Martin, watching from near the other end of the long table, marveled at Celine's ability to calm Pierre. She had, it seemed to him, taken on a new role in the last month or two. His mother Rose seemed literally to have taken a back seat. She no longer sat next to Pierre at breakfast; she deferred to Celine in a way Martin had not noticed before.

"Have you heard from Germany?" Martin asked him.

"Emil won't be sending the Janus specifications," Pierre said. "Not until I've agreed to terms."

They were all looking at Pierre now. This was the first time they had heard of terms. The double head of Janus had always been the symbol of the separate but equal association between the two Coburg companies. Was the Janus press now about to tip that balance?

"What are Emil's terms?" Celine seemed most naturally the one to ask the question.

Pierre looked at her, then down the table. "All right," he said. "We'll talk about it." He paused to organize his thoughts. "A machine that will revolutionize banknote printing is in existence. It was developed and is owned by Emil. Admittedly, I did not put money into it. I have no claim to it other than a brotherly agreement made at the beginning of this century that we would share any technical developments."

"So . . . ?" It was Celine again. "Is Emil reneging on that agreement?"

"Emil is sitting pretty in Europe with German government contracts coming out of his ears," Pierre said. "Already Poland has a new, mostly Coburg currency. Now Norway, now Denmark. As the German army marches, my brother simply picks up more contracts. He should change his company symbol from Janus to Midas. Everything he touches turns to gold! Emil's terms will be given to me when I go cap in hand to receive them. I was summoned by cable this morning to meet him in Europe"

"Will you go?" Martin asked.

"Hell, no!"

On May 10, 1940 the German army invaded Holland and Belgium. Day after day the New York *Tribune* carried unbelievable headlines. The French army reeled back. The British began to evacuate their troops from Dunkirk. By early June, Italy had joined Germany and was moving into the south of France. The French government had evacuated Paris; Bordeaux was now the capital. Then, a month after the German offensive began, France surrendered.

As those blows rained down on the countries of western Europe, so Pierre Coburg reeled. Perhaps the changes in him had not all come in one month, but it was in one short month that they were evident to those around him. All that ebullience and sometimes brutal energy seemed to have drained out of him. He walked alone in the gardens. Every servant knew that he had to be called the moment a radio news bulletin was announced or the *Tribune* arrived. He drank much more than usual. He declined offers to dinner parties and canceled others. Nobody now, including even Celine, seemed able to get close to him. He was suffering a mounting rage of jealousy.

When Rose and Celine talked, as they did more and more that spring, they had no doubt that this cancerous jealousy of his twin brother was at the root of Pierre's difficulties.

"Let me tell you," Rose said as the two women sat together in her second floor sitting room, "let me tell you that Pierre has *always* thought of Emil as his younger brother. Now he's not sure."

"He's very sure," Celine said, "that he's being overtaken by his twin brother."

Rose looked at her coyly. "Does he talk to you much?"

"Not like he used to."

"Does he . . ." Rose left the sentence unformed. "Do you . . . ?"

Celine shook her head impatiently. "Up until a month, six weeks ago, Pierre liked to touch me some nights when we were up in the library. We were getting on fine. He was talking. Little company secrets. Stuff about him and Emil. He got drunk, he got frisky."

Rose's eyes glistened. "And . . ."

"And that's as far as it went. The news from Europe is a turnoff. He's just not interested."

Rose pretended to think for a few moments. "Perhaps," she said. "Perhaps you should try again."

"What the hell for?"

"I've got a nasty feeling," Rose said, "that we could be talking about our future."

"You think our future depends on me getting Pierre into bed?"

"I think our future," Rose said, "depends on you persuading Pierre he has to go to Germany to talk to Emil."

"He'll never do that. He's got far too much pride."

"You can put it to him that Emil is a member of a belligerent country. It's not safe for him to leave Europe. Suggest they meet in Paris. Yes, why not? It belongs to the Germans but it's not Germany. Yes, Paris."

"Somewhere in France, maybe," Celine said thoughtfully. "That just might be possible."

Rose nodded emphatically. "Face to face I would still back Pierre against Emil."

Celine sprang up and paced the room. Her mother watched her. Watched her silk dress swishing around her knees, the movement of her hips . . . men loved that movement. She no longer had anything much to offer Pierre herself. Not at least what he wanted—that young, free swaying of the hips. But Celine had it. And was ready to use it.

A little encouragement from her mother. A little advice about how . . . "Another thing. Make sure you go with him to France. Not Martin. Play it right and this could be our chance."

Celine stopped in the middle of the room. Her face was set. "I want you to take up that weekend invitation with the Lawsons," she said.

"They didn't say when exactly."

"Make them say this weekend. I've seen you do it before." Celine smiled sardonically. "And get them to invite Martin as well."

"Martin won't go. You know he hates the Lawson girl."

"I need the weekend," Celine said. "That's the deal."

"It was good of Martin to go with her to the Lawsons," Celine said, pouring a brandy for Pierre.

Her grandfather grunted indifferent agreement, his thoughts miles away. She turned and walked towards him, warming the brandy snifter with the palm of her hand.

He sat staring, mostly at the fire, in his favorite library chair. He wore a terry cloth robe and pale gray cotton pajamas. Until Celine had appeared he'd thought he'd finish his cigar and go to bed. Today's news had been disastrous. France was to be divided in two by the victorious Germans. Both sides of the new line would need a completely new currency system. New printing contracts for Emil's Imprimerie Coburg now added up to a considerable proportion of the new currencies for Norway, Denmark, Holland, Belgium and, in all probability, the two entirely separate parts of France. The French North African colonies were certainly also going to change currencies.

Celine sat on the arm of his chair. Her robe draped itself over his arm. He flicked it aside irritably and took the glass of brandy she offered.

Celine's finger scratched at the V-shaped hair at the neck of his pajamas. "Do you know you're a very hairy man?"

He sipped his brandy. "You know what the world's going to look like by 1943, Celine?"

"No." She left her hand where it was, but kept her finger still.

"Do you realize that in a year or two Coburg Banknote could be finished?"

Celine rearranged her position on the arm of the chair. "Just because of this war?" she said.

"Listen," he said as he gulped at his brandy. "The Bureau of Engraving prints the currency of the United States. No way in there. De la Rue in London effectively prints for the countries of the British Empire. No way in there. Japan now controls an important part of China militarily and commercially. No way in there. The German victories have put every new European contract within the grasp of Emil. No way in there. So what are we left with?"

She scratched gently at the curling gray hairs on his chest. "What *are* we left with?"

"Not much," he said.

She slid her hand just inside his pajama jacket.

He looked up at her. For the first time in weeks his brow cleared. He grunted, smiled.

She slid her hand further down so that the fingers passed over the hair on the dome of his stomach. "I think you have to meet up with Emil," she said softly. "I'll go with you if you want."

"I'm not kowtowing to my own twin brother," he said.

"It wouldn't be kowtowing. After all"—she massaged down to the elasticated waistband—"what you say is true only if the situation remains as it is. But just imagine FDR wins this election and takes the United States into the war next year. What happens then to all Emil's contracts and plans if the United States and Britain win. Which they will."

He looked up at her smiling. "It's a strong argument."

"To put to Emil when you meet him in Paris."

Pierre nodded. "He needs us because he needs insurance for the future. I could offer that in return for the Janus specifications." He grinned broadly. "I'm feeling better."

"So I see."

It was the first time either of them had recognized in words what her hands were doing to his thighs.

"Celine honey," Pierre said, pretending shock. "I'm your *grandfather.*"

"Are you going to let that make a difference?"

He laid his hands across her stomach and unbuttoned the large pearl buttons of her pyjamas. The silk fell open.

Neither of them had heard the door of the library open.

The cry of horror was incoherent with shock and anger.

As they swung their heads towards the door, John Coburg was already half running down the long library towards them.

Their hands were still half hidden in cotton or silk pajamas. They dragged them out as John Coburg reached them. "Get up to bed Celine," he screamed. "Now, go up now. *Now!*"

She stumbled to her feet and looked down at Pierre. But he had not moved.

"Now!" her father screamed again. And she turned and fled from the room.

The two men faced each other, the son's face a bright unnatural red; Pierre's pale and suddenly darkening. They were both thinking of the night John Coburg had been caught with Jack Aston.

"I don't care . . . I don't care about myself or what I've done," John stammered. "But I promise you this. If anything like this happens again. Even if I think anything like this *might* happen again, I'll call the police."

Pierre got to his feet and walked past him. The long robe concealed the fact that he was trembling with anger.

"I'll do it," John Coburg shouted as his father reached the door. "I'll finish you for good. I'll call the police."

Carefully closing the door behind him, Pierre left the library.

CHAPTER 16

~ ~ ~

Pierre's decision not to take her with him on his trip to see Emil was a heavy blow to Celine. She knew the reason of course. She knew her father had received a new lease of life as he relished the role he had adopted as watchdog over her. He seemed to see very little of Jack Aston these days. He was drinking less. Watching more.

And Pierre was afraid, there was no doubt about that. To have the police called in by his own son would be a scandal he could not successfully surmount. In Rose's view, her husband ought to be hounded out of the house.

"Listen, Celine," she said. And Celine turned wearily. All her life her mother's instruction, suggestions, interventions had been prefaced by "Listen!"

"Listen to what for God's sake," she said. "Martin's going with him to meet Emil. I'm not. Because my father is threatening Pierre with the police."

They were in Rose's sitting room a little before lunch in the early summer of 1940. The *Tribune* had that day carried pictures of Hitler sightseeing in Paris.

"We could have done something about it. We could have drummed *him* out. Told him to go off and live with his darling Jack Aston or else."

"It's too late," Celine said. "Pierre's changing. These last few months have hit him hard."

"He doesn't look his old self," Rose said. "His doctors have told him he's a candidate for a heart attack if he doesn't let up a bit."

174

"That won't stop him." Celine poured herself lemon water and walked across the room to the window. The gardens of Island House were at their most magnificent. Across the tops of the trees the ocean sparkled blue-gray in the sunlight. Below her the grooms were taking out the horses for their daily exercise. Her own pair of Irish setters romped elegantly across the lawns. She turned her head. The chauffeur was driving her white Bruzzelli sports car into the rear courtyard for its monthly service. She heard her mother's voice behind her, but she had no desire to listen. After Pierre, all this, she was passionately convinced, belonged to her and to her alone. She thought for a moment of dispossession, inevitably by Martin, and moving to an apartment, however large, in Manhattan, and her stomach knotted. She loved banknotes, she loved contracts, the fight for new orders, meetings, urgency, success. The only way for a woman to get to the top of a corporation in America was to own it. That she was utterly determined to do.

In her orderly, logical fashion she sorted the opposition into three groupings. Pierre, of course, was free at any time to dispose of the company to whom and in any way he wished. But, without interference, she believed that she could ensure that his will was in her favor. Martin was the most intractable problem of the three. He was changing, getting older and more sure of himself. The problem of Martin could only be dealt with through Pierre. But the hub and pivot of her difficulties, she saw, was her father. While he held the sword of Damocles over Pierre, Celine knew that she could not hope to regain her influence over her grandfather. Therefore, John Coburg had to be dealt with. She considered consulting her mother, then quickly rejected the idea. But she would get her mother's help.

She turned from the window.

"Really Celine," Rose said, "you can be so cold. I

was talking to you, darling. And you stand there as if you're deaf."

"I was thinking," Celine said slowly. "I now know what we must do."

Rose watched her in silence.

"You're going to help me."

"Of course, darling," Rose said uncertainly.

"Wait until you hear what I want you to do."

"Anything."

"I want you to invite Jack Aston for drinks."

"No. Why in God's name?" Rose flared, then stopped. "Clever Celine. They haven't been seeing too much of each other lately, your father and Aston. Push them back together. Then put the gun to his head. One breath of scandal and we'll have him jailed for five years for sodomy."

"Go ahead and invite dear Jack," Celine said. "After all, we're practically neighbors."

At dawn the Pan American Clipper banked over Estoril and followed the line of the north shore of the Tagus as it began its descent on Lisbon airport. Pierre had slept much of the flight, rising with the sun in the forward cabin windows and now, shaved and dressed, he looked better than he had for months.

Martin had slept less well. It was not the narrow, rather hard, airliner bed that had kept him awake, nor the steady drumming of the engines. Much more it was the thought of seeing Alexina again.

It was now almost a year since he had seen her. He was now just nineteen-years-old; she less than a year younger. He looked back on last summer in confusion. The politics, the bizarre night with Elisabeth, the Führer at Lingfeld, the break with Alexina, and finally the outbreak of war. The rush of events against which he had first fallen in love and then slept with a woman, a different woman, made his head swim. His decision now was to be a neutral in politics, to stand above, to be, as many people in the United States yearned to be, isolated from what was happening in Europe. But close to Alexina. If she would let him.

The airplane bumped and powered across the slender concrete runway, then swung left and taxied into the early morning sun towards a line of white airport buildings.

As Martin emerged from the cabin and came down the steps behind Pierre he was surprised by the number of aircraft on the apron bearing the German cross. He could see no Portuguese airplanes, no Spanish, one or two Italian light transports, but mostly the silver-bodied, three-engined Junker 52, the workhorse of the Third Reich.

Entering the airport building, he was astonished to see Elisabeth Oster coming towards them. Pierre smiled and stepped forward to clasp her in his arms. "My dear girl," he said, "how good of you to meet us."

When she was released by Pierre, Martin kissed her decorously on both cheeks. Pierre clearly knew she was coming to meet them. Equally clearly, he had not considered it worthwhile telling Martin. It was just another of those examples of his grandfather's return to the breezy, confident Pierre of last year. Face to face with Emil he believed he could dominate him.

Elisabeth was laughing. "Pierre didn't tell you," she said to Martin as they were escorted by porters to a large German Embassy Mercedes. "My part in the war effort is a posting to our embassy in Lisbon. There are worst postings."

"I'm sure," Martin said. "And how is Rolf? Was he with the army in France?"

Martin thought her face clouded slightly. "No, Rolf is on special duties in Poland. Yes, important special duties."

The car moved smoothly down the road towards the center of Lisbon. "Tonight," Pierre said, "I'm taking

Elisabeth to dinner." Martin waited while Pierre
paused for effect. "You Martin," he added, laughing,
"are going to entertain Oliver Sutchley."

"Sutchley?"

Pierre nodded. "The man who looked after you in
London last year. Since he's English and works at the
British Embassy here in Lisbon, it's not possible,
thank God, for him to dine with myself and Elisabeth.
So the honor falls to you."

They drove in to where the German Embassy sat at
the end of the grand boulevard. Martin was fascinated
by the sheer impudent size of the swastika waving in
the early morning breeze. It curled and uncurled,
folded and unfolded in a lazy demonstration of the
new confident power of Hitler's Germany.

He pulled his eyes away from the flag. "Will it be
difficult to get a French visa?" he asked from polite-
ness rather than real concern.

Elisabeth's laugh trilled. "Difficult? Difficult to get
a visa to France? Why should it be difficult. After all,
Martin, it is the German Embassy that now issues
them."

Pierre turned to her. "We travel by train or boat?"

"We have arranged a Portuguese steamer to Bordeaux, which is at this moment the seat of the French
government of Marshal Pétain. From Bordeaux you
take a train inland to Brive-la-Gaillarde and from
there another train to Paris."

"And what are the conditions like traveling in
France?"

She squeezed his arm. "All French resistance has
ceased, of course. But we have some conflicting
reports."

On the morning Pierre and Martin landed in Lisbon,
Alexina Coburg was driving a Renault van through
the backstreets of a working-class suburb of Paris. It
was a gray dawn matched by the long gray streets of

garages and factories and blank walls with peeling
posters urging Frenchmen to remember the Marne or
Verdun.

Alexina was frightened. She had crammed her hair
into a leather peaked workman's cap and smeared a
thumbmark of motor oil on her cheeks. But she was
never going to persuade anyone giving her more than
a casual glance that she was a young Paris mechanic.

There were no German soldiers to be seen, no road-
blocks, no gendarmerie. The ancient van bounced
over the cobblestones as Alex scanned the corners for
the turn-off into the Rue Gassin. It came sooner than
she supposed. Braking hard, she swung the Renault
left and saw ahead of her a factory courtyard with a
sign reading: Imprimerie Gerassimov.

Again there was no sign of life in the street. It was
as if this part of Paris was deserted. Or perhaps waiting, watching from behind half-closed shutters.

She shuddered at the thought and turned the van
into the Gerassimov yard. Almost immediately, a rusting metal-plated door was pulled back. She moved the
van forward even before the screech of the doors'
metal rollers had ceased. Seconds later the van was in
the glass-roofed plant and the door was being pushed
closed.

She got out of the van. Her schoolfriend Andrée de
Bretagne ran forward to kiss her, stopped and burst
out laughing at Alex's feeble disguise. In the darkness
behind them Monsieur and Madame de Bretagne rose
anxiously from the wooden crates on which they were
sitting. A long gray-green German Army staff car
stood behind them, the occupation swastika on the
hood.

There was no laughter now. "So far so good," Alexina said crisply.

Andrée, a pretty, dark-featured girl, was opening
the back of the Renault van.

"Enough food and bottled water to get you down to

the Pyrenees, with one stopover," Alex said. "Three
blankets and three sleeping bags. One hundred liters
of gasoline. One spare tire. Tools. A bottle of English
whiskey with the label removed. Four liters of *vin
ordinaire*. Bread. And . . ." She knelt on the oil-
stained cement and reached under the back of the
van, from which she pulled a shotgun.

"Let's pray we won't need it," Monsieur de Bretagne said.

Andrée's mother hugged Alexina to her. "You're a
marvelous girl," she said. "A marvelous girl."

Behind them there was a clatter on the iron staircase. Emil came down, his face unsmiling. "You
should go now, Georges," he said to Andrée's father.
"Every hour that passes the organization of our Military Government improves." He indicated the upper
window he had been watching from. "It's clear outside," he said. "No patrols. Go south through Orleans, then head for Tours. My friend the general says
the roads are clearer that way." He shook hands with
de Bretagne and embraced his wife.

"We know what this means to you, what you have
done for us," de Bretagne said.

Emil smiled. "I can't think of it as treachery," he
said. "Not betrayal of Germany. If there's any truth
in all this madness I suppose I'm doing it *for* Germany. Not against."

Alexina and Andrée embraced. *"A bientôt,"* they
told each other, and Alex stepped back to watch the
de Bretagnes climb into the rocking Renault van.

Emil had the plated door open. As the Renault
passed through it, he and Alexina ran quickly to the
army staff car and climbed in. While Alexina cleaned
up her face and threw the workman's cap out of the
window, Emil drove rapidly through Argenteuil
towards the center of the city.

After a few minutes they both began to relax. The
sun was rising, throwing color onto the Seine on their

right. "Please don't get me into this sort of thing again," Emil said, laughing now. He stretched an arm and hugged her to him. "Or yourself."

"No promises," Alexina said.

He glanced at her and read the determination in her face. Releasing her he said: "You know the dangers. You know no influence I have can help if it became a police matter, a Gestapo matter."

"I know. But you believe it's right too, don't you?"

"At one time I didn't." Without looking at her he said: "Madame de Bretagne was right. You are an extraordinary girl."

Martin met Oliver Sutchley that evening, by arrangement, in the bar of the Hotel Bristol. He remembered Sutchley as a tall, stoop-shouldered, brown-haired Englishman. Tonight he was dressed in a well-cut dinner jacket. In the first ten minutes in the Bristol bar he had drunk three martinis.

"Don't think of me as unpatriotic, old boy," he said over the fourth martini. "But I'm a realist. And Winston bloody Churchill isn't."

"You think he isn't?"

"Did you hear his last speech? The German Army's at his throat. Twenty miles away across the channel there's the best army in the world and the biggest and most modern airforce. And what does the lunatic say?"

Martin shrugged. "What did he say?"

In a Churchillian growl Sutchley intoned: " 'We shall seek no terms, we may show mercy—we shall ask for none.' Did you hear that? On the edge of defeat."

Martin shifted uncomfortably. It sounded pretty crazy to him, but it was surely what people wanted to hear. They didn't want to be told their government was desperately looking for terms. That's what had finished France, when Marshal Pétain announced on his own initiative that he was seeking peace terms. The best of soldiers don't fight on after that.

"You and I, old boy," Sutchley was saying, "we understand each other. We've got to stick together, okay? Pray for peace and we'll be all right." He ordered another drink. "It's not going to be long now. Churchill or no Churchill."

Martin declined Oliver Sutchley's offer of dinner. An hour with him was enough. Perhaps he felt it was some sort of disloyalty to Alexina to hear someone talking so warmly about the German dictator she despised. Or perhaps it was just that as a patriotic American Martin Coburg could not relate to this shifty, opportunist Englishman. Walking through the echoing colonnades of Lisbon at midnight, Martin stopped to look at the floodlit swastika flying high over the German Embassy.

CHAPTER 17

~ ~ ~

France in mid-summer of 1940 was in a state of unbelievable chaos. As the German panzer divisions had sliced through Holland and Belgium and then rolled back the British and French armies in northern France, the Great Exodus had begun. Fueled by incredible rumors of spies, of parachutists and of the insensate cruelty of all German soldiers, thousands then hundreds of thousands of Dutch, Belgian and French civilians began to leave their homes. It mattered nothing that the reality of the German advance was quite different: there were no parachutists dressed as nuns, no Germans in French peasant garb, no Hunnish fury unleashed upon the defenseless population. Yet, nevertheless, the exodus continued to grow. Great towns like Lille in the north of France saw the flight of over a half of its inhabitants and as the countryside around emptied, the townships and villages south of Paris were engulfed by a tide of fleeing people. Hungry, thirsty and desperate, seventy thousand refugees surged into the small Correze town of Brive-la-Gaillarde; further south Cahors on the river Lot, population thirteen thousand, was swamped by a vast refugee army marching on the town. Over forty thousand people, exhausted, many old and sick, all at the limit of their endurance, camped in the market squares or besieged the railway station for news of trains going even further south.

Pierre and Martin Coburg found themselves plunged into this unbelievable chaos. By the end of June, eight million people had traveled north to south, the length of France, until then the greatest single migration in the history of Europe. By the beginning of July and the signing of an armistice a large proportion of those refugees were now fighting to return north to reoccupy farms and city apartments that they had abandoned only weeks before.

The French railway authorities tried to run a service, but with the French Ministry of Transport camping in a hotel without telephones in Bordeaux, it was an impossible task. As Pierre and Martin rattled west in a wooden slat-seated local train from Bordeaux, they both knew that it might take them weeks to complete their journey to Paris.

On the sixth night out of Bordeaux they stopped in the small town of Souillac on the Dordogne River. The engine was uncoupled for use elsewhere and they joined a thousand travelers surging downhill to find food and accommodation in the center of the town.

The small stone-flagged squares of Souillac were crammed with people camping under the covered market or living from cars without gasoline or carts whose horses had been sold along the way. Thousands streamed through the narrow alleys off the Route Nationale 20, or fought for water at the single public pump in the Place du Puits.

As thousands tried to move north by road, tens of thousands more were brought in by train from Toulouse or Bordeaux. Beyond the tiny market town of Souillac, for reasons nobody knew, there were no trains running north to Paris.

On the cathedral square the dust danced in a shimmer of midday heat. The medieval cathedral, almost Moorish with its array of domes, stood before them. Pierre was sweating until great dark patches spread from under the arms of his pale gray suit. "There," he pointed as if he were personally responsible for positioning the man, "a German sentry."

They crossed towards the German corporal who stood, his rifle held by the sling on his shoulder, his forage cap tipped forward against the sun.

Within five minutes, they were drinking schnapps with a young officer in the signals room. Within less than half an hour, after much winding of handles and shouting into black bakerlite mouthpieces, Pierre was speaking to Emil in the Georges V in Paris.

"Pierre, you old devil," Emil could be heard bawling, "where are you?"

"We're at a town called Souillac on the Dordogne River," Pierre said. "Very pretty, but with no possible chance of a train north to Paris."

The line crackled and hissed. Martin, sitting on a stone bench in the high vaulted room, struggled to hear what Emil was saying. Did he hear Alex's name mentioned? Did Emil say he had brought Alexina with him?

Pierre was yelling into the handset. "You'll what? You'll do what?"

Through more crackling and hissing Pierre listened, nodding, then gestured to the lieutenant to take the line. He turned away to Martin. "We're in luck," he said. "Emil was just entertaining General von Henzinger at lunch in his suite. The general will put suitable accommodations in this area at our disposal."

"But how do we get to Paris?" Martin said.

"We don't. There's a small flying club airfield less than twenty kilometers from here. Emil will fly down from Paris. The mountain's coming to Mahomet."

Martin, restrained himself for a moment, with difficulty, then blurted out: "Is Alexina coming with him?"

Pierre grinned hugely. "She'll be a pretty young woman by now, eh?" He took Martin's shoulder in the painful grip that had tortured him as a child. "Don't you worry, my boy. There'll be plenty to occupy you while Emil and myself are talking business."

*   *   *

Beyond Souillac, where the Ouysse River cuts its way
through the limestone cliffs or follows a twisting path
through bald rocky hillsides, the Château de Belfresnes stands guard at what was once a critical crossing point. Among the many châteaux of this much
fought over region, Belfresnes passes almost unno-
ticed. It is small, with perhaps no more than a dozen
bedchambers. But it is built high on an incomparable
limestone cliff and its courtyard juts out onto a terrace
with a view across the river to line after line of blue
hills.

In 1940 the château was lived in by a Hungarian
woman of an uncertain past who called herself the
Countess Boritza. She was by now in her sixties and
had lived at the château since the Great War, with
an international selection of lovers. When the young
German officer explained that he was to requisition
the château for a few days during which important
meetings were to take place there, the Countess was
delighted. She would be paid; she would be able to
continue occupying her suite of rooms in the high turret; and she watched with pleasure the superbly built
young German soldiers unpacking bedding and food
and crates of wine for her important visitors' greater
comfort.

Emil and Alex arrived the day after Pierre and Martin. From the terrace Martin had watched their car
and its motorcycle outriders twisting through the hills,
disappearing behind limestone rocks and reappearing
to climb the steep road toward the château.

Alex, in a wide-brimmed straw hat and a cream
muslin dress, was seated next to Emil in the back of
the open car. The driver was old Wilhelm from Lingfeld. Running across the main hall to meet them, Martin nearly knocked over the countess.

"Young man," she said in her highly accented English, "young man, why are you in such a hurry. Stop a moment."

Martin stopped. "My apologies, Countess," he said hurriedly. "I was going out to meet the new arrivals."

He had already turned towards the door when she hooked his arm with the handle of her ivory walking stick. "Martin," she said. "You must escort me out to the courtyard. Give me your arm. We shall greet the newcomers together."

It was not by any means the picture he wanted to present to Alex after nearly a year apart, but he had no choice. He offered the countess his arm and very slowly, her stick tapping on the ancient terracotta tiled floor, they passed under the main arch and out into the blazing sunshine. At that exact moment the outriders roared into the courtyard with the Mercedes directly behind.

He thought he saw Alex smiling. Certainly Emil was finding it difficult to hide his amusement.

Martin slipped his arm out from the countess and formally presented Emil and Alex to her. While Emil bent over the old lady's hand, Martin came forward to kiss Alex on both cheeks.

"What chaos," Emil said. "What indescribable confusion. Paris is beyond anyone's comprehension." He was talking to the countess. "You are very kind, Madame, to allow us to use your beautiful château for a few days. My brother, he's here already of course." He turned to Martin. "Where is the rascal?"

"He's upstairs in his rooms," Martin said.

"Now tell him our guests are here," the countess said gaily to Martin. "And I will take Herr Coburg and his most beautiful daughter for an aperitif under the trees."

Emil smiled and offered his arm. With Alexina they went off to the orchard where the countess took her daily glass or glasses of Suze in the shade.

It was almost twenty minutes later that Martin returned and delivered the message that Pierre would take a bath and then join them for lunch. For a brief second Martin was sure he saw Emil's eyebrows rise. Then he leaned forward, smiling. "A glass of something for you, Martin?" he said and gestured to the soldier-waiter who was serving them. Leaving Martin to give his own order, he said to the countess: "I was saying, Madame, whole *quartiers* of Paris are empty of people."

"But of course," the countess said. "They're all down here in the southwest. But tell me, the theaters are still open, the restaurants, the nightclubs?"

"Yes, in the midst of the administrative confusion and with half a million German soldiers swarming all over the city and the *banlieue,* life continues."

Martin turned his head and found that Alex was looking at him. He smiled and slowly she smiled back.

A half-smile.

"You ask me what will happen, Madame," Emil continued more seriously now, "and all I can say is that I don't know. Will France become two countries? Yes, I suppose so. Perhaps. Perhaps not. Most important of all, what will the United States do? Will President Roosevelt be reelected do you think, Martin?"

Of course Emil was talking about the twenty million counterfeit dollars.

"I think," Martin said carefully, "that the president's chances have increased since March. The opposition have not been as effectively organized as I'm sure they hoped."

"I see," Emil nodded. "It is possible that the isolationists in America are short of funds."

Martin smiled. "I think it's possible, Emil."

"Now, Madame," Emil said as he made a sudden turn to the countess, closing off his line of questioning to Martin. "What are your own plans now that peace has returned. Will you stay in this most beautiful château? Will you leave for Paris or Berlin? Will you go back to Budapest, a city I so much enjoy? What will you do?"

"Monsieur Coburg," she said, "I am a penniless old lady. I had once thought, not so long ago, Monsieur, that the Château de Belfresnes was my dowry. Now I face facts. It is my pension. I shall sell it and take an apartment in Paris, where I will end my days in delicious depravity."

Her rouged cheekbones stretched taut. Her red lips pouted. She ran her hand across the thin red-blonde hair. Alex was staring.

"My darling Alexina," she said. "To you growing old is inconceivable. To me it is a pain in the back when a gentleman, so rare these days, decides to lower his weight upon me. Ah," she laughed as Alex blushed. "Do you think then my darlings that age deifies a woman? When I am cut do I not bleed?" She stood suddenly. "Come Monsieur Coburg, let's go in to lunch. Let's drink *énormement* of the excellent champagne you have provided. Let's pretend for an hour or two that there's no war, no business meetings, no growing old."

With Emil accompanying her, they set off for the château.

Alex's eyebrows shot up. "Are all Hungarian women like that?"

"God knows."

"It's good to see you again, Martin." She spoke quietly.

"It's a year almost," he said.

"Since the day Elisabeth and Rolf were married."

She was underlining that moment, the night before the wedding. Putting it between them before ordinary affections could smudge or obliterate it.

He was determined not to let her. The sunlight dappled her hair as they stood together in the orchard. "Alex," he said slowly, "you never answered my letters."

"No. Not letters like that. I saw no point."

"Did you read them?"

"Some."

"Don't you understand now that I thought you were going to marry Gregor?"

"You're saying that's why you slept with Elisabeth?"

"For God's sake I didn't *know* it was going to happen. Emil dropped me at that house in the woods."

"And the fairy princess was waiting for you!"

His face tensed angrily. "You knew it was going to happen. Why the hell didn't you warn me?"

She shook her head bitterly.

"Well why?"

She looked down at the table, her fingers drumming on the cloth. "Because I wanted you to have the choice, I suppose."

She moved around the table and looked out through the apple trees to the stone wall enclosing the orchard. "When I realized what Emil and Pierre were planning, I thought I was going to go mad. I tore into Emil. I told him that all this Waldviertel myth was nothing but medieval slime that had to be washed off. Abandoned. Women weren't filthy vessels to be cleansed by the holy penis of the lord or the priest or the first invited. It was a sick ancient custom, a custom designed for men. For their own salacious pleasure. In the Waldviertel it was, as often as not, a cover, an excuse for incest."

She broke off, tears in her eyes. "And you fell for it. When I realized it had happened I could have killed Emil, you, and Elisabeth for submitting to it." She looked up. "Or maybe that wasn't too much of a sacrifice."

"Alex . . ." He moved toward her.

She shook her head, keeping the table between them.

"We've got a few days," he said. "And you didn't,

after everything that had happened, decide to marry Gregor."

"That decision was taken out of my hands," she said. "He was killed in Poland."

"I'm sorry, Alex."

She nodded slowly. "But I wasn't going to marry him."

He was silent for a moment. "We can't start at the beginning," he said. "I understand that. But we can make a new start. If you want to."

They walked together through the orchard, the sunlight dappling her white dress. More than anything he wanted to reach out and take her hand. She seemed to know this as the back of their hands brushed against each other and she looked up at him and smiled briefly before looking away.

"Tell me about this last year," he said. "Did you ski? Did you skate at Hollenheim?"

"I spent the winter in the north," she said more brightly. "A nursing course in Hamburg." She laughed and the shadows seemed to pass away. "I learnt what very, very hard work is. Lectures from seven in the morning till midday. Practical work on the wards from two until six or sometimes eight. I got to know lots of girls from all sorts of different backgrounds. Girls who wanted to be more than just a hausfrau or a breeding machine for the New Germany."

They passed through the ancient archway into the sudden cool of the wide hall. The thunderous voices of Pierre and Emil could be heard from the dining room, with the countess's high screech of pleasure interwoven between. There was much laughter and the frequent clink of glasses.

"Thank goodness," Alex said as they paused by the door, "the two brothers are getting on well together."

"They won't let business get between them," Martin said.

She looked at him gravely. This time she did brush the back of his hand, slowly and deliberately. "Let's have lunch," she said, "and listen to some disgraceful dreams of Imperial Budapest."

CHAPTER 18

〜 〜 〜

The discussions between the two brothers began after lunch the first day and continued until late in the evening. A cold tray with cheese and beer was ordered up into the room that had been set aside for the meetings. Martin and Alex dined alone with the countess. They had by now decided she looked like a giant bat with her rapid, swooping movements and the dresses that fell in great folds from her arms and floated and fluttered behind her. When she failed to elicit from them anything about the meeting of the brothers, she began to recount her stories of Budapest before the Great War. An unending succession of counts and archdukes had given her priceless jewelery, had asked for her hand or tried to gain entrance to her boudoir. "I am not a *putain*." she assured Alex and Martin with a screech of laughter, "but if men behave in such a silly fashion should we women not profit from it. My dears, I was from a family of great breeding, but little money. Some in those Hapsburg days boasted that they had never made love for love. But they were just *putains*. I, darlings, never made love for anything but love. If I accepted small presents from someone other than my lover, it was only if Count Esterhazy's shade of ruby suited the color of my hair, or if Count Balaton's diamonds, though large, were not too vulgarly set."

"And did this life end with the Great War?" Martin asked.

"Not at all," the countess said. "I was still a young

woman. Vivaciously attractive. Men wrote to me from the front telling me they would die for me. Some did. No, the life didn't end with the war but in the 1920's it moved. Opera and shooting parties gave way to skiing and tennis in the south of France. I think the truth is, darlings, that it became a little vulgar."

When Martin and Alex stood outside her room later that night they were overtaken with gales of laughter. The champagne and burgundy had done their work; the strain of listening gravely to the old countess was lifted. Any phrase that had been used by the countess was enough to start them laughing again. "I am not a *putain*," Alex said.

"Certainly not if the diamonds are not too *vulgarly* set," Martin responded.

A sound on the staircase stopped their bantering. They both looked along the landing to where the countess was standing beside a huge Chinese vase.

They faced her, overwhelmed with embarrassment. Then she came forward, smiling, and kissed each of them on the cheek. "Oh my darlings," she said. "Why shouldn't you laugh, even at me. You have so little time."

Their embarrassment faded. The American boy and the German girl looked at her, baffled.

"Time?"

"So little," the old lady murmured.

For a moment the three of them stood in the wide corridor. The countess smiled toward Alexina's door. "Spend it together, don't wait," she said as she flounced past them and disappeared at a turn of the corridor.

They stood awkwardly, facing each other. "Well," Martin said, "I'd better say goodnight."

Neither of them moved.

"But what if she's right?" Alexina said.

Martin touched her hand, then ran his fingers up her arm to the rich curve of her shoulder.

She moved closer to him. Reaching to put an arm around his neck, she kissed him. The simple pressure of their lips brought their mouths open and their tongues danced slowly together.

The following morning the four Coburgs breakfasted at the long refectory table out on the terrace, while the old countess ate smoked salmon and scrambled eggs in her room. The atmosphere was, for Martin and Alex, unnerving. The two brothers were not their normal selves.

Looking out over the gorge with its sparkling river, Pierre was ebullient in a way Martin had never quite seen before. There was an element of theater in the way Pierre behaved, pacing the terrace with his coffee cup waving in his hand.

Emil, on the other hand, was unusually quiet. Not withdrawn or angry, but thoughtful, answering Alex or Martin with a slow smile.

Perhaps, Martin thought, as the two men retired with their briefcases and papers to the room upstairs, it was that Emil was quiet and confident; and Pierre was less certain of the way the discussions were moving.

In the great kitchen below the ground the soldier-cooks the Wehrmacht had provided were packing an elaborate picnic basket. Sepp Jurgens, the senior cook, stood over them counting in the items, the Puligny Montrachet for the main course, the Château Margaux to drink with the cheese. He was a small fat man whose waistline reflected his occupation. He was eating a great sandwich of French bread and cured ham as he waved his arm to encompass the stone-vaulted room. "In the old days," he said, "they knew a thing or two about building kitchens, don't you think, young sir?" he said to Martin.

"I'm not sure," Martin said dubiously, in deliberate provocation. "It's not much like an American kitchen."

"An American kitchen," spluttered Sepp as pieces of bread flew from his mouth. "An American kitchen. How could anyone cook a decent dinner in an American kitchen?"

"I guess it's been known," Martin said smiling.

"Hah, you play jokes with me, young friend. But what I say is true," Sepp insisted. "Look at these ovens, look at that fire! Can you make fifty loaves at a time in an American kitchen? Could you roast an ox?"

"No."

"Exactly my point. Now look at this." He swung open a wooden door. "My refrigerator!"

Martin and Alex peered into a huge dungeonlike room. With only a narrow aisle left to reach the stacked shelves at the back of the stone room, the flagstones were piled with blocks of ice. The intense cold seeped into the kitchen.

"Go in, go in," the cook urged them.

Martin took Alex by the hand and together they stepped into the icy rom

"Why is it so cold?" Alex said.

Martin pointed towards a flight of rough-hacked stone steps in the back of the room. From them a draft of cold air came like a steady wind.

"Let's go see," Martin said.

They could see that light came from below and as they approached the top of the stairs they could hear the roar of water.

"Some sort of underground river," Alex said as they started down the steps.

Ten steps down they stopped in astonishment. A huge cavern opened up before them through which a river surged. Electric lights in the roof of the cavern threw weird shadows on stalagmites and stalactites, columns of limestone whose strange rondels made them seem as if they had been fashioned on a giant lathe.

They reached the bottom of the long, twisting staircase. The stone floor was damp as they crossed it and then followed the course of the river until the electric lights gave way to splintered beams of sunlight hitting the rock above their heads.

Forty or fifty yards further, away from the roar of the underground river, they reached the cave mouth. Thick foliage half obscured the sun and they pushed through the bushes to find themselves at the base of a narrow gorge. Bright purple flowers swamped their senses. They stood in one another's arms until they heard the German army cook calling to them, then they turned and slowly made their way past the roaring river, back up the stone steps to the kitchen.

"See, you young moderns," Jurgens said. "You think a cook should be content with an icebox the size of a hatbox. Or four sniveling gas flames on a stove. Here, drink a glass of schnapps with me before you go off on your picnic." He poured three large glasses of schnapps, looked around at the other three cooks, grunted and poured for them, too.

Sepp lifted his glass. "To the American kitchen," he said. "May it never come!"

They took an army *kubelwagen* and drove down the twisting road among the yellow rocks to the bridge. Beside it one of the château's flatbottom boats was beached and tethered to a post. Alex untied the rope and dragged the boat to the water's edge as Martin hauled the picnic basket from the back of the *kubelwagen* and crunched across the pebble beach to place it on the boat.

The sun blazed down from a sky that was empty but for a few white rags of cloud and a tiny Storch spotter plane reporting the movement of refugees on some distant road north. They launched the boat and pushed off with one of the blue-and-red-banded oars. Alex insisted on rowing downstream and Martin sat in the stern of the boat, the tiller rope in his hand, the brim of his straw hat tipped over his eyes. Watching Alex, seeing the fall of her breasts as she bent forward to row, the glitter of sweat on her arms, the light puffing of the lips as she took the strain, he thought he had never felt so happy. From the look on her face when she rested the oars, he thought she felt little different from him.

They rowed and floated downstream until they came to a deep cove in the riverbank where the cliffs lifted clear from the water to a height of hundreds of feet. Above them three separate streams gushed over the cliffs and plunged down into the river. There was shade there from great chestnut trees that grew around the cove, and the fall of water created an extraordinary coolness in the air.

They tied up the boat and unloaded the picnic basket. Taking the rug that was strapped inside the lid, Alex spread it on the ground beneath one of the chestnut trees.

Martin had turned to watch the falling water, bouncing and sparkling on the rock, when he was suddenly aware she was no longer there. Calling her name, suddenly nervous, he brushed through a screen of bushes and stopped. She was poised for a fraction of a second, naked, on a jutting rock. Then her legs bent slightly and she propelled herself outwards, until she cut into the water below.

She had not seen him and he stepped back quickly behind the rock. It was not that he had not imagined her naked body before. Many times of course. But he had no conception of what the effect on him would be, seeing her like that.

He went back quickly and was kneeling forward, unpacking the basket, as she swam around the rock. He stood up and walked to the edge of the flat slab of the jutting limestone. Only her head was above the surface. Below, her brown body rippled in the clear water. "Are you coming in?" she said.

He nodded, beginning to unbutton his shirt. She slipped under the water, turned and swam along the line of the rocks. He undressed quickly and dove in.

For half an hour or so they chased and flirted in the water, pretending an indifference to their nakedness. When a fisherman rowed slowly past and seemed likely to choose the cove to stop, they waved and called and splashed about until he decided to move on.

It was a flawless day. The trees waved above them in a soft breeze, the cigales chirped and trilled in waves of sound. When they had driven off the fisherman, Alex swam towards the bank. Holding herself afloat by one hand on a jutting rock, she called to Martin. He turned and swam toward her. "Look the other way," she said. "I'm getting out."

He turned his back obediently and began to swim in a wide half circle. As he came back in the direction of the bank he could see that she was standing on the flat limestone slab, her towel wrapped around her tight across the breasts and tucked in underneath her left arm. Her legs were bare to above the knees. Her hair was already drying into thick golden strands.

He reached the rock and she threw him his towel and turned back to the picnic basket. He climbed out and wrapped the towel around his waist. The sun beat down hot on his shoulders; high above the river a pair of buzzards circled slowly in a dance of love.

They were both silent now, highly conscious of the tenuous fastenings of their towels. They stretched out on the blanket opposite each other.

Minutes passed. Several minutes.

He reached forward slowly. She knew what he was about to do and she made no attempt to stop him. With the tips of his fingers he brushed her towel over her left breast at the point it was tucked in. The end loosened. Very slowly the towel fell from her.

She rolled forward slightly on her hip and stretched

for the fastening of his towel. It fell away quickly. "Equal," she said, looking at his erect penis.

They were too afraid to make love. But for an hour they kissed and fondled and rolled on top of each other until one extra movement of her hand, one extra movement of exquisite friction against her belly and his spasm sent the sperm shooting.

She lay back gasping, one hand between her legs.

He looked down at her mouth shaped as if to scream. Then she jerked her knees up. Moaning.

For moments they lay together until the sun began to sear his back and his sperm dried on the golden bloom of her skin.

They loaded the picnic basket into the boat and Martin took the oars. It was a different journey back. The current was strong and progress slow. Huge gray-black clouds brought the rumble of thunder over the hills. The water slapped the side of the boat. The fisherman, content with cloud shadow, watched them curiously as he hung his line from the back of the boat.

They reached the stone bridge, tied up the boat and carried the picnic basket to the *kubelwagen*. They had hardly spoken a dozen words since they left the cove.

The storm burst upon them with the ferocity that only weeks of blazing sunshine can produce. As they ran for the shelter of the stone bridge, the rain was already slashing down, the thunderclaps following hard upon the flashes of lightning.

From under the arch of the bridge they watched nature wreak its frenzy in the sky as rainwater gushed and coursed down the rocky bank. They sat on the ledge of cut stone a foot or two from each other and watched while, framed by the arch of the bridge, the storm moved away and the rain began to slacken.

"Do you think they'll come to an agreement, Emil and Pierre?" she said suddenly.

"They're brothers," he said. "They understand each

other. They're from the Waldviertel. They're bound by a tradition they can't escape."

She was, he saw, looking at him strangely.

"Perhaps they're no longer bound by the same tradition," she said.

He put his arm around her waist and drew her close to him. "What do you mean by that?"

"Emil's changed, you know. He told me how much he regrets what he did last year. Involving you as Elisabeth's first invited."

"He can't regret it as much as I do."

She shook her head. "It's not only that. Not as narrow as what it did to you and me. Emil's seen for himself what Adolf Hitler really is. Where he's leading Germany."

"From victory to victory," Martin said, and immediately regretted saying it.

She looked at him for a moment. "He's leading Germany back into some Wagnerian make-believe," she said. "All mists and soldier-peasants and blood feuds. He's leading German civilization to utter destruction."

"Maybe you live too close to it."

He could see she was angry.

"I think you believe," she said, "that it isn't important which Germany to support. Perhaps you don't really think there's any difference between the Germany of Goethe and the ordinary baker's wife or student and the Germany of these swaggering bullies who make people clean the manure off the streets with their bare hands. Simply because they're Jews. I've seen that, Martin, in Vienna, with my own eyes."

"Once and for all," he said, "I am not a Hitler supporter. And I'm not letting you back me into that position."

"With Hitler, if you're not for, you've got to be against."

"Oh, it's as simple as that?"

"I think it's got to be."

He shook his head, exasperated. "A lot of Americans feel the way I do, Alex. They're a million miles from being pro-Nazi but they have the feeling that Britain and France have brought a lot of this on themselves."

"Is it Britain and France's fault," she flared, "that SS men are forcing people to clean the streets with their bare hands?"

"Jesus," he said, "there are New York cops who ought to be in the penitentiary. They're exceptions. They happen in every country."

"In my country, for the moment, they're not exceptions. They're state policy. They're part of a huge Nordic myth based on dimwit philosophers and pseudo-racial scientists. A lot of us at Munich University, professors and students, believe they're evil. You've got to take a stand, Martin. You, me, Emil, Pierre—we all have to."

The rain had stopped but water dripped from the stones of the arch above their heads. The sun reappeared to dry the wet stone. A lizard emerged from a crack beside him and darted and stopped and darted again towards the light.

She stood up, watching the sunlight glance through the raindrops dripping from the bridge. "What you did with Elisabeth is unimportant. Except to me, of course. But the Waldviertel myths are what Hitler's Nazi Party is about. Don't you understand that he's dragging Europe back into the fog of deceit and cruelty that we've spent centuries trying to struggle out of?"

She walked slowly from under the arch and climbed the slope towards the *kubelwagen*. As he walked beside her, she said: "I thought Americans rejected all this foul slush."

He saw what she was saying as a direct challenge to his loyalty to Pierre. "I don't see that the ideas of

Hitler and the Waldviertel have anything in common,"
he said stubbornly.

"Nothing in common," she exploded. "His family
came from there, for God's sake. There have been
peasants named Hitler or Coburg in those hills for five
hundred years. Adolf Hitler was soaked up to his neck
in it."

"Pierre Coburg is not Adolf Hitler," he said furiously. "And you're not going to persuade me that he
is." He watched her get into the *kubelwagen*. Her face
was set. She sat with her hands in her lap not looking
at him.

He suffered a strong sense of defeat. But there was
anger, too. Perhaps Emil had changed. But Pierre still
believed in bonds created by the wild tracks of the
Waldviertel.

First his father, Martin realized, had rejected the
family myths; then Alex, and now Emil himself. He
climbed into the driver's seat and started the *kubelwagen*. It all seemed to fit so well, the idea of a new
Germany rising through the mists of its own ancient
past. Something in Martin responded. Was that totally
wrong?

They drove back the short distance up to the château without speaking. Inside, at one of the great
twelve-drawer desks, an ancient Frenchman in a black
frock coat was reading through a document, his lips
moving, the French sentences emerging as a bee's
drone. Emil was standing by his side. The countess
was sitting on a Louis Quinze chair, her legs crossed
as if she were twenty-five rather than sixty-five, smoking a cigarette from an ivory holder. There was no
sign of Pierre.

The old Frenchman finished his reading, removed
his pince-nez and looked up at Emil. "The document
is complete, Monsieur. If the parties will sign."

Martin and Alex watched as first Emil and then the
countess signed the pages of stiff pale-blue-paper.

"Ca y est!" said the Frenchman.

"You have made me so happy," said the countess.

"I fell in love the moment I arrived," said Emil.

Martin and Alex looked on in bafflement.

"Now the document of gift," said the Frenchman. "If Ma'moiselle would sign here." He looked towards Alex.

She came forward, half led by Emil.

"Just sign," he said. "Just sign."

She bent and put her name to a single sheet of the blue paper. As she looked it over she drew in her breath sharply.

"A little birthday present for you, my darling," Emil said. "From this moment you are the *châtelaine* of this most beautiful château."

Martin watched in silence. He knew that for Alex it should have been one of the happiest days of her life.

CHAPTER 19

It was a hot night full of the sound of cigales and the wheeling, fluttering of huge moths.

The four Coburgs dined at a small table on the stone terrace overlooking the river. Soft light fell from the château windows above them. A pair of candles in brass candlesticks flickered on the table.

Emil and Pierre had hardly spoken. Alexina made one or two attempts to gain their interest, then furtively put her hand on Martin's leg. "Perhaps Martin and I should take our coffee into the drawing room," she said to Emil.

He glanced across at Pierre who was pouring himself brandy. Pretending not to have heard. Pretending he didn't care.

"No, stay," Emil said. "Someday the House of Janus will belong to you two. Stay and hear."

This time Pierre's head came up. He swirled brandy in the balloon glass. Then nodded.

Alex's hand tightened on Martin's leg, communicating alarm.

Emil took the brandy decanter from beside Pierre and poured a glass for himself. "I want to be as fair as possible in describing our differences. If Pierre wants to correct me, he's at liberty to do so."

Pierre grunted into his brandy, turned his chair, crossed his legs and looked out into the dark hills on the other side of the river.

Martin felt the tension in Alex. He realized suddenly that she knew something at least of what had passed between the two brothers.

"I believe," Emil said softly in English, "that the rule of Adolf Hitler will bring first Europe and finally Germany to its knees. I won't deny that Alex's arguments have been important in persuading me. Every German and everyone like you, Martin, who loves Germany, must face the truth. Wherever in the world this man sprang from, he must be destroyed. And he sprang from the Waldviertel."

"So what difference does that make?" Pierre growled.

"Perhaps it means we have a special responsibility," Alex said.

Pierre ignored her.

"We have a responsibility to do all we can to prevent Hitler's rush to disaster. We are beginning to hear horrible stories of the fate of the Jews in Poland. I have received information that plans are being drawn up to attack Russia. We are a country ruled by a lunatic. As one simple German industrialist I know what I can do. I can't shoot him, I can't foment rebellion—but I can print banknotes. One-thousand-mark bills for the Reichbank. If I were to increase the supply . . ."

"It's a crazy idea," Pierre said savagely.

"No. It will work," Emil said deliberately. He turned to Martin. "You know, Martin, that the strength of a nation's economy depends on many things. One of them is confidence in its currency. So . . ." He held both hands in the air. "I will flood Germany and Europe with one-thousand-mark bills. Genuine ones printed by me. Distributed through banks in Europe. Within six months Hitler's currency will be gravely compromised."

"Within three months," Pierre said, still looking out at the hills, "you will be in jail—and the name of

Coburg, your name and mine, will be dirt in every central bank in the world. And what for—nothing.''

"Pierre," Emil exploded angrily, "It's time for the truth. You know that every major nation in the war is investigating economic warfare."

Pierre swung round and faced his brother. "Let me tell you a story," he said. "Six months ago John Steinbeck, the writer, went to see Roosevelt. His idea was that if the United States entered the war on Britain's side we could break the German economy by printing billions of counterfeit Reichmarks. Secretary Morgenthau and the British Treasury even believed it would work."

"My idea exactly," Emil said.

"We turned it down flat," Pierre said as the palm of his hand hit the table. "We turned it down because it's a weapon like poison gas. It can blow back on your own side."

"You mean, Pierre," Emil said quietly, "that the banknote printers of America and Britain turned it down because you feared for your reputations after the war."

"You know as well as anyone, Emil, that our business depends entirely on trust. A company known to have printed counterfeits even on government orders would never receive a foreign contract again."

"In this case, to strike a blow at Hitler, the risk is worth it." Emil looked at his twin brother with steel in his blue eyes.

"You will ruin yourself." Pierre's voice was a harsh whisper. "And you will ruin *me*."

"Pierre," Alex said softly. "When the United States comes into the war, and we all know it will, the name of Coburg will be honored as one of the first to resist Hitler."

"The contents of graves are honored," Pierre said savagely. "Corpses, dry bones. You're not going to do that to the Coburgs, Emil."

Emil looked down at his drink. Martin took the decanter and poured brandy into the two remaining balloon glasses.

"Let Martin and Alex hear my proposal," Emil said.

"Oh yes." In the candlelight Pierre's face was flushed with anger. "Having smashed his own company to smithereens, he now wants half my company. A fifty-fifty share in Coburg Banknote."

Martin gaped.

"In return for the Janus," Emil said.

"Which is rightly part mine anyway."

"Which you refused financing for."

In the silence around the table a nightjar shrieked across the river valley.

"I have made arrangements," Emil said to Martin, "for Dorotta, Alex and myself to escape as soon, or even before, the Gestapo knows what's happening. My plan is to come to New York and to join Pierre as a partner. Together we will make the House of Janus greater that it ever was. We will take on the aristocracy of banknote printing. And we will win."

Pierre slammed the table. "No. Because we'll be seen as the Coburgs, the people that committed the greatest sin possible in our world. Forgery."

"There are greater sins by far."

"Who will care? You will destroy the Coburg name." He stood up, towering in his anger. "I will not have it, Emil! Do you hear? I will not have it!"

Martin and Alex stood together on the terrace, disturbed, frightened by what they'd seen.

"They'll never come together on this," Martin said.

"Of course not. Pierre's thinking of one thing only, the future of Coburg Banknote of New York."

"What's so wrong with that," Martin said defensively. "What Emil's planning to do goes against the basic trust governments must have in their currency printers."

"It's show, Martin. All front, you know that. You've seen them wheeling and dealing in China. You've seen them bribing for contracts. They're bucaneers, adventurers. Except now, suddenly, Emil sees there's something more important than the House of Janus."

"It's crazy," Martin muttered. "He's risking himself, Dorotta and you for a temporary disruption of the German currency. It's childish!"

She hit him. A stinging blow across his cheek. "It's not childish if you're a Jew on the run. Or a student at Munich University in Dachau concentration camp. It's not childish at all if your nine-year-old Hitler Youth son denounces you for anti-government talk!"

He was looking at her in shock.

She became silent. Tears streamed down her cheeks.

"I promised to drink a digestif with the countess," he said. "Maybe I'd better go."

She nodded, looking at him, willing him to make one step towards her. "I'm sorry," she said.

He turned away and walked quickly towards the staircase.

The blow fell less than an hour later.

"When you and Alexina are married," the old countess had said, "you must come to stay with me in my apartment in Paris."

"We won't be married," Martin had told her, the wine and whiskey now having a marked effect on his speech. "I told you. She thinks I'm a barbarian. She's devoting her life to opposing Hitler. Like a nun, damnit . . ."

The countess looked at him. "She's not alone. Many hate what's happening in Germany. Many fear it. It is not something to be neutral about. Alex is right."

"Listen," Martin said, recklessly pouring whiskey.

"I'm not a card-carrying Nazi Party member. I'm not even German, for God's sake."

"Your beautiful Alexina is saying that doesn't make any difference. She's saying that evil must be seen to be evil."

The internal telephone rang and the countess lifted the ivory and silver handset beside her chair. For a few moments she listened. "Yes, he's here," she said. "Yes, I will give him your message."

"Your grandfather wants you downstairs. Immediately it seems. They have been searching for you all over the château."

She watched Martin drain his glass. "Your château as well," she added, "when you and Alexina are married. It was Emil's intention from the first time he saw it, you know."

"What intention?"

"That Château de Belfresnes should be for both of you. He has told me how happy that would make him." She laughed. "Ah, what strange people you Coburgs are! Look at Emil and Pierre, two great brutes hulking around the château talking, talking, laughing, laughing, fighting, fighting. Murder in their eyes one moment, the love of two brothers the next."

They walked to the door of the turret room. "There are some good things about having a tradition too."

"Alex doesn't think so."

"That's because we need to choose from the past with great care. I'm not sure," she kissed him on the cheek, "that you Coburg men are very good at that."

He left the room and stood on the landing looking out of the arched window at the sweep of the river between the cliffs. He was drunk. He was angry, miserable, repentant, apologetic all at the same time. Most of all he was desperate to see Alex. He came down the winding staircase, his shoulder banging against the stone walls. He walked unsteadily along the lower landing until he reached the head of the main staircase. He could hear his grandfather's voice thundering through the lower floor. He focused with difficulty on the suitcases stacked in the hall and saw that some of them belonged to him.

Below him there was much banging of doors. Emil's raised voice shouted in German. "Very well, if you want to behave like a spoiled child, behave like one."

Pierre's voice, in English, roared as he entered the hall. "So much for the spirit of the House of Janus."

He appeared below, looked up, and saw Martin. "We're leaving," he snarled. "Now."

Martin came down the staircase. "I must say goodbye," he said.

"We're leaving *now*."

German soldiers had began to take the suitcases outside.

Martin stood his ground. "I won't go without saying goodbye," he said.

Pierre looked at him as if he was about to hurl himself at his grandson. Then, suddenly, strangely, his shoulders seemed to droop. "I'll wait for you," he said, "outside in the car."

Martin found Emil and Alex in the salon. They had been talking earnestly together and stopped when Martin entered. "I've come to say goodbye," he said.

Emil stood up and clasped Martin to him. "Goodbye Martin," he said. "I fear it will be a long time and perhaps in very different circumstances before we meet again. In the meantime do not let Pierre do anything he would regret. He's an impetuous man."

Again he pressed Martin to him, then released him and walked quickly out of the room.

As the door closed behind him, Martin turned towards Alex. She stood upright, her hands resting lightly on the back of a Directoire chair.

"There's nothing more to say, is there?" She smoothed her hands along the walnut rail of the chair.

"I don't know," Martin said. "I'm pretty drunk and

I'm not sure how clearly I'm seeing things, but I've been talking to the countess."

"She's a survivor."

"She's also got a lot of common sense."

"She told you to go back to New York and forget the Waldviertel and the whole dirty business here in Europe."

"No."

"What did she say?"

"I think she said we're all part of what's happening. British, French, Germans. Americans as much as anyone else."

"It's what I said."

He shook his head. "Not quite," he said. "The countess says we shouldn't throw away the past. We should choose from it what we want. Like a young woman, she said, going through the jewelery she has inherited from her grandmother."

She came from behind the chair and stood in front of him and slid her arms around his neck. "Perhaps," she said. "Perhaps."

Her body pressed close to his. "I will always love you," she said. "I think I always have."

Out in the courtyard Pierre was hitting the horn. A long series of harsh blasts.

"You must go," she said.

Then she kissed him.

CHAPTER 20

~ ~ ~

Reaching the beach, Celine put the mare into a gallop. She found it difficult not to laugh out loud with the exhilaration of the moment. On the third finger of her left hand the diamond flashed in the sunlight and was answered by the sparkle of the waters of the Sound.

Island House stood on its long slope of hillside, set out like the drawings for some English eighteenth-century home and garden. From the beach she turned and rode at a canter up the slope of the broad gravel alley, which brought her to the front of the house. Merchant, one of the grooms, had seen her coming and was there to take the mare.

"Is my mother at home?" Celine asked him, already on her way towards the front door.

"No, Miss," the groom grimaced at her back, "she left for lunch with Mrs. Tindale about an hour ago."

Celine stopped and turned. She was bursting with impatience to tell someone. "Is my father in?"

"I believe he's in his rooms, Miss. He went fishing early and I seen him come back about ten. Didn't go out since."

She turned away and entered the house. Her father was coming down the stairs.

"A good ride?" he asked. "Where did you go?"

"Along the beach. I like to get down to a good gallop." She pressed the bell at the head of the servants' stairs. When she heard one of the maids coming up the uncarpeted stairs she called down to her.

"Bring a bottle of champagne and two glasses up to the library."

"You've got a friend coming in for lunch?" Her father asked, rifling through the mail set out on a silver tray.

"No. I thought you and I could share a bottle together."

His eyes were raised to her in surprise. He smiled. "Very well." He opened the door to the library. "And to what do we owe this?" he asked, following her in.

"It's not unusual to drink a glass of champagne to celebrate, is it?"

"Ah," he nodded. "You've heard from Pierre and Martin. The discussions with Emil went well."

"No," she smiled slowly.

"But they've arrived in Paris?"

"No, they never made it to Paris. They met Emil in southwest France."

"But you've heard nothing since?"

She opened a cigarette box and slowly took a cigarette. "Not a word."

"If it's not success in commercial battle, what are we about to drink to?"

"You've always told me commercial success isn't everything."

"Perhaps because it.always eluded me."

He knew from the barely controlled smile of triumph that she was taunting him. It was a familiar smile he had seen a thousand times on his daughter's face when as a child she had gone behind his back to her mother to have an unpopular instruction countermanded. But they had drifted so far apart that she no longer had the power of irritation or pain. He sometimes asked himself if his newly assumed role of the watchful father was not more of an attempt to get even with Pierre than it was to protect his own daughter. Looking at her now as she lit her cigarette with those slow mannered movements she had copied from her mother, John Coburg realized how much he disliked her.

"As you know, Celine, commercial success isn't the only type that's eluded me."

She waited while the butler entered the library with an ice-bucket and champagne glasses on a tray. He opened the bottle, poured two glasses and withdrew. They took a glass each.

"You must have felt it a success when you prevented Pierre taking me to Europe with him." Again that smile.

"I did what I thought was necessary," he said carefully.

"What I choose to do is my business," she said in a flat, hard tone.

"You're nineteen," he said. "Unmarried. Whether I like it or not I'm responsible for you."

She laughed. "No longer," she said.

"Is that what we're drinking to?"

She nodded, lifting her glass. "That's what we're drinking to." She raised her left hand, stretching her fingers to display the diamond. "To my engagement," she said. "Jack Aston asked me this morning to marry him."

They had emerged into the horror of the real world a few miles from the château. The great surge of humanity that had brought Dutch, Belgian and northern French down to the Dordogne and the Lot rivers was now fully reversed. Like water in an unsteady pot, millions of refugees were now flowing back north to their homes and farms. It was impossible to proceed against this tide of tired, angry, worried and distressed humanity. The first night they slept in the car. The next morning they began to edge forward again, Martin at the wheel, Pierre gray-faced and burning with anger.

Hour after hour they moved forward fitfully, then

stopped. The sun beat down, bringing the temperature
inside the car to intolerable levels. Somewhere before
Cahors the limousine came to a halt. A broken-down
cart blocked their way. An implacable stream of hag-
gard faces flowing in the opposite direction offered no
hope of persuading them to pull over.

"Pierre," Martin said, the steering wheel burning in
his hands, dust and sweat pouring down his face, "let's
go back. Let's go back to the château for a few days
until this madness is over."

Pierre sat slumped in the passenger seat. He had
removed his jacket and rolled up his sleeves. His collar gaped loose. In eight hours they had covered less
than twenty miles of the two-hundred-mile journey to
the Pyrenees.

"If we turn back," Martin urged him, "we can go
with the flow. By nightfall we'll be back at the
château."

"We'll find a hotel here," Pierre growled.

Martin looked at him. A hotel? Was his grandfather
crazy? With the population swollen by millions, what
chance would there be of a hotel room?

"We've got money," Pierre said, still looking straight
ahead through the thick yellow dust on the windshield
at a peasant struggling to right his collapsed cart.
"Money talks."

Martin took a pull on the water bottle. He felt hung
over, his temper on a short leash. "Face it," he said
angrily, "we're not going to find a hotel room
tonight."

"Listen to me, Martin," Pierre said after a few moments. "I can't go back. I can't go crawling cap in
hand to my own brother. I've burnt my bridges. I
called him every name it's possible to call your own
brother. Get me back to New York City, Martin. I
don't care how the hell you do it, just get me back
there. I should never have made this trip. I should
have stayed where I was. Negotiate from strength,

Martin. Always negotiate from strength. Just get me back home."

Martin looked at the huge figure next to him. His great head had slumped forward. He lifted his cigar to his lips and drew on it. "What a goddam mess," he said, smoke breaking untidily from his mouth. "What a goddam mess."

Martin sat with his hands on the wheel. To feel pity for this huge figure so dominant in his life, was so unfamiliar that he felt sick to his stomach. He restarted the car and began to turn it around.

"We're not going back to the château," Pierre said.

Martin shook his head. "No. We're going back until we can turn west through the villages off the main road.

"West?"

"To Bordeaux. It's still being used by U.S. shipping. We'll be able to pick up a berth there."

In the library at Island House, Celine had watched her father's face crumple. He had not cried tears, but he had cried nevertheless. After a few moments he looked up at her. "Why, Celine? Why did you do it?"

"That's not a question a father usually asks his daughter when she announces her engagement to the most eligible bachelor in the Hamptons."

"Stop fooling with me, please. Jack is twenty years older than you. We both know he's not your type."

"What type is he, Dad?" she asked coldly.

He swallowed. "I think you know what I mean. He's a quiet, gentle person. He's not interested in business. He lives very much his own life. He. . .

"Jumped at the chance to be engaged to me," she said.

"He's always wanted children. He's always felt he owes it to his family to have children."

"You know what Jack Aston is," she said sharply.

"He's bisexual. One side of his nature fights the other. He's not a happy kink."

"I asked you why you're doing this."

"You sound as if you don't approve. He's your best friend, isn't he?"

"He's my best friend, yes."

"Of course you'll give me away," she said briskly. "Jack and I are thinking of the early fall for the wedding."

He closed his eyes in pain.

She stood up. "He likes girls, you know. He likes me. He's not a difficult man to deal with. Simple in fact. Maybe even simpleminded."

"What are you saying all this for? What is this all about?"

"You don't imagine I'm gasping with love for a seedy, middleaged fag, do you?"

"I don't think you love Jack, no."

She nodded. "Good. That's clear. Now, you can have him back on one condition. You move out of this house and you stay out. I want no interference from you, do you understand?"

"My God," he said, "I knew you had no morals but I had not quite realized how totally devoid of humanity you were."

"It's too late for lectures."

"Yes." He placed his untasted glass of champagne on the tray. "When will you tell Jack you're breaking off the engagement?"

"As soon as you've packed your bags and gone."

"So that you can have Pierre to yourself."

She nodded crisply.

"To do whatever foul things you want to with him."

She looked at him for several moments. "I'll choose how I run my life," she said. "Now you go and pack."

They reached Lisbon a week later by a Panamanian registered freighter from Bordeaux. One hundred and thirty-five passengers had bought sleeping room on the deck, mostly German Jews who had settled in France and who were now forced to be on the move again. Disembarking at Lisbon, bearded, indescribably filthy, Pierre and Martin shuffled forward in the long line waiting for their entry papers to be completed.

A taxi from the port area cost them their last American money. They were able to check in at the Hotel Bristol because they were known from their last visit; otherwise they would have been turned away on sight.

Pierre had hit rock bottom. He was convinced that Emil was intending to destroy the Coburg Banknote Corporation. On the journey to Bordeaux and then Lisbon, long periods of total silence had alternated with a garrulous excitement during which he talked for hours, speculating, cursing Emil, vowing he would get even. Then he would drop into maudlin reminiscences of their boyhood in the Waldviertel. Of shooting rabbits together or illegally trapping deer when the winter was hard and food was desperately short.

"He has no pity, my brother Emil," he had said as they were waiting on the only bridge across the Garonne River into Bordeaux. A mass of carts, trucks, and private cars with mattresses tied to the roof solidly blocked the ancient bridge. Between one vehicle and the other there was so little room that people entering the city on foot were obliged to clamber across the top of vehicles to reach the other bank of the river.

"I could stop him even now," Pierre said almost to himself. "A word in the right ear . . ."

"For Christ's sake," Martin said, "you could cause him real trouble."

"And what's he planning for me? I told him. Ruin. Ruin is what he's planning for me."

For a moment he fell silent. Disheveled, unshaven, the wings of his white hair flying loose, he sat nodding his head. Martin ached to see him so diminished.

Then, sitting in the by now battered limousine in

the relentless heat, with the angry shouts of frustrated people and the neighing of crowded, frightened horses all around them, Pierre again began to rage against his twin brother. "Goddam him, Martin, he's arrogant. He can't let history take its course. He wants to intervene, shape it."

"And you?"

"All I want is to own the greatest banknote printing business in the world," he said without irony.

Suddenly the traffic moved again, jerkily at first, then flowing out off the bridge in a cacophony of blaring horns, shouting men and neighing horses, into the heart of the Armistice capital of France.

At Lisbon Airport Martin was informed that it would be at least two weeks before two seats would be available on the Pan American Clipper service to New York. He haggled, he pleaded a sick grandfather, he offered money. But in the end he could do no better than two tickets for mid-July.

For Martin the two weeks passed strangely. Part of each day was spent drinking with Oliver Sutchley in the Bristol bar. Part was spent telephoning the German Embassy to see if Elisabeth had returned from a period of leave. Mostly, he was concerned with his grandfather. Pierre now passed all day in his hotel room, much of it in bed, his energy and vigor seemingly drained from him. Sometimes in the evening he would drink whiskey, and then his mind would seem to ramble through memories of his sometimes stormy relationship with Emil, from their village childhood to the betrayal of the last days. "Coburg Banknote," he said, "has always been more successful than Imprimerie Coburg."

His lips trembled with anger. He gulped at his whiskey, sucked hard on his cigar. It seemed nothing would control the trembling. "But what will anything matter in a month or two. Emil will have pulled us both down. No Central Bank in the world will give a banknote contract to the Coburg *forgers*. The House of Judas!"

He scratched at his gray stubbled chin. "He must be stopped, Martin. For God's sake we've got to stop him!"

Martin saw that he was close to sobbing.

Pierre's behavior affected Martin strongly. He looked at his grandfather sitting up in bed with a bottle of whiskey and noted the rheumy eyes and the twitch of the chin that once meant impatient decisiveness and now seemed all but uncontrollable.

He was not sure if he felt love for him. Not sure any longer that he felt respect.

But he did feel deeply moved that life should so build him up and the avenging angel, in the form of his own twin brother, cut him down so hard. Was it pity then that was the cause of the turmoil inside him?

At night he walked the elegant eighteenth-century streets of Lisbon. Oliver Sutchley would be waiting for him in the Bristol to share a nightcap and explain why each day's news made Britain's defeat more certain. His contacts with the German Gestapo intelligence units, highly active in Portugal, were growing every day. Even Martin, who didn't like the man, felt bound to warn him that the British would shoot him as a spy if he didn't behave more circumspectly.

Below all this, occupying every available chink in his thoughts, were his feelings about Alex. He had reached the devastating conclusion that he could not love her.

A girl who would destroy Pierre's life achievement for her own nineteen-year-old's political ideas.

Who would risk destroying everything Martin felt for her.

Who was recklessly arrogant with the love he had wanted to give her. How could he love her?

He was too inexperienced to see that his seesaw

reaction to Alexina was not the result of her political
views or even some sense that she and Emil had
deeply wounded Pierre.

Instead, it was the impossibility of facing life without her that he was reacting to, cultivating an anger
against her, feeding on it until all elements of rational-
ity were gone.

These were the nights he would feel a massive burst
of rage against her as he roamed the streets of the
Portuguese capital watching the drifting streetwalkers
among the ill-lit colonnaded squares of the city.

Rambling, drunken sessions with Oliver Sutchley
seemed his only release.

It was a few days before they were due to leave Lisbon. Martin had been lunching alone in the dining
room of the Bristol. He sat at a table in the middle
of the room, which he had come to see as neutral
territory. On the right, in a favored section under the
great windows, the Germans occupied a group of tables.
On the left, in a dark corner of the dining room re-
flecting their current lack of success in the war, sat members of the British Embassy, the captains of merchant
ships, port wineshippers on their way home to join the
army. In all public places where the Germans and British met, at least one policeman was always present.

Martin was about to leave the table when he heard
German voices in the hotel lobby. Looking up he
saw Elisabeth Oster leave a group of Germans and
hurry towards him. He stood up. From her face as
she approached he realized something was desperately wrong.

She stopped before him. In a voice that was
strangely flat and formal, she said, "Martin, I've just
returned from Germany. A most appalling thing has
happened at Lingfeld. Emil and Alex have been denounced to the Gestapo."

CHAPTER 21

~ ~ ~

They had driven down the gravel driveway to the house with old Wilhelm waving as they passed. The trees were bright summer green and the sky between their gently moving tops was blue with a scud of faint white cloud.

Six members of the household, women in black dresses and white aprons, lined the terrace steps. The housekeeper who, now that most of the younger men were with the Wehrmacht, was the senior member of the staff, came out across the terrace. She came to a stop in front of them, her face unsmiling.

"Where is my wife?" Emil's voice boomed out as he crossed the terrace. "Has she gone into Munich for the day?"

Alex noticed the housekeeper's eyes were red. She had been crying. Or perhaps had just not slept well.

Emil and the housekeeper exchanged formal greetings. "Madame Coburg is not here," she said.

Alex could see the tension in the woman's face.

"In Munich, uh?" Emil said. "The shops. Although when she sees what we've brought back from France for her . . ."

"There are two gentlemen here," the housekeeper said quickly as two men in gray suits emerged from the French windows and walked across the terrace towards the steps on which they were all standing.

A strange cold breeze seemed to surround Alexina. Men like this, men in gray suits that were neither well nor badly cut, but tailored more with the neutral competence of a uniform, men like these she had seen emerging from the arch under the medieval town hall on Munich's Marienplatz. It was said that the *Geheimes Staatspolizei,* the police force everybody called the Gestapo, rented the cellar rooms of the old building from the municipality.

The two men came to a stop in front of Emil and Alexina. They were not young or clean-cut as somehow Alex's terrified imagination was insisting they be. One was about forty, with the round face of a country shopkeeper. The other was younger, pale-faced, his oiled dark hair combed back in straight slicks along the side of his head.

"Madame was taken away yesterday," the housekeeper whispered quickly.

The man with the black hair came toward Emil. His lips seemed to Alex to move before the words emerged. He had long yellow teeth. "Emil Coburg," he said.

"Yes."

"Inspector Krebs of the Munich Gestapo. You're to come with me."

"Do I have the right to ask why?"

"No."

"Am I under arrest?"

"If you like," the Gestapo inspector shrugged his indifference at the letter of the law.

"Can I bring a bag?"

"No."

"No clean clothes?"

The man's red lips parted. The yellow teeth smiled. "We'll send them on," he said.

His round-faced companion nodded.

"Our car's around the side of the house," Krebs said. "Get a move on."

"Alex . . ." Emil turned towards his daughter. Krebs came forward and delivered a loud open-hand smack to Emil's cheek. "Get going," he said.

Emil turned in shock. His back was to Alex.

"And you," Krebs said. "Alexina Maria Coburg."

"Yes." She felt an overwhelming need to act with dignity. Krebs's assistant was already pushing Emil towards the car parked at the side of the house.

Alex drew herself up in anticipation of the inspector's next question. He smiled. "Get your fat ass across there," he said as he jerked his head to the car. In that moment she realized that the battles of the future, beyond those for life or limb, would be for some shred of dignity to sustain her. "Goodbye Frau Kessling," she said to the housekeeper, shaking hands with her before Krebs could stop her.

"Goodbye, Fräulein," the housekeeper said, emboldened by Alex's manner.

Taller than the man, Alex looked down at him, her lips compressed. Then she turned quickly away and walked ahead of the Gestapo inspector towards the waiting car.

At two-thirty in the afternoon on the day of the arrest, Pierre returned from the Lisbon Gestapo office on Avenida Lisboa. Like many Americans fleeing through Portugal, he had been astonished to discover that what was a foreign police organization was housed in such a large and prominent building. But no government on the continent of Europe any longer had the power to refuse a Gestapo request.

Martin was waiting for his grandfather in the bar of the Hotel Bristol. He watched Pierre come towards him shaking his head.

"There is nothing to be done," Pierre said heavily.

"You saw the head of the Gestapo himself?"

"Yes. A thickly built chap with a dirty collar. He wasn't helpful."

"Did he tell you anything at all?"

"He told me it was not Gestapo policy to discuss arrests. Or even to confirm them."

"You offered him money?"

"It didn't work."

"Good God," Martin said. "You were there over three hours. Didn't he say anything?"

"Yes," Pierre said. "He finally agreed that Alexina had been arrested. Emil and Dorotta as well, on the basis of the *sippenhaft* law. Family guilt."

"So where is Alex now?"

He was silent. Then, in a strangely even voice, he said, "In some Gestapo basement I suppose. Being questioned."

"She was denounced, Elisabeth said. That means by someone."

"My Gestapo friend said, finally, that Alex had been interfering in racial matters. You know what that means. It means she's been helping Jews. Did you know that?"

"I knew she had. Elisabeth knew as well."

"Maybe others, too," Pierre agreed. "Too many others."

"Will they go to prison?"

Pierre was silent.

"Did he say that, the Gestapo man?"

Pierre shook his head. "They're finished, Martin. Finished."

For the first time, Martin's imagination lifted from reprimands by lecturing magistrates, to single nights in police cells, to month-long sentences. "Finished," he said, dry-mouthed. "What do you mean, finished?"

"It's a very tough regime," Pierre said. "It doesn't like opposition."

"What does finished mean?" Martin's voice rose.

"Don't give me the melodrama," Pierre said harshly. "You know what finished means in Germany today."

"That's what the Gestapo man told you?"

"He told me a lot of things, Martin," Pierre said, draining his Americano and pushing his glass towards the barman for another. "I took him to lunch."

"You took him to lunch?"

"When I saw how the ground lay, I realized I was going to need his good offices."

"To get them released."

"No," Pierre shook his head. "That's beyond possibility now."

"Then what?" Martin said. "If we can't get them released why do you take a goon like that to lunch, for Christ's sake?"

Pierre looked at him. "You're a good boy," he said. "But you're young. You don't understand. If there's nothing we can do for Emil and the others, certain steps have to be taken."

"What steps?"

Pierre turned away from him, took his Americano and slowly half-turned back. "It was my solemn duty," he said. "I made an offer to the Gestapo for Imprimerie Coburg, its engravings, plant and patents."

"You bastard!" Martin swung on his bar stool to face his grandfather. "Are you a goddam ghoul? Your twin brother is taken by the Gestapo and you go right off and make them an offer. Not an offer of every goddam penny you own to get them released. You make them a slimy offer for the Janus patents you want to get your hands on!"

Pierre got off his bar stool and turned towards the door. But Martin was already standing next to him, his hand gripping his grandfather's arm. "Denounced," Martin said, "denounced by whom?"

"Take your hand off me, boy," Pierre said icily. "Or I'll knock you down."

"You won't. You'll sit back on that goddam stool and you'll tell me exactly what happened. And I'll tell you now that if it was you that denounced them, I'll kill you."

They faced each other, in shock. They knew that in the last ten seconds their relationship had changed forever.

"I want you to tell me," Martin said in a hard, quieter voice. "Did you?"

Pierre faced him. "Did I? No." He paused. "Did you?"

"For God's sake!"

Pierre threw some money onto the bar. "For two weeks you've been mooning around the bars of Lisbon. Drinking too much. You've been talking to Sutchley, haven't you?"

"To Oliver Sutchley? So what?"

Pierre started for the door, Martin hurrying after him. "Sometimes I wonder just how bright you are, boy. Oliver Sutchley speaks to the Germans, you know that."

"I knows he's pretty pro-German. What's that got to do with it?"

"You didn't get drunk with him?"

"I have, yes."

Pierre stopped at the elevators and gave his floor to the attendant. "Did you ever talk about Alex?"

"Probably."

"Boasted a little about what a hell of a girl she was? About the Jewish family she'd helped in Paris?"

The elevator arrived and Pierre stepped in and turned to face Martin. "Did you, boy? Is it just possible?"

Aghast, Martin watched the elevator doors slide closed.

They hauled the body of John Doyle Coburg out of the sea off Montauk Point. He was unconscious, but his oiled cotton windbreaker, acting as a rough life jacket, had brought him to the surface. Of the two fishermen in the boat, one was Dr. Stephens of Montauk, a man who had seen more drownings and near drownings than he could remember. The principle he worked on was to assume life still existed, however much death was indicated. In this way he had saved many from drowning. In this way he condemned John Coburg to a life John had no wish to preserve.

Only Jack Aston was prepared to look after the brain-damaged husk of John Coburg. In the years to come Aston was to be seen lowering his invalid friend from the back of the pick-up truck he had had specially converted, and wheeling his chair to the clapboard general store at Springs.

Late at night the airport lobby at La Guardia was seldom crowded. The cream-colored carpet, which ran the length of the room, was soft underfoot. Gleaming leather cases were being carried by neatly uniformed young men. Passengers for Chicago and Minneapolis drifted from the restaurant towards the flight gate.

Celine stood at the Pan American desk and stared down at the young man in his powder-blue uniform.

"The Lisbon Clipper was early, Miss. Landing was half an hour before schedule."

"Where are the passengers now?" she asked icily.

"Those waiting to be met are in the Clipper Lounge, Miss. Some are still clearing customs."

"Page Mr. Coburg for me," she said. "Tell him I'll be in the President's Bar."

The clerk checked the list. "There were two seats booked in the name of Coburg on the Lisbon flight, Miss."

She nodded.

"But only one seat was taken."

She frowned suddenly. "Only one seat?"

"It appears Mr. Martin Coburg didn't make the flight, Miss."

PART II

DANIEL

CHAPTER 22

I was a civilian. I could, of course, say that I was a civilian *again.* But it meant nothing to me. I had no life before the military. After nearly a year in a New Hampshire veterans hospital undergoing examinations, profiling tests, gradings and assessments, I was discharged with a disability pension and moved to New York City.

I took a job in an antique shop on Fifth Avenue and within a few months graduated to private dealing in English furniture for the ever increasing number of the New York wealthy. At the same time I found myself to be financially adept. With the advice of one or two of my clients, I used my Army backpay as stake money in the surging graph line of American post-war industry.

But it wasn't long before I was ready to move on. I never knew clearly why, but I felt uneasy in the city, challenged every day to remember when I had been here last, irked by the familiar unfamiliarity of streets, even of whole neighborhoods. Why in God's name did I seem to know Harlem better than other parts where I might plausibly have lived or worked? Why was the road out to Long Island charged with that flickering excitement I associated, perhaps wrongly, with a buried memory? But beyond this I had other reasons for wanting to move on. I was beginning to drink too much. Bad company began to stick to me. I glimpsed a vortex that could have sucked me in.

California beckoned. The names held no signifi-

cance for me, beyond a certain West Coast magic—
Santa Barbara, Santa Monica, Malibu, even Los
Angeles itself. 1 was sure I had never been there, sure
that it was right to start again clean. Despite all those
wild nights in New York I was aware of a strong conventional streak in myself.

Another Christmas passed but I hung around in
New York for a month or so after I had made my
decision. I had an Army Medical Board session for
pension confirmation to attend in New Hampshire that
March and there seemed no point moving west before
that matter was wrapped up.

One night I was in a bar when a fight broke out. It
was a mixed bar, and with bewildering speed the sides
split into white and black. I ducked a flying bottle and
was hit by something that cracked against the side of
my head. I slumped back against the wall, sliding
towards the floor. Out of the confusion a boot swung
at my head, missed and tried again. Someone next to
me held off my assailant with a chair, swinging it over
my head. "This isn't our fight," he said. "Grab a
chair. There's an exit door behind you."

I barely had time to realize that my rescuer was
someone white, shorter than me but with huge shoulders and a barrel chest. Each of us with a chair extended towards the erupting room, we fought our way
back through flailing fists and the mean glint of knife
blades to the exit.

I fell out of the bar into a freezing fog and walked
across the road as the sirens whooped up from the
East River. My companion was still carrying his chair.
Placing it in the deep shadow of a shop doorway he
extended a hand. "Vik Zorubin," he said. His thick
lips split towards his enormous ears in a savagely
friendly grin. He was one of the ugliest men I had
ever seen.

In the street three howling cruisers screeched to an
untidy halt.

I told him my name. "You saved my ass," I said. A taxi pulled up, blocked by the police cars. I pulled open the back door. "Let's go somewhere quiet," I said. "I'll buy you a drink."

We paid off the taxi at a nearby restaurant decorated with red-checked tablecloths and chianti flasks. Zorubin had said he was hungry for spaghetti and I'd offered dinner instead of a drink. His quick reaction in the bar made it seem right.

It was a time when men asked each other immediately how they'd spent their war. "Third Army," I said. "In France and Germany."

"What did you make? Lieutenant? Captain?"

I nodded. "Captain. How about you?"

His heavy mouth pulled into a smile. "I was an old guy for infantry," he said. "Nearly forty when I shipped to Italy. Platoon sergeant. Wounded. Invalided out while the war still had two years to run."

Our spaghetti came with a flask of Classico. "What did you do?" I asked him. "Go back to your old job?"

"With the Boston Police Department?" he said. "There's no going back there with a stainless steel kneecap."

"So how did you use your year's start on the other guys?"

"I drank a lot of vodka," Zorubin said. "Old Polish family habit."

"And . . . ?"

"I applied for a job with Pentagon Records. A civilian job."

"They turned you down?"

"No. I joined the European section three days before the invasion of Normandy. After that, if I'd had a heart it would have broken. We were inundated with letters from parents of kids who had made the landings and disappeared." His vast rubbery face screwed up. "Missing in action. M.I.A.s. Harder for the parents than killed outright. At least for some parents, the parents of those who don't come back in the end."

I called over the plump Italian girl who was serving us and ordered a half of vodka. I could see Zorubin wasn't enjoying his wine.

While he grunted his thanks, I asked him if he was still with the Department of the Army.

"No," he said. "I resigned the day the war ended, and went over to Europe. As an ex-cop I felt our missing person investigations were worse than useless. They raised false hopes, they confused names . . ." He paused. "I became a professional searcher."

"For M.I.A.s?"

"Ghoulish, you think, Captain? Like robbing war graves?"

"No," I said slowly. "I don't think that. What sort of success rate do you have?"

"Minuscule," he said. "But sometimes I'd find a guy in an old German prison camp in Poland. Or living in a mountain village in Italy not sure yet whether the war's over. Sometimes."

"It's kind of an odd-ball occupation," I said carefully.

"I'm an odd-ball."

"Just M.I.A.s?"

"I trace missing soldiers," he said quietly. "I trace long lost girl friends. I trace what's left of the families of American Jews. I trace French men and women who were transported to Germany and have never been seen again. And I trace Germans for other Germans who lost them in the night and the fog that settled over Europe for five years."

"Don't give me a hard time, Vik, because you take on German clients."

"I'm anticipating," he said grimly.

We got drunk or drunker. He made no effort to disguise the fact that he was a loner, taking his pleasures where he found them, burning up his emotions on the hopeless tragedies of postwar Europe.

"Where are you from, Dan? You've got a lot of class."

"Kansas City," I said. "But that's going way back."

"Rich family?"

"So, so."

"Brothers?"

"No."

Zorubin caught the moment's hesitation and looked up.

"No brothers," I said.

"Sisters."

"No."

"Tell me if I'm asking too many questions."

"Ask away." I signaled for the check.

He poured the last of the wine for me as I paid the waitress.

"Great spaghetti," he said. And then added, apparently out of the blue: "Where did you go to school, Captain?"

"Princeton," I flailed wildly at an answer.

"Samuel Barford?"

"Uh?"

"The President."

"Oh, sure," I said. And realized I had fallen for it.

He sat back, finishing his drink. "None of my business, Dan. Sorry. Fifteen years a cop, old habits die hard."

What the hell was I holding back for? Why *not* tell him? "You're getting there Vik," I said. "In a sense I'm one of your people. One of those lost in the fog."

"Tell me."

I finished the Chianti. "A few minor problems with memory," I said.

"Intermittent amnesia?"

I shook my head, relaxed again now. "Nothing intermittent about it, Vik. I am one of those rare and

beautiful cases of what the doctors call global amnesia.
They also say it could last."

Zorubin thought for a few moments. "Do I offer
my services? Or do you ask for them?"

I twirled the empty glass. "Neither," I said. "This
is one amnesiac who's far from sure he wants to
remember."

Zorubin shrugged.

I stood up. "Good to meet you, Vik."

He pushed out his heavy-knuckled hand. "Nice time
I had," he said.

My psychiatrist during the time I had been a patient
at New Hampshire's Eastlake Veterans Hospital was
Major Rob Baxter, a fresh-faced enthusiast of about
the same age as me. I knew over the months before
my discharge from the Army that he had come to see
me as a career opportunity. Material for a Pulitzer
Prize winning study of a genuine global amnesiac. I,
in turn, had come to see him as an amiable nuisance,
discomforting me as he scratched away in blank areas
of my mind.

After I had completed my testing on this last visit
to Eastlake, he gave me a drink and viewed me sadly
across this desk. "We've come to a dead stop, Dan.
The tests show no single area of breakthrough."

"Too bad."

He tapped his file. "I've got a bit of material here,"
he said. "I'm in a position to make a few educated
guesses."

I shook my head.

"Maybe not," he agreed. "We've become good
friends, Dan, over the time you've been at Eastlake."

I thought that was going too far but I nodded posi-
tively. I knew he was sorry to lose his only total amnesiac case, but I had no plans to keep in touch.

"Keep in touch," he said.

"Sure."

"Promise."

"Thanks for all your help," I said as I lifted the glass.

"One thing, Dan, has always bothered me about you."

I waited.

"Your lack of curiosity."

It did more than bother him. It left him anguished that his plans for co-operation on his case study were being tossed aside by my cavalier indifference. Yet there was a core of truth in what he said.

I fumbled through my shirt pocket for a cigarette. I had to face the fact that I had no wish to discuss my lack of enthusiasm for detective work. I didn't really want to know who I was. I had been presented by chance and a 2.5 kilogram Teller mine with a unique opportunity to construct my own being. Perhaps I *was* running away from something, but at this point in my life at least I thought of myself not as evasive but as uniquely privileged.

On the basis of Baxter's innumerable profiles I had sketched a background for myself, a sort of safe retreat if ever I found myself cornered. During my time at Eastlake I had written it out at night in my room, checking reference books and street maps as laboriously as if I were an illegal resident constructing my *storia vitae*.

Working from the back copies of the Kansas City *Star*, I checked and memorized my story until I had it word perfect. My name is Daniel Lingfield. I was born in 1920 in the West Bottoms, Kansas City. My father was of second generation German extraction and was killed in an accident in the Kaw River packing plant where he worked when I was seven. My mother was Irish. She died shortly after my father, and the family was split up. I vaguely remember brothers and sisters but perhaps I'm just romanticizing. I joined the U.S. Army in 1939 and was commissioned shortly after the outbreak of war in December 1941. I shipped to Europe after D-Day and am the sort of reluctant hero that hates talking about his war experiences. I learned decent French on our progress through France and perfected my German during the time I spent in Germany. I was badly wounded just before the end, hospitalized just outside Munich and discharged with the European Theater medal early in 1946.

Not a bad life story. I could fill in details. Anything I wanted, from the Goat faction of Kansas City politics to Harry Truman's failed haberdashery venture at Twelfth Street and Baltimore in the 1920s.

I left Eastlake for the last time just ahead of the heaviest snowfall that winter. As the train bore me toward New York and I looked out on the gray, snow-bound townships of New England I felt that surge of something that spoke of new beginnings, a new life.

I had time to see Vik Zorubin once more before I moved west. We met in the bar of his Polish-run hotel and I allowed myself to be persuaded into sharing a chilled carafe of pepper vodka. I found in myself a strange affection for this hard, shabbily dressed man driven by the tragedies of a war most Americans were trying desperately to forget.

"What's your next assignment, Vik?" I asked him. "Something in Europe?"

"My next assignment?" He gave me a sidelong glance. "I've been asked to check on a young French woman. Her husband served out the war as a submarine captain based in Liverpool. He got back to Paris to find she'd disappeared."

"Paris in the spring? You'll take the job?"

"No, I don't think so," he said, scowling up at me over the frosty glass.

"Why not?"

"One thing, I'm pretty sure I could tell the guy

what happened to his wife without a long, expensive search."

"And the other thing?"

"I want to work for you."

"Oh no, Vik," I said. "I'm a happy man. I've got a great future ahead of me. I don't want to be saddled with a past."

"What are you afraid of?" he asked calmly.

"Nothing."

"Something you've remembered," he persisted. "Something you've half remembered."

"For Christ's sake, Vik"—I could hear the tension in my voice—"leave it alone."

"It's your life," he shrugged.

"You're right, goddam it." I knew I was shaking like a madman.

He hunched his heavy shoulders. "Someday you'll want to find more. When you do . . ."

I nodded. "Sure," I said. "You'll be the first to know."

CHAPTER 23

In the spring I moved west to Los Angeles and signed
up to teach in a school in Anaheim, successfully bluff-
ing and faking my way through the paper qualifica-
tions I was supposed to present. I gave Colonel Buck
as my principal witness and he came through as I'd
hoped. By the beginning of the 1948 school year I was
teaching German at Putney High School, living the
easy life of southern California on my salary and
nearly fifty thousand dollars invested in Coca-Cola,
the Boeing Aircraft Corporation and a real estate
company that specialized in land for golf clubs. In the
evenings I went to art school to learn to paint.

I wasn't fully well. Apart from the persistent loss of
my past, I was, I came to realize, disturbed. I slept
well at nights only if I took sleeping pills or five or
six Malt whiskies. I dreamed dreams of an intensity
that made me wake with my heart racing—and yet
seconds later no details remained, only a strange sort
of vacuum of fear.

Bella Felperin worked at the school. She was a few
years older than me, a shapely dark-haired woman
with a sudden Martha Ray smile and very beautiful
brown eyes ringed by enormous gold-rimmed glasses.
We met regularly—she was head of the Foreign Languages Department—to talk about students and I
found her all the things a good teacher should be,
maybe even a little too owlishly serious at times.
There seemed no point in hiding my admiration.
When she passed I looked. I didn't gape but I didn't

try to look away. If she was aware she showed no sign.

Then one evening after a Department meeting, six or seven weeks into my time at Putney, we were walking along the top gallery when she stopped and swung around to face me. "Listen," she said. "What do you do evenings, when the brats have all gone home?"

Her tone threw me. "Not a lot," I said. "Apart from preparations for the next day's classes."

"Very worthy," she nodded crisply. "Will you buy me a drink sometime."

"How about tonight?"

"Tonight'd be just fine." She smiled her Martha Ray smile. "Easier than you thought, wasn't I?"

She drove me out to her own favorite bar so I had little time to reflect on Bella Felperin's change of pace. But there was a slight smile on her lips that suggested she was aware of my surprise.

"You like southern California, do you, Dan?" she asked me as we rode out along the ocean.

"After New York it's a paradise."

"You don't give a lot away. That's usually the sign of a bad war, I've noticed." She was her sober, schoolmistressy self with no trace of the sassiness that had appeared for a moment there on the top gallery.

I watched her as she drove, expertly swinging the Ford under a sign that read The Fisherman's Trawl and into a parking space in the lot. "Not too bad a war," I said carefully.

She switched off the engine and took off her glasses. Somehow she made it seem a significant act. "Better?" she said, smiling.

The Fisherman's Trawl was, not surprisingly, done up with nets and carefully selected pieces of driftwood. Dark glass picture windows looked out across a mournful sepia ocean. Bella greeted the guy behind the bar and a few regulars and we settled in comfortable benches with a view across the ocean and two Bloody Marys to break the ice.

"On a first drink like this I think people ought to come clean, don't you?"

"Come clean about what?"

"We all have our little foibles."

"Tell me yours."

She placed her fingertips together under her chin in a conscious parody of her schoolmarm self. "I like other women," she said. "Does that bother you?"

I took a breath. "I'm not thinking I just wasted the price of a drink, if that's what you mean," I said.

"Uhuh," she shook her head. "I mean you're not shocked?"

"I'm not shocked," I said. "But thanks for telling me."

"I don't like a guy to think I'm coming on to him . . ."

"When you're not."

"When I think I'm not."

"You mean you're not sure?"

"I'm very screwed up," she said matter-of-factly. "But I'm fun to be with."

She was. She drank a lot. She flirted indiscriminately with men and women alike and she was constantly in some sort of trouble. She had two separate personalities. The serious, devoted high school teacher was not recognizable by the time the small hours arrived in a bar or at a beach party. In the months that followed she came to count on me as some sort of prop. More than once I spent the night persuading the police not to charge her for some disturbance that usually involved offending public decency. At parties I talked her and myself out of innumerable tight corners. I was, mostly, the big brother.

Mostly, because, despite her proclaimed preferences, from time to time we made it together. But we both recognized it for what it was, as lust rather than passion. As a necessary part of the process of becoming just very good friends.

California in those years after the war was a land of immigrants. Americans had come in from all over the United States to grab a share of its lifestyle. The people didn't talk too much about where they came from; they were far too hyped up about just being there. It made life easier for me. In New York I had to field questions ten times a day. In California nobody was really interested in my past.

Except Bella. From the moment I told her about the blank screen that rolled before waking up in a hospital in Germany, she couldn't let it rest. She couldn't understand that I had done nothing since my discharge from the army to find out who I really was.

"So the army wrote all the next-of-kin of every soldier missing in action on that last day of the war?" she said when I first told her the story. "Yet none of them identified you?"

"None."

"How many were there?"

"Missing in action? Maybe fifty on our front."

"You've got to do something about this, Dan."

"You're drunk." I said.

She was on one elbow stretched on the sofa in her apartment. "Dan, you've got to do something about this." She swung her legs down and sat up opposite me. "You must see a doctor."

"I'm seeing one next week in San Diego," I told her. "I have an annual Medical Board. They test me, they tell me I'm still crazy and go on paying me money. I don't need another doctor. I've got a good deal with the one I've got."

"That's what you think, Dan." I realized with alarm that she had slipped out of her weekend persona. This was Miss Bella Felperin, Head of Languages, speaking. "Trust me," she said. "I'm your friend, right?"

I nodded into my drink.

"You think you come over complete, whole. But you don't. There's something missing."

"A whole bagful of marbles?"

"I'm serious, Dan. The way you live, the way you keep everything, everybody at arm's length. The way you have me as your only real friend."

I stood up. "Leave it, Bella," I said.

"You could have had a wife, maybe even kids."

I shook my head. "Why did no one answer?"

"Some military screw up. Okay, no wife. But parents, brothers, sisters. You can't just let them go, Dan."

There were big tears in her eyes. She lifted her glasses and palmed the tears away with the heel of her hand. "Okay, okay," she said, "half the lost marbles are mine. But when you've got a family somewhere I think you're desperately wrong not to go looking."

CHAPTER 24

A week later I drove down to San Diego and presented myself to the army clerk in the foyer of the low white ranch-type George C. Patton Military Hospital. He gave me a ticket and directed me along a polished corridor to waiting room 3. I opened the door and stepped inside to hear a deep rumbling greeting from the figure in the corner.

He stood up. Broad shoulders shrugged into his gray gabardine raincoat. Flat, mobile lips parted in that extraordinary smile. "Good to see you again, Captain. Not entirely by chance," Zorubin said. "I rang around to see when you were doing your next hospital board and fixed my trip out for the same day."

I shook his heavy hand. I felt real pleasure at seeing him. "How are you, Vik?"

"Good," he said. "So you like it out west?"

"Young man's country," I said. "And what are you doing here?"

"No end of clients," he said. "With the war long gone you'd think they'd tail off. No. The more prosperous people become the more they're ready to spend on a long shot."

I looked at his dusty gabardine coat and the edges of a thick jacket and cardigan I could see underneath. He wasn't dressed for California. "How long are you staying?" I said.

"I have a doctor to see here, a plane at two o'clock

and a Pan Am connection to make for Frankfurt, Germany at eight o'clock tomorrow morning."

"You lead a busy life. When we're through here I'll drive you to the airport. We'll get a quick drink and a sandwich before your flight."

At the airport the bar was all chromium steel and pink ribbed glass. Zorubin scowled at the barman and asked for vodka. "You know, Captain," he said, "that story you told me in New York really turned me on."

I collected my Glenmorangie and we walked across to the long, smokey pink window from where we could see the DC-3s taxiing on the runways.

"This is the place, Vik," I said. "You live a different life out here. Maybe the sun helps but mostly it's just far from Europe. It's so far away the kids here aren't fascinated by it. They don't know what happened. They don't care."

"You think that's healthy, Captain?"

"It suits me."

He grunted. "It would. You just quoted your epitaph. He didn't know what happened. He didn't care."

"You never give up, do you?"

He put down his glass and slowly mashed his thick hands together. "I'm interested, Dan. When I'm interested I stick with it. Have you ever seen this?"

I watched while he delved into an inside pocket and brought out a folded sheet of paper. "I dug it out of the Department of the Army when I was lost in Washington. Thought you'd like to run your eyes over the names."

He handed me the paper and I unfolded it. It was a list of every U. S. officer killed on May 8, 1945 in the Southern German/Austrian sector of the front. I cast my eye over Abel and Batson, Burrows, Cicino, Coburg and Cohen . . . Harman, Harrow, Hill and Hutzmann . . . Quarterman, Yeatman, Zoliewski and Zoller.

I folded the paper and handed it back to him. "And no bells ring," I misquoted.

He sat back and watched an airplane for a few minutes. As it roared away toward the perimeter he turned back to me.

"Why did you go to all that trouble, Vik?"

"To dig out the paper? No great trouble if you know your way around the Department of the Army. I thought you'd be interested."

"I'm not, Vik."

He shrugged. "Why not?"

"I'm not one of your clients, Vik."

The thick lips pursed. "Not everyone gets to choose."

I sat back in astonishment. "Listen," I said. "If I want you to stay out of my life, you stay out."

"Don't cut up rough, Dan. Your case intrigues me. What you were doing in those last days of the war I haven't got to yet. Quite a few members of the U.S. Army would have done the disappearing act if they'd had the opportunity."

"Disappearing act? For Christ's sake, Vik, you think that's what I've done. You think my amnesia is a cover story?"

Zorubin smiled. "I don't know, maybe I never will. If you're a genuine missing person, Dan, you've got my services whenever you want them, free. If you're not, then I'm just going to put your case on hold."

He finished his drink as his flight was announced. We shook hands. I felt a strong need to tell him. "For whatever reason," I said, "the amnesia's one hundred percent genuine."

"I hope so, Dan," he said. "I don't make a lot of friends."

I stayed in the restaurant and watched the stocky figure cross towards his waiting airplane. The sun glinted on his short gray hair and sunk into the thickness of his raincoat, which flowed untidily open in the slipstream. He stood aside as an old couple mounted the metal stairway and he must have seen my outline through the pink. He raised an arm and waved.

The truth was, as Bella said, I didn't make a lot of friends either.

"Listen," Bella said, "maybe you want to marry me."

We were huddled around a storm lamp on a cold stretch of beach eating paté sandwiches and drinking some good California red wine. Bella had sworn it was going to be a warm, romantic night.

"Have you thought about the possibility?"

"We would drive each other crazy," I said.

"We can't live like this," she insisted. "People are talking."

I burst out laughing. People never stopped talking about Bella. Luckily, none of it ever reached Putney High School.

"I'll give up women," she promised.

"Listen, I'll think about it."

"This is an offer that could go cold on you, you know."

"I know that, Bella." As ever, I was unsure how serious she was.

"We could have kids." She stopped, sandwich poised. "No, no kids."

"No kids?"

"Not until you find out who you really are. They've got nothing on my side. They have to have something on yours."

Partly to divert attention from the marriage talk, I told her about meeting Zorubin in San Diego.

She listened carefully. "You really like this guy," she said, at the end of the account. "Why don't you take up his offer?"

"I guess I'm scared."

"It's good to hear you say that. Any idea why?"

"Sure. Whatever I find out will turn my comfortable world upside down."

She nodded, lifted the wine bottle to her lips and drank. "About time," she said.

"You really believe that?"

"I believe you'll be a recluse, a zombie, in five years if you don't find out."

I sat back while she poured wine down my throat. Then I pushed the bottle away and wiped my mouth with the back of my hand. I could taste damp sand grit. "Next vacation," I said, "I'm going to Europe."

"You'll get Vik Zorubin on the case?"

"Not yet. I want to go to Lingfeld again."

"The place you were picked up?"

"I want to go there and ask a few more questions."

"Great." She threw the wine bottle into the basket. "Let's go."

"Where to?"

She was already scrambling to her feet. "Either we can drive out somewhere and get married by special license . . ."

"Or?"

"There's this terrific orgy I heard about out at Pacific Palisades."

We went to the orgy.

CHAPTER 25

To be back in Munich filled me with excitement and trepidation in about equal quantities. Many things had changed. There was no longer an American zone. The British and Americans had merged their two zones into what was soon to become the Federal Republic of Germany. GI's were everywhere, in bars and cafes, strolling in civilian clothes in groups of five or six down the Leopoldstrasse, driving in seemingly endless convoys out to training fields beyond the town.

There had been some rebuilding but many areas of destruction still remained. Yet there was, I was soon aware, a sense of new hope about. The United States had proposed the Marshall Plan, the greatest single piece of international generosity ever known. The Deutschmark offered the hope of a stable currency and Germans were already working for a new future.

But much of this was not yet evident. The people in the streets looked gray-faced, their clothes were mostly worn thin, there was acute overcrowding because of the bombing and the large numbers of German refugees who had been brutally driven out of their Sudeten homeland by the Czechs. Yet somehow, around me, I felt the real stirring of hope, the anticipation of a new Germany being born.

I checked in at a small hotel in Schwabing, the more raffish area of Munich near the University, and took stock of my position. Strangely, having come all this way from California I was uncertain what to do. I knew that now, in the chánged circumstances, Elisabeth Oster would no longer watch me, cold and frightened. In all probability she would quite simply call the police and have me thrown out. I had no right to be there. No right to insist on being there.

And yet I was drawn out along the Perlacher Forest road towards Lingfeld.

Six hours after my plane had landed at Munich Airport I had installed myself in my Schwabing hotel, eaten lunch, hired a car and was on my way to Lingfeld. It was late afternoon on a mild spring day. I soon left the city behind me. Along the country roads there was little motor traffic. Farmers in creased green Bavarian hats drove carts pulled by lean horses. On the tiny farms scattered across the hillsides women worked and sometimes waved as I passed. At the Lingfeld 5 kilometers sign I almost turned back. For a moment I experienced a return of the feeling that urged or perhaps warned me to seal off the past. I had come to believe there was to me more than my rational surface self, whatever I had been told about my not being a psychopath. I didn't think that I was, or had been. But when these waves of irrational fear rolled over me I flinched like a child.

At that 5 kilometers post I forced myself on. The curiosity to see what effect Lingfeld would *now* have on me was as strong or stronger than my fears. At the great stone gates I turned and stopped the car. The shrapnel holes in the stonework had been repaired. A neat white sign with black lettering read *Haus Lingfeld,* replacing the one that had warned against mines. I looked up the drive towards the house. It had been freshly regraveled and the gardens beyond the line of linden trees were well kept.

I had been staring so intently in the direction of the house that I hardly noticed the movement to my right. When I turned my head I saw nothing but the darkening shadows of the bushes beside the drive.

I made a move to put the car in gear and again

something caught my eye. And with it a rustle of leaves and the crunch of a footstep.

I climbed out of the car, now keeping my eyes on the patch of bushes where the sound came from. This time I caught the movement. A head ducked into the bushes as I dived forward. My hand went out, broke through a curtain of leaves and caught the cloth of a sleeve. I pulled hard and a small, wizened man came bursting out of the shrubbery. Saliva dotted a gray stubble, small bright eyes blinked in alarm. He gurgled and began to cackle nervously.

I let him go. "I'm sorry to frighten you, sir," I apologized, half ashamed myself that I had been frightened of a crazy old man. "Do the Osters still live here?"

He nodded. "Wilhelm," he said. "I'm Wilhelm." He dived back into the bushes and disappeared from view.

I got back into the car and drove slowly up the driveway. The wide roadway had not changed but the house had obviously undergone major repairs. The roof and upper floor window frames had been completely renovated. For some reason I particularly remembered the line of machine gun bullet holes in the stonework of the lower facade. Today in the light of a setting sun I could see the bullet scars were gone.

I stopped the car and got out. A woman was walking down the long slope of the parkland to my right. Two young golden Labradors galloped and pranced in front of her.

It was, I saw immediately, a very different Elisabeth Oster from the woman I had last seen in the shell of this house four years ago. The clothes were clearly different, new, probably London-made country tweeds, the shoes equally expensive looking. But it was the set of her head, the imperious look of inquiry, the immaculate makeup and perfectly cut hair that struck me most. She was a woman now of perhaps forty or a year or so more, remote, controlled, self-confident. But she nevertheless made one simple mistake. She pretended not to recognize me and as one of the few thirty-year-old Americans with a healthy thatch of white hair I am, if nothing else, pretty unforgettable.

She came down the stone steps from the terrace, the dogs romping around her. "Good afternoon," she said cooly in German. "Can I help you?"

We stood looking at each other for a long moment. Like old lovers who had long ago ceased to amuse or attract each other.

"I asked you if I could help you." She changed to English. "You're American are you?" she said, looking at my clothes. "Perhaps you're lost."

"No," I shook my head. "Not lost." I paused and she now began to look uncomfortable. "I think you remember me, Frau Oster."

"No."

"I think you remember at the very least a night just after the war when I came here."

With a minute facial movement she indicated assent. "What are you doing here?" she said.

"I'm taking a vacation in Europe."

"Then why have you come here? To Lingfeld?"

I extended my hand. "My name is Lingfield," I said. "Or rather my given name. You must understand that for me this house is a starting point."

She shrugged irritably.

"I wondered if seeing the house again would jog my memory, some detail, however small."

"And has it?"

"Not the house, no." I was sure I saw relief in her expression. I timed it carefully. "But seeing you again is different."

The alarm showed clearly on her face now.

"Will you invite me in?"

She shook her head.

"Are we to stand out here talking?"

"We have nothing to speak about," she said.

"I think we have."

"Will you please leave now?" she said almost shrilly. "Will you please leave before I call someone to escort you out."

"The old man, Wilhelm?"

It was meant to be no more than a cheap jibe on my part. The effect on her was devastating. She stood for a few moments in obvious confusion, obvious distress.

"Perhaps we'd better go into the house after all," I said.

It was a rough shot in the dark, but she immediately nodded a sort of defeated agreement and turned to lead the way back up the terrace steps.

We entered through tall French doors that matched equally tall windows on either side. The main entrance hall was to the left and the servants' quarter, where the Osters had lived in candlelight and cold blasts from broken doors, was somewhere deeper into the house.

There were no broken doors now. No candlelight. She switched on a blazing candelabra and six or eight small table lamps from one switch. She stood in the middle of the room, breathing heavily, making no motion for me to sit down. Then she turned and quickly took a cigarette from a silver box and lit it with a snap of a table lighter. "Go on," she said.

But now I was at a loss. It was easy to see that she thought I knew more than I did. The wrong sentence could re-establish her confidence. "I saw Wilhelm at the gate," I said.

Again, that expression of panic crossed her face. "Wilhelm is half-witted," she said. "We keep him on as an act of charity."

My mind was racing. She was implying Wilhelm had been at the house for some years. When he had stuttered his name I had taken it as a crazy old man's statement of introduction. "Wilhelm, I'm Wilhelm." But what in fact if it was a reminder? To me. I recast the words in my mind. "Wilhelm, I'm Wilhelm." Was the implication meant to be—"don't you recognize me?"

"He recognized me," I said.

She nodded dumbly.

"From when I was here," I added unnecessarily.

She puffed her cigarette and walked across to the mantle, leaning one hand against it and looking away from me, out through the long windows to the park. "Yes, you were here," she said.

I felt an incredible surge of triumph. "When," I said. "When was I here?"

"Don't you remember?"

"No."

"Then I've no intention of unnecessarily adding to my own embarrassment."

I decided to go for broke. "Shall I say it or will you? We slept together."

She went pale but she didn't answer.

"If I have to ask all over the village of Lingfeld I intend to find out," I said. "It's part of my life, goddam it. It's not something I'm going to let go because of your embarrassment."

She turned toward me. "It's not a story I enjoy retelling," she said.

I looked around desperately. I needed a drink. I gestured to the decanters on a side table and she shrugged indifferently. I poured myself a large whiskey. "Will you have one?"

She shook her head.

I sat on the arm of a chair looking up at her. "I knew I'd seen you before," I said deliberately. "More than that I know that you and I . . ."

She waved her arm angrily. "What else do you remember?" she said vehemently. "Anything, anything at all?"

"I think you'd better tell me the story," I said.

"You remember nothing of those last days of the war?" The words had an elusive ring.

I stayed silent.

"You don't remember the chaos when German women and children were ejected from their homes by the new Czech government and forced to march through the snows into Germany while the war still raged around them? You don't remember the thousands who died on the road from starvation or cold?"

I shook my head.

"No, you wouldn't," she said bitterly. "Nobody does. Because this time the victims were German."

I remembered what Zorubin had said about the hundreds of thousands, millions even, of Germans who had died on the forced trek from Poland and Czechoslovakia at the end of the war.

"When the roads became too clogged with carts or bodies or sometimes by the fighting that was still going on all around us, the Czech army police established vast camps for us in the woods or used old German army barracks. My accommodation," she said, "was rather special. I was taken to Theresienstadt."

I knew the name.

"Yes, Captain. To the old concentration camp where the Nazis had murdered their last victims only a few days earlier. The camp was pressed into service again by America's allies, the gallant Czechs."

"Who was in military control of the area?"

"We're talking about the last days of the war. Small pockets of German soldiers were still holding out. The SS of course were fighting for their lives. But the American Army was in the area, General Patton's Third Army had advanced almost as far as Prague and, to their credit, Captain, they were shocked by what they saw. By what they saw being done to German women and children. Teams of American officers came to our camp."

I walked over to the decanter and poured myself another drink.

"We began," she said, "to feel slightly less abandoned by the world, slightly more human. When the American officers came, the women dressed themselves as best they could, they made the best of themselves, you understand."

"I think so."

"Will you let me spell it out for you, Captain. The word spread. An officer could take a few hours off from his unit and choose any woman out of ten thousand for a *chocolate bar.*"

"I see."

"When *you* arrived at the camp, Captain, I had eaten one half a cabbage in twelve days. You gave bread, some cheese—and of course a chocolate bar. I was your choice, Captain. And I counted myself very lucky."

"My name," I said. "What was my name?"

"Do you think I cared? You wore a khaki uniform. You had the power of life and death over me because you were dressed in that uniform. Your pockets were stuffed with enough food to keep me alive. What did I care about your name?"

"And Lingfeld," I said quietly. "What was I doing here?"

She paused. "I had begged you to help me get out of Theresienstadt. I told you that my husband had a house here not far from Munich. You promised to pull some strings as you put it. You made the price perfectly clear. Within a few days I was released, turned loose on the road again. I made for Lingfeld of course. The war was falling apart. The German Army unit at Lingfeld left warning of minefields. It was, as I later discovered, the last day of the war. I hourly expected soldiers to appear. Perhaps Americans, perhaps Russians, I didn't know. Then a single jeep appeared and turned into the driveway. You had come to collect, Captain. But you never got as far as the house."

It was a story told with something that was either passion or desperation, I couldn't tell which. It was a story that left me feeling bad. But not totally convinced.

CHAPTER 26

～ ～ ～

I left Munich and drove across Austria toward Italy. So perhaps I had behaved like a million other soldiers, American, British, French, at the end of the war. Not so much rape by force and threats but sex for chocolate bars, sex for food, sex for a piece of paper that allows a girl to travel home. So my nightmares were because I had induced Elisabeth Oster to sleep with me. Slightly less than rape, a good deal less than an act freely entered into. But then a world war was ending and civilized values were still a long way from being re-established.

It made it easier, I guess, that I disliked Elisabeth Oster, but not much easier. I stayed a week in Venice wandering through galleried palaces until, driven by a sense of emptiness, I drove south to Florence and on to Rome. In a bar on the Via Veneto my indecision ended. I recognized I was in bad need of company. I bought another drink and placed a call to California. When it came through I realized how much I'd missed the sheer friendliness in Bella's voice.

"What did you find out?" The line crackled over the thousands of miles.

"Nothing," I said. "Or nothing much."

"Come on, Danny." She called me that when she wanted to chivvy me along. "You can tell me."

"Listen, Bella," I said. "How would you like to spend some time in Europe."

"Europe," she echoed.

"Rome, London, Paris."

"Paris," she said.

"My treat."

"I'll make arrangements with the school," she said. "I haven't seen Paris since I was fourteen-years-old."

Paris was wonderful. An escape from a world still recovering from war. Not like London, which I'd passed through, still battling, fighting a war they were barely aware had already ended. Not like Moscow or Leningrad or Kiev, licking wounds in silent hatred. Not like New York or Los Angeles with a trace of guilt that they had escaped the whirlwind. Paris had put the war behind it. It was over. France, they said, with a little help from its friends, had triumphed again.

So I took a hotel room at the Georges V and ordered some flowers and a bottle of '28 Krug and some whiskey to be sent up. It was a bright day with still a sparkling of frost on the cobblestones of the Champs-Élysées.

I took a taxi to Le Bourget airport, still nothing more than long prefabricated huts.

The flight from New York had just arrived and I walked across to watch the baggage room. The porters delivered a mountain of leather cases onto the trestle tables and a group of very American-looking passengers trailed in. It was only at that moment, seeing the dark-haired woman in the new red coat waving furiously across thirty yards of baggage room, that I remembered Bella's words. As I waved back I thought how strange it was that she had never mentioned visiting Paris before. I shrugged myself off the wall that was taking the weight of my shoulder. When she came through the barrier I put my arms around her and hugged her until her feet left the ground.

In the taxi to the George V she snuggled up close. "I got a lot to ask you," she said, her hand delving, unbuttoning my shirt.

"I've got something to ask you," I said. "What were

you doing in Paris before? I thought you'd never been outside the state of California."

"Hell, that doesn't matter," she said. "A flying visit with my parents."

I looked at her. "That's a half truth."

She nodded, still delving. "I'm going to tell you all about it this trip. But not yet. What happened in Germany?"

"I turned out to be just one more of the licentious soldiery. I went to Lingfeld looking to get laid."

"End of story?"

I hesitated. "I'm not sure. There was a photograph, framed, standing on a table at Lingfeld. It was a pre-war shot of Elisabeth Oster on a tennis court somewhere in southern Europe. Tennis skirt, racket in hand. A very flattering picture."

"But . . . ?"

"In the background, pretty much out of focus, a man was standing next to the net. Her partner, I guess."

"Did you know him?"

I pulled her hand out of my shirt. "I don't know Bella. I've wracked my brains. Somehow I can't get clear of the idea that the out-of-focus tennis partner was the same man who visited the hospital shortly after I came out of my coma. Only then he wasn't a German tennis player, but a very pukka officer from the British Army in Austria, asking me damn fool questions like had I ever been to Lisbon."

She was delighted by the hotel and we decided, since it was still mid-morning, to take a walk, have an aperitif and lunch on the Boulevard St. Michel. It was a soft spring morning and Paris is the easiest city in the world in which to walk. We came down the Champs-Élysées, wandered through the Tuileries Gardens, skirted the Louvre and crossed the Seine at the Pont Neuf. Walking, Bella turned and looked at me quizzically. "We're not, by chance, on some sentimental journey, are we?"

"No," I assured her.

"Because I wouldn't like that."

"It's you who's been in Paris before," I reminded her.

She nodded, saying nothing.

We selected one of the dozens of small restaurants and sat down and ordered an aperitif. "I think you should tell me," I said.

She nodded. "So do I." She lifted her glass and sniffed suspiciously at the Suze she had ordered. "But if I do it's going to break the spell. You're going to see me for what I am. No longer as a sexy, bright, whacky Jewish girl with the sun of California in her veins."

"You mean you've got dark secrets too?"

"That's what they feel like, Dan."

"You were born in Europe?"

"Strike one. I was born in Berlin. I was fifteen when Hitler came to power. By then it was no surprise to my father."

"He knew?"

"Everybody did. It was a bandwagon."

"Your father had the money to do something?"

"And the foresight. The year before, he had brought the family to Paris on vacation. While we were here, he bought a small apartment in Neuilly and made arrangements to transfer funds from Berlin if it became necessary. The rest of the family laughed at Berhardt's bolthole."

"Not for long."

"Not for long. On that last election day we were packed, ready to go. My brothers and sisters, all six children, sat on packing cases waiting to leave for the station. But my father had insisted on doing one last thing before the result was declared. He went with my mother to the home of her youngest sister and begged her and her husband to come with us. My aunt refused and my parents set off from home. At the Brandenburger Gate their car was stopped by Nazi supporters. They were beaten up. He died in the gutter."

I signaled the waiter to bring us whiskies, and took the untouched glass of Suze from her hand.

"My mother lingered on for six months. By then treatment for Jewish people was getting difficult . . . there were plenty of doctors but drugs and simple equipment were getting difficult to find." Bella sat back and took the whisky straight from the waiter's tray. She drank it without water.

"You were taken in by relatives?"

She smiled bleakly. "No problem there. There are Felperins around the world, unfortunately."

"Unfortunately?"

"Yuh. Unfortunately. All around. In places like Warsaw and Cracow and Budapest. Even Paris. Two of the boys stayed with my aunt in Berlin. Suzie came to Paris, Becky went to Warsaw. Lisa was in Budapest."

"And you?"

"Offers came in from London, New York and this place called Hollywood where some of the Felperins were busting into movies. Fifteen-year-old girl, I thought, Hey, I'm going to be a movie star. So early one morning . . ."

"You left for America."

She sat looking wanly at the passersby.

"What happened to your brothers and sisters?"

"You know what happened," she said without turning her head.

I reached over and held her hand. "We'll walk a bit," I said, "and find ourselves another place for lunch."

She stood looking towards the Seine while I dropped coins onto the tin table. Tears rolled slowly down her cheeks. "You escape," she said, "but you're never free."

That evening we went to a little dance theater in St. Germain and watched Roland Petit's Ballets Parisiens. At a cafe we drank coffee and cognac under the budding trees and watched the mix of students, West Africans and parachutists with red berets drift by. Then we walked and leaned on the granite embankment and looked across the river. Barges with brightly painted wheelhouses chugged along before us. Fishermen fished. Booksellers sold books from their high mounted wooden boxes. We were closer, closer than we had ever been. I knew because that frantic quality in her had gone. Ever since this morning, when she told me about her family, she had walked through the day different, more at peace.

I wasn't in love with her, somehow that was beyond me at present, but I was uniquely fond of her. I think I would have done anything to save her hurt.

That first night we had sandwiches and coffee sent up to our room, made a little easy love and went to sleep.

She was awake before me the next morning and had ordered *café au lait* and croissants before I was really fully conscious. I struggled up on one elbow and stretched for the coffee, listening to the sound of splashing water in the bathroom. The sun slanted through a crack in the curtains with the promise of another fine spring day.

After a few moments she emerged from the bathroom fully dressed in a yellow jacket and skirt. She pulled the curtains back and the sun now flooded in. She looked happy and she came over to the bed and gave me a good morning kiss. "I could grow to endure this life," she said.

"Me too." I put my hands behind my head and lay

back, eyes half-closed, luxuriating in the warmth of the sun and the soft opulence of her scent.

The boiling coffee hit me with the force of a fire hose. I half rose from the bed, my chest burning, to see the look of uncontrolled fury on her face.

"You disgusting bastard," she said. She snatched up a heavy brass bedside lamp and swung the base at my head. I rolled across the bed as the lamp thumped the pillow. Screaming like an animal, she threw the breakfast tray across the bed.

"Bella, for Christ's sake . . ."

"Shut up," she screamed. "Shut up, you lying bastard." She stood back, breathing heavily. "Loss of memory," she snarled. "God, you lying swine!"

Crossing the room, she jerked open the door. I scrambled into my clothes in total confusion. I ran outside into the corridor. The elevator had reached the ground floor. I recalled it and it stopped twice on the way. By the time I got down to the ornate, gilded lobby she had disappeared.

I was aware that people were staring at me, but I was so dazed I just sat at one of the tables and looked blankly towards the door. After a few moments, I ordered a black coffee and a large cognac and tried to make some sort of sense of what had happened.

Had she been saving up that moment for its maximum shock? Impossible. She had walked out leaving her luggage, even leaving her coat and purse. I drank the cognac and ordered another. What exactly had happened? She had come out of the bathroom and pulled the curtains. She had been relaxed, smiling, and she had leaned over and kissed me. I think then she must have picked up the coffee pot to pour herself some coffee. I wasn't one hundred percent certain because I was lying back, my eyes half-closed against the sun streaming in through the window. Then what in God's name had happened to bring her to that stunning pitch of fury.

Nothing. Absolutely nothing.

I left the lobby and took the elevator up to our floor. As I emerged into the corridor a sudden thought struck me. She had ordered coffee and croissants while I was still asleep. She had ordered a newspaper, too. A copy of *L'Aurore* was lying folded on the bedside table. Was there something she had seen in the paper? Something even about me?

The room door was still open. I crossed to the bed and snatched up the paper. The main front page story was of negotiations to form a new government. Below that was a story about the end of meat rationing in England. A picture of a Tour de France cyclist. A long speech by the mayor of Lyon. Nothing that could possibly relate to me. I turned the pages and scanned every item but I knew by now it was hopeless. The single important fact was that Bella had not opened the newspaper between the time she came out of the bathroom dressed, relaxed and apparently perfectly happy, until the time she had hurled the boiling coffee at me.

I sat on the edge of the bed looking at the things scattered about the room. Pieces of jewelry on the dressing table. Stockings and yesterday's blue dress thrown casually on the sofa, a pair of high-heeled shoes by the bathroom door. My eyes roamed the room desperately looking for an explanation.

I picked up her purse. There was nothing unexpected. A little French money, fifty dollars in fives and ones. A neat leather case, scented with perfume, carrying credit cards. Keys, lipstick, that sort of thing. Her suitcase was equally unrevealing. Clothes, more makeup, all those female necessities for a dirty weekend.

I am not deeply intuitive. I can now recognize memories of the past trying to surface. But intuition plays no part in my life. Yet, today, in my bafflement and frustration, I was taken with the image of Bella walking first down the Champs-Élysées on the same route we had taken yesterday. I was suddenly energized. I left her a note if she returned and another message with the concierge. Then I ran out onto the Avenue Georges V and down towards the Champs-Élysées.

It was Sunday morning and the sidewalks and cafe tables were not crowded. In her striking yellow suit I was unlikely to miss her. Following yesterday's route, I ran through the Tuileries Gardens almost certain I would see her sitting alone on a bench. But the gardens were empty except for an old man sweeping the gravel and a busy flock of pigeons pecking at the areas he had just disturbed.

I skirted the Louvre. The traffic was thicker here along the river. I had slowed to a fast walk now. Crossing the Seine, I reached the Boulevard St.Michel and the small restaurant we had had the aperitif in yesterday. It was my last chance.

The tables were empty. The zinc bar inside was supported by three or four old Frenchmen in suits and plaid shirts. I turned away with a deep sense of shock.

I took a taxi back to the Georges V and hurried across to the concierge's desk. No messages, but there is someone waiting for you upstairs, Monsieur. I ran for the elevator, pressed the floor button, came out and turned towards my room. A gendarme was standing outside. "What's happened?" I said. "What's going on?"

"Monsieur Lingfield?"

"Yes."

The gendarme opened the door of the room. Inside was a plainclothes policeman and another uniformed gendarme. The most awful sense of foreboding kept me quiet.

The inspector picked up Bella's American passport from the table and leafed through it. "Miss Bella Felperin has been staying here with you?"

"Yes."

"We hear she left the hotel about nine this morning in a state of some agitation."

"Yes. What's happened, for God's sake?"

"She was wearing a yellow dress?"

"A bright yellow suit. Has there been an accident?"

The inspector's face was impassive. "Why was Miss Felperin so upset?"

"I'm not sure. Hell, I don't know at all. Why are you asking me these questions? Why are the police involved?"

"There was some disagreement between you . . ."

Something warned me that it would be easier to say yes. I nodded. "It was trivial, I said."

"I have bad news for you, Monsieur," the inspector said, pocketing Bella's passport. "A woman in a yellow dress was seen to wade into the Seine this morning by two small boys. By the time they persuaded anyone to believe them, the woman had disappeared."

"Why," I said slowly, "apart from the yellow dress do you think it's Bella Felperin?"

"We found this on the riverbank, Monsieur."

He held up a crumpled Georges V napkin. It was stained with lipstick, mascara and, perhaps, tears. She had snatched it up as she left the hotel, dabbing at her eyes as she walked down to the Seine.

"You haven't found her?" I asked quietly.

"No," the inspector shook his head. "Many people have jumped into the river from the Pont Neuf in the last few years. They usually turn up within six to eight hours at the bend of the river at the Pont d'Iena." He smiled bleakly. "The bodies can be seen from the Eiffel Tower, Monsieur."

As we drove across Paris to the Pont d'Iena the weather changed. Clouds covered the sun not in wispy puffs of white but in great thick slabs of gray. Once there I passed the most melancholic hours imaginable. I shared a pair of binoculars with a young gendarme and we stood at the rail of the first stage of the Eiffel

Tower and searched the water between the Pont d'Iena and the iron framed bridge a few dozen yards to the east. At about four o'clock in the afternoon the gendarme nudged my arm and handed me the binoculars. A brief shaft of sunlight played on the surface of the river. Below the sheen of the water the yellow skirt billowed gently.

"Là voila," the gendarme said. And we went down to ground level to inform the river police.

I came back to the hotel and ordered a bottle of brandy to be sent up to my room. I would take a shower, go to bed and drink myself to sleep. I took off my clothes and stumbled into the shower. There was an angry red patch of skin on the left of my chest and when the shower water hit it I flinched in pain. When I had finished I dried myself carefully but the skin was still stinging. Then I remembered that Bella had some moisturizing cream in her night bag and I rummaged about until I found it. Carrying the pot back into the bathroom I opened it and began to apply some of the scented cream to the reddened skin on my chest. The burn extended across the left and continued around under my arm. I took a glob on my right finger and lifted my left arm. The burn was worst in my armpit. I examined it carefully. I held up my arm until it caught the light from the shower—and I fell back in thunderstruck dismay.

Deep in the armpit, hidden but for a trick of light, was a tatoo. Even backwards in the mirror I could read it: SS 79461.

I dropped the pot of cream. For five years those tiny inked SS runes had remained hidden from surgeons, from lovers, from myself. And then in that angle of sunlight, as I stretched back in the bed this morning, hands behind my head, in that blaze of sunlight the SS soldier's marking had been visible to Bella. So her lover had followed the same Hitlerite path as the men who had murdered her parents, her brothers and sisters. . . . My heart was thudding like wild, uncoordinated drums. Hideous images of myself filled my mind. Elisabeth Oster's story was, as I had come to believe, a pure invention. I now knew that when my body was picked up, far from being a U.S. soldier who spoke fluent German, I was a German SS-man who spoke fluent English!

CHAPTER 27

~ ~ ~

I flew to Berlin as soon as I had completed formalities with the French police in the morning. I now saw myself as a hunted man. I did not dwell too long on why Elisabeth Oster had lied. I assumed it was some attempt to protect her husband. Had Rolf Oster and I been associated in the past, had we been SS comrades? If so I could understand that he, having somehow acquired his denazification clearance, certainly didn't want me around. Any story, I could imagine Elisabeth Oster saying, was better than the truth. So what had Oster been involved in? What had I been involved in *with him?* What was the truth?

In Berlin it was the days of the Anglo-American airlift. Five thousand airmen had kept a whole city supplied with food and fuel and medicines. Every two minutes airplanes from the airfields of southern England were landing, every ten minutes they were unloaded by Germans working around-the-clock shifts. It was the first time since 1945 that the Anglo-Americans and the Germans had really worked together.

In the climate of anti-Stalinist feeling it was easier for small SS self-help offices to open up. Some, like the one near the Spandau Prison, dealt mostly with claims for injury pensions and stayed clear of politics. I got the address by posing as a freelance journalist at the press center at the airport. I then took a taxi straight to the seedy bomb damaged building which gave away no more than the name of the occupant of

the upstairs rooms: Herr Peter Helm. It was the name
I had been given at the press center.

I mounted a dusty stairway and entered an office
with a two-inch crack down one wall, leftover from
the bombing, and a small torn carpet on bare boards.

Behind a desk sat a large man with a badly scarred
face. He had no right arm and the sleeve of his jacket
was tucked into the pocket. He shook hands with his
left. "Sit down, Herr Lingfield," Helm said, his smile
restrained by suspicion. "You are a journalist?"

"A freelance journalist."

He complimented me on my German and gestured
me to a seat. He plunged into the problem as he saw
it, straight away. "Do you understand the position of
the former SS soldier?"

"You tell me."

"The problem is simple," he said. "The SS was declared a criminal organization at the end of the war.
Membership was a criminal act. What the Allied authorities assumed is that membership was a *voluntary*
act. But, in fact, by far the majority of Waffen SS
soldiers were ordinary conscripts. Soldiers like any
other."

I listened in silence.

"Of course, you have come here to write yet another article about the SS. Is it too much to ask, Herr
Lingfield, that you discover the facts first?"

"No," I said. "I'm here to discover the facts, at
least to discover the facts about one particular SS
man."

He looked at me and sighed. "You are a Nazi-
hunter, am I right? You work for a Jewish organization
in New York or London and you have an assignment
to trace Oberscharführer Braun or SS-man Schmidt.
How can you expect me to help you find the real
criminals who no doubt existed in our ranks, if the
organization you represent refuses to listen to the
truth?"

I took out a pack of cigarettes and lit one. As an afterthought I offered one to Helm. He shook his head contemptuously.

I had hoped to get somewhere without revealing that I was asking the questions about myself, but I saw now that that was a naive hope. This man would give nothing except a defense of the SS.

I stood up and took off my jacket while he looked at me in surprise. I unbuttoned my shirt and he waited, somehow knowing what was coming. I pulled aside my shirt and he rounded the desk and peered for a moment at the number printed in my armpit.

He smiled and clapped me on the shoulder. "You know," he said, "there was something I liked about you from the beginning."

I left the office, escorted down the narrow stairs by Helm. He had been a Major in the Totenkopf, the Death's Head Division, and had lost his arm in the fierce fighting around Demiansk, on the Russian Front. He told me that my story was safe with him, but before taking action he required me to go to ex-SS Doctor Lutze who would examine my tatoo and confirm that it was genuine.

I crossed Berlin for the brief but careful examination and I phoned Helm's office a couple of hours later.

"Don't come over now, comrade," he said. "Wait until dark. I'll meet you at the Gasthaus Beck."

"Has Lutze been in touch with you?"

"Doctor Lutze has confirmed that it is genuine."

My heart sank. It was as if I had been told that tests on an incurable disease had proved positive. "Why wait until dark?" I pressed him.

"Be patient," he said. "It is better this way."

I walked through the still shattered backstreets of Spandau Old Town until the light began to fade. It was easy to see that Berliners felt themselves to be in the center of international tension, the front-line against the Russians. They were tough, shabbily dressed but immensely determined. They were mostly Berliners but I could hear from their accents easterners among them from way out, from what was now called Poland. All that stood between them and the new horrors of Stalinism was President Harry Truman's will to resist. I sat in a small garden before a ruined church. Germans hurried past me on their way home from work and I felt some distinct, moving affinity with them. But I still had to repeat, softly to myself. *I am a German*. I am a *German*. I did this, but found to my bitter amusement that I was whispering in *English*.

I reached the Gasthaus Beck as darkness fell. It was no more than a long room with an oak bar and a few tables along the far wall. The innkeeper was a big man who was very definitely in charge of things behind the bar. The dozen or so customers were all men of about twenty seven to thirty five years of age. I wondered if they too were former SS men.

When Peter Helm came in a few moments later he was greeted by customers and innkeeper alike with marked respect. I had no longer any doubt that nestling under the left armpits of most of the men in this bar were the tiny SS runes and service number.

Helm ordered two beers and the innkeeper hurried across to take them to a corner table. A sign passed between them, which concerned me. It was a movement of eyebrow and mouth but it said not to worry, the stranger is one of us. The innkeeper extended his hand to me and shook mine vigorously. "I can offer you hot sausage, bacon, cabbage and the best dumplings in Berlin. Yes?"

"Why not?" Helm said. "My young friend and I have a lot to talk about. And some more beer Franz."

"Coming, Herr Oberst."

I watched Helm as he drank deeply and then set the glass down on the scarred oilcloth table. With his

index finger he traced the black marks on the cloth.
"It won't always be so," he said. "I give it a year
before we can crawl out from under cover. Two million trained men linked by an indissoluble sense of
comradeship. The Allies are going to *have* to call on
us very soon."

I said nothing and he took my silence for respectful
agreement. "First let's get down to work," he said.
"Where are my notes?" He fumbled in his inside
pocket, glancing up to the mirror above my head, a
mirror I suddenly realized that gave him a view of the
door. "There are several cafes like this in the district.
Strangers aren't welcome," he said. "Especially
strangers asking questions about old comrades."

He laid his notes on the table and the tension in my
body became close to unbearable. "My name," I said.

"Martin Johan Coburg."

I drank some beer and sat back. *Martin Johan
Coburg.*

Martin Coburg.

The innkeeper brought a great pot of hot sausage,
cabbage and dumplings. He set out plates and knives
and forks.

"Martin Coburg of Lingfeld, Bavaria," Helm said.
"Born in March 1921." He smiled. "I assume the
name you gave me, Mr. Lingfield, was not a
coincidence."

"Not as it turns out," I said.

The innkeeper replaced our beers. "There is a sug-
gestion in your record that your mother was American. I can get you your Family History Certificate if
you wish. Details of your racial purity back to 1715."

I shook my head.

"Yes," he said. "What difference does it make
now?" He consulted his notes. "You enlisted in Munich as a Freiwillige, a volunteer, in June 1940. You
received three *A*'s in preliminary training and were

sent to Bad Tolz, the SS officer training school near
Munich. From there we have no record of service."

"Is that unusual?"

"Very. We take a pride in the completeness of our
files."

Waves of despair passed over me. I found it impossible to face the fact that I was not American. After
all, I had been American all my remembered life. I
finished my beer. "So that's it," I said.

Helm looked at me strangely. "No, not quite it.
There's something else. I was told this afternoon that
in our file your name has a green star beside it."

"A green star. What does that mean?"

"A green star in our records means that at one time
you must have made an application to serve on the SS
guard detachment of one of the concentration camps."

I was beaten. It wasn't difficult to guess now what
I wanted to forget. Sickening images of myself as a
camp guard churned my stomach. I could no longer
deny the truth. My damaged memory could no longer
hide it from me.

Helms had taken a thick brown envelope from the
side pocket of his jacket. "You don't figure on any of
the Allied wanted lists. But they are still incomplete."

"I see." I was watching the brown envelope.

He placed it on the table and pushed it towards me.
"These papers are the only record of your service in
the SS."

I took the envelope. I couldn't bear the thought of
opening it in front of Helms. I'm not sure that at that
moment I could bear the thought of opening it at all.
I felt I knew more than enough about my past.

After that I bought a few drinks and heard a few
stories of the mud of the Rasputitza and the bitterness
of the Russian winter. By nine o'clock they were singing songs and I shook hands with my new comrades
and slipped away into the night.

I was miserable beyond belief. It was raining and,

as an economy measure, the only streetlights were at the intersections. Among these gaunt, dark streets there was no chance of a taxi. But I remembered a train station just across the gardens and I made my way there in rain and deep despair.

I stumbled into the lighted station. I caught a glimpse of myself in a mirror and recoiled. I was already the hunted man, my hair stuck down with rain, mud on my coat, my collar turned up, a furtive uneasy look on my face.

I bought a ticket and went onto the platform. There were few people waiting. I sat on a bench, my legs shaking. In my pocket was the brown envelope. I knew I must burn it without opening it.

A few more people came onto the platform. I sat staring at the sign on the arched brickwork across the tracks—Spandau. I thought of the Nazi war prisoners in the prison somewhere close to here. I thought about war-guilt and pleas of *befehl ist befehl,* orders are orders. I thought of that brown envelope in my pocket.

I pulled it out and tore at the adhesive flap. Nobody was paying any attention to me. Somehow I thanked God that there were no letters. The top item was an SS paybook, green with worn silver lettering: SS Untersturmführer M. J. Coburg. I opened it. I was staring down at a picture of myself. Or at least of a very young man who was unmistakably myself. You could almost feel the pride in those black SS collar tabs. Born March 1921. Issued January 1941. The boy in front of my eyes was still less than twenty-years-old. I turned to the next item. A recommendation by someone named SS Brigade-Führer Holz for a cadet award Second Class, dated January 1941.

Underneath that a photograph. Six uniformed young men outside a cafe, smiling, waving at the camera. And one of them appeared to be me. A fresh-faced but unsmiling young boy.

I pushed the photograph and papers back into the

envelope and put it in my jacket. A train roared into the station and stopped on worn squealing brakes. I stepped through its open doors without even asking where it would take me.

The train was crowded and hot with the dampness rising from everybody's coats. I took a strap and stood swaying like a drunk to the movement of the train. My eyes wandered across the torn and disfigured advertisements from another age. The train rattled around a bend and the cars straightened themselves into line as we approached a station. I could see the next carriage was equally crowded with straphangers. I saw an old man with a brown parcel under his arm; I saw a young girl with a long pretty face. And I saw, looking straight at me, Vik Zorubin.

I turned my face from him. Without thinking, I pushed my way through the press of people. At the next station I got out and ran for the stairs. I heard a shout behind me. Or maybe I thought I heard a shout. I was not thinking clearly, only that he was the bounty hunter and I was his prey. I was in a more brightly lit part of Berlin. There were a lot of American and British soldiers on the sidewalks. Cafes were brightly lit. A club advertised non-stop jazz.

I looked behind me several times. There was no sign of Vik Zorubin. I entered a cafe and ordered schnapps and beer. Had I really seen Zorubin? I began to be less certain, I began to think that when the mind gets as tortured as my mind had been it is capable of seeing anything, feared or loved makes no difference. And my mind *was* tortured, close, I would guess, to the limit of what I could take. I must go back to California, I knew that. I must remake my life as Dan Lingfield. I must forget Martin Coburg. I must build up enough life to expunge him from my mind. At a movement next to me I turned.

Zorubin was standing at the bar beside me. I kept my hands deep in my pockets. His huge hands were flat on the bar in front of him. "It's been some time," he said.

"It has."

"You don't seem pleased to see me, Captain."

"I'm not sure," I said. "I'm not sure what sort of terms we left on."

"If I remember," Zorubin said, "I still had an open mind." He smiled that enigmatic, alarming smile. A man easy to like, easy to fear.

"What happened to *you*, Captain?" He was looking at my hair and mud-spattered coat.

"I went back with a girl," I said. "She and some guy tried to roll me in a park."

He smiled totally without sympathy. "You got enough left to buy me a drink?"

"Sure. Schnapps?"

"If it's as close to vodka as I'm going to get."

I ordered drinks for both of us. "What took you over to that part of town?" I asked carefully.

"I do a lot of work there, Captain," he said. "There are a lot of SS joints there, little clubs, hangouts, that sort of thing. Sort of an SS final redoubt."

I didn't look at him as I fumbled out the money for the drinks.

"Still happy enough not to know who you are?" he asked.

I shrugged, trying to assume an indifference I did not feel.

"You still don't know?"

I shook my head. "I told you a long time ago, Zorubin, that I'd no wish to know who I was. I'm just me. Whoever I was, whatever I said, whatever I did, it wasn't me, get it."

He smiled that strange stretching of his dark, rubbery face. "Okay," he said, shrugging. "So you mean you don't want me to tell you who you really are?"

I froze. Very slowly I turned towards him. "You think you know who I really am?"

"I'm sure." He finished his drink and snapped a heavy finger and thumb at the barman. The man came running with the schnapps bottle.

I stood at the bar, my mind too confused to think straight.

"Your name's Coburg," Zorubin said. "Martin Coburg."

Quite suddenly my head cleared. I knew there was every chance that I was fighting for my life. "Martin Coburg," I said, repeating the name as if I was hearing it for the first time.

"Suits you, uh?"

I looked into those unfathomable dark eyes. "What makes you think my name is Martin Coburg?"

"It was simple," Zorubin said. "The way my investigations often work out. I was in Munich some time back, working on a completely different trace. My client was a rich French girl who was trying to trace a friend, a German girl from the Munich area. The two girls had become best friends at their school in Switzerland before the war."

I couldn't see where this was leading, but I drained my schnapps and nodded for Zorubin to go on.

"Now get this," Zorubin said. "My French client gives me the name and address. The German girl's name was Coburg. She lived in a mansion called Haus Lingfeld outside Munich! With her parents and her mother's younger sister, Elisabeth."

"Elisabeth. Elisabeth Oster?"

"She lived there. But Haus Lingfeld was owned by her brother-in-law, Herr Emil Coburg."

"So what led you to me?" I said hesitantly. "What made you think *my* name was Coburg too?"

"The original list of guys killed or missing on the last day of the war. You saw the list."

"The U.S. Army list."

"Sure. You don't remember the names, but I did.

There was a Coburg on it. Captain Martin Coburg. 327th Infantry. U.S. Third Army."

I gasped. "U.S. Third Army. I was a captain in the U.S. Army!"

He grinned. "My apologies, Dan. And my congratulations, Captain. I had come to think your story might be much more murky than that!"

I walked with Zorubin along the Ku'damm toward my hotel. My head was buzzing unmercifully. From time to time he glanced at me, then looked away, continuing his slow rolling walk. He was, I realized, giving me time to get accustomed to my new identity. He didn't, thank God, know how impossibly complicated that seemed to be.

It was I who reopened the wound. "On the last day of the war parts of the Third Army were in the Munich area."

"Parts of the Third Army were all over the goddam place. I guess Captain Coburg took a couple of hours off from the war."

"To drive to Lingfeld."

"To find news of his cousins."

"Elisabeth Oster's my cousin?"

"So was the missing German girl I was commissioned to find, Alexina Coburg."

"What about this missing German girl?" I said carefully. "Alexina Coburg."

"Hell of a good-looking girl. I've seen pictures."

"What do you know about her?"

"What do I know about her? Not much I guess. She and my French client, Andrée, were great friends prewar. Used to visit with each other in France and Germany. The last time Andrée saw Alexina was in Paris in 1940. Alexina and her father Emil Coburg helped Andrée's family, who are Jewish, to get to Spain."

"And then?"

"And then I don't know."

"You don't know what happened to her?"

"She vanished. Without a trace."

"What about her father?"

"Him too. The whole family."

"Except Elisabeth Oster."

"Except Elisabeth Oster," Zorubin nodded.

"And what does she say?"

"She says it was wartime. She had been posted to the German Embassy in Lisbon. She knew Emil Coburg was an anti-Nazi. Alexina even more so, it seems. Elisabeth says that when her letters started coming back marked 'Address Unknown' she went to Germany. Haus Lingfeld was shut up. The staff dismissed. Elisabeth's conclusion was that Alexina and the rest of the family had gone underground."

"And nothing else is known?"

Zorubin nodded. "Yep," he said. "I traced the record through. Alexina and her parents were executed in a sub-camp of Mauthausen, Austria, August 2, 1940."

CHAPTER 28

〜 〜 〜

I flew back to New York keyed to a fever pitch of excitement. I was Martin Coburg.

Somewhere I had a life story.

The Coburgs were rich. That much Zorubin had told me. They were the owners of the Coburg Banknote Corporation. That single fact made so much understandable, such as my obsession with checking banknote serial numbers and guessing the length of time a bill had been in circulation from the wear at the folds.

During the lengthy flight across the Atlantic, I had had time to realize this wasn't going to be just the return of the long-lost son. The Coburg family, whoever it consisted of, had chosen not to know me. For whatever I had done I had become a pariah. The SS tatoo under my arm was enough to explain that to me.

I could have left it there. But as we came in to land at Idlewild my heart was pumping wildly.

I wanted to know. I wanted to know why the Coburgs had not just openly rejected me. My SS background was enough to justify that. But why had they gone to such lengths to bury my connection with them? What did *they* have to hide? For my sanity I needed to uncover these years of mystery.

About the Coburgs.

About parents, or brothers or sisters who had left me unclaimed in that hospital.

I hauled my bag myself, half running through the brightly lit airport lounge out to the taxi rank.

I dragged open the door of a cab, threw in my valise and slid into the backseat. "Take me to New York Public Library," I said.

"You come back for the good weather?" the driver said for openers.

I barely heard him. I had already unzipped my bag, checking for a notebook, pencils.

The librarian, a tall earnest young man, reverently placed the thick envelope of clippings on the desk in front of me.

"This is your material on the Coburg family. Of course, we have a whole collection on the Coburg Banknote Corporation."

I told him the clippings would be fine and slid the wad of newspaper from the manilla envelope.

Staring at me was a picture of a man. Big face, good-looking. Blonde or white hair. He could have been me in thirty, forty years time.

It was captioned "Death of Pierre Coburg in Washington, DC." Dated yesterday!

I read the story beneath the caption. President of Coburg Banknote. Aged sixty-nine. Died of a heart attack during a meeting at the Bureau of Printing and Engraving. His granddaughter, Miss Celine Coburg, twenty-eight, became president of the company at an emergency meeting of the board held that morning in New York.

I turned the clippings. There were a mass of stories on Pierre Coburg. For over twenty years he had been one of New York's most eligible bachelors. Reports of liaisons were an inch thick; another thick wad of clippings showed him sailing and skiing. Always with a good-looking woman nearby.

Some serious items, too. An invitation to the White House. Dedication of a memorial to the victims of Waldviertel Concentration Camp. His appointment as president of the Security Printing Association of America.

His death had been a minor news event. His death and his granddaughter's succession. The stories were all accompanied by a photograph of a tall, blonde girl, looking more like a model than a company president.

Several items recounted the sad story of the death of her twin brother on the last day of hostilities in Europe.

So this young woman was my sister. The good-looking old man was my grandfather.

Did I have a father and mother still alive?

I read back into the recent past. This was a bad time to have a death in the company. Coburg Banknote were competing for a huge order from the Bureau of Printing and Engraving. The U.S. Army in Europe and Japan was to have a currency of its own. Scrip it was to be called, an anti-blackmarket device dreamed up by the Treasury Department.

The order was clearly gigantic and, as I saw from the *Wall Street Journal* clippings, it carried prestige. A great deal of it. New standards of speed and color were to be required. Paper waste was to be less than four percent.

Already, three months or more before Pierre Coburg died, Celine was chief negotiator for the company.

Interleaved with stories about banknote companies and printing contracts throughout the world there was a lot of material on Celine. A lot of photographs. Not surprising when you saw how unsexy her competition was. But she was also, evidently, a very clever and tough lady. All the stories made that clear.

I leafed back. She was a favorite for this winter's New York Woman of the Year Award. She spoke in a Sarah Lawrence debate on "A Woman's Place." She gave prizes and endowed a chair of business studies at a women's college in Kansas City.

Despite Pierre Coburg's lengthy obituary, it was
crystal clear that Celine had run the company since
the war's end.

Her company?

Now here was something. A clipping from a technical journal, Print and Printing News. Turmoil in the
normally calm backwaters world of banknote printers.
A brilliant young Italian engineer named Rino Giori
was developing a new multicolor machine. A possible
world-beater. De La Rue in London was interested.
The story went on to give more information about the
race to produce a hairline register multicolor press.
Rumors that the British were far advanced had proved
groundless. No American company was seriously in
contention. Except . . .

Except that Coburg Banknote Corporation of New
York owned all rights and patents of the former Im-
primerie Coburg of Linz, which had belonged to
Pierre's brother, Emil Coburg. He and his family had
disappeared into Waldviertel Concentration Camp.
Thus the dedication of the monument to the victims
and a donation to the Waldviertel Survivors
Association.

My pulse rate was up now.

I read on. It had been widely known before the
war that Emil Coburg was working on an advanced
banknote printing press. Even the name was known.
Emil Coburg had called it the *Janus*.

But the Janus had disappeared. Sometime in the
war the Janus had been moved from the Coburg factory at Augsburg. It was worth, ultimately, millions
of dollars to its patent's owners, Coburg Banknote of
New York.

Buried treasure.

The tall librarian came over to tell me politely that
the section was closing. My excitement must have
come over as a slightly threatening desperation. He

told me I could keep the file until he had cleared the out-tags.

I didn't ask him what the out-tags were. I flipped back quickly in the pile of clippings to 1945. There it was. The Coburg family, grandfather Pierre, John and Rose Coburg, my parents, and, oh so sad, Celine, watching the coffin of Martin Coburg, killed in action, being lowered into a Long Island grave.

The empty coffin.

The librarian coughed genteelly, I was the last customer. But there was one more thing I had to do, one more item I had to find.

I flipped the old yellow clippings, square, rectangular, folded flat. There it was. November 16, 1945. Print and Printing News again. Washington *Post,* a small story. *Wall Street Journal,* a fourteen by ten: American Military Government Court, Munich, Germany. Today Pierre Coburg's claim was upheld to inherit the estate of his brother Emil Coburg, formerly of Lingfeld, West Germany.

The *Wall Street Journal* noted that the real estate value was negligible but the rights, royalties and patents of Imprimerie Coburg could prove to be of great value.

Except, as Print and Printing pointed out, nobody knew where the patents were. Nobody had found patent, specifications or machine itself.

The Janus remained a buried treasure.

I stuffed the clippings back in the envelope and carried them over to the desk.

I was exhausted. I thanked the librarian and picked up my bag. Outside in the cool air I stumbled down the broad stone steps. It was still messy. It was still fog-bound. But a shape was emerging. A shape that began to scare the hell out of me. Like those images of a top-hatted Jack the Ripper in a London fog.

I knew I was close to evil. I could feel its breath on

my cheek. I hailed a taxi and told the driver to take
me to a hotel. He asked which.

I told him the *Pierre*.

It was only a moment or two later that I realized
it was my subconsciousness acting out a bit of black
comedy.

I didn't choose the day I arrived at Island House for
the first time as Daniel Lingfield. I didn't choose the
timing of my visit, but I don't think I regretted it
either.

I drove towards Montauk from the Hamptons
knowing I must have done this a thousand times. But,
as I looked across the countryside and to the ocean
on my right, Long Island might well have been a tiny
peninsula jutting from the underbelly of Australia. I
recognized nothing.

Perhaps four or five miles from Island House I
stopped to check with an old couple walking arm in
arm along the straight hot road.

"Island House?" the man said. "You go straight
down this road and keep the ocean on your right. But
keep your eyes on the left. Island House is the big
one just after the crossroads. You can count on three
miles. Maybe four."

As I thanked him I could see his wife was nudging
him in the ribs. He turned to her, mildly irritated.
"What is it, Em?" he asked.

Her eyes never left me.

"Well, thank you," I said again.

"You're Mr. Martin, aren't you," she blurted out.

There was silence in the singing heat. The engine
of my hired Plymouth turned over fretfully. "Yes," I
said slowly. "I'm Martin."

She backed away. Just one step, then stood her
ground. "We all thought you were dead," she whispered. Her husband had grasped her arm and was
pulling her away from the car.

"You worked at the house." I guessed.

"In the kitchen, Emma Hardy. You remember me?"

"Of course," I said. "I'm pleased to see you remember me. I was in the hospital for a long time after the war. I'm not a ghost, Emma," I said lightly.

She relaxed. "Didn't think you were a ghost, Mr. Martin. Just nobody told me you were still alive."

I got back into the car. Emma Hardy had recognized me. But the family at Island House had written to the army that my picture was not me. The army had left nothing to chance. They had sent out to each next of kin on the army's missing persons list something like an actor's composite of half a dozen pictures of me, close-ups, full-lengths, in uniform and in civilian clothes. But they'd done even more. They had meticulously recorded what we called my profile: that I spoke fluent German, that I was familiar with, and had certainly visited, Kansas City many times, that I knew something of the chateaux system of Bordeaux wines, even details of books they were able to establish that I had read.

And yet with all this, nobody at Island House had recognized me. Like Elisabeth Oster, they had deliberately lied. There was no other possibility.

Emma's husband was tugging her away. "We won't keep you, Mr. Coburg. You won't want to be late."

"Late?"

"For the funeral," Emma Hardy said. "Late for the funeral."

Island House was bigger, older and genuinely more impressive than I had imagined. It was a mansion house that dated from around 1840, with fine bowed windows on either side of the pillared front door, and wisteria climbing to the elegant second floor balconied windows. From where I parked my Plymouth I could see extensive gardens with shaded graveled alleys running down towards the foreshore.

I was standing beside my car when a movement at the far end of the driveway caught my attention. I turned to see a long black hearse leading a procession of three black Rolls Royces. The convoy crackled slowly across the gravel drive and came to a halt at the front porch. I was perhaps thirty or forty yards distant. The driver of the hearse got out and mounted the wide arc of stone steps that led up to the house. His companion left the passenger seat and rounded the hearse to open the back. I stood in the bright sunlight as the birds flitted and twittered around me and a faint flavor of ozone was carried to me from the ocean.

I took a couple of steps forward but stopped as the glazed double doors of the house opened and four men came out holding a coffin, which they carefully carried down the front steps and slid reverently into the hearse.

Men and women dressed in black came out slowly and assembled on the top step, watching as the hearse doors were closed on the coffin of Pierre Coburg. I could identify the principal actors from my reading of the clippings. The man in the wheelchair, thin-faced, haunted, was my father John Coburg. The older woman more or less next to him seemed to stare down indifferently at the scene before her. She was my mother, Rose, a tall and still beautiful woman in her late forties. Next to her was my sister, Celine. Everything about her physical being reminded me of someone my memory could not reach out to.

This young woman had a very special quality. A cutting edge that was apparent in the way she stood, in the way she gestured to the black-coated mortician's assistants to carry my father's wheelchair down the steps, the way she indicated with a lifted finger who should travel in the second Rolls Royce.

When members of the family had been allocated their cars, the convoy, led by the hearse, moved away down the drive. At the corner of the stable yard and at an upstairs window maids watched it go. A gardener stood and removed his cap.

I got into my car and waited so that I could follow at a distance behind the convoy. As the limousines swung left at the gates to the driveway I saw the face of Celine Coburg looking back at me from the rear window of her Rolls.

We drove at an appropriately funereal pace east toward Montauk Point. At the gates to the cemetery of the tiny clapboard church of St. Peter-in-the-Fields, two burly men stood in black jackets and striped trousers. The hearse passed through. The leading Rolls stopped for a moment as some words were exchanged between the gatemen and one of the occupants. The graveyard was on a light slope. It was small, not more than fifty yards by fifty yards, and the scar in the earth where Pierre Coburg's coffin was to be interred was close to the gate.

I accelerated slightly as the last Rolls passed into the cemetery and braked rapidly as one of the black jacketed men swung the gate closed. My fender was a few inches from it.

"This is a family occasion, sir. The press have been asked to restrict themselves to this evening's press conference. All the papers have agreed," he added.

"I'm a member of the family," I said.

"I'm sorry, sir, Miss Celine's orders are perfectly clear."

"I told you," I said. "I am a member of the family."

The polite but strongly built man gave me a heavy push in the shoulder. "Take off," he said, "I can smell a journalist a mile off. No goddam respect."

Next to me a light pleasant New England voice said: "Beyond the pale, Martin. Like me you're beyond the pale."

I turned round to see a tall slim man, not young but with a young air. His thin brown hair stirred in the ocean breeze. "You don't know me?" he said. It was a question.

"No, I'm afraid I don't."

"You really did lose your memory."

"Yes sir."

"If I told you I was Jack Aston, would that mean anything to you?"

The retainer at the gate was out of earshot. "You recognize me as Martin Coburg?" I said.

"I'd be more or less prepared to swear in court that you were Martin, yes. Although the Coburgs would destroy me if I did."

I absorbed that slowly. "But outside of a courtroom you'd say I was Martin Coburg?"

He smiled. "Or a very close imitation."

We stood beside the chest-height stone wall that surrounded the cemetery. The ceremony was about to begin. The members of the family were arranging themselves around the large open green marble vault. I could just see from where I stood the inscriptions cut deep into the marble.

"Your grandfather much favored the idea of family vaults," Jack Aston said. "He even had the ashes of his parents brought over from Austria."

As the sunlight fell across the stone, I could just barely read the inscriptions: Aloys Coburg 1841–1895, Paula Coburg 1856–1880, Martin Coburg 1921–1945 and Pierre Coburg 1880–1949.

"They say,"—Jack Aston's voice was edged with hatred—"that the stonecutters worked all night by flashlight to get the vault ready for Pierre."

"You seem to have no great love for the Coburgs," I said as I turned to him. "What did they do to you?"

He smiled bitterly. "Would you like to hear what they did to *you*?"

CHAPTER 29

It was almost dark when I drove over to Island House. So much of the past raced through my mind. It was like someone recalling his early childhood, uncertain whether he remembered an event from the past or knew it only from hearsay. Jack Aston had spared nobody. Certainly not himself. I knew of his relationship with my father; of his brief engagement to Celine. I knew of Pierre's avaricious sexuality, of his affair with Rose and almost certainly with Celine. I knew of the Waldviertel Coburg past, of Emil and Dorotta and Elisabeth and Alexina. I knew of the growth of Emil's company; I knew of the Janus printing press and that I was present on Pierre's last desperate trip to, as he saw it, save the Coburg Banknote Corporation. I knew much but my weakness was that I didn't know how much. Or how little.

I stood in the hall at Island House examining the detail of floor tiles and plaster cornices in the hope that they might suddenly bring the past to life. When the butler returned it was to tell me that Miss Coburg had no intention of seeing anyone today. If I wished an appointment I should telephone her secretary at Coburg Banknote in New York City.

I told him no. I was going to see her *now*.

He bristled but I could see he was scared.

I pushed him aside and opened the door he had used. I was in a book-lined room, long, elegantly lit with table lamps, an impression of Persian carpets and leather armchairs. Next to the fire Celine was standing with Rose. Each held a glass in hand.

"You know who I am," I said as I walked towards them.

"I know who you claim to be," Celine said. Her mother, *my* mother, was nervous. Celine was perfectly relaxed.

"You can't keep this up," I said.

She smiled an infinitely superior smile. "Of course," she said, "it's possible you're right. It's possible you are Martin Coburg. How shall we ever know?"

I had imagined everything from sullen defiance to screaming denials. I never thought I would be confronted by an indifferent shrug of the shoulders.

She signaled to the hovering butler to leave us. "I'll ring if I want you," she said. "I'll deal with this."

I walked over to the drinks table and poured myself a Scotch. For the first time her composure cracked. "This is *my* house," she said, in a voice close to a snarl. "You wait until you're offered a drink."

I turned towards her, drink in hand. "I don't know whose house it is at the very moment," I said. "We're going to find out."

"There was a will," she said coolly, "a simple will. The business and property came to me."

I sipped my Scotch. "You know that a will may be declared invalid on the basis of the legal doctrine known as 'undue influence.' "

"Not relevant," she snapped.

I looked at my mother. She was pale and licked her lips nervously.

"Who took over," I said softly, "as Pierre's mistress when his son's wife could no longer offer enough *zest?*"

Rose was a caricature of a woman trapped. Her breath hissed in. Whiskey spilled from her glass. She shot a wild look at Celine.

"Who was Pierre's mistress after *you?*"

"I don't know what you're talking about," Rose said feebly.

"I'm talking about undue influence," I said. "I'm getting very close to talking about incest."

Something gurgled in my mother's throat. Celine came forward. "Your suggestions are distressing to my mother. What do you want?" she said contemptuously, "money?"

I had never seen such a steely quality in a woman.

"I want to know how it was that my grandfather, my mother and my sister failed to recognize my photograph when the U.S. Army was trying to establish my identity in 1945."

Celine smiled. "But of course we recognized the photograph." Her swift change of tactic had put her on top again. "I'll tell you."

"Let Rose tell me."

Panic signals flashed from Rose to her daughter.

"*I'll* tell you Mr. Lingfield," Celine said. "Just listen. When the letter from the army arrived, my grandfather, Pierre Coburg, called together the close family, Rose, myself and John. Our problem was to decide how we should answer the letter."

"Why not just say, it's Martin Coburg."

She ignored my intervention.

"The photographs *could* have been Martin Coburg. Same height and general build."

"Less than three percent of American soldiers were over six-foot-two," I said.

"We're talking of individuals, not percentages," Celine said coldly. "Then there was a knowledge of German, which of course Martin had. And there was a familiarity with Kansas City . . . for what that was worth."

"Put all the items together," I said, "and it was worth a lot."

"We had to judge, Mr. Lingfield. And we judged that Daniel Lingfield might well be Martin Coburg."

She shrugged. "There was quite simply no way of knowing."

Did she know she'd trapped me? Did she know that the evidence nestled under my arm? Did she know that, to produce that evidence I would have to admit to a piece of the past that still left me paralyzed with guilt?

"So what was there for us to do? Pierre wrote a brief note saying the photographs were not immediately recognizable.

"*She* wrote the letter," I pointed at Rose. "And it said the photographs did not resemble her son. I phoned the Department of the Army this morning."

"What difference does it make who wrote the letter," Celine said crisply. "The letter was written. We all stand by it."

"My father too?"

She pursed her lips. "Ask him?"

"You bitch."

"Why ask," she said casually, "if you know that he's incapable of recognizing his breakfast. He has been for years."

"I also know how it came about."

She put down her drink. "If you have any practical suggestions, I'm prepared to consider them. If you're short of money I'm quite prepared on the basis of this genuine doubt that exists to make you an *ex gratia* payment from my personal account. I am prepared to provide you with seventy-five thousand dollars. But don't make the mistake of believing that you have just completed a successful act of blackmail. Legally, *nothing* belongs to you, Mr. Lingfield. Now please leave."

I had never hated anyone this much. I wanted to reach out and hit her. I saw that my mother's confidence was surging back. She looked at Celine proudly.

"I'm not leaving without an answer," I said with much more assurance than I felt.

Celine nodded slowly. "I see," she said, "that you're determined to rattle the skeletons in the Coburg family cupboard."

"Why not?"

She raised her eyebrows. "Have it your own way," she said.

I was distinctly nervous. To be without a full memory of your own past is sometimes easy, comforting almost; but sometimes deeply disturbing.

Especially when faced with this young woman's totally confident smile.

"You seem to be under the impression," she said, lighting a cigarette as she spoke, "that your family abandoned you in 1945."

"Am I wrong?"

"We certainly chose not to recognize your photographs. Of course we all knew it was you. But there was nothing new in our attitude." She paused for effect. And she got it. "None of us had spoken to you since the beginning of the war. None of us intended to speak to you ever again. So what possible reason could there have been for us to recognize the photograph? In Pierre Coburg's eyes you were no longer a Coburg."

"No longer a Coburg," I said. "Why not?"

The only sound in the room was Celine blowing smoke across the glowing tip of her cigarette. "Did your very partial memory tell you that you were a member of the SS?" she said scathingly.

I poured myself another drink.

"Of course it did. And I suspect your memory told you a great deal more." Then, with a sudden unnerving transformation, her face flushed purple in anger. "How dare you talk of undue influence with respect to your grandfather's will? How dare you even come back here when you betrayed half our family to the Gestapo?"

I dropped my glass.

"Oh yes," she hissed. "Before you left Portugal for the SS, every detail of the help Emil and Alex were giving to Jewish friends was on the desk of the Lisbon Gestapo. Passed on by you to a pro-Nazi Englishman named Oliver Sutchley. Does *that* name ring a bell?" she said with searing sarcasm.

It rang more than a bell. I saw him clearly now, the British officer standing beside Colonel Buck asking what seemed damn fool questions about Lisbon. He was checking, of course, on how complete was my loss of memory. But was he checking for himself—or for the Coburgs?

"This is Sutchley's account of what happened?"

"It is." She smiled, cold as ice.

"For God's sake why should I do that? Why should I betray my own family?"

"You were young, ignorant and loyal. Loyal to Pierre. You told Oliver Sutchley that whatever happened Emil must be stopped. His plans to issue counterfeit German money would have destroyed the House of Janus. Both sides of it."

She knew she had me reeling. I tried to formulate the questions.

But there was no mercy in this woman.

"Get out," she snapped. "Before I set the dogs on you."

I stumbled out to my car and drove quickly away from Island House, along to the Point. I parked looking out to sea and thought that the only person I really wanted to talk to about all this was Vik Zorubin. But that, in the nature of things, was out of court.

I hated Martin Coburg. I hated the bastard.

I put the car in gear and drove at a dangerous speed towards the cemetery at Montauk. My headlights threw great shadows from the overhanging trees and I felt engulfed by a horrific nightmare or piece of surrealist theater. The cemetery gates were open and I drove in, slewing to a stop on the gravel in front to the Coburg family vault.

The headlight burnt into the green marble: Martin Coburg 1921–1945.

Sitting there in the car I blinked with fear. I was thinking of Martin Coburg as someone else. But that arrogant young patrician in Lisbon was *me*. I could ask more questions, I could get more answers, but the only way to deal with the dangerous schizophrenia that was threatening me was to leave Martin Coburg buried with the grandfather for whom he had betrayed Alex and her parents.

I turned the car around and drove slowly down the coast road. I deliberately didn't stop at Jack Aston's house. I could not bear to see him or my father now. I drove with a mind completely blank with pain; I drove with every intention of driving away from Long Island forever.

I passed along the ocean road west until I could see the distant dome of light over New York City. I told myself what I had done I could never undo. However much my young self made my flesh creep with revulsion, I was now Daniel Lingfield of Los Angeles, California. No part of me had ever been Martin Coburg of Island House, Long Island.

My mind eased a little. The guilt I felt was someone else's guilt. To believe that was the only way I could stay sane.

I drove through Queens and the image of the words on the green marble came up before my eyes. Almost as a hallucination in the headlights before me. I saw the deep incisions in the dark stone: Martin Coburg 1921–1945.

Let it be.

CHAPTER 30

⌒ ⌒ ⌒

Definitely.

I had made up my mind.

I would go back to California on the first flight to-morrow morning.

Unless I phoned Zorubin in Berlin and asked him to come over and work for me.

No, I had made up my mind. Let it be.

Definitely.

I awoke next morning with a hangover composed half of alcohol poisoning and half of self-loathing.

Had I really done it? Had I really sent the German side of the family to their deaths? Had I really done it because I thought Emil Coburg was about to destroy his brother Pierre by printing counterfeit bills? Had I done it in my naive belief that the punishment for smuggling Jews into Spain was just a withdrawal of government favor, government contracts?

Martin Coburg was a self I didn't know then. He might have felt, believed, any of these things. But one single idea returned again and again to my mind. If it wasn't me—who was it?

I lay in the big double bed and projected onto the screen of my mind pictures of Pierre from the newspaper clippings. Did he do it? Did *he* betray his brother to the Gestapo and yet still send contributions to the Survivors of the Waldviertel Association? Was he that evil? The press clearly didn't think so. His presence at the Waldviertel memorial ceremony was worthy of a news item each year.

My mind drifted. I called the desk to get the times of the flights to Los Angeles this morning.

While I waited I thought what I had to do to clear up and leave New York.

Forever.

I phoned Jack Aston. I thanked him for all he did for my father. I thanked him for what he'd told me about the Coburgs, about myself.

"What are you going to do?" he said.

"I'm going back to California."

"And?"

"And nothing, Jack."

There was a long, long silence on the line. "What happened," Jack said flatly, "What happened when you saw Celine?"

I saw no reason to be easy on myself. "She took me by the scruff of the neck," I said, "and she bounced me off a couple of walls and threw me out of the house."

"What did she tell you, Martin?" the voice on the other end of the line intoned quietly.

"She told me I was responsible for the deaths of Emil Coburg and his wife—and Alexina."

"Do you think you were?"

A long pause.

"Do you think you were, Martin?"

"Yes," I said. "I think I was."

Somehow telling him about my SS tatoo stuck in my throat. "I've reason to believe it," was all I could get out.

"You believe that *that* was why you never saw Pierre again after he returned from Europe. You believe he would have nothing to do with you?"

"It makes sense, Jack," I said in anguish.

"It makes no sense at all," he said quietly. "It doesn't explain Pierre's will. I'm something of an expert on Coburg wills," Jack said. "I've had to be, in your father's interest. Pierre's will remained in your favor until the U.S. Army reported you dead in 1945. After that he changed it. Apart from fairly minor bequests to Rose and your father, Celine became the main beneficiary.''

I had remained his heir until I was reported dead in 1945!

That didn't seem to be the act of a man who had cut off his grandson in 1940 in the belief he had betrayed the German side of the family.

"Don't give up, Martin," he said.

I knew what he was saying. I knew he wanted me to take up the sword against Celine. But I had no answer for him at that moment.

I said goodbye. It was a poignant moment. I didn't expect to talk to him again.

I jumped as the phone rang. I picked it up and a young woman's voice told me I could get an American flight to Los Angeles from Idlewild at midday. I said yes. Packed my bag. Carried it down to the lobby and paid my bill. Let it be, I said to myself. Let it be.

I left the hotel. I was fleeing back to the sunshine emptiness of my life in California. A life now without Bella's friendly support. I had been defeated by Celine. I was on the run.

I took a cab and told the driver I wanted Idlewild. We were driving in silence down Fifth Avenue towards Rockefeller Center. The line of automobiles bunched, moved on and came to a stop. The driver cursed. My head was turned to my left. I wasn't really looking at the imposing stone face building just twenty-five feet away. The bronze plate beside the entrance was too big to be discreet, too classy to shout the company name to the world. Silvered lettering read: Coburg Banknote Corporation.

I grabbed my bag and jumped out of the cab. The driver yelled even as my five dollar bill fluttered in through his window. Taxis were hooting behind us. A loud central European voice was yelling at me.

I ran through the traffic and reached the sidewalk. Bag in hand I stared up at the building.

The doors were plate glass. The uniformed doorman opened one side and I walked in. Oak-panelled. Marble-tiled. Another uniformed figure sat at a broad desk. I crossed the lobby and swung my bag onto the desk in front of him. "I want you to look after this," I said in a manner so lordly Oliver Sutchley would have been proud of me. "Which is the executive floor?"

"Fourteen, sir," the man said. "Can I have your name please?"

"Coburg," I said. "Martin Coburg."

He recoiled, half nodding. As far as he was concerned I was a distant member of the family.

By the time he had rounded his desk I had stepped into the elevator and pressed the button for the fourteenth floor.

The layout of the executive floor made it easy. Two receptionists' desks formed the corridor. A door marked Arthur C. Jansen was on the left; another carrying the name Merril Soames was on the right. At eyeline level in the middle, was the most imposing of the three mahogany doors, with thicker architrave and an eighteenth-century pediment, and on it in brass letters was the name Celine Coburg.

I walked in. Behind me both receptionists had risen from their desks. In front of me, an attractive forty-year-old woman, becomingly severe in her black dress, was standing with the telephone to her ear, a yellow pencil tapping her teeth.

I walked past her, too.

Through the inner door and into a room with large windows in two walls looking over Rockefeller Center or back toward Central Park. There were white paneled walls, and from one of them hung a bad portrait of Pierre Coburg. Photographs in silver frames rested comfortably on polished side tables.

Celine rose from behind the desk as I turned the key in the door behind me.

She said nothing. She wasn't frightened or alarmed. She didn't even give the impression she was put out. She picked up a telephone and said, "Betty, don't have someone break the door down yet. I'm giving Mr. Lingfield five minutes. After that, have someone standing by."

She pointed to a chair. She smiled. "Sit down," she said. "What can I do for you?"

Perhaps I was too baffled to speak. I told myself I was too angry. The truth is I just didn't have her experience in these one-on-one confrontations. Eyeball-to-eyeball, they'd started calling it in the business world.

Instead, I said slowly, "I think I've got a shock for you."

She pursed her lips. I felt somehow I'd said the right thing. This was a woman who wanted to be in charge. Who mostly *had* been. Something coming out of left field she would find hardest to take. I was going to have to remember this in my dealings with her.

I waited.

"What sort of shock?"

I lit a cigarette. "I've decided," I said carefully, "that I'm going to face the past. My past, Pierre's past. Your past. I'm going to go on and on—and if necessary on again, until I find out what really happened."

"I've told you what happened," she said coolly. "After your gross betrayal of the German Coburgs to the Gestapo, Pierre refused to see you again."

"Is that so?"

She said nothing. But I could almost see her flinching.

"He wouldn't have anything to do with me?"

She nodded.

"And yet his will remained in my favor."

Now she did flinch.

"Pierre left it that way"—I tried to keep my tone level—"until the army announced my death. *He* didn't think I betrayed his brother's family."

She took a deep breath. "What counts is that he did alter the will."

"What counts," I said, "is whether or not you and my doting mother ever showed him the photographs and data the army sent you."

She smiled. "And that you'll never know."

Someone began knocking on the door.

"That I know already," I said. "And I'm as near as damn sure it wasn't me who talked to the Gestapo in Lisbon."

The phone rang and she picked it up. "Mr. Lingfield's leaving in a moment or two," she said.

I took the key and unlocked the door. I could feel the presence of secretaries and security men on the other side.

"I won't give up," I said. "This is where my life ends or starts. So far I don't know which. But I won't give up."

"Keep me informed," she said, her tone less casual than the words.

I turned the door handle. "I'll keep you informed. You'll know from moment to moment just how much your grip's loosening on all this." I waved my hand at the paneling, the silver framed photographs of prime ministers and presidents. "I'll call you, write you, cable you."

She nodded.

"Funny thing," I said. "When I left my hotel I was on my way to Idlewild to pick up a flight for California."

"And now?"

"Now I'm still on my way to Idlewild. But my flight's going to be to Paris. I'm starting back in Europe, Celine. Anybody who knows who turned the

Coburgs over to the Gestapo is going to be in Europe."

Her face was completely without expression. I opened the door. Two uniformed security men took a step forward. I turned back to Celine. "I'll keep my promise," I said. "As soon as I've got anything I'll cable you. Step by step you'll *know*."

CHAPTER 31

~ ~ ~

Cross the river at the Pont d'Iena. Run along the embankment. Look down from the rear window of the Paris taxicab to where Bella's yellow skirt billowed in the gray-brown river.

I got out at the Boulevard St. Michel and sent the cab to check my bag into a small hotel on the Rue Rappe.

Paris held no magic for me. It was drizzling. Two o'clock in the afternoon. Cool rather than cold. But the booksellers along the embankment were wearing mittens.

I started making my way through the crowds of students and clerks and shop girls streaming back to work after lunch. Here and there a group of Foreign Legion paras in red berets sat at a cafe table. Tall, blue-black Africans sold leather belts from open suitcases on the sidewalk; Arabs offered couscous from brightly colored street stalls; the smell of garlic and black French tobacco hung in the air.

At other times I would have loved this place. But the memory of Bella Felperin was too strong and that sense of isolation that can afflict Anglo-Saxons in Paris hung heavily upon me.

I turned at the Rue St. Severin and started counting the numbers opposite the church. The blue-and-white plate, that number I was looking for, seemed to apply to a small burgundy-painted secondhand book store. The windows were not that clean and the lights inside were dim. I pushed open the door and looked over my shoulder at the clang of the overhanging bell.

Nobody came out from the back room. I looked around at the walls lined with high bookshelves. The titles passing rapidly before my eyes were twentieth-century French and Anglo-American poets and novelists. In front of me a poster in English and German read: A meeting of the Waldviertel Survivors will take place above the Café de la Republique on Friday, May 2, to commemorate the liberation of the camp. Members of the Association and of any other survivors' associations will be welcome.

Waldviertel. A chill passed through my veins. The bottom part of the poster carried a simple black-and-white, pen-and-ink drawing of a barbed wire fence and gnarled hands clutching at it.

I stood there for perhaps a full minute, my head bowed, desperately conscious of the tiny tatoo in my left armpit.

At some point I was aware that a man was watching me through the open door that led into the back room. As he came forward, I saw that he was not tall but wiry, his face dark, lively, serious without being somber. "I'm Hans Emden," he said. "Can I help you?"

"You're connected with the Association?" I nodded toward the poster.

"I'm secretary of the Paris branch."

"My name is Dan Lingfield," I said. "I would like to make inquiries about some people who were imprisoned in . . . Waldviertel."

I had almost choked on the name. Nausea ebbed and flowed through me.

He nodded. Not really encouragingly.

"The family name was Coburg," I said.

I saw his face tighten.

"Emil and Dorotta Coburg and their daughter, Alexina."

Immobile, he nevertheless seemed out of breath.

"And you, Mr. Lingfield, who are you? A journalist perhaps."

"No."

"A private investigator?"

I knew he was playing for time. "I'm a member of the family," I said. "My name was once Martin Coburg."

"I see."

I let the pause sink in. "You were in the camp yourself?"

"I was in Waldviertel," he said. "Yes."

In a shaft of sunlight dust sparkled. We stood for a moment in silence among the books and the smell of coffee drifting from the back room.

"Did you know the Coburg family?"

"Thousands passed through the camp," he said. "Mostly we didn't even know each other's names."

"Do you have records of any sort?"

"We have a rough and ready *Todtbuch*, a Death Book." He turned and drew a heavy ledger from a shelf behind him.

He opened it with his back to me, leafed over pages that crackled drily, and turned back toward me. "Coburg. Here they are." He placed the book on the desk. His hand remained on the page.

I ran my eyes down a list of names entered in a coppery ink in a continental hand.

So many names.

Then, Coburg, Emil (Executed 9.7.40); Coburg, Dorotta (Dead on arrival 9.7.40); Coburg, Alexina (Dead on arrival 9.7.40)

He closed the book with a snap. "That's all we have on record," he said.

I knew something was badly wrong. You didn't treat a relative with this cold disconcerting manner. No word of sympathy, nothing. Just "Coburg. Here they are," and a Death Book dropped on the desk in front of me.

The catch spring hit the hanging bell over the door. An old woman came into the shop with a brown paper parcel under her arm. "Do I disturb you, Hans?" she asked in German.

"No, no, come in Magda," he said. He took the parcel from her and unwrapped the books. Opening them one by one, studying the title pages, flipping them over to examine the bindings, he muttered to himself. "These are very good, Magda. Very good editions. I can offer you three thousand francs and still do very well on the turn."

"Give me a thousand and not a pfennig more," the old lady said briskly. She turned to me. "The man's a fool," she said. "At least to old ladies."

They settled for fifteen hundred francs. To me her interruption had helped to defuse some of the tension I felt.

Emden walked into the back room and I heard a cash drawer opening. I leaned forward and took the Death Book. Opening it I found the Coburgs. Against Alexina's name, after *Dead on arrival,* was a note that had been obscured by Hans Emden's thumb. It read: See Anna Breitmann.

Hans Emden had emerged from the back room, a tin mug of coffee in one hand, three five-hundred-franc notes in the other.

Breitman, Anna (Dead on arrival 9.7.40). Papers given to Coburg, Alexina (9.7.40).

Hans took a long drink of his coffee, his dark eyes watching me over the rim of the tin mug.

I closed the book. "Why?" I asked him.

He shrugged and handed the notes to the old lady. While she protested he had overpaid her, I said: "What happened to Anna Breitmann?"

"Anna," the old lady said. "Anna was an angel.

One day I remember, she gave me two salted mackerel, *two*. Stolen from the SS cookhouse."

Emden took her to the door. Closing it after her, he looked back at me. "Not all survivors want the details about them known," he said.

"Alexina told you that?"

He didn't answer.

He shrugged. "She survived."

I found myself battered by strange emotions. By an extraordinary elation that this girl was alive. This girl I could never remember spending an hour with.

"When did you last see her?"

Emden put his head on one side. "She came here once or twice," he said. "I don't know where she is now."

"In Paris?"

"I said I didn't know, Mr. Coburg."

I turned toward the door and stopped. "I mean her no harm," I said.

"Good."

Silence hung thicker than the motes of dust between us. I knew I was going to get no more from him.

I glanced at the crude wooden donations box beside the desk. I reached for my pocketbook.

"Get out," he said, his face as gray as death. "Leave us alone."

I did two things.

First, I went to the post office in the Rue Gaspar, called Vik Zorubin in Berlin and asked him to take the next flight to Munich.

Secondly, I kept my promise to Celine. My cable read: REAL GOOD NEWS STOP OUR COUSIN ALEXINA COBURG ALIVE AND WELL IN PARIS STOP MORE LATER STOP MARTIN.

Vik Zorubin arrived at Munich Airport wearing what looked like a dark blue Navy surplus trenchcoat and carrying a scuffed leather Gladstone bag. His shoulders rolled, his great rubbery face split in a grin. "So I'm on your payroll," he said, extending his hand. "Where do we start?"

"Before we start, Vik," I said as we walked through the concourse, "I've got the rest of the story to tell you."

"Okay," he said as he spied the bright red-and-white coffee shop in front of him. "Tell me over a cup of coffee."

I nodded. "That way you don't leave the airport. When you've heard what I have to tell, you might want to turn and catch the first flight back to Berlin."

"Oh no," Zorubin protested with that unique brand of menacing amiability he could conjure up. "I wouldn't go home without visiting the mountains, gazing at a few ski girls and roughing you up a little."

We sat down in the service area and a girl in a red imitation stewardess uniform brought us coffee.

"Away you go," Zorubin said, his thick-fingered hands flat on the white table between us.

I told him everything. When I reached 1940, I told him Pierre had come back from Lisbon alone. I had stayed in Europe in a crazy, young man's attempt to see Alex again. There was only one possible way of getting into the camps except as a prisoner.

He looked at me hard-eyed. "So you joined the Allgemeine SS," he said.

I nodded. "I joined the SS."

He said nothing for about thirty seconds. He stared at me with his dark expressionless eyes for what seemed to me a very long time indeed. Then he said: "How long have you known that you were in the SS?"

"Since I met you in Berlin."

A half smile. "You had been to see Colonel Helm in Spandau Altstadt."

"He told me that my SS number"—I touched my left armpit—"meant that I was Martin Coburg, that I had volunteered in August 1940, and disappeared a few months later."

I lit a cigarette. He pulled an obscure Russian brand called *Stravka* from his pocket, slowly tore open the cheap paper packaging and took out a yellow corn-paper cigarette. "Let's go back a step," he said. "So you didn't join the Allgemeine SS to fight for the Führer."

"You know I didn't."

"I know." He took a lighter and laboriously flicked at the wheel with his thumb. On the third or fourth try the spark became flame. "What made you call me in Berlin?" he said. "Why not leave all this safely buried?"

"Yesterday I went to the Waldviertel Survivors Association in Paris. Alexina survived the camp."

For once his face registered something clearly recognizable as surprise. "She's in Paris?"

"Almost certainly. But I can't get any further without your help."

Zorubin got his cigarette lit, scowling at the taste. He sat back. He blew a smoke ring and it hovered like indecision between us. "So my job would be to find Alexina Coburg."

"If you'll take it."

He scowled again at his cigarette. "You're not holding out on me?"

"Holding out?"

"You're not holding anything back?"

"You've got it all, Vik."

"Okay," he said. "On one condition. If anything comes out that suggests you were an enthusiastic camp guard, I turn you straight over to War Crimes."

I stretched out a hand. He took it and squeezed till the knuckles cracked.

CHAPTER 32

~ ~ ~

We made plans. Zorubin would go straight to Paris and do all the conventional police work on a trace for Alexina Coburg or Anna Breitmann. I would drive out to Haus Lingfeld to confront Elisabeth.

Zorubin and I stood next to the Avis desk at Munich Airport. "You're sure you don't want me to provide some muscle," his heavy voice rumbled. "You're not going to let her walk over you again."

I smiled. "Thanks pal, for the vote of confidence."

His flight was being called for the second time.

"See you in Paris tomorrow."

He treated me to his savage smile and we parted.

I watched with some affection the powerful shoulders making space for himself through the crowded airport lounge. He had not been in favor of my seeing Elisabeth alone but I had some idea, perhaps hazily derived from my patrician background, that this was one woman I could deal with more effectively by myself.

I hired a car and drove across Munich and along the Perlacher Forest road. Something was happening at Lingfeld. A U.S. Army convoy was parked along both sides of the narrow village street. Further on, as I approached the entrance to Haus Lingfeld, I could see trees demolished and huge Army earth-moving equipment parked around the entrance to the drive. I turned up toward the house. Soldiers were everywhere, unloading prefabricated wooden sections of dark green huts, digging out drainage channels and fixing telephone lines. I stopped the car and walked towards a large open-fronted tent. Inside, bare light bulbs hung above a captain and sergeant bending over plans.

When I explained I knew the owners of the house, the captain offered me coffee. Lingfeld, he said, had been bought by the army for a new armored divisional headquarters. The lay of the land made it perfect for a tank park. The plan was to dig into the limestone hill to provide sheltered parking for the division's tracked vehicles. To hear him talk so casually about ripping out the side of the hill had a strange effect on me. I asked what they planned to do with the house.

"That's coming down," he said. "That old house is no protection against a Russian air-strike," he said. "We're replacing it with a deep bunkered command post."

All this had been arranged long before I last spoke to Elisabeth. She had said nothing to suggest such changes were under way, but why should she? Why should she tell me, of all people, that Lingfeld was to disappear. She certainly was not going to leave me a forwarding address.

I asked the captain if he knew anything about the former owners of the estate, but he was cheerfully ignorant of anything but the task ahead. He walked with me back to my car. "When this complex is completed," he said, "a whole armored division will be able to parade on a reinforced apron there," he gestured with a sweep of his arm across the park. "You ever seen that, sir?" he said. "It's a magnificent sight."

I looked out across the rolling parkland, its slopes patterned with oaks and elms.

It wasn't a bad sight as it stood.

I thanked the captain and got into the car. It was pointing up the driveway so I just drove the fifty yards or so to the crest. What remained of Lingfeld stood starkly before me. I had the impression of peering at a gigantic skull. Contractors had removed the ornate doors and window frames, statuary had been stripped from the terrace, carved stone had been pried out of the facade.

I made no attempt to stop the car. I put my foot down, turned fast across the gravel forecourt and drove through the bustle of military activity back to the Munich road.

I checked with Army Acquisitions in Munich, which had arranged the purchase of Lingfeld, but they had no forwarding address for the Osters. I spent time at the Munich *Daily* but their story covering the sale was no more than a few lines with no mention of where the Osters had moved on to. I passed the best part of another day asking questions in Lingfeld village but nobody evinced much enthusiasm or interest in the Osters. By contrast, memories of the Coburgs and their daughter ran deep.

I went back to my hotel that evening still fired with a determination not to let the trail go cold, but with no real ideas about my next step. At the desk I gave my room number to the brown-uniformed concierge. As he handed me my keys he said: "And there's a message for you, sir. Frau Elisabeth Oster called this afternoon. She asked you to call her back." He handed me a slip of paper with a local number.

Elisabeth Oster answered the phone herself. "I understand you were making inquiries in Lingfeld village this morning," she said.

"I have a whole lot more questions for you," I began.

"Very well." She cut me short. "This time I'll do my best to answer them."

Within less than an hour I was being shown through a luxurious one-story building to a secluded riverside garden.

Elisabeth rose from a chair and put aside her book. There was something less than a smile on her face, but she was not entirely unwelcoming.

As I reached the shaded garden table on the riverbank, she came forward and, to my astonishment, kissed me soberly on both cheeks. By that single action she told me she was up to date on my re-entry into the Coburg family.

For some moments neither of us spoke. Then she gestured for me to sit down. "You know Lingfeld's gone, I suppose."

I nodded, watching her.

"The best thing," she said. "By far."

"Perhaps."

We sat down, facing each other across the white-painted garden table. "I don't know how deep you're in this but we have a lot of talking to do," I said.

Shadows of defeat played about her face. "I'm in very deep, Martin. I went along with the whole deception."

"Why?"

She shrugged. "I had no choice. Or at least I felt I had no choice. I was doing it for Rolf."

I frowned. "And now you're not?"

"No."

A kingfisher swooped down the middle of the shaded river. "Where is Oster?" I said.

"He gave me Haus Lingfeld as a divorce present."

"Generous? Or not?"

"Not. It was the price of my silence."

"About what?"

"About so many things."

"About Alex being alive?"

"That too," she said.

"You know where she is?"

"No." Elisabeth's shoulders dropped. "She came back to the house just after the war. I sent her away."

All the rustling sounds of the riverbank were silenced by the sudden splash of a jumping fish. I could imagine the loathing in my expression, but she was a hard woman, easily capable of rejecting dislike. Again she shrugged. It seemed the closest she was going to come to an apology.

"Why?" I said. "Why, for Christ's sake after all she'd been through!"

"Rolf told me to. He told me that unless I sent Alex away the American Coburgs would withdraw his denazification papers. You see Martin, Rolf had a very . . . uncertain . . . war."

"A lot of people had an uncertain war," I said savagely.

She seemed to ignore my anger. "I don't think of him as a murderer, not even now," she continued. "But he certainly did not deserve the papers Pierre got him."

"How did Alex fit into this?"

"The clearance papers were given to Rolf on condition that we frighten her away. In the atmosphere of 1945, it was not difficult."

"But why?"

"Because of the court action. Pierre's claim to inherit his brother's estate."

I shook my head. "They wanted everything."

"They always did."

"Pierre too?"

"By the end of the war Pierre was a shell of what he had been. An old man long before his time. Celine," she said with undisguised bitterness, "decided everything."

"So Alex was scared off."

"She was officially dead, executed at Waldviertel."

"What did you tell her?"

"I told her what I was told to tell her. That the American Coburgs were determined to acquire Emil's estate. That her life was in danger. She believed it because of what had happened."

I took a deep breath. "You were in Lisbon in 1940. Do you know who denounced Emil and his family?"

"I know," she said quietly, "whose name I gave to Alex. Yours."

"It wasn't me," I said.

She shook her head impatiently. "We all know who did it. Oliver Sutchley denounced Emil and Alex to the Lisbon Gestapo chief. What we don't know is how he got the information to use against them."

Oliver Sutchley. The English officer who had come to the hospital in Germany, claiming he was checking for missing members of the British Army. Checking on what was left of my memory, in fact. Checking for Celine.

"Why should Oliver Sutchley denounce them?"

"Working in Lisbon, he expected a German victory. In the Nazi world a good denunciation bought a lot of credit."

"So we still don't know how he found out that Emil and Alex had helped the Bretagne family escape from Paris?"

"Celine's answer is that you told him."

"Do you believe that?"

"No."

"Who then?"

"I've got no answer for you," she said. "Celine wasn't even in Lisbon. Pierre loved his brother as much as he envied him." She paused. "No, it wasn't Pierre . . ."

I was acutely aware that the finger still pointed at me. "So the answer is to find Oliver Sutchley," I said.

She shook her head. "Sutchley's dead," she said. "He died in London a few weeks ago."

She leaned forward and, removing a beaded muslin from a jug of iced water, filled a glass and pushed it across the table towards me.

"Have you ever seen Alex since the end of the war?" I asked her. "Do you know she's still alive?"

She hesitated for a moment or two, pursing her lips. "Yes," she said, "she's still alive."

"Where. Where is she living?"

"When I last heard," Elisabeth said carefully, "she was a dancer. In a Paris cabaret."

"A dancer?"

Elisabeth shrugged.

"Do you have an address?"

"Of course not. Would she risk the Coburgs knowing her address?"

I lit a cigarette. We sat in silence for a moment, her eyes never leaving my face. Then she leaned forward and pushed the glass she had filled closer to me.

I took it and sipped. There was a little white wine in it, a refreshing iced drink. "Why don't you inform the German courts that the original Military Government order was invalid. That at that time Alex was still alive?"

"It's all past," she said. "It's all a part of my life I want nothing to do with again. I'm like a lot of Germans of my age group. I didn't kill or encourage killing. If I was guilty of anything it was a sort of mindless patriotism. And then the war ended and all the lies began."

"Why don't you inform the German courts that Rolf's clearance was false and that Alex is probably still alive?" I repeated harshly.

She was pale now, even regal in her straight-backed attitude as she sat opposite me. "It's not the first time you've come to me as my conscience."

"When you phoned me at the hotel you knew what I wanted from you?"

She hesitated.

"You knew I was going to ask you to give evidence in court."

"Yes."

"You'd already decided that you would?"

She paused for a long time. "You know Rolf is to marry again?"

"Will you go to court?" I said insistently.

She stood up. "Yes," she said, "yes I will."

"What's changed," I said, "since I last saw you? The divorce?"

"More than that."

I waited.

"I've decided," she said, "that's good enough isn't it?"

"As long as you don't change your mind."

"I won't. I phoned immediately after I called your hotel in Munich. I told him I was intending to give evidence."

"I still don't understand what made you change your mind."

"Because," she said, "after all the torture I went through to save him, he is hoping to marry Celine."

As the afternoon sun fell on the cheap lined paper, I wrote a cable to Celine at a stand-up desk in the Lingfeld post office. It read: ELISABETH DISAPPROVES MARRIAGE PLANS STOP WILL TESTIFY STOP MARTIN

I knew I was on my way.

At six-thirty the next morning the door to my Munich hotel room opened without ceremony and four men entered. One was the hotel manager; the others were undoubtedly policemen.

I became fully conscious, stumbled into my robe and sat down on the edge of the bed while the inspector showed all the documentation. "I have some important questions to ask you," he said. "I'd sooner do this at police headquarters."

I got dressed and was taken to a service elevator at the back of the building, which took us down to a small courtyard where two police cars were waiting.

Ten minutes later I was sitting across the desk from the inspector and one of his assistants in the interview room of the Marienplatz headquarters.

The opening questions were brisk. The inspector clearly knew the answers in advance. But when I told him I was in Munich on personal business I knew I had said the wrong thing.

He made a note on the pad in front of him. "You hired a car at the airport"

"Yes."

"What make?"

"A red Taunus."

The inspector was suddenly silent.

"What's this all about, Inspector?" I asked with the same desperation and the same words I'd seen in a hundred movies.

A few seconds passed. The silence was some sort of signal to his assistant. While the inspector watched my face intently, the assistant said: "Last night Frau Oster was found in the woods by the riverbank. She had been there some time."

I looked at him, then at the inspector, incredulously. "Dead? She's dead?"

"She received multiple fractures of the rib cage," the assistant intoned, "a fractured left ankle, and a greenstick fracture of the left femur."

"But she's alive?"

"A savage attack, Mr. Lingfield," the inspector said. "There were also severe injuries to the head."

I could see he was playing with me, using a degree of professional skill the purpose of which I couldn't understand. "Will you tell me if she's alive or dead for God's sake?"

There was another of those silences while the inspector stared hard at me.

After a three second pause the assistant said: "Dead."

CHAPTER 33

I was held for twelve hours in the Munich police station until one of Elisabeth's maids volunteered the information that she had seen a second car arrive, long after I had left the house in my hired red Taunus. This second car, a black Opel, had been parked off the road near the house. The maid had not seen the driver.

Within a few hours the black Opel was found abandoned in a parking lot on the outskirts of the city. It had been reported stolen on the day Elisabeth was killed. There was no doubt that it was the murder weapon. Its front fender was badly dented and splashed with blood to which adhered tufts of Elisabeth's hair and strands of her clothing.

The Munich police were efficient and gracious about their error. By questioning the staff of my hotel it was quickly established that I was in the center of Munich when Elisabeth was killed. A few minutes later, the recipient of ungrudging apologies, I was walking free across Marienplatz.

I flew back to Paris and found Zorubin at his hotel. He had had good cooperation from the French police but they had produced no lead on Alexina. We took a cup of coffee in the red leather and brass studded hotel dining room and I filled him in about Elisabeth. He nodded several times as I recounted the story but his face remained impassive, unshocked. I realized that as a cop in Boston he must have heard a thousand such stories.

"What did the guys in Munich think for motive?" Zorubin asked, hunched forward, his huge hands clasping his coffee cup.

"Robbery. The murderer lifted a necklace from around her neck."

"You assume that was just a red herring, right? But it might not be. In most police work the obvious answer is the right answer. There's not a·big Agatha Christie element in most killers. But just sometimes . . ."

I ordered croissants and some more coffee.

"The problem is, Captain," Zorubin grimaced, "even if the killing was connected to her promise to take the stand in court against the Coburgs, it could not have been your cable to Celine that led to the murder. You can't arrange a murder contract in a few hours." He gave the waitress his most wolfish smile as she placed a wicker basket of croissants on the table.

"That leaves the finger pointing at Rolf Oster," I said. "He already knew that Elisabeth was willing to testify."

Zorubin grabbed a croissant in his huge hand. "My guess is that Celine Coburg and Oster had already decided Elisabeth's fate. When you told Celine you were coming to Europe," he savaged his croissant, "she saw you as the perfect fall guy, Captain."

We were in an area of Paris I knew nothing about, an area of long cobbled streets lined with garages and decayed factory buildings. Tattered posters covered everything; ancient Defense d'Afficher signs were themselves half plastered over with announcements of Communist Party meetings or fights or vaudeville performances. Sometimes a school or a branch of the Credit Lyonnais stood out from the grayness of the roof tiles and the kaleidoscope of peeling wall posters. In the back of the taxi Zorubin looked out and grunted as we passed the Metro Porte St. Denis. The weather was trying hard to match our bleak surroundings.

We paid the driver of the blue Renault taxi, and got out in front of a warehouse. The sign above the door in front of us read: Musée de la Danse Moderne, Porte St. Denis.

We entered a dark green clapboard building and followed a long corridor until we reached a half-glazed door. The room beyond was cavernous and dark but for a series of crude floor-mounted spotlights that illuminated line upon line of carefully framed posters for the Folies Bergeres, the Moulin Rouge and the Lido.

A human version of the American bald eagle, perched on a high stool, turned, eyes sharp, as we entered the room. She was a woman of incredible age, almost hairless, the flesh of her face so far attenuated that the eyes had become deep-sunken and the nose a thin, hooked beak.

"Bonjour Messieurs," she said in a surprisingly strong voice. "Come in. You're my first visitors today."

I had the strong impression we were her first visitors that week or even that month. An intermittent draft carried pieces of paper trash the length of the room or swirled them around her stool. "I am able," she said, "to guide you through the history of cabaret dancing in France without moving an inch."

Zorubin grinned at her. "They all say no one knew the game like Madame Champellet."

I shifted my feet about uncomfortably. "Were you long in cabaret dancing yourself, Madame?"

She leaned from her stool and selected a switch from the bank of them on her desk. Lights flicked on, illuminating a set of photographs of perhaps the 1880s. Madame de Champellet was unrecognizable as the elfin figure posed in a photographer's glade or dressed as an improbable Roman legionary.

Zorubin turned and walked through a searchlight

towards her. "Now Madame," he said, his arms spread as he approached the old lady, "let us move forward in time."

"Ah, the twenties," she said. "Men love the twenties, the skirts so short, the morals so loose."

"I mean after the war, Madame," Zorubin said firmly. "This war."

"We're looking for someone." I came towards her perch. "We're looking for a particular dancer."

The old woman stopped her restless shuffling.

"A girl named Alexina Coburg," I said. "Or perhaps she called herself Breitmann. A German girl."

Madame de Champellet nodded slowly. Among her myriad creases it was difficult to say, but I think she was frowning. "There was a girl named Breitmann who danced with the Folies Bergères up to a few years ago. She called herself Alex. It's fashionable to have what they think of as an English show-name. Yes, Alex . . ."

Both Zorubin and I stayed silent, afraid to disturb her train of thought. But a great bubble of hope was rising inside me, that this bizarre old lady was about to direct us to Alex.

"The thing I remember so well about Alex," Madame de Champellet said, "was her magnificent legs. Quite the most magnificent long legs in Paris. A strong well-built girl, yes, the physique of a born show dancer. Though she never got beyond the chorus line or at most a feature in a tableau."

"Do you have a picture of her?" Zorubin asked.

The old lady shifted and humped her shoulders without replying. Her lips were moving in an effort to galvanize her formidable memory. "I would propose," she said at last, "the spring lineup at the Folies Bergères in 1946."

She flicked switches and lights flashed around us. One single spot settled midway up the warehouse wall. A slight adjustment brought one girl after another into view. The fifth was inscribed simply, Alex. She wore the plumed headdress and five-inch heels of a show dancer. Her costume was minimal and revealed an extraordinarily beautiful body against the tawdry setting of gold lamé curtains. For a moment I stood feeling strangely breathless in my small moment of triumph. It was really Zorubin's expertise that had got us here and the old lady's phenomenal memory that had produced the picture of Alex. But I felt it my own triumph to have conjured this beautiful girl from the mists of my past.

Madame de Champellet had found Alex but did she know where she now worked?

"Do you know where she went from the Folies Bergères?"

The old lady's head rolled on her scrawny neck. "The dance never saw her again after that year. It's possible she left Paris."

"To join another troupe?"

For a long time she thought, her lips again mumbling through the pages of her memory. "She spoke English well I remember. And of course the studies!"

I looked at her, no longer following her eccentric train of thought.

"She studied a great deal while she was in Paris, Monsieur. She enrolled at the Sorbonne I recall. It was her ambition not to be a dancer forever, you see."

"What did she plan to be, Madame?" I asked her.

"She spoke very little about herself. She was a German aristocrat, I'm sure, but she said little. Whatever she planned for herself I don't know, but she was far too beautiful not to be some exceedingly lucky young man's wife by now."

My heart sank. A married Alexina would be that much more difficult to trace. But I knew that was only part of what I felt. Mostly it was some raw emotion, not a million miles from jealousy. How could I feel like this about a girl whose only existence for me was the accounts of others and the already fading photographs of Madame de Champellet?

It took half a day at the chaotic Sorbonne to discover that Alexina Anna Breitmann had studied International Law and had received her license in 1948. After that no one knew anything about her movements. We talked to girls from the Folies and the Bluebell Girls. Some knew Alex but none had any idea into what walk of life she had disappeared. Yet there was a theme running through the answers we were able to get. As a West Indian girl named Jo Metcalfe, who seemed to have been one of Alex's closest friends, said: "She left in such strange circumstances that it'd be hard to say anything with certainty."

We were sitting at a cafe table below an enormous plane tree outside a former grainstore where the Bluebell Girls practiced their routines.

"What were the strange circumstances, Miss Metcalfe?" Zorubin asked. "You mean she just disappeared?"

The girl nodded her dark curly head.

"When you say she disappeared, do you mean of her own choice?" Zorubin asked carefully.

The girl grinned. "She wasn't white-slaved as the phrase goes, if that's what you mean. Leastways I don't think she was."

"So tell us how it happened," I prompted her.

Jo nodded. "She wanted out. We all knew that anyway. In the nicest possible way Alex was a very superior lady. She wasn't going to dance in a chorus line until replacement day. She wanted to cut completely loose."

"What about a guy?"

I watched Jo nod slowly. "There was a man who used to take her out sometimes. A Frenchman. Much older then her. Polite, rich, lost one arm in the Great War—*that*'s how old he was."

"You remember his name?"

A long pause. "Carsac . . . Barsac . . . sorry . . ."

"A Parisian?"

"He had an apartment here. But it's not where he lived." She was thinking hard. "His real home was on the Riviera. Cannes, Nice, some place where he picked up a nice suntan."

"So if you had money to put on it," I said, "where is she now?"

For some moments Jo considered. The birds burst out of the plane trees and hurled themselves across the square. A demonstration of *infirmières* in white coats trailed through the square carrying bedsheets on poles bearing the inscription: Reinstate Docteur Marly.

Nobody took a lot of notice.

Jo held her face in her long brown hands. "She married him," Jo said. "That's what I'd guess. After that I've just no ideas at all, gentlemen."

We sat in Zorubin's hotel room. Me on the edge of the bed drinking coffee. Zorubin pacing, barefoot, shirt open to a hairy chest, a tumbler full of vodka in his hand.

Elisabeth's death had given me a bad jolt. As Zorubin said, it was time to start looking over my shoulder. I had been in touch with the Munich police again but they had nothing. No leads. They were inclined to think it was exactly what it looked like, a sneak thief in a panic. I knew it wasn't.

I also knew I was being followed.

Between Zorubin's hotel and mine it was an easy five minute stroll along the river. Tonight, as I had walked along the Quai de Montebello, I had become aware of a black Citroen slipping along the curb behind me. When I stopped, the Citroen stopped. When I turned to stare at it the headlights flicked onto full beam. Then as I began to run back down the quay towards it, the Citroen swung away in a tight U-turn across the cobbled street and sped off along the river. It could have been an unmarked police car.

It could have been.

Zorubin's voice brought me back to the hotel room. "We're nearly up with her." His vocal chords seemed to throw the words at the flimsy bedroom walls. "My guess is she took the old guy's offer and moved down south. It would account for the absence of farewells or forwarding addresses."

"Maybe," I conceded reluctantly.

He nodded vigorously. "She was ashamed to tell the girls. She'd come on strong as someone who didn't sing for her supper. And now she's singing for a life-long meal ticket."

"You really see it that way, Vik?"

He looked at me with that hard, relentless stare. "Face it, Captain," he said. "It fits."

Perhaps I just didn't want to hear it, but my gut feeling was against Alex getting married, against the idea of her singing for her supper. "You take the South of France, Vik," I said. "I'm going to hit the Sorbonne again. Some fellow student must know what happened to her."

He came down to the lobby with me—shoes, no socks, wide open shirt, glass of vodka. Madame, behind the brass and mahogany counter, sniffed disapproval.

Zorubin stopped one step above me and silenced the Madame with one of his savagely suggestive grins.

"Best of luck in the south," I said. Carsac . . . Barsac . . . Nice, Cannes . . . it didn't seem a lot to go on.

It must have been obvious, from my face, what I was thinking.

He turned his ferocious grin on me and put his arm around my shoulder. "We're on the road, Captain," he rumbled into my ear. "Take my word for it."

CHAPTER 34

Leaving Zorubin's hotel I looked quickly right and left. There was no sign of the Citroen. I walked quickly down the street. Across the Seine, Notre-Dame rose above the thin river mist. Lights sparkled behind stained glass. I fancied I heard organ music and voices singing.

The Citroen of course could have been nothing. A curb crawler looking for a streetwalker. A family admiring, as I was, the masterpiece in stone across the river.

But I still looked around me. Cars passed; couples strolled along the embankment; two gendarmes examined the silk women's underwear in Lutèce. Normal.

I turned onto the Boulevard St. Michel, walked quickly through the drifting crowds, and turned into the sidestreets between there and the Rue de Seine.

I had been walking fast. Now I slowed down, caught my breath and took out a cigarette. I was outside my hotel, a small Paris hotel, with pre-war glass globes at either side of the entrance. A gust from the river took the flame off the top of my lighter. I watched, over the flame, the long black nose of a Citroen edging forward from behind a domed lottery kiosk.

I walked quickly up the steps of the hotel between the lighted globes. Pushing open the door I stepped inside.

The Citroen was parked across the road, that much I could see from the window opposite the lobby bar. I peered hard at the figure at the wheel but the street lights were too dim to make out more than a shape. Then the driver's door opened. One, two, three, four pug-nosed King Charles spaniels came tumbling out followed by an old lady, unsteady on her feet.

I went over to the bar, pulled up a stool and ordered a pastis. While the barman was pouring, the patron came across waving a pale yellow envelope. "A cable for you, Monsieur. Télégramme Express."

I took the yellow envelope and tore it open. The cable read: ARRIVED PARIS RITZ STOP URGENT WE MEET STOP CELINE.

I could not restrain my delight. I laughed out loud, surprising the barman and the patron. Celine was in Paris. Drawn there by my cables. By the fear of what I might discover next.

I came through the revolving door on the Vendôme side of the Ritz. Once settled at a table in the panelled Little Bar I ordered a Scotch and asked for Miss Celine Coburg to be given a message that her brother was waiting for her.

She came down five minutes later wearing an ice blue dress under a pale mink coat draping her shoulders. Several customers turned on their bar stools to watch her as she sat on the deep sofa next to me and ordered a Vichy water from the waiter who was almost immediately by her side.

For a moment we sat in silence.

"So what are you doing in Paris?" I said, unable to suppress my sense of triumph.

"I've a meeting with the Regents of the Bank of France," she said casually.

"When was that arranged?"

She smiled grimly. "When I was on the plane," she said. "Okay, I'm here to see you. Cards on the table."

The waiter delivered the Vichy water and fussed about with canapés and ashtrays before withdrawing.

"Cards on the table," I reminded her.

She nodded, playing with her hotel key marked President Wilson Suite. After a long pause she said: "So you believe that Alex is still alive."

"*I* know it," I said. "*You* know it."

She picked up her glass and sipped at the Vichy water.

"You know it," I said, "because you bribed Elisabeth to warn Alex off when she came back to Lingfeld from imprisonment at the end of the war."

"That's what Elisabeth says."

"Said."

Either she was a great actress or she really didn't understand. "That's what Elisabeth said when you saw her in Germany?"

"That's what Elisabeth said just before she was killed."

Her face was without expression. She needed long years of training for a performance like this—whether or not she already knew Elisabeth was dead.

"She was killed," I said, "the evening after she promised to testify against you. Against the theft of Emil's estate."

She smiled brilliantly, "Overdose?" she said. "Morphine was her solitary pleasure I understand. What did the police have to say?"

I looked away from her.

"Do you know where Alex is?" she asked after a long silence.

"I will in a day or two," I said.

"And what then? Why should she talk to you after what you've done to her?"

"Don't think I'm going to take your word for that."

She looked at me somberly, a look I was to remember afterwards, for her a disconcertingly candid look. "You were a young arrogant patrician," she said. "Crossed in love and bitterly angry at what Emil planned to do to Pierre's reputation. You denounced them Martin. Not Pierre or me. You." She paused. "I asked you what will happen when you find Alex."

"Then you and the Coburg Banknote Corporation will be taken to court for theft of the estate of the Imprimerie Coburg."

"Why should anyone want to steal a couple of old, deserted factories? One of them a burnt-out wreck."

"Why should anybody want to steal the Janus?" I said.

Again she paused, nodding unhurriedly. "I see you've done your homework."

"I have. I know how much you need that press. For the new U.S. Government scrip contract, for half a dozen new currencies up for bids in Europe. And I know about brilliant new presses being developed that will leave Coburg Banknote a company without a contract to its name."

I think she flinched. I like to think so. "Does Alex know where the Janus is?"

"She must," I said. "Emil must have hidden it immediately before his arrest. It follows."

She inclined her head. "Whoever finds it, whatever their legal claim, could sell it on the black market. Any of the toffee nosed banknote printers in the world would snap it up. Most of them without questions."

"That would include you."

"I guess," she said slowly, "the time has come for you and me to make a deal."

"A deal?"

For a moment I thought my mind was playing tricks. I saw her lips pout, her legs swing out and back. All those tiny devices she must have used a hundred times throughout her career. "You're crazy," I said. "I'm your brother."

I watched the lift of the eyebrow, the sulky, disappointed line of the mouth. "We always meant a great deal to each other, you and me."

"I don't believe it."

"We're Coburgs. We don't have to play by other people's rules."

"You don't have to play by other people's rules. You and Pierre and even Rose."

"And your father," she said. "Don't forget him."

A passing hotel guest let his eyes linger for a moment on Celine.

"It's the only way to save Coburg Banknote." She was brisk now. "Fifty-fifty. We run the company together, you and me."

I was shaking my head.

"You find Alex," she leaned forward, the mouth a tense curved line. "You find Alex and you buy the Janus patents from her."

"You believe you can pull me in," I said. "As you did Pierre?"

"I believe what I'm offering you is what you want."

"Jesus Christ."

"Do you understand what the Janus is worth?" she said.

"Probably not."

"Then let me tell you. The possessor of that machine," she gave the word a clear sensual connotation, "commands a fortune. Almost any banknote printing organization in the world would want to bid for it."

"So Alex is going to be a rich young woman."

Her eyes narrowed. "Martin, if that machine falls into other hands, if Coburg Banknote is excluded from its use, it would be a catastrophe."

"Not for me."

I could almost see her swallow hard. She drove the hardness from her face. "We're on the same side, you and me. We must work closely together."

The wave of revulsion that passed over me deprived me of speech. I stared at her.

Perhaps she thought it was in fascination. She put her hand on mine. "It's the only way now," she said softly. "The only way to save the company."

A great wave of anger rose in me. "Don't you know that *I* don't give a damn for the company? Don't you know that even if it were mine I'd get rid of every goddam dirty share of it as quick as I could?"

Her eyes were shining. The calm was shattered. Tears, rage, disbelief, everything passed in front of me. She was gripping my hand, kneading it, like a rejected lover. "Martin," she pleaded, "Martin, don't say things like that. A business deal. A simple business deal. You and me against Alexina."

I pulled my hand away and stood up. "You're mad, Celine," I said.

She stood up beside me, a tall striking young woman.

"You're not clinically insane. You're not certifiably mad. But when the courts strip you of all the trappings of power, when you're reduced to a prison number, not even a name, then I don't think your mind will be able to take it. No deals," I said. And turned and walked through the bar toward the Vendôme exit.

I could feel the blood coursing, the pulse at the base of my neck throbbing. I was experiencing a form of elation I could not remember before.

Celine was cracking. Her fear of my finding Alex was all I'd hoped it would be. Then my spirit dropped again as I remembered her thin-lipped insistence that it had been me who had denounced Emil's family. There are times, even listening to a compulsive liar, when you believe. I'm not sure how close I was to being convinced it was me, but however much I wrestled with the idea I found it impossible to throw it off. Of course Celine would deny she had done it, or Pierre had done it. Until I could shake myself free it was the one single hold she had over me.

And yet, still, something deep in my instinct said she was not lying. At this one single moment she was telling the truth as she believed it to be.

I caught a cab outside the Ritz and rode across the river to my side of town. At Rue Jacob I paid him off and took a beer standing up against the bar at a small cafe.

It was late. I finished my beer after midnight and walked on down the Rue Jacob. It was a misty night with very little traffic about. Ahead I could see the two hotel globes glowing creamily.

In front of me where a building jutted out I could see my shadow outlined against the wall. I saw, with a kid's delight, my shape double and treble until I was thirty feet tall.

I swung around in horror. The headlights of a black Citroen were needling towards me. There was no old lady and her pug-nosed dogs in this one. Coming from directly behind up on the broad sidewalk, the Citroen gave me no chance of jumping clear.

There was no calculation in what I did. One step sideways and the rounded wing thwacked against my thigh.

I span around and slumped back against a doorway to a shuttered shop. The Citroen had turned; the headlights were again drilling into me.

As the car leapt forward, I ran. Behind me the tires screeched. The engine roared. Shadows of my fleeing self were thrown across the facades of the old houses.

I flung myself sideways into an alley, slid to my knees, scrambled up and ran again. Wildly, down the dark cobbled alley.

One moment I could see almost nothing, just the shadowed outline of dustbins, the shuttered windows, the deep doorways. Then a flare of white light engulfed me.

And the Citroen came screeching down the alley, overturning dustbins, so close I could almost *feel* it.

I had time to see that, ahead, the alley ran into a small square. I had time to see low old timber warehouses and the sharp detail of a rustling tin Michelin advertisement.

Then the car hit me. I went up, my raincoat billowing, was hit again by the top of the windshield and rolled over and down across the covered spare wheel.

I lay dazed in darkness.

And in silence. There was no sound of the Citroen's engine.

I tried to open my eyes but blood was running copiously across my eyebrows. The Citroen was standing in the square in front of one of the warehouses. The driver's door was opening.

I fought to blink the blood out of my eyes. There were footsteps approaching. A woman's shape, tall as Celine, came across the cobblestones towards me. I made the effort of a drowning man. I mobilized every single muscle in my body. I pressed down with my hands and feet and with a hoarse gasp I threw myself up and forward.

The impact bowled her over. I could hear her scream of pain and shock as I stumbled to my feet.

She was already up running for the car. My legs carried me a step or two, but my weight seemed to haul me backwards.

The Citroen's engines roared. The headlights flared in my face. This time I fell. As I hit the ground I saw, at eye level, the wheels hiss past me.

I lifted my head. The black car swerved, hit one side wall of the alley, ripped off a door panel as it careened on, bounced from one side to the other trailing sparks and pieces of torn metal. When it crashed it seemed to climb a door frame, the front wheels six feet off the ground.

I dragged myself up. In the silence I could hear something dribbling. I walked forward. Gasoline was bubbling from the gas cap. Then a sheet of flame rose with a dull roar.

I ran forward. The driver's door had burst open.

The fire and fume obscured everything but a shape. I gripped a wrist and an ankle and pulled. The shape tumbled over me. Flames jetted from burning wheels. I leaned down and pulled with my last vestiges of strength. When she was safe from the fire I collapsed next to her.

Smoke-smudged and distressed by pain as her face may have been, I had no difficulty in seeing it was not Celine. No difficulty at all in recognizing it from the photograph as Alexina Coburg.

CHAPTER 35

~ ~ ~

What counted first of all with her was that I had thought it was Celine.

She told me I had shouted Celine's name as I hauled myself off the cobblestones. And again at some point as she ran for the car.

We sat in my hotel room with cups of hot coffee, she leaning forward from the single armchair, me on the edge of the bed. The fog between us was thicker than anything that could have come off the river at the bottom of the street. It was a fog of fear, of suspicion and doubt.

She had washed the streaks of oil from her face and pulled back her hair into a chignon. In a dark blue sweater and blue skirt she looked wracked with indecision, deeply unhappy and totally desirable.

I poured brandy into her coffee. We had talked all night. Outside, the rising sun showed as a lemon yellow line against the slate roofs of Paris.

She was exhausted. "I'm full of hate," she said. "Only a saint could survive a place like Waldviertel without hate and revenge as consolations. When Hans Emden told me you were in Paris, that you were looking for me, I was terrified. But I was glad too."

"But you thought I was dead. Why were you glad to discover I was alive?"

She stood up and walked towards the window, her arms folded, her face turned away.

"Why glad?" I repeated.

"Because ever since I left the camp I have known

I need revenge. For Emil and Dorotta and all those others who were betrayed during the nightmare."

She turned to face me. "You can't possibly understand."

"Tell me."

"In a place like that," she said, "you either submit or you burn with hatred. It's the only emotion that can overcome the heart-stopping fear of what each day will bring."

I got up and poured her fresh coffee. "Your hatred was directed at me."

"At all the American Coburgs. I knew it was one of them. Perhaps Pierre, perhaps Rose and Celine. Perhaps even you."

"And when you were liberated?"

"Hans Emden and I walked to Munich. I remember I was sad because I could never feel for him what he felt for me. In the ruins of Munich we divided our remaining food. He set off for Hamburg to see if his mother had survived."

"And you headed for Lingfeld."

"Of course. It was a few days after the war ended. I was filthy, still in striped prison rags. I'd taken boots from the corpse of a German soldier and in those I stumbled across the woods."

"I know what Elisabeth told you."

"She gave me money, some jewelry to sell, and she told me to disappear forever. She told me that the Coburgs would stop at nothing now."

"And she told you it was me who betrayed you to the Gestapo."

She nodded slowly. "But she also told me you were dead. With one lie she deprived me of the last thing I had, a focus for my hatred."

"So when Hans told you I was still alive you were glad . . ."

She shuddered. "I was afraid too, of course. But

when you came looking for me at the bookstore, I knew I *had* to do something."

"You've got to believe I meant you no harm, Alex."

She paused, letting her head drop. "You pulled me out of a burning car," she said slowly. "The truth is that one part of me believes you. But the other part needs my hate."

"You've got to know," I repeated, "that when I came to the bookstore I meant you no harm." I took a deep breath. I knew I had to put it into words, almost as much for myself as for her. "I can't say that it *wasn't* me who denounced you. I just don't know. I can only say that now I mean you no harm."

"You mean it might have been Martin Coburg. But it wasn't Daniel Lingfeld." She shook her head. "That's too easy," she said. "That's far, far too easy." She walked back to the window, holding her coffee cup, watching the red rim of the rising sun.

I stood behind her. Very carefully I reached up and put my arm around her shoulder. For a minute or two we stood there. She was biting her lower lip. Tears were running down her face. "Oh God, my God . . ." she whispered into the dawn light.

I left for London that same morning soon after I had put her into a taxi.

She was exhausted, somewhere suspended between belief and disbelief. We both needed time.

I also needed information. Someone in London must have talked, boasted, got drunk with Oliver Sutchley. Sometime, awash with pink gins, he must have said something about his relationship with the Coburgs.

By midday I was being served lunch on the Golden Arrow from Paris Gare St. Lazare to Victoria Station, London. I had armed myself with copies of the *Herald*

Tribune, the *London Financial Times* and Time Magazine.

Business pages were all full of the new U. S. scrip contract, which the Department of the Army was just about to award to Coburg Banknote, another stop along the way of what seemed to be Celine's unimpeded progress. She was already a favorite subject with editors, the only corporation president you could photograph who had the glamour of a movie star.

More than that, Coburg Banknote had greatly changed under her presidency. It was now a public company and had expanded its Kansas City plant to make it capable of accepting the biggest currency contracts. The company's contacts with Washington were recognized as exceptionally tight during the post-war Democratic administration of Harry Truman. Indeed, Celine and her executive vice-president, Merril Soames, had, it seemed, sloughed off the slightly raffish impression of Coburg Banknote that had derived from Pierre's sticky fingered delving in the China trade. This week, my twin sister, the president of Coburg Banknote Corporation, smiled confidently from the front cover of Time Magazine.

More confidently than she had in the Paris Ritz.

It was seven in the evening before I got to London. I checked in at the Regent Palace Hotel, dropped my bag in my room and took a taxi to Chelsea Barracks, the headquarters of His Majesty's Brigade of Guards.

I had some initial difficulty with the guard commander, a tall, awesomely military Irish Guardsman, but within half an hour I had talked myself into the office of the adjutant. He was an equally tall young man who looked and sounded as if he had just stepped out of the pages of P. G. Wodehouse but I saw that he wore an impressive row of medals on his chest and three discreet red wound stripes on his service dress cuff. He was, himself, he explained, a Coldstreamer.

I must have raised my eyebrows.

"We're Irish Guards, Scots Guards, Welsh Guards, Grenadier Guards and Coldstream Guards here," he explained. "A headquarters unit for the whole Brigade of Guards."

"So you would not yourself have known Sutchley," I said. "He was Grenadier Guards."

"He was," the adjutant said, pouring me a whiskey and adding water. "But he was known all right. Not liked, but known. Owed you money, you said?"

I nodded. "Two thousand pounds. Dates from his days in Portugal."

"The horses, I expect," the adjutant said. "Well, I can't make any promises, old chap," he said carefully, "but we do carry a small fund for this sort of eventuality. We'd need an I.O.U. of course."

"A fund," I said, puzzled.

"We don't like Guardsmen to have outstanding debts. Even a bounder like Oliver Sutchley."

I explained quickly that I was not trying to get an old debt repaid by the fund. Perhaps his family would honor the obligation, since Sutchley was dead.

"Pushing up the daisies," the young officer agreed nonchalantly. "Drunk in Soho last month. His usual haunt. Tottered out of a pub and collapsed." He smiled. "Not a pretty tale."

"No," I conceded.

"Appalling chap."

I nodded. "His wife lives in London?"

"Yes. Pleasant woman. Good family too. But all downhill once she met Sutchley. He introduced her to Soho."

"She spends a lot of time there?"

"She's one of the Soho crowd. Boozing, betting, banging each other and pretending to be artists. I suppose one or two of them may be, God knows. But if you want to talk to her, that's where you'll find her."

I finished my whiskey and thanked him for his help. We walked out across the wide parade square where long columns of young men in khaki were being drilled by a ferocious sergeant-major. "You'll do your best, old boy," the adjutant said, "if there is any unfortunate publicity, to keep the name of the Brigade out of it."

I promised. At the gate the Irish guard commander stamped to attention and saluted me as I passed.

It was a twenty minute walk to Soho. Perhaps I had been here before. But this visit offered no familiar feeling. The narrow courts and alleys were paraded by frowzy streetwalkers who seemed to believe it was enough to be a woman to be desirable. The pubs were better. I moved from one to another, drinking a half pint of bitter beer and asking the barmen if any of them had known someone named Oliver Sutchley. Or knew his wife. By my fourth or fifth pub I had established that, though Vera Sutchley was known in most of the pubs in Soho, she was clearly no better known for paying her debts than her husband had been.

The Fitzroy Tavern was a Victorian pub full of mature mahogany and decorative cut glass. It was also full of BBC radio producers and young sailors short of money at the end of their leave.

I eased my way up to the bar. "Tyrone Power," someone murmured in my ear. "Have you ever had your portrait painted?" whispered another.

At the counter the barman was middle-aged, Irish and definitely heterosexual. "Yes sir," he said as if he'd spent his youth in the Irish Guards.

I ordered a large Glenmorangie and stood savoring its unique smokey taste until my whole tongue was alive with the flavor. Eyes flickered towards me and passed on. I stood around for a couple of minutes watching the drift of men through the bar. I doubt if there were three women in the whole pub.

The barman came down the bar. "It's a quiet night tonight, sir," he said. "Most Saturdays, it's more like something out of Dante's Inferno."

I asked him if he wanted a drink.

The barman relaxed, one hand on the bar, as he surveyed the clientele. "Thank you, sir. I'll have a beer."

"You ever get a woman named Vera Sutchley in here?" I asked.

The barman nodded. "The red-head," the Irishman said. "Keep your hands on your wallet. She's over there in the corner."

I paid for the barman's beer and turned towards the corner he had indicated. A tall red-haired woman of about forty stood with two men in tweed jackets. She was handsome in a drink-worn, slightly raddled way. Her clothes were, I guessed, originally expensive, but she managed to convey that faintly down-at-heel look of someone teetering on the brink of alcoholism.

For a few moments I watched her. She talked with some animation, waving a gin and tonic in her hand. Concentrating, I could hear a few phrases in her beautiful bell-like voice. "The four-thirty at Ascot . . . ran like a wet dream . . . last but one . . ."

"Did your husband ever talk to you about the time he spent in Portugal?" I asked her when, ten minutes later, we were settled in the corner of a very different pub on the edge of Mayfair.

"You're a rather lovely young man," Vera was saying, "but I'd like to know where all this is leading."

"There are some things in his life," I said, "that I need to know more about. Have you ever heard of the Coburgs?"

"I've heard of them, yes."

I hesitated, wondering if it would be premature to give out more information. "I'm Martin Coburg," I said. "Does that mean anything to you?"

There was no coquetry now. "Martin Coburg, the memory man."

"That's what your husband called me?"

She nodded. "So you're one, too?" she said. "A Coburg?"

"You don't like them, I see."

"I've no reason to," she said. "They stopped Oliver's pension when he died."

"He was receiving a pension from Coburg Banknote?"

"Yes."

I took a second or two to absorb that. A pension. For keeping quiet? "I'll give you two hundred fifty dollars," I said.

She inclined her head.

"I want to know the lot," I said. "Everything. Especially about his time in Lisbon."

"You know he was actually in touch with the Germans?"

"In Lisbon?"

She nodded. "Early on in the war when he still thought they were going to wipe the floor with us."

I was throbbing with excitement. "Did he ever tell you about 1940 when the German Coburgs were arrested?"

She raised her eyebrows. It wasn't a question. She knew.

"He had something to do with it," I insisted.

"A mailman, he said he was. Okay. He delivered the bomb. He told the Gestapo that the German Coburgs had treasonably informed Pierre Coburg about the counterfeit twenty million dollars."

I had to take it slowly. "You mean the German Coburgs were not denounced for helping Jewish families escape to Spain?"

"Oliver wasn't a petty traitor," she said, her lips curling. "If Oliver decided to rat on his friends, he'd rat big."

There was a long, long pause. Oliver Sutchley could not possibly have known about the twenty million dollar counterfeits unless either Pierre or I had told him.

"Sutchley delivered the bomb, you said. Who put the bomb in his hand?" I asked finally.

"The memory man," she said flippantly. "You did, of course."

My heart jumped in my chest.

She laughed. "Come back to my place and I'll tell you how it happened."

We went straight back to her flat in Maida Vale, a big, rambling, shabby sort of place. The dishes were still in the sink, underwear and bras hung on a string across the bath.

"Gin and tonic?" she said.

"Why not? So what are you going to tell me?"

She smiled, lit the gas fire and went over to pour the drinks. "You think I got you up here for my own low motives?"

I was silent. Too much misery flooded through me to care. I took the wad of dollars from my inside pocket. The bills were secured by a band of broad blue paper tape. I wasn't sure her information had been worth it but I dropped the thin pack on the table.

"Wait a minute," she said. She went into the bedroom. Through the door I saw her plucking at the bedsheets, straightening them.

I called through. "Vera," I said. "I'm going."

She came back and stood in the doorway. "He really did believe in the German cause," she said.

"You mean the Nazi cause."

"Of course, but Oliver was not a clever man. Not a thinker."

I stayed silent.

She began to wander round the room touching small objects, vases, picture frames, cigarette packets. "He was devastated by the knowledge that he was mediocre. His family had been explorers and writers and sea captains for five hundred years. But poor Oliver was simply mediocre."

"What was his job in Portugal?" I gave her a cigarette and lit it.

"Emil Coburg had tipped the FBI that he had been ordered to work on counterfeit twenty-dollar bills intended to buy American politicians. Oliver was responsible for routing the bills through Lisbon. He did it. But it seems he also wanted to get in well with the people he thought were to be our new masters. He passed over the information about Emil Coburg's tip to the local Gestapo."

I was taking deep breaths. "You mean Sutchley did this on his own? You mean none of the American Coburgs denounced Emil and his family."

She smiled. "No. But they were prepared to pay Oliver a pension to make sure he would swear you did it."

Even in my self-obsessed relief I could see the pain she had suffered. "When did you find out?" I said. "When did you discover what he'd done?"

She laughed, a tight, bitter movement of the garish lips. "The day after he died," she said. "Widow's unhappy task, you know. Sorting through the papers. Looking for cash to buy a bottle of gin, actually." Her face hardened. "When I found out, I sent the bastard off for a pauper's funeral."

I sat down on the sofa. She gave me another drink. "Have you proof, Vera? Evidence of all this?"

She went across to a bureau, an eighteenth-century piece of mahogany, and began opening and closing drawers.

"Got it."

She was holding an envelope in her hand, a long gray official-looking piece of stationery.

"I think you should have this." She handed me the gray envelope.

I pulled the letter from the envelope. It was from the City and Provincial Bank. It assigned a number to a safety deposit box Oliver Sutchley had left in their care.

"The relict," she said, "of Oliver Warburton Sutchley. You'd better have it. I checked for money and handed it back to the bank. Family photographs of better days. But there are a few papers. All the evidence you need."

It was Saturday evening. Nothing could be learned from a British bank under any circumstances on Sunday and I wanted to be back in Paris as soon as possible. "Will you get the box for me on Monday?" I asked her.

"Okay. And then what?"

"Will you send it to the Hotel Clemenceau, Paris?"

"Okay."

She stood looking at me, then took a pen from her purse and scribbled on a copy of *The Sporting Life* the address I had just given her. "I've got an old friend who works for Air France," she said. "If you want I could get it to you before Monday evening."

"I'm counting on it." I leaned forward and kissed her on the cheek.

"That's all?" she said.

"That's all, Vera."

"Change your mind?" She looked towards the bedroom.

"I guess not," I said.

"A screw to remember?"

I shook my head.

She smiled. "I always thought the moment Oliver was gone from my life I'd get lucky."

I was standing at the door. "You have," I pointed to the two hundred fifty dollars.

"Who'd want to remember that?" She crossed to the door and opened it. "Goodnight gorgeous," she said in her beautiful voice. "Go now before I rip your fly."

*   *   *

I took the night boat-train from Victoria Station back to Paris. I suppose I had never felt like this. Amid the shouting of railwaymen and clanking of steel wheels, the train was run onto the ferry at Dover. I slept fitfully, then lay in my bunk staring up at the lights flickering on the ceiling. All the dreams and images of guilt were only slowly leaking away. I had to force my mind to release me, force my mind to accept that I was not guilty.

I woke sweating in the confined compartment. We were stationary at a French station. A hanging clock face was set at three in the morning. The hour of the wolf, Vik Zorubin told me the peasants of Waldviertel say. The hour when most people die.

The train pulled forward, steel buffers clanked on steel buffers, steel wheels shrieked on steel rails. Men shouted. A pale blue light illuminated a rail sign reading Rouen—St. Jean. I turned in my narrow bunk. I dreamt of columns of men and women shuffling past me, their heads bowed, the dawn mists rising like sulphur fumes around their feet. So many, a voice was chanting, I had not known death had undone so many.

I awoke finally as the train pulled slowly through the Paris suburbs. The night had purged me, cleansed my mind forever of the guilt that had beset me ever since that moment I woke in the army hospital outside Munich. As little as I knew about the way the mind works I felt that this one last night of perturbation was necessary. I was free; a new life was beginning.

After our night-long talk Alexina had left me without giving her address. Some part of her fears about me had not been stilled. When I had asked her how I could contact her she had told me to go to Hans Emden's shop.

I was on the doorstep as soon as Hans opened the door.

He didn't seem any more pleased to see me.

"Alex told me you would put us in touch."

He walked back to the counter and turned to face me. "That depends on what you've got to tell her."

"You know I've been to London."

He nodded, his dark eyes never leaving my face.

"Tell Alex to call this number." I passed over Vera Sutchley's phone number across the counter. "She can ask Mrs. Sutchley any questions she wants."

He glanced down at the piece of paper, then up at me. "All right," he said reluctantly, "wait at the cafe across the street."

Half an hour later I paid off my cab and entered the glass and concrete building through the wide swinging doors. For a moment I stood among the bustle of young German students and middle-aged businessmen. I found an official who checked my name with someone on the phone and directed me up a wide winding staircase and left into a waiting room. I thanked him and went up to the gallery above. A notice read: Visas for the Federal Republic. I entered the empty waiting room slightly mystified. It was large, with ornate cornices and two long windows looking down on the square below. A double door, half open, led into another room from where I could hear a typewriter clacking busily. I took a seat on a modern Danish teak sofa. In front of me travel magazines were piled on a coffee table.

Through the partly open double doors I could see into the inner office. A middle-aged secretary walked past the opening. I heard her knock on an inner door and say: "Mr. Daniel Lingfield is in the waiting room." And Alex's voice said formally: "Thank you, I'll see him now."

The door opened. She looked totally different from the last time I saw her. Instead of the pale washed face and torn sweater I was looking at a young woman in a dark well-cut coat and skirt, her tawny blonde hair held back loosely, a pair of heavy black-rimmed spectacles in her hand.

She came forward. "I'd prepared all the speeches," she said. "All the apologies. Now they've flown from my head . . ."

"You phoned Vera Sutchley?"

"As soon as Hans gave me your message."

She paused, looking at me across a distance of six feet. "Can we ever recover from the past?" she said.

CHAPTER 36

～ ～ ～

We moved from place to place like desperate nomads, talking all day. I needed to absorb the detail of her life to know my own.

On a bench in the Jardin des Invalides we held hands while she talked shudderingly of Waldviertel.

It was a short journey in miles, she said, but it had taken over fifteen hours. With sixty-five people packed into each cattle car the day's heat was unbearable. No water had been provided, no food. The prisoners crowded into this fetid hell knew only that they were traveling east but the constant stops, the rattling progress for fifteen minutes before the long train again hissed to a halt, confused even those who were trying to guess their destination.

In cattle car number 72, Alex and her father had stood pressed tightly together. They had seen Dorotta driven into another cattle car. By nightfall on the next day Alex was convinced that the woman pressing against her back was dead. She had tried to speak to her, clearing her throat of dust and the acrid smell of their slatted prison, but the woman no longer even moaned. Alex knew, too, that a child and an old man had been trampled underfoot as they were all driven relentlessly onto the train. Somehow the feet of these crushed, terrified people had worked the two corpses into a corner. But that had been in the early hours of the journey, before the prisoners needed every ounce of strength to keep themselves alive.

By the following night most of the prisoners were

locked in some private delirium. Some women, less tall than Alex, were already dead. Nobody talked any longer. Some muttered in their standing sleep, some screamed.

With the first thin light of dawn, Alex and Emil had turned their heads towards the barbwired gap above the low door. Gradually, they were able to make out the shape of trees, then of small farm buildings. Then suddenly Alex heard a strange gurgle in her father's throat. She remembered clearly throwing her weight backwards against the dead woman behind her so that she could half turn to face Emil.

He was laughing!

"Oh, my darling Alexina," he said. "It's that meaningless irony of the gods. They're taking us back home."

After a few more minutes the train had rattled and clanked off the main line onto a single track spur through the forest. There was still no edge of sun in the eastern sky. A paleness streaked with gray gave enough light for Alex to see that they were pulling up at a long platform whose surface was roughly constructed of logs. Boarded walkways for the gray, menacing figures of the guards ran along the length of the high barbed wire that edged the far side of the platform. Between white Death's Head SS symbols was written in huge Gothic letters the name, *Waldviertel*.

An order had been shouted, a single incomprehensible word, and the gray figures seemed to hurl themselves at the cattle car, dragging back bolts, thundering on the sides with the base of their whips, shrieking at the prisoners, dragging them from the cattle cars.

Men and women who were barely strong enough to move stumbled down onto the rough surface of the platform, legs jerking like marionettes before they fell to their knees and were whipped crawling forward to join the line already stretching the length of the train.

It seemed to Alex to be a deliberate recreation of the entry to Hell. Prisoners jostled and pushed as they flinched away from the guards' whips, screams of fear and anguish filled the woods. The dead and the dying were already being dragged from the train. Over two thousand people cowered in terror as a perfect dawn broke across the eastern hills.

Among the huge snaking line of people she tried desperately to cling to Emil. But a whip fell indiscriminately across her back and, as she flinched away, fell, crawled and stumbled up, she looked around to see his gray head turning, searching for her until he too was lost in the great dark mass.

It was shortly after they had been marched to the huge sandy Appel Square that she saw Hans. He came out of one of the low wooden administrative buildings that surrounded the square. He was wearing a prisoner's striped jacket but carrying a whip under his arm. He was walking slowly, reading from a sheet of paper.

Hans Emden was greatly changed since Alex had last seen him as he had turned to make his way to the Swiss border. His face was gray and his eyes were sunken. His head was shaved. His movements were sharp and nervous. He had that thin vicious quality of stamped tin.

"The prisoners with the whips are kapos," somebody had whispered. "Be careful, they can be worse than the guards. Pass it on."

Alex had passed the information on, her eyes never leaving Hans Emden's face as he walked towards the great dark mass of people on the Appel Square.

The kapos screamed and kicked and whipped them into long lines. Hans Emden, she saw with dismay, was as harsh as any, acting under the negligent eyes of the dozen SS officers in charge.

She knew he had seen her. She knew that as he shouted and pushed the prisoners into line he was aware that he was moving toward her. She saw, too, that he did much more screaming and pointing than actual beating. She had, for a second, a small glimmer of hope.

He was standing before her, looking down the long line of prisoners. His hand fumbled for her. "Anna Breitmann," he said as he pushed papers into her hand. He bawled for them to toe the white marks, and ran forward. Then, still shouting orders, he walked backwards down the line. "Give me your transportation papers," he said from the side of his mouth.

She fumbled in her coat, found the papers and pressed them into his hands. The line was forming up now, raggedly at first, men and women who had never been soldiers learning to dress ranks in seconds rather than days.

"You're on the execution list for tonight," Hans had spoken like a stage ventriloquist, staring along the line. "Your name is now Breitmann. You'll be all right."

A group of SS officers had assembled at the far end of the front line. Hans ran toward them, stopped and bowed his head. Alex watched as the officers moved down the line. Even today, she said, she could remember the names of those prisoners called just in front of her: "Altmann, Kurt . . . Siedman, Sophia . . ." the SS officer had droned. With each name, Hans had stepped forward to present papers. "Greim, Christina . . ."

"Dead on arrival," Hans said as he presented the woman's papers. She was the next in line now. Her mind was blank with terror.

"739182," the officer said.

Hans stepped forward. "Coburg, Alexina. Dead on arrival Herr Leutnant." He handed over a fold of papers.

"Breitmann, Anna," the officer yawned.

"Present, Herr Leutnant," Alex had said.

The officer yawned again and passed on down the line. For a second only, Alexina's eyes had met the dark, blank eyes of Hans.

We got up and walked through pigeons pecking at the dusty gravel, then sat again at another bench as if movement was necessary to match or quell the turmoils of memory.

"After the war," Alex said, "I kept sane. God knows how. The only life I knew was as a camp inmate. Then I found I could make a living as a dancer, the only job I could get in Paris that didn't ask for a work permit. All the time I studied until finally, at the beginning of this year, I passed the International law examinations and those for the German Consular Service. Then one day, what seems a hundred years ago now, Hans Emden told me that you had been to his bookstore."

She was breathing heavily now. "All those emotions I thought I had suppressed, all those emotions that centered on you—love, hatred, fear—everything erupted to the surface. For twelve hours I was paralyzed, literally unable to move. When I recovered I had refined all my feelings into one—hatred. Hatred for you. Disgust at the very idea that you had lived when so many died."

We stood up again, propelled by strange gusts of feeling we could neither predict nor control. She reached up and hooked her fingers in the back of my collar, caressing me as we walked.

"You have no idea what it's like not to be alone," she held tight to me.

"Celine is desperate," I said. "She won't be able to resist a claim from you to hand back Emil's estate."

She frowned. "For what it's worth. The Imprimerie Coburg is now nothing more than a couple of not very valuable building sites."

"But the rights to the Janus," I said. "They're worth a fortune."

"Not unless we *have* the Janus."

"Emil didn't tell you where he'd hidden it."

"He had no time to hide it," she said. "He was arrested the moment we got back from France."

"We know Celine doesn't have it. Are you saying it just disappeared, got bombed, dismantled for scrap?"

She shook her head slowly. "You don't remember?"

"Remember what?"

"That Emil relied on you to hide the Janus if anything happened to him. He asked you that in France."

Then suddenly it hit me. "Is that why I joined the SS, to go back after you were arrested to hide the Janus?"

She stopped and put her arms round me. "It looks like it," she said. "It's the only explanation that makes sense."

We walked slowly along the Seine. We had talked the whole afternoon. Walked and talked.

As the sun set we had dinner in a small restaurant below her apartment on the Ile St. Louis. We ate mostly in silence now, drained by the extraordinary day we had spent together.

I had never met anyone like her. Someone with the same ability to speak so frankly, to risk rebuff. She had told me what she had felt for me when we were little more than children at Lingfeld. Then she told me, with that stunning frankness, what she felt now. "We've lost too much time for it to be otherwise," she said.

We left the restaurant and turned through great green painted carriage doors into a courtyard within the ancient building. Ornate cast-iron staircases led up to galleries with apartments leading off them. We climbed the staircase. Lights burned in the windows all around us. People moved inside their apartments—families, couples.

"But to destroy Celine," Alex said, as if following a train of thought in her head, "we must first find the Janus."

We became lovers, perhaps because we always had been. Standing with our arms around each other's waist in her apartment on the Ile St. Louis, looking down on the Seine and the flickering reflection of the barge lights on the water, we had talked ourselves to a standstill.

It was somehow inconceivable to both of us that I should go back to the hotel. I turned towards her and kissed her mouth. Perhaps we both remembered that first time, that brief moment of reconciliation at the Chatêau de Belfresnes. Then we broke apart and walked together into the bedroom.

CHAPTER 37

～ ～ ～

Naked, she was superb. We lay facing each other in the narrow bed, my fingertips traveling a patternless course over her body. Her mouth was drawn back in pleasure as I smoothed my hand across the minute golden hair of her belly and down between her legs. "I must get up," she said, her arm tightening around my neck. I kissed her breast and, moving, let my tongue reach deep into her armpit.

I released her and she sat up on the side of the bed. Then laughing, she propelled herself upwards and ran towards the shower.

I lay back in the bed and let the scents of lovers rise around me. I knew that what I had found was far more than my past. I knew that this tall, slender girl with dark blue eyes, with long brown arms, with swelling breasts and blonde pubic hair, was to be my future, too.

I lay back in bed as she came out of the shower and I watched her cross and recross the room until she looked up, saw me watching her and smiled, her hands full of underwear. "Lunch is out," she said. "We're entertaining a Franco-German group of industrialists at the embassy. I'll be able to leave by two."

"I'll be here waiting for you."

She stepped into her briefs and moved smoothly into a showgirl grind and bump across the room. "At heart," she said laughing, "I'm a dreadful tart." As she expertly slipped into her bra, she added "I rather enjoyed what I was doing to the men at the Folies."

She came across to me and sat on the bed. "Be warned," she said, "when we're married."

It was the first time either of us had talked about a future that was not concerned with retribution or revenge. It was the first time in all the tumult of the last twenty hours that either of us had dared bring our future into the open.

I pulled myself up onto one elbow and caressed her thigh as she leaned over to kiss me. "Will you be Mrs. Alexina Lingfield," I said.

"If you ask me to."

"Will you marry me, Alex?"

"I will," she said, tears rolling from her extraordinary Coburg eyes.

I took a shower, got dressed, made coffee and used Alex's phone to call my hotel. The patron told me there were no parcels from London but that a Mr. Zorubin called trying to contact me. He was at his hotel in Paris.

I called Zorubin straight away.

"Where the hell were you?" his voice rumbled down the line. "I got back last night and I've been calling you ever since."

"I was with Alex," I said.

It took a moment for the news to sink in.

"You've found her?"

"More truthfully, she found me. She works for the German consulate."

"Jesus. And the printing press. The Janus?"

"She doesn't know where it is. But listen to this, Vik, she is damn near certain that Emil Coburg made it my responsibility."

I could hear what I took to be vodka gurgling into a glass. "Okay, Dan," he said, "let me give you my report. I've got an idea we're going to be able to put two and two together."

"I can come over right away," I said.

I'll give it to you on the phone. The South of France was a bust. Nothing, no trace. No problem now because you found her."

He paused to drink. "Okay. I took a ride up to Munich. An idea had been eating at me for days. Your SS records office in Berlin told you that after your officer training at Bad Tolz you disappeared from the records, right."

"His idea was that I was doing something unspeakable in Russia."

"But in fact," Zorubin said, as much triumph in his voice as ever I'd heard, "in fact you were hightailing it for home. You deserted."

"After I'd taken care of the Janus, if Alex is right."

"She's right," he said flatly. "Let me tell you about Munich. I've got some pull with Archives. Old records of SS court martials. What do I find? One Untersturmbahnführer Martin Coburg sentenced to death in absentia. For desertion."

"Where does that take us?"

"To France strangely enough. Listen, desertion was the main charge. Half a dozen minor charges covered illegal use of passes and movement orders . . ."

"And?"

"And appropriating a Mercedes truck and vehicle low loader. Things the German army hauled armored cars or even small tanks on."

"I've got more nerve than I thought," I said. "You mean I had the Janus on the back of the low loader?"

I was intensely excited now. We only needed one more detail. Did Zorubin have it? "Vik," I said. "Did the court-martial record say anything about where the Mercedes truck was found?"

"Yes," he said. "In France."

Then it hit me. "Near the Dordogne river," I said. "It has to be."

"It means something to you? A little place called Souillac?"

"It means a hell of a lot to me, Vik. It means I hauled the Janus to the château Emil gave to Alex."

I gave Zorubin details and asked him to drive down to the château straight away. Then I phoned Alex and caught her just before she was going in to lunch. When I told her she gave a whoop of delight that must have startled, or inflamed the industrialists.

"We've won through, Alex," I said. "It's taken a long, long time, but we've made it."

There was a long silence on the end of the line. I could see her face; I could almost read her thoughts. "I'm thinking of Emil and Dorotta," she said.

"I know."

"It's strange to think," her voice was low, "that, after all these years, we've got what they wanted for us—the Janus and each other."

"Listen, Alex," I said. "I want to wait here in Paris until Vera Sutchley's package comes. We're going to need the Sutchley papers to use against Celine."

"Okay, darling," she said. "I'll ditch the industrialists and drive down to meet Mr. Zorubin at the château."

I was exhausted with sheer exhilaration when I put down the phone.

Alex and I were on top.

Nothing could stop us now. Certainly not Celine. However many bundles of corporate lawyers she assembled.

I poured myself a Scotch and phoned Celine. Perhaps it was a childish gesture. But it was something I needed.

That so cool voice. A change of mind?

"I'm sitting in Alex's apartment," I said. "I know where the Janus is."

She didn't hesitate. "Come over right away," she said.

Putting down the phone, I drank my Scotch and rang my hotel. Still no package from London.

I wanted that package. I wanted the complete documentary proof of my innocence. But I also wanted to get a car and drive down to the château right away.

One more Scotch. Phoned the hotel again without luck.

And decided to go around to see Celine.

Why?

I guess I wanted to taste my triumph before the lawyers held us at arm's length.

I wanted to see Celine hurting.

I came off the Vendôme and into the Ritz through the Little Bar. At the rental cars desk I made arrangements for something fast to take me the five hundred kilometers down to the River Dordogne.

"We have a Jaguar, Monsieur."

"That's fine," I said.

"I'll check that it's free."

I took a Vichy water at the bar while I was waiting, and thought of Celine. I held all the cards. Some of them had fallen into my hands, some had been put there by Vik Zorubin. Some I had dealt myself. But the woman upstairs knew that she had a reckoning to face.

I sipped my Vichy and wondered at the thoughts that must be going through her mind.

The clerk at the desk raised his pencil in the air. "The Jaguar is free, sir."

I paid him and asked him to bring it around in five minutes. Then I straightened my jacket and took the elevator up to the President Wilson Suite.

I felt jubilant. The soft green carpet comfortably absorbed my footsteps. I stopped at a window and looked down on the Place Vendôme. I had a moment's regret that Alex was not with me. But I knew there would be time.

Leaving the window, I followed the discreet gold-on-walnut sign pointing me to the President Wilson Suite.

I turned at the second sign and faced the two white double doors.

One was open. Ajar.

I walked forward and stopped. Pushed the door until it swung fully open. Light streamed across a Chinese silk carpet in the parquet hall.

I called out. Then walked forward and pushed at the main door facing me. As it swung slowly on its hinges I saw, on the pale carpet, slowly revealed, the body of Celine. Her neck was broken. It was clear from the gigantic yellow-and-blue bruise at the neck and the rag-doll angle of her head.

By some automatic reflex I swept my eyes across the room looking for the weapon. A Bouchon bronze perhaps, a candlestick. Nothing.

I knelt down beside her. There were no other signs of the struggle, no cuts on the hands or torn clothing. She had been struck one massive blow with a heavy object. Maybe even from behind.

I stood. Very, very slowly the shock began to ebb. Thought processes began to grope for an answer. I stepped back towards the door, turned and walked out into the corridor.

Alex! I knew her so little. I knew her not at all. Had she killed Celine because she had to do it? Because somehow, this way, she had assuaged her thirst for revenge.

I remembered the words she'd used. "I need my hate."

Oh Christ. Alex! Had the Coburgs won after all? Had the face of the Waldviertel reared up in her mind in the moment of our triumph?

I rode the elevator down to the street. I walked through the bar. If the rental car clerk spoke I didn't hear him. My mind was blank.

The Jaguar stood at the entrance to the Little Bar. I got in and drove back to the Hotel Clemenceau. My temples thundered as I tried to rerun my last phone call with Alex.

I pulled the Jaguar to a halt outside the Hotel Clemenceau and ran up the steps between the glass globes, still lighted in daylight, and into the lobby.

The proprietor was emerging from a back room. He carried a tattered brown paper parcel tied with string, crudely sealed with red wax.

I took it from him wearily. A wave of fatigue flooded me, unbalanced me.

Perhaps I stumbled. Certainly the proprietor was holding me by the arm. "Some coffee, Monsieur?" he said.

I sat on a barstool while he got the coffee. The package from London was on the copper counter. I fiddled with it without interest. I knew the contents.

I tapped the corner of the parcel making it spin on the smooth copper surface of the bar. Nothing in it could be of importance now.

I plucked at the string and watched the red wax crack and tumble onto the shining copper.

I was within a millisecond of thrusting the package aside as the proprietor approached with the coffee. But my finger was hooked under a fold of brown wrapping.

I tore the paper towards me. Then tore again. From inside the crumple of cheap brown paper and string I drew a slender cigar box. The proprietor put down the coffee on the bar.

I flipped the cigar box lid. On a pink card, a note in an italic hand read: The earthly remains of Oliver Warburton Sutchley, gentleman, wastrel and bum.

I had the feeling it was written in Sutchley's own hand.

My mouth was dry. I let the pink card flutter onto the bar and looked down again at the cigar box. On top of a pile of papers was a wedding photograph of Oliver Sutchley and Vera. At the age of twenty-five his essential seediness had not yet shown through. Vera displayed a wide, hopeful smile. I turned the photograph and dropped it onto the bar. Underneath it was a thick pack of documents secured by a rubber band. I slid a few out. They were large, ornate Russian share certificates all dated long before the 1917 revolution.

Family photographs. Victorian upper middle-class men and women certain that two thousand pounds a year from slum rents evoked the world's respect. Photographs of Sutchley at Eton, dark-eyed and evasive despite the Eton jacket and silk hat. Two franked tickets for the *Orient Express*. A carefully folded silk handkerchief . . .

More photographs. Mostly of garden parties against a background of Lisbon rooftops. Some single girls.

I was looking down at two typewritten pages of coarse orange foolscap paper spotted with the brown marks of woodpulp. The top page carried the black eagle wings on either side of the swastika set in a circle.

The paper was headed: Preliminary report to Gestapo Headquarters organization. The typed address was 1, Avenida Lisboa, Portugal. July 1, 1940. It began:

As senior Gestapo officer attached to the Reich Embassy in Lisbon I have the honor to report: that on June 30 last the Embassy received an approach from Captain Oliver Sutchley of the British Embassy, a man known to Gestapo Hauptampt, Lisbon. The purpose of Captain Sutchley's approach was given as the offer of information of the greatest importance to the interests of the Reich. Because the informant is British and because he is known to us as one sympathetic to our cause, I personally made an arrangement to meet him at a hotel in the Lisbon outskirts we employ as a discreet house.

Mr. Sutchley's information (the full details will follow this report) concerned an alleged attempt by Ausland Organization in Berlin (since confirmed from that quarter) to introduce one million twenty-dollar bills counterfeited in Germany by Imprimerie Coburg G.M.B.H. into the United States. The reported intention is to use the funds to support all possible alternatives to Roosevelt's candidacy in the coming November U.S. presidential election. The essence of Captain Sutchley's information is the allegation that this matter has been treasonably revealed to the Americans by Herr Emil Coburg himself. Full report attached.

I looked at the Gestapo affidavit. On the grainy orange paper, stamped with the imprint of Gestapo Hauptampt, Lisbon, and signed by Sutchley and the interviewing Gestapo officer, this document had all the chilling authenticity of the murderous betrayal that it was. Oliver Sutchley was beyond vengeance, but my stomach still twisted at the careless sweep of his signature. The sheer evil embodied in the ill-typed statement on its war economy orange paper left me breathless, my hands sweating. I folded the document. Staring up at me was a circular stamp of Gestapo Hauptamt.

Then the most terrifying shock I have ever experienced tore through my body and made me cry out loud in horror. *The Gestapo officer signing the document was Viktor Heinz Zorubin!*

CHAPTER 38

I drove out of Paris like the man possessed I was. Possessed by a dreadful fear that Zorubin would reach, *must* reach the château and Alex before I did.

I had tried to telephone from the hotel but there was no line. The local operator in Souillac had volunteered the information that the Château had been empty since an old Hungarian countess had left there during the war.

The Jaguar was powerful and fast. The strain of its roadholding on corners was revealed only by the screech of tires as I sped south across Paris. I saw red lights flash by me and saw other cars braking to a last minute halt. Blaring motor horns followed me down the straight avenue named after General Leclerc and across the cobbled Place d'Orleans.

I was now out onto the open road, the Nationale 20 to Orleans, Limoges, Brive and Souillac. Zorubin had started his journey immediately, I assume, after he had murdered Celine.

I allowed myself to think as the tires pounded the road and the plane trees flashed past. Zorubin, whose strange physiognomy imparted an unusual charm to his manner, his way of walking, even the way he sat, the huge hands flat on the table before him.

In that single moment reading his signature in the hotel lobby, the charm had disappeared. I saw now his twisted, rubbery smile as infinitely threatening. It had been a long haul for him. I cast my mind back to the way we had met, or the way he had organized our meeting. I barely remembered now his cover story of service with the Boston Police Department and, of course, I had never for one moment thought to check. Or even to question his faint accent. Enough good Americans still retained some trace of a European past. Nor had I ever questioned our meeting in California. And the coincidence so much later that he should be working for a French Jewish family trying to locate Alexina. He had invested years in the search for the Janus. Presumably as Celine's man. But Zorubin was nobody's creature. The moment he had discovered the location of the Janus nobody was safe who had an interest in it—Celine, me . . . Alex.

My head was thumping, pacing my heart as I thought of the ferret tenacity with which he had pursued Alex.

As I raced through Orleans and onto the Châteauroux-Limoges road I blew a tire. Like on a Coney Island Big Dipper operated by a madman I was swung once, twice, nearly blacking out, grazing trees and an oncoming truck until the skid lost its frenetic energy.

The car came to rest in the entrance to a field a few feet from the road. I climbed drunkenly out, my head spinning, my legs trembling. By the time I had changed tires and got back onto the road I had lost nearly fifteen minutes. In my imagination I saw Zorubin's rubber smile of triumph.

I roared through Limoges with a Renault police van on my tail. But the Jaguar streaked away at the southern suburbs leaving the occupants of the trundling van to decide whether to phone ahead or to look for some other wrongdoer. It was nine-fifteen. By my calculation I had something in the region of an hour to cover one hundred thirty kilometers, the last part a twisting hill road along the Dordogne gorge.

I couldn't know that Zorubin was already turning into the courtyard of the château.

EPILOGUE

~ ~ ~

Alexina's red sportscar turned into the cobbled courtyard of the Château de Belfresnes and came to a stop beside the Simca with the Avis sticker on the rear window.

Getting out, she walked slowly across the dark courtyard absorbing the scent of juniper and lime from the black hillsides around.

Absorbing the memories of the first time she was here.

The great front door was open and she passed through into the tiled hall. Only as her eyes became more accustomed to the dark could she make out the outline of the staircase and the gallery above. Then the moon emerged from behind a cloud and threw a long panel of light across the hall floor.

It was dank, eerie. But she told herself any house of this age, empty for seven or eight years would be eerie.

She called out. "Is anyone there?" Then, "Mr. Zorubin, Mr. Zorubin . . ."

A crash and clatter greeted the words, slate sliding from the roof. On the gallery a flashlight clicked on and a moving shadow came to the rail.

She could see he was a formidably square-shaped man. The head huge and round and cropped quite short. "You're Vik Zorubin?" she called up to him.

"I'm Zorubin," he said. He came down the stairs towards her, the flashlight bobbing. She found, to her surprise, the man exuded a strange chill. Surprise because Dan had described him differently.

He stopped on the top stair. He had still not yet asked her name, although he clearly knew who she was. "I've checked the generator," he said. "This part of the house is dead. For the kitchens and cellars it's working okay. Feeble but okay. So where do we start looking?"

She had to remind herself that this man was a friend of Dan's. She said: "I'm Alex Coburg," and held out her hand.

"Sure," he said. "We'd better get moving."

She let her hand drop.

"Now this machine must be twenty feet at least. Mounted on the long loader maybe even more."

She noted the heavy rumble of his voice.

"That suggests to me a barn maybe, a garage cut out of rock, this sort of thing."

"I've been thinking on the drive down," she said, almost reluctant to tell him, preferring to wait until Dan arrived. "I've been thinking there aren't too many places here to hide something that size."

He smiled suddenly and she thought she got some idea of what Dan meant. It was a strange smile, wolfish and yet compelling. It told you this is a man you wanted on your side.

"When Dan and I were here before," she said, "we were shown a room through the back of the kitchen. As I remember, it led down into some system of limestone caves."

"Caves?"

She smiled, trying to lighten the moment. "This is the best known region of Europe for caves. Almost every village here has its own *grotte*. Some of them run for miles underground."

He nodded. "Okay, let's take a look."

It was no good. She could not like the man. Or, at least, could not warm to his brusque manner.

She led the way downstairs to the huge kitchen.
There was electric light there, dim and sometimes
flickering, but enough light to see the great iron stoves
she remembered. And there, the door into the cold
room.

She pushed it and stepped through. Zorubin followed her.

They walked between the long lines of now empty
shelves, then down the rough-stone, puddled stairs.
From below the draft of cold air hit her in the face.
A few steps lower she could hear the rush of water.

At the bottom of the stairs the huge cavern opened
up before them. Dim flickering lights in the cavern
roof threw shadows from the twisted columns of limestone. A narrow river plunged and twisted between
jutting rocks.

Zorubin stood beside her. "Is there any way in here
from the road?"

"Yes, there's an entrance to the cave system just
off the track up to the château."

"Okay," he said and started forward.

The river turned away at this point but an arch of
stone revealed electric light beyond. Zorubin ducked
through the arch and emerged into a long, flat-bot-
tomed cavern. At the far end moonlight showed
through a thick screen of bushes.

In front of them, the shape of a huge machine stood
under a tarpaulin on an old German Army six-
wheeled long loader.

She felt no jubilation. She was watching the face
of Zorubin as he flicked his flashlight over the dimly
outlined tarpaulin. She found she could not fathom
his expression.

He walked up to the loader and kicked at the flat
tires, then he reached up to one of the tarpaulin ropes
and agilely pulled himself up onto the low platform.

She was cold now: Unhappy. Uncertain about this
man.

She watched him take an Opinel wooden-handled knife from his pocket, heard the click of the blade into position, then saw him slit the tarpaulin in great downward strokes.

She could not force herself to ask him why.

As the tarpaulin fell away she saw the Janus exposed, the dark green paint cracked and flaking, the metalwork tarnished in the damp atmosphere of the cave. She wanted to turn and walk away. To run even.

Her eyes never left him.

She had, with a tremor of fear, the impression of something almost lustful as his hands roamed over the machine, pulling out drawers or sliding sections, muttering, grunting.

She took a step backwards. He had found something, maybe what he was looking for all the time, the steel nameplate screwed onto the flank of the machine.

She took another step away.

"Stay where you are," he said, his eyes fixed on the nameplate.

She turned. And ran.

Behind her she heard him leap from the platform as she raced for the bottom of the stairs.

Dan Lingfield's Jaguar took the winding road on screaming tires, the headlights fingering the limestone rock shapes and the stunted hanging trees. A pale yellow moon hung in the sky and light skeins of cloud drifted across it. Dan could see, across the gleaming river on his left, the outline of Château de Belfresnes' turrets and battlements high on the cliff.

Crossing the stone bridge he accelerated rapidly up the narrow road towards the château. Beneath the wheels rock chips were thrown up clattering against the underside of the car. As he skidded around a bend the château loomed for a moment silhouetted against the lighter sky. Then he was in the courtyard, two pairs of automobile rear lights winking a reflection as he braked.

The great medieval doors were wide open. As he ran from the car he could see some sort of light in the hall. In the mad panic to get to Alexina the menace of Zorubin had become diffused, no longer a human figure with powerful rolling shoulders and huge, blunt-nailed hands, but something that hung over the château, something that occupied any or all the rooms, the staircases, the mouldering, cobwebbed landings.

He was in the main hall now, running across it, heading for the stairs. Somewhere above he could hear something, movement, scuffling perhaps, and rapid footsteps.

The light in the hall came from a flashlight rolling across the tiled floor. He snatched it up as he reached the stairs, the light throwing huge shadows of balusters and newel posts on the crumbling plaster of the floors above.

The scream was short, momentarily piercing, an animal cry that put ice in his spine. Then the most terrifying series of screams his imagination could conjure. And a dreadful baying sound, an animal in pursuit.

Then silence. A complete engulfing silence. Without realizing it he had stopped on the first landing. His flashlight threw a long oval of light across the floorboards. He called in a voice that was no more than a harsh, barely human croak. He called Alex's name and heard no answer. He walked forward, shocked by the realization that his legs would hardly carry him. The ringing in his ears speeded and slowed, speeded and slowed. He called again and heard only that terrible grunting from above, a shuffling sound he could not identify.

And silence.

Running up to the next landing he saw that the moonlight flooded through open French doors from the terrace beyond. Perhaps the doors were still swinging, but he knew someone had passed through them only seconds ago. He threw himself forward and stopped dead. The sound was from *behind* him now, a ferocious high keening like an animal in a steel trap.

The flashlight jerked across the wall as his arm turned, and the beam settled up the last flight of stairs.

Zorubin sat there belching blood. His arms hung limply, the hands flat on the stairs. His head lay to one side, half severed by a great gash from which his blood pumped.

It seemed to Dan that he was shouting for Alex, but he had no way of really knowing. Zorubin's button eyes were on him, indifferent it seemed to his draining life blood. Did he laugh? Or make some sort of ghastly attempt at laughing? Then he shuddered violently again and again as if he were suffering some prolonged orgasm. Slowly his weight took him forward and he pitched towards Dan down the last few stairs and rolled dead at his feet.

No passage of time had any significance. At some point he heard her sobbing. Against the moonlight from the terrace he saw her moving. The French door swung as she leaned against it. In the dim light he saw her face and bare arms were covered with blood. From her hand something clattered onto the flagstones. Automatically the beam of light sought it out. It was a kitchen cleaver, the wet blade chipped and bent.

Sale of Daniel Lingfield's major shareholding in the Coburg Banknote Corporation and Alexina Coburg's one hundred percent ownership of Imprimerie Coburg and its patents in the revolutionary Janus intaglio banknote printing system was put in motion immediately. The proceeds, which would run to nearly fifty million dollars, were principally to be assigned to survivors of the Waldviertel Concentration Camp, Upper Austria, and distributed through Herr Hans Emden, now president of the Waldviertel Survivors Association.

Several smaller donations were to be made to the garden staff and domestic servants of Island House, Montauk, Long Island.

In Harlem a young man named Joe Williams who, until suffering a serious accident, was considered an up-and-coming cruiserweight fighter, had been informed that he was to receive the sum of seventy-five thousand dollars. The news reached him, coincidentally, just one month before the lease became available on the late Henry O's luncheon club on Lenox Avenue.

To Rose Coburg events had moved at an astonishing speed. Within days of Celine's death she had been informed that the house and company were to be put on the market. She had been told not to expect a share of the proceeds.

She had packed four large suitcases that day and a

jewel box and told a maid to get someone to help her take them down to her car. She allowed herself a final glance around the room and out across the gardens to the ocean beyond.

Leaving the bedroom where her small son had first found her in bed with Pierre, she had descended the great Gothic staircase for the last time. At the door to Pierre's library she stopped, shuddering.

She desperately needed another drink.

The maid was still upstairs trying to find someone to help her down with the suitcases. It was bad form to be seen by the servants drinking in the afternoon.

She paused in the hall. Of course there was brandy in the decanter on the library table. She pushed open the doors and went in. She was careful to close them after her. Quietly crossing to the drinks table, she took a decanter and poured herself a good measure.

Averting her eyes from the center of the room she sat down in what had been Pierre's favorite chair.

It wasn't as though a daughter had died. She had never really loved Celine in that way. She raised the brandy to her lips and let the spirit burn across her tongue. She was surprised to see that the glass was almost empty.

She looked up now at the plain coffin on the long library table and heard the sounds of funeral cars on the gravel outside. Of course Celine had been wicked. She had been wicked to have kept Alexina from her inheritance; and to have sent the U.S. Army photographs of Martin back without showing them to Pierre. She had been wicked to hire that monstrous ex-Gestapo man who had murdered Elisabeth and finally murdered her.

Rose poured another brandy. You would have thought Celine cleverer than that. Strange that: she had never realized that all along Zorubin was working for himself.

She was drunk when the men in black suits came

to take the coffin, waving her glass to give them permission.

She didn't clearly remember being driven to the graveyard. She saw in a haze Jack Aston maneuvering her husband's wheelchair; she thought she saw a black man with a broken nose; she saw people from the company she vaguely recognized. She saw her son and Alexina, his arm around her shoulders.

When the service was over, Rose left Island House forever.

They had all gone. Rose to God knows where; Jack Aston and John Coburg back to the cottage; Joe Williams to Harlem; ex-Colonel Buck to the new clinic he had just opened in Denver, Colorado.

Dan had shaken the last hand, thanked the last person for coming. Now he looked around and saw Alex, a tall figure in black, standing alone before the wall of green marble that fronted the vault. He walked slowly back down the gravel path and stood next to her. Their eyes moved down the incised and gold-lettered names:

Aloys and Paula Coburg.

Pierre Coburg.

Then, Martin Coburg 1921–1945.

He thought he felt the girl beside him shiver.

And finally, Celine Coburg 1921–1949.

He took Alex's hand and they looked up at the heavy gold lettering at the head of the green granite block: Vault of the Coburg Family of Waldviertel, Austria, and Long Island, New York.

Then they turned away.

Let it be.